She had been secretly waiting for this moment for a long time...

Nikki had never been this close to Toly's rock-hard physique. They were both tall, and they fit together as if they were made for each other.

Toly smelled wonderful. Nikki loved the feel of his hard jaw against her cheek. It sent darts of awareness through her body. The temptation to turn her head and kiss his compelling mouth was killing her. Toly didn't let her go and she could have stayed in his arms all night.

"If you hadn't been involved with someone else, we could have relaxed like this before an event long before now," he whispered into her hair.

Her heart jumped to think he might have been thinking about her on a more intimate level over the last few months, too. Still, he'd never let her know. They were all friends and she knew Toly kept his cards close to the chest.

But with the way she was feeling right now, he had to know she didn't want to be anywhere else...

MONTANA
★ COUNTRY LEGACY ★

THE RANCHER'S
CHRISTMAS PRIZE

---　✗　---

Rebecca Winters

Amanda Renee

Previously published as *Roping Her Christmas Cowboy*
and *A Snowbound Cowboy Christmas*

HARLEQUIN

(H) HARLEQUIN®

Recycling programs for this product may not exist in your area.

ISBN-13: 978-1-335-20955-9

Montana Country Legacy:
The Rancher's Christmas Prize
Copyright © 2020 by Harlequin Books S.A.

Roping Her Christmas Cowboy
First published in 2017. This edition published in 2020.
Copyright © 2017 by Rebecca Winters

A Snowbound Cowboy Christmas
First published in 2017. This edition published in 2020.
Copyright © 2017 by Amanda Renee

This edition published by arrangement with Harlequin Books S.A.

For questions and comments about the quality of this book, please contact us at CustomerService@Harlequin.com.

Harlequin Enterprises ULC
22 Adelaide St. West, 40th Floor
Toronto, Ontario M5H 4E3, Canada
www.Harlequin.com

Printed in U.S.A.

CONTENTS

Roping Her Christmas Cowboy   7
by Rebecca Winters

A Snowbound Cowboy Christmas   209
by Amanda Renee

Rebecca Winters lives in Salt Lake City, Utah. With canyons and high alpine meadows full of wildflowers, she never runs out of places to explore. They, plus her favorite vacation spots in Europe, often end up as backgrounds for her romance novels—because writing is her passion, along with her family and church. Rebecca loves to hear from readers. If you wish to email her, please visit her website at rebeccawinters.net.

Books by Rebecca Winters

Harlequin Romance

The Princess Brides

The Princess's New Year Wedding
The Prince's Forbidden Bride
How to Propose to a Princess

Holiday with a Billionaire

Captivated by the Brooding Billionaire
Falling for the Venetian Billionaire
Wedding the Greek Billionaire

The Billionaire's Club

Return of Her Italian Duke
Bound to Her Greek Billionaire
Whisked Away by Her Sicilian Boss

The Billionaire's Prize
The Magnate's Holiday Proposal

Visit the Author Profile page at Harlequin.com for more titles.

ROPING HER CHRISTMAS COWBOY

Rebecca Winters

To the continual existence of the rodeo, a tradition of the American West that's part of our DNA. May it grow and flourish through the centuries to thrill young and old alike, as we watch exceptionally gifted men and women working with their magnificent horses in a symphony of unparalleled harmony.

Chapter 1

"Come in my office and sit down, Mr. Clayton."

"Thanks, Dr. Moore." Toly Clayton had driven the half hour to Missoula from the Clayton Cattle Ranch outside Stevensville, Montana, for an appointment with a neurosurgeon. He'd just undergone an electromyograph to get to the bottom of the numbness that had attacked his lower right forearm and hand.

"The needle I inserted in your arm muscle recorded electrical activity when it was at rest and when it was contracted. The procedure helped me determine that you have a nerve, not a muscle disorder. How long did you say you've been team roping?"

"I've done that and tie-down roping since my early teens."

"That would explain the numbness that has come on. The constant strain over the years from roping has caused the nerves to be partially compressed or stretched. You say it has happened twice in practice?"

"Yes. Once in October, and again a few days ago. It was frightening to experience that loss of feeling. It only lasted a few minutes, but it was enough to prevent me from throwing the rope with any accuracy."

"Did you feel sharp pains or discomfort in your forearm just before the onset?"

"No. That's what worries me. Both times when it happened, I had no warning."

"You told me in the examining room that you've had no sign of this affecting your feet or legs."

"None. Does that mean I can expect that to happen too? What's wrong with me?"

"You have a very mild form of peripheral Charcot-Marie-Tooth, a slow growing motor sensory neuropathy. It's inherited through a gene carried down in the family. Do you know if you've ever had it in yours?"

"Not that I'm aware of."

"Some people don't even know they have it."

"If it should happen while I'm throwing the rope during a performance at the National Finals Rodeo in December, everything's over for that round and, of course, my partner suffers. We don't get second chances."

"I understand, but if such an incident occurs, you'll still have strength in your upper arm."

"I'm afraid that won't be enough. Is there a medicine to stop this from happening?"

"Not that has been invented yet."

"You mean there's no cure for it?"

"No, but medical science is always working on a cure. I've been doing some research and can tell you they're making strides with a new surgical technique."

Adrenaline filled Toly's system. "You mean there is one?"

"It's been in the experimental stage for quite a while. The results aren't a hundred percent yet."

"What kind of results are you talking about?"

"In a few cases, surgery has slowed down the process. In a few others, it has stopped it."

"What's entailed?"

"The surgery would replace the damaged nerves in your forearm and hand with a new protein that would stimulate nerve cell growth. If successful, it could revolutionize the problem for those afflicted."

"So there is some hope."

"Of course. I'm still doing research on it. The procedure is being done in Paris, France, by a team of neuro and vascular surgeons."

Paris... "If it were possible for me, how long would I have to stay there?"

"Two to three weeks depending on complications."

"When the rodeo is over, I'd like to be a candidate."

"I'm afraid it couldn't be that soon."

"But you will call me when you know anything, and make the arrangements for me?"

"I'll get back to you after I've looked into it more. Just remember it's possible that you'll never have more than the occasional manifestation in your right arm. Call me if you have any more questions, and good luck!"

"Thank you, Dr. Moore. Once the rodeo is over I'll be a full-time rancher and need to get better. You have no comprehension of what it would mean to me to fix this problem."

"If not cured, at least slowed down. We'll talk again soon."

Toly left the doctor's office determined that surgery would help him. Right now he could only hope that he and his partner, Mills, survived the punishing ten days ahead of them.

Anything could go wrong during a rodeo, but the thought of his hand not working for a few minutes had him the most worried. The condition had only manifested itself twice so far. He had to hope against hope it wouldn't come on during their performance.

To Toly's relief, Mills hadn't realized what had happened in practice and he didn't want him to know. Toly didn't plan to tell anyone, not even his family. All he had to do was get through Finals and pray another incident during an actual round didn't cause them to bomb.

Too bad this hadn't happened six months ago. Perhaps he could have gone in for the experimental surgery and be recovered long before Finals. But there was no chance of that now. After the rodeo he would tell everyone he was going off on a month's vacation to do some sightseeing for a change.

If the operation wasn't successful, no one would be the wiser. Life would go on the same. He'd wait until the doctor found another team of surgeons to help him beat the disease.

"In case you're a listener just tuning in, this is Jeb Riker from KFBR Sports Radio in Great Falls, Montana. It's Friday, December 2, here in Great Falls, Montana. We've been broadcasting our Christmas show from the Ford dealership here in town since two o'clock this afternoon.

"What a turnout we have had to meet the three rodeo champions from our fair state headed to Las Vegas for this year's Wrangler National Finals Rodeo championship!

"All you dudes out there, come on in and meet the beautiful Nikki Dobson. She was last year's Miss Rodeo Montana, and this year's second-place finalist for the coveted national barrel racing championship. I don't see a ring on her finger yet, guys.

"Guess what? She isn't the only eligible celebrity who hails from the Sweet Clover Ranch here in Great Falls. We've got her twin brother Mills Dobson in house. He and his partner, Toly Clayton, from the Clayton Cattle Ranch in Stevensville, Montana, are the reigning team roping champions on the circuit headed for Las Vegas. Ladies? Get ready for this announcement. Both are still single!

"Guys and gals? Don't miss this opportunity to meet these celebrities up close and personal. The next time you see them, they'll be in Las Vegas where they're scheduled to win national championships and be entered into the ProRodeo Hall of Fame."

Wouldn't it be a miracle if that happened. Knowing what he knew now that he'd been to see the doctor, a miracle was what it would take.

Toly looked around the showroom with its lighted Christmas trees, noticing that Nikki had been swarmed by every male in sight. She stood an exquisite five foot nine in her cowboy boots. With her long curly black hair and crystalline gray eyes, she *was* a sight! Ever since he'd asked Mills to be his team roping partner to compete on this year's circuit and had met her face-to-face, she'd blown away all the other women he'd ever known.

In his teens he'd had lots of girlfriends, but his dream had always been the rodeo, ruling out any serious involvement with them. Over the years he'd met literally hundreds of women on the circuit. This last year there'd been a dozen or so who'd caught his eye and he'd done some line dancing with them before moving on to the next rodeo on the circuit.

But always in the back of his mind, the vision of Nikki Dobson got in the way. However, there were several reasons why he'd never acted on his attraction to her. For one, he knew from Mills that she'd been in a relationship that hadn't worked out and was still dealing with her pain.

For another, she was Mills's sister. Though they'd never talked about it, from the time Toly and Mills had hooked up to be team ropers together, he'd sensed that Mills wouldn't like it if Toly showed a personal interest in Nikki. Much as he wanted to, Toly knew he needed to be careful not to let anything affect his friendship with Mills while they were in a competition to win.

Mills and Nikki had lost their parents in a car accident three years ago. Toly had never met them, but he admired the twins who'd overcome their grief and had gotten on with their dreams to be rodeo champions.

Until he retired from the rodeo at the end of this month, Toly would continue to keep it friendly with Nikki. Knowing Mills's feelings, he'd decided not to explore a closer relationship with her…provided she was even interested. He thought she might be. But that was something he had yet to find out while they were all in Las Vegas.

For the next half hour, he kept signing pictures as more fans continued to pour into the dealership. The ladies offered their phone numbers. Toly just kept smiling while they took pictures of the three of them with their phones. Soon they'd be able to call it a night. He wanted to get to bed early. Starting in the morning, they had a thousand-mile drive ahead of them with the horses.

But he never lost track of Nikki who was still being mobbed by guys snapping pictures of her. He imagined she'd had to ward them off since her teens.

"Let's get out of here," Mills suddenly muttered.

Toly jerked his head around. He'd been concentrating so hard on Nikki, he hadn't realized his friend had walked over to him. Since a month ago when the girl Mills had been dating had broken up with him, he'd grown dark and morose. You couldn't even talk to him.

"We'll have to say goodbye to Jeb Riker first and thank the manager of the dealership."

"Yep."

The two of them walked over to talk to the radio announcer broadcasting from the back of a new truck. Toly thanked Riker for the great promotion and send-off. They were joined by the manager whom they thanked and chatted with for a few minutes.

Out of the corner of his eye he could see that Nikki was still involved with her fans. Since she'd come in a separate vehicle from him and Mills, there was no reason to wait for her.

They pulled on their sheepskin jackets and ate another hot dog before working their way through the throng of supporters to the entrance. Once outside, they walked through the brittle snow left by several storms and climbed into Mills's Dodge Power Wagon truck.

The temperature registered twenty degrees and would probably drop to fourteen overnight. Las Vegas sounded pretty good right now with a temperature hovering near sixty degrees.

Mills gunned the motor and they took off, passing Nikki's Silverado truck parked half a block down the street. The silence lengthened on their way to Dobson's small Sweet Clover Ranch on the outskirts of town.

"Want to talk about it yet?"

"Nope."

Toly pushed his cowboy hat back on his head. "If you change your mind, I'm your man."

"Thanks, but I won't."

Until a month ago Mills had been dating Denise Robbins, a girl from Great Falls, for about four months. When she'd unexpectedly called things off, she'd knocked the heart right out of him. Until their breakup he'd never seen Mills so happy. Her action couldn't have been worse for him. At their last two rodeos, his timing had been a little off. Toly had tried to get him to talk about it with no success.

Somehow Toly had hoped Denise would show up at the Ford dealership this evening to make up with him. Toly could have sworn half the town had turned out. She was a former barrel racer and couldn't have helped but hear about it being advertised. With Finals only a few days away, for her to pick this particular time to part ways couldn't have been more cruel.

En route to the Dobson ranch house, Toly received an email notification on his phone from their agent, Lyle. When he checked it, he saw that Lyle had forwarded him an email from Amanda Fleming. She must have gotten his email address off the website that his agent ran for them.

Toly figured she must have sent it from her office at the hotel in Omaha, Nebraska, where they'd met three weeks ago. He and Mills had stayed there while his rig was getting serviced. She had invited Toly to have a meal with her in the hotel after their event and he thought why not. The next day he and Mills left for their next rodeo.

Her email explained that she would be in the stands during the competition in Las Vegas. She hoped they'd be able to spend at least one of the evenings together.

He frowned. She hadn't been on his mind since he'd left Omaha and knew what that meant. Only one woman had the power to remain in his thoughts and not go away no matter what else was going on. That woman was back at the Ford dealership.

Toly was sorry he'd eaten dinner with her. In a few days he would send her an email via Lyle. At that time he would tell her that every night was uncertain because of the gold buckle ceremony and parties after each rodeo. Perhaps there might be a night he was free, but he wouldn't know until he'd ridden in his event. He would have to see. Hopefully she would read between the lines. Toly had no desire to be rude to her, but knew their relationship couldn't go anyplace.

After Mills drove them up to the ranch house entrance, they both went inside and grabbed a snack in the kitchen while they made final plans for the next day.

Toly kept listening for Nikki to come in, but it wasn't meant to be. Furthering his disappointment, Mills informed him that their crew, Andy and Santos, would be driving her horses in their rig. His sister would fly down on the sixth, negating any hope Toly would be able to talk to her at rest spots along their route to Nevada.

Earlier in the day, Toly had made the 190-mile drive from Stevensville to Great Falls in his rig with the horses and he was tired. After staying at the Dobsons' tonight, they would load all four of their horses in the morning and take off on I-15 for their three-day trip all the way to Las Vegas.

The crew would be staying at a hotel near the Thomas & Mack Center and meet up with them on the sixth at the equestrian RV park. It was the place he reserved every year so he could sleep in his rig rather than at a hotel.

This year Mills would be living in the Dobson rig parked next to Toly's rig. Nikki would be staying at a hotel, but during the day she'd drive out to the RV park to exercise her horses. Toly felt a heightened sense of excitement, knowing that she'd be around for those ten days. He would have a legitimate reason to talk to her, coming and going.

After texting his mom that he'd be heading out in the morning with Mills, he said good-night and clicked off. He wouldn't be seeing his family again until everyone flew down for the final night of competition on the seventeenth to celebrate en masse.

Turning to Mills he said, "I'm going to go on up and hit the hay."

"Before you do, come in the den with me for a minute."

Wondering what this was about, he followed him through the cedar-plank-and-brick ranch house to the room where all the Dobson family pictures, awards and trophies were on display.

"Sit down for a minute."

"Sure."

Toly perched on the end of the couch and waited for his friend to speak. Though Mills had darker gray eyes than his twin, their black hair and basic features were so alike it was positively uncanny. They took after their mother he could see in the photographs, but got their height from their father. Every time Toly looked at him, he saw Nikki.

"I've been an ass for the last month. Sorry."

"Forget it, Mills."

"I wish I could." He started pacing, then stopped. "I thought I knew Denise. Geez—how wrong could I have been! I could have taken it if she just plain didn't like me anymore, but her timing after we'd made plans to celebrate when it was all over... I had big plans," he murmured.

Toly had an idea what they were and was heartsick for his friend. "I know, dude. It surprised the heck out of me. I thought you two were tight."

"Join the club. It makes me wonder something. I keep asking myself, did she shut me down right before Finals because *she* didn't qualify and that's why she dropped out?"

"Whoa. I don't believe that, and neither should you."

"I have a reason for saying what I did. As you know, I met her through Nikki. They'd been contestants at the same time for the Miss Rodeo Montana Pageant the year before and became friends. Five months ago she invited Denise to the ranch while I happened to be home that weekend."

"I remember."

"The chemistry between us was amazing. Though you and I were on the circuit part of the time, she and I talked on the phone for hours when we couldn't be together. I thought she was the one."

"Don't I know it."

Mills planted himself in a chair. "What you don't know is how devastated she was when she didn't place in that pageant. For the first two weeks into our relationship, it seemed like all she wanted to do was talk about her disappointment. Then the subject changed when she told me she'd decided to drop out of barrel racing. I'm afraid I didn't immediately connect the dots."

"So what are you saying?"

He took a deep breath. "I'm not sure, but I'm wondering if it's because she's been comparing herself to Nikki and doesn't want to be around her anymore, which means shutting me out. I guess I never told you Nikki made a clean sweep of all the categories in the pageant, including personality, appearance and horsemanship, and she won the Queen Speech award. The folks would have been so proud."

That didn't surprise Toly, who shook his head. Deep inside he had to admit Nikki would be an almost impossible act to follow.

"Look, Mills—even if your supposition contains a kernel of truth and she has some envy issues, I can't comprehend that she would deny herself the happiness you two have found since meeting each other. It doesn't make sense."

"Maybe it does because deep down Denise is more into herself than I'd realized. I found out from my friend José that he went to the same high school with Denise. She was big into barrel racing back then and ran for Miss Teen Rodeo three years in a row."

"How did she do?"

He looked at him. "She never placed in the top three."

"Neither did the majority of the other contestants."

His friend let out a sound of frustration. "But I don't think she ever got over it."

Toly got to his feet. "If that's really true, and you believe she's too obsessed with past failures to see a bright future with you, then she did you a favor by breaking up with you. Let me give you a piece of advice my big brother once gave me. He fell in love with his high school girlfriend and planned to marry her after college.

"But she met an actor from Hollywood while she was in Europe who swept her off her feet. After she came home, she ended it with Wymon. He thought she'd wanted a ranching life with him. It shocked him to realize he could never have given her what she really wanted. But before he finally got over her, he nursed a broken heart for a long time and grew bitter.

"I'm telling you this because when I first got into tie-down roping on the circuit—before my brother Roce and I started team roping—Wymon sat me down because he was worried about me. He knew how much I liked the ladies and feared I might get dazzled too soon by a woman who could never love me. My brother feared that if I wasn't careful, I'd be like he had been and wallow in pain instead of getting on with life."

Mills stared at him. "What did he say to you?"

"To quote him, 'The last thing you ever want to do is get hung up on one of those rodeo beauty queens. They're in love with their own image and probably have been all their lives. The dude who's hooked and can't see through it is doomed to be an afterthought, if that.'

"Later on, I realized he'd said that while he was in a bad place, but after hearing what you've just told me, maybe there was some truth to his words." Toly didn't know what else to say. His friend needed to try to get over Denise or he was going to be miserable for a long time.

Mills stood up. "In the beginning I would never have thought of her like that. But the more I think about it, there has been a pattern of high expectations and bitter disappointments she can't get over. Your brother might have had a point when he gave you that advice."

"Mills? What's important is that you move on for your own happiness."

"You're right. Thanks for the talk. I'm sure as hell not going to let her ruin what you and I have worked so hard for. I promise I won't let you down."

Toly patted his shoulder. "You couldn't do that. See you in the morning. Try to get a good sleep."

It was great advice to give Mills, but Toly knew he wouldn't be falling off anytime soon. He went back to the kitchen, hoping Nikki would come home so they could talk. No doubt some guy was detaining her.

Starting tomorrow morning, Toly wouldn't be seeing her for the next three days. He wished they were all driving down to Vegas together, but Mills had never suggested it. From the moment the two of them had starting riding the circuit together, Toly had sensed Nikki was off-limits to him. Naturally he was friendly with her when they were all together here on the ranch, but he kept things professional. That's why they'd all gotten along so well.

But Toly wanted more than that. The only thing saving him was the knowledge that the three of them would be together in Las Vegas for ten whole days and nights. He had plans despite what Mills wanted.

After waiting another twenty minutes while he watched the news on the small TV in the kitchen, he decided Nikki might not be home for hours. Not if that dude at the dealership was holding her up.

She could sleep in tomorrow while he and Mills had to take off early. So much for a talk with her before he went to bed. That would have to wait. *Hell.*

Chapter 2

At three o'clock on Tuesday afternoon, the airport shuttle pulled up to the magnificent new Cyclades Hotel and Casino in Las Vegas, Nevada. Four huge, white rounded windmills with their pointed brown roofs and blades—the famous trademark advertising the Greek islands—formed the facade around the entrance. A sign on the marquee said, Welcome Wrangler National Finals Rodeo Finalists.

December 6 was finally here. Nikki climbed out of the limo following her two-hour flight from Great Falls, Montana, and was instantly met with whistles and a barrage of photographers taking pictures. She ought to be higher than a kite to be here at last, on the verge of possibly winning the national championship. But her spirits couldn't have been darker. Not after the conversation she'd accidentally overheard between her brother and Toly Clayton the other night at the ranch house.

She hadn't been able to put it out of her mind and would have given anything in the world for her loving parents to still be alive so she could talk to them about what Toly had said. She was afraid he'd been referring to her when he'd made certain remarks. But there was no such miracle for her and somehow she had to find the strength to get through this experience on her own.

Being a finalist required she had to be prepared to look the part. That meant wearing specific brands like her white Stetson, Justin cowboy boots, and Wrangler jeans and Western shirt. It also meant putting on a smile when it was the last thing she felt like doing.

A doorman reached for her two suitcases and accompanied her inside the lobby decorated with Christmas trees and thousands of twinkling white lights crisscrossing the ceiling. She'd almost forgotten the holiday season was upon them. He put her luggage next to her and went back out in front.

One of the clerks at the counter approached her. "Welcome to the Cyclades Hotel."

"It's good to be here. My name is Nikki Dobson."

The clerk's smile broadened as she signed her into the computer. "You're one of this year's barrel racing finalists. Congratulations!"

"Thank you."

"We have the Delos Island suite ready for you and a rental car. When you're ready to pick it up, their office is down the north hall next to the double doors leading to the indoor pool and gym.

"If you'll follow the bellhop, he'll show you to your room off the east patio. You'll find literature on the coffee table to answer any questions you might have. Here's your card key."

Nikki thanked her again. The bellhop picked up her suitcases and she followed him past a coffee shop and the crowded casino to a set of glass doors at the other end of the lobby. They led outside where a charming, miniature Greek village greeted her vision.

The whitewashed cubed houses built next to each other, with some being double storied, had been designed in the Cycladic style around several swimming pools lined in Greek tiles.

What a stunning change from the high-rises of many other hotels! She liked the architecture and was glad she didn't have to deal with crowded elevators and happy people. After the blizzard she'd left behind in Montana, she had to admit the high-fifties temperature here in the desert felt balmy by comparison.

As soon as she was shown to her two-bedroom suite with its blue-and-white decor, she paid the man for helping her with her bags. If Mills got tired of sleeping in the rig, he could spend a night here in the other bedroom. But in his depressed state, she had no idea what her brother would want right now.

Once she'd closed the door, she sat down on a chair by the coffee table in the small sitting room to text Mills that she'd arrived at the hotel. She knew he was expecting to hear from her.

Next she phoned Santos and Andy, the crew all three of them were sharing. They'd driven her rig and quarter horses here from the Dobson ranch. She knew from an earlier text that they'd arrived at ten that morning and had pulled into the RV equestrian park in Las Vegas. It had several big arenas, nine barns and all the amenities to work with the horses like steer dummies and practice barrels. It saved having to go over to the Thomas and Mack Center all the time where the National Finals Rodeo was being held starting the day after tomorrow.

"How's it going, Santos?

"Despite a flat tire and a long wait while a herd of migrating elk crossed the highway, we're fine."

"Do I want to know how bad it really was?"

"Nope. You've got enough on your mind."

What would she do without their crew. They were her greatest support. "Is Bombshell settling in?"

"She's good. So is Sassy. But Duchess is missing you."

"I'm not surprised. Now that I've checked in to the Cyclades Hotel, I'll pick up my rental car and drive over so I can exercise her."

"That'll perk her up."

"If all goes well, I won't be riding her during the competition. But I need to keep her happy and in shape, just in case of a problem." Though Duchess was fast, she required more cosseting than the other two.

"You can always expect something will go wrong, Nikki."

"Don't I know it."

She'd learned that when her parents had been killed, and again when she realized she couldn't marry Ted, not to mention the pain inflicted when she'd overheard a certain conversation the other night.

As for her rodeo experiences, she'd been riding horses on her own from the time she was seven. Her childhood dreams were all to do with riding in the rodeo one day. At fourteen she'd competed in the teen rodeos. At eighteen she'd started college and had begun competing on the state and national circuit.

For the last six years Nikki had gone through everything that could go right *or* wrong personally and professionally during her exhausting schedule. It still wasn't over and anything could happen until this competition came to an end after ten grueling nights. Then she'd retire in order to promote the rodeo in a brand-new way with her brother who was also a rodeo champion along with his famous team roping partner.

When the pro rodeo championship finals were over, Mills planned to retire as well and go into business with her. The two of them had talked about it a lot. Neither of them had been lucky when it came to romantic relationships that were destined to last. His recent breakup with one of her best friends, Denise Robbins, had torn him apart. She was glad that when Finals were over, they had each other to rely on for the future.

"Any sign of Mills yet?"

"Yeah. He and Toly pulled in at noon and parked their rig next to yours."

She guessed he hadn't had time yet to answer her text. Technically it was Toly Clayton's rig. They'd lived out of it while doing the circuit this last year. He was the youngest son on the renowned Clayton Cattle Ranch located at the base of the Sapphire Mountains outside Stevensville.

"I'm glad they got there safely."

"Their horses are stalled right by yours. It's a good thing you guys made reservations last January. The place is full up."

"We knew it would be."

"I've already spread several bags of soft shavings in all three stalls. Andy filled the buckets with water and is measuring their intake. When the vet comes around tomorrow, he'll want to check them."

"There's nothing you haven't thought of. Thanks, Santos. I couldn't do any of this without you guys." She got to her feet. "I'll freshen up here, then be over."

"In that case, I'll saddle Duchess and put a soft bit on her."

"Terrific. See you soon."

Nikki hung up, realizing she'd be running into the drop-dead gorgeous Toly Clayton before long. Knowing how he felt about her, it was the last thing she wanted, but being around him was inevitable.

After a year of seeing him coming and going, both on the circuit and at the ranch, she'd thought they were all good friends. But just the thought of him now cut her to the quick.

The other night, on the way to her bedroom after coming home from the Ford dealership, she'd passed by the den, surprised anyone was still up. Toly's words had drifted through the crack in the door.

The last thing you ever want to do is get hung up on one of those rodeo beauty queen types. They're in love with their own image and probably have been all their lives. The dude who's hooked and can't see through it is doomed to be an afterthought, if that.

Stung by words she would never forget, Nikki had run down the hallway to her bedroom so they wouldn't know she'd been in hearing distance. She'd lost sleep that night wondering what that conversation had all been about. But she'd had enough time since Friday to believe that what Toly had said was probably his general opinion of rodeo queens.

In this business he'd met and dated any number of them over the years. After apparently finding all of them wanting since he was still single, it might explain why he'd never tried to get to know Nikki better.

She'd known pain when she and Ted Bayliss realized their relationship couldn't go anywhere. He was a big advertising executive from Laguna Beach, California, who'd asked her to marry him. But he wanted her to move there where they would lead a different lifestyle with his friends that had nothing to do with horses. As he'd said, she could always go back to her ranch on vacations and ride her horses with Mills.

When she told him about the elaborate plans she and Mills had talked about once they'd both retired from the rodeo, Ted recognized that marriage wouldn't have worked for them no matter how attracted they'd been to each other. He had a business rooted in Southern California he couldn't leave. It would mean Nikki would have to uproot herself, something she couldn't do. At that point they stopped seeing each other.

For a time it was hard to accept that there could be no future for them, but she'd finally gotten over it. That's why it surprised her how much she was still hurting over Toly's comments to her brother. It didn't make sense. She'd never been on a date with him or spent hours of time alone in his company, let alone had a relationship with him like she'd had with Ted.

She would love to get into a discussion with Mills about how he felt over his friend's blanket repudiation of women like Nikki who'd been steeped in the rodeo world all their lives.

But in order to bring up the subject with her brother, she would have to admit that she'd overheard the two men talking. She hadn't meant to eavesdrop. After a few seconds she'd fled the scene, but her good intentions didn't matter because Mills would have seen it as an intrusion on his privacy.

After mulling it all over, Nikki wasn't sorry it had happened. What she'd learned had removed the blinders. Toly might be Montana's favorite rodeo champion and a bona fide heartthrob, but his insensitive remarks had ensured she would never be one of *his* worshippers. She didn't care how many gold buckles he'd garnered, or the fame he'd won before he'd ever asked her brother to team rope with him.

Too bad Toly had been her brother's idol for years. The fact that he'd chosen Mills to be his team roping partner for the current year had been a dream come true for him. Though Nikki had every desire to see them win the national finals championship, she would avoid Toly as much as possible.

Nikki wished the side-by-side reservations for their rigs hadn't been made eleven months ago. She couldn't do anything about that. But fortunately she'd be staying at the hotel and not in her rig where she usually slept. The rest of the time she'd be putting her horses through the paces at the park, keeping her distance.

In ten days' time Toly Clayton would be long gone and she'd never have to see the Sapphire Cowboy again. According to Mills, that was the nickname Toly had been given by a journalist at the *Billings Gazette* years ago when he'd performed as Montana's champion tie-down roper. She'd seen pictures on the billboards driving in from the airport that featured the Sapphire Cowboy on several of them.

Somehow, some way, she had to put him out of her mind. The fact that she was having such difficulty had to mean that on some subconscious level she'd thought a lot more about him than she would have admitted.

Clearly the negative indictment of rodeo queens had been the last thing she would ever have expected to hear on the eve of her hoping to win the national barrel racing championship. That's what you got for listening to something you shouldn't have. *It's your own fault, Nikki. Learn from it.*

On that note Nikki finished the diet soda she'd grabbed from the minifridge and changed into well-worn jeans and a white, long-sleeved cotton pullover. Once she'd stashed her riding gloves in her tote bag along with a bag of peanuts for herself, she put on her white cowboy hat and left the room to get her rental car.

After she'd picked up the Honda Civic held for her, she left the hotel and headed to the RV equestrian park on Flamingo Road. Las Vegas was packed year-round, but during the pro rodeo finals, the traffic was beastly and it could be a nightmare if you hadn't made reservations for everything months ahead of time.

She found the park and wound her way through to their black-and-gold rig parked near one of the barns. The long white Clayton rig lined up on one side of it had always been Toly's hotel. When she'd first met him, she'd heard him say he was allergic to hotels.

Nikki pulled behind the Dobson rig and got out. So far she didn't see anyone around. Good! She walked around the side and unlocked the door to the trailer section. Before she visited her horses, she needed to load up on some treats for them. They'd been separated three days and needed her love and attention in order to perform at their peak.

A few minutes later with her pockets stuffed with

goodies, she walked the short distance to the barn where her horses had been stalled. She greeted Bombshell and Sassy with treats. Tomorrow her three horses would be moved to the stalls at the Thomas and Mack Center for some practice runs.

"There's my Duchess," she crooned to her red roan quarter horse and received a volley of nickers and nudges that made her chuckle. "I missed you too." She fed her some apple-flavored Pony Pops and untied the lead rope to back her out of her stall.

"That's the kind of welcome that makes me jealous," sounded a deep male voice behind her.

Nikki knew who it was. No surprise here when his horses were stalled in the same barn. After taking a deep breath she mounted Duchess, then reached in her jeans pocket for another Pony Pop and turned toward him.

Toly Clayton stood there at six foot three in his boots wearing his signature black cowboy hat that covered a head of dark blond hair. His light green eyes almost blinded her with their intensity.

Damn and blast if her heart didn't rap out a double beat without her permission despite her pain. "I have an idea that will fix all your problems. Why don't you give Snapper one of these on me?"

She tossed the treat to him. To his credit he caught it neatly. They didn't call Toly the greatest header of all the team ropers on this year's circuit for nothing. He was the one who roped the head of the steer. Mills had won the same distinction for being the greatest heeler. His job was to rope the hindquarters. They were both experts. "See you later, Toly."

Nikki rode away, unable to believe he could act like

nothing was wrong after what he'd told Mills about her in private. How could he have looked at her just now like she was someone special?

Where did he get the gall to let her think he wanted to be with her and talk to her when deep down he'd mocked her in a particularly cruel way that had cut deep? Now that they were here, she'd be giving him wide berth!

Toly had seen her enter the barn while he was tending to Snapper and wanted to say hello to her, hoping to talk to her for a minute alone. But after tossing him the treat he put in his pocket, she didn't give him a chance to invite her to eat dinner with him and Mills later in his rig.

Though he knew how anxious she was to exercise her horses after being separated from them for three days, he sensed that something else had prompted her to ride off without a normal exchange of conversation. That wasn't like her usual friendly self. Probably nerves had caught up to her this close to the first night of competition coming up the day after tomorrow.

He couldn't help but admire her expertise as she rode Duchess out of the barn. Nikki used a barrel racing saddle with a taller horn and rounded skirt for more stability and control. She had a natural seat that made her look like she'd been born in the saddle. It caused her to stand out when she rode. The fact that she was incredibly beautiful only amplified that picture.

Toly had copped one of her signed posters at the dealership and had folded it inside his jacket so neither Nikki nor Mills could see what he'd done. The photographer had caught her rounding the third barrel at lightning speed during a circuit performance. He planned to put it up in the tack room of the barn at home where he kept some of his favorite mementos.

As soon as she disappeared, he went back to Snapper's stall. After breaking the treat in half, he gave part to him and the other half to Chaz in the next stall. He'd already put both quarter horses through their paces. The two had speed and instincts that made them invaluable.

Once he'd made sure they were watered and had enough hay in their nets, he left the barn. The crew would check on them later. It was four thirty and the sun had just gone down over the horizon. It would be dark before long. Tomorrow the vet would meet him and Mills at the barn to give their horses a thorough exam.

He looked in the direction of the arena. Nikki would be over there putting her horse through a series of backup and turning drills. He would love to watch her, but didn't obey the impulse. She would be back soon.

Toly headed for his rig, but noticed Mills hadn't returned yet. They'd arranged for a rental car and he'd gone to do errands and pick up some steaks to cook. That gave Toly time to let himself inside for a shower and shave before dinner.

A half hour later he got to work on a salad and baked potatoes. He'd learned a long time ago that cooking helped him to relax. As he was whipping up biscuits, Mills came in with the steaks for their dinner and put them on the counter.

"Thanks."

"Sure." He removed his parka. "I saw Nikki's rental car in back. I didn't know she'd texted me until a minute ago. Did she say she'd come to dinner?"

Nope, but Mills didn't need to know what had happened. Toly was still trying to figure out the reason for her unusual behavior. He took the wrapping off the meat to throw them on the kitchen grill.

"I only saw her in passing and didn't get the chance to ask her to dinner. She was in too big a hurry to exercise Duchess. Why don't you call her and tell her it's ready if she wants to join us."

Mills pulled out his cell phone. "That horse has emotional problems. I'm afraid Nikki has taken them on."

"She's a true horse lover."

"Dad used to say the same thing. Sometimes she takes it too far."

"Why do you say that?" Toly put the pan of biscuits in the oven.

"Because she treats them like they're her children."

Toly had noticed that for a long time. It was one of her traits he most admired. "Maybe that's why she's going to win the national championship this time round. There's nothing wrong with those horses knowing they're loved. She's ranked second in winnings and is depending on them to bring her to number one."

"What I'd give to see that happen! No one deserves it more than she does."

Toly couldn't agree more. Both brother and sister deserved that honor. He'd spent a lot of time on their ranch training with Mills, hoping to see as much of Nikki as possible. When she was there, she worked harder to perfect her circles and figure eights than anyone he'd ever seen. The self-discipline she imposed on herself was the reason she was a champion.

Whatever disappointment she'd suffered in love, she hadn't let it affect her standings or work ethic. Toly would like to know a lot more about her personal feelings, but Mills hadn't shared that information with him. Being Nikki's twin, the two of them were careful to protect the other's privacy.

Though it was commendable, Toly was finding it more and more aggravating because his desire to get closer to her had met with a setback earlier in the barn. Something had gone on that hadn't felt right to him and he was determined to get to the bottom of it.

Mills disappeared to talk to her. Toly was forced to live in suspense until his friend came back to the kitchen. "She'll be right over." He started to set the table.

Surprised at the relief he felt to hear that news, Toly turned the steaks and checked on the biscuits that were almost done.

"Later on she has to attend a WPRA party at the MGM Grand," Mills added, "so she won't be able to stay long."

Toly ground his teeth in frustration because after she left, it meant he wouldn't see her again until tomorrow. Throughout the next ten days she'd be staying at the Cyclades Hotel every night. Damn.

The Wrangler party for the finalists Nikki had to attend at the MGM Grand would be one of the big highlights during her stay in Las Vegas. For one particular reason tonight that had everything to do with the man in the rig next door, it would be her pleasure to dress the part of rodeo queen to the hilt. She'd brought an overnight bag with her in the car that contained her outfit.

After exercising her horses, she showered in the rig and put on her new Wrangler cream scoop-neck dress with the elaborate crochet back. It fell to the knees.

She paired it with ankle-high Italian leather boots in a sand color.

After Mills told her that he and Toly had invited her to come for dinner, she went overboard on her makeup. A rodeo queen's whole purpose in life was meant to knock a man's eyes out, right? She'd do her best to live up to Toly Clayton's preconceived notions, maybe even surpass them. That would be a novel idea. Nikki brushed her hair, leaving it long and flowing. After fastening her new lacy gold chandelier earrings, she put on her dressy cream felt cowboy hat. She'd bought a new handbag to go with her dress and put her wallet and keys inside. One more look in the mirror. The result made her smile. She was ready to do her worst.

She left her rig and walked around to Toly's. They knew she was coming so she let herself in without knocking. Something smelled good. Since her brother wasn't known for his cooking, she had to assume Toly was the chef. Unless they'd bought takeout.

Nikki found them in the kitchen putting food on the table. "Good evening, gentlemen." She put her bag down on the end of the counter. They both turned their heads toward her.

A tangible silence filled the trailer's interior.

"Well, don't all speak at the same time," she teased. "Wasn't I supposed to come for dinner?"

Mills's eyebrows lifted. His face wore the most comical expression she'd ever seen. "Good grief, Nikki."

"What's wrong?"

"Nothing," he said quietly. "You look…nice." He had a hard time getting that word out, making her want to laugh.

"Thanks. Where do you want me to sit?"

"Right here." Toly galvanized into action and pulled out a chair for her. She felt his eyes taking inventory of her face and figure as she sat down. Maybe she *had* accomplished her objective and dazzled him just enough to make him choke a little on his own words.

Mmm. Steak and potatoes. Biscuits too? "Isn't this exciting? All three of us here in Las Vegas at last?" Nikki glanced at Toly. "By the way, did my Pony Pop do the trick?" she asked after they'd started to eat.

He passed her the tossed salad. "I had to split it two ways, but they both seemed happy enough."

"Next time give them their own packets and see what happens. I've got a ton of them in my rig. You're welcome to help yourself to as many as you want to sweeten things up."

"I'll remember that. Thanks."

Mills eyed both of them. "What are you two talking about?"

"Duchess was overjoyed to see your sister earlier. She gave me a Pony Pop and told me to feed it to Snapper. Maybe he'd be more excited to see me."

Nikki could tell her brother was bewildered, but she was quite enjoying herself and continued to eat. "This dinner is delicious."

"Thanks," Toly said. The man didn't sound happy and she couldn't have been more thrilled. "Would you like a homemade biscuit?"

So he *had* done all the cooking. "Much as I'm tempted, I don't dare. You cowboys don't know how hard we cowgirls and rodeo queens have to work to watch our figures. After trying for so long year after year to stand out in order to be noticed, I'm afraid I'll always be worrying about how I look. It's kind of what we live for, you know? But this steak and salad were perfect for me and have hit the spot."

Mills had stopped eating. He looked sick.

She smiled at Toly. "My congratulations to the cook who's a team roper too. Imagine me thinking you only knew how to make coffee when we were at the ranch."

Delighted to have delivered that last salvo, she pushed away from the table and got to her feet. "Now I'm afraid I have to go. Sorry I won't be able to help you clean up, but I'm sure you understand I can't be late for the photographers. This party is important because they're setting up a special photo shoot that could open doors for me. You have no idea how eager I am to explore all my new possibilities. Good night, guys. Thanks again for inviting me."

With her cheeks hot from being so worked up, Nikki reached for her purse and left the trailer. She hurried behind her rig and got in the rental car. On her way to the MGM, Nikki relived the last half hour in her mind and was shocked by the way she'd acted. It was like another person had emerged and taken over.

Obviously Toly's conversation with her brother had gotten under her skin and tonight her anger had spilled over. She was incensed for all the women she'd competed with who loved the rodeo and wanted to enjoy every part and aspect of it.

The men who lived and died for the rodeo were no different. They just didn't line up on stage and get chosen as the best or the worst by a committee. Toly Clayton had been strutting his stuff around the country for a long time. His huge fan base fed his ego and was his judge. Who was he to put labels on the women who loved the rodeo and found fulfillment in their own way?

But on the drive to the MGM Grand, her thoughts always came back to the Toly she'd gotten to know over the last year. That Toly had been so fun to talk to. Between rodeos, they'd come back to the ranch and sat around the table in the kitchen to eat after working out.

He was a fascinating conversationalist. They'd exchanged stories about what had gone on while they'd traveled the circuit. He knew everyone's scores and who to watch. So did she. She'd loved the times when the three of them could be together and share their lives. Nikki had grown to look forward to every meeting with him.

But no longer…

She blinked away the tears threatening and pressed on the gas, anxious to get tonight over with.

Chapter 3

Toly could no longer enjoy his meal while he was trying to put two and two together.

Mills had stopped eating and threw his head back. "What in the hell was all that about? I could swear that wasn't my sister who was eating dinner with us a few minutes ago."

"I hate to say it, but I think I know."

"Then you're a prophet."

"Answer me one question. Is Nikki's bedroom upstairs or on the main floor of the ranch house?"

Mills blinked. "The main floor at the end of the..." He groaned and got to his feet. "That's it! She came home the other night after leaving the dealership and overheard us talking about Denise on the way to her bedroom."

Toly closed his eyes tightly. "If she'd listened to our whole conversation, she wouldn't have been angry."

His friend nodded. "You're right. Hell. She heard just enough to send her off the rails. In my whole life, I've never seen this side of my sister."

"Except that she wasn't mad at you. That whole performance tonight was for *my* benefit." It explained how strangely she'd acted at the barn. Now that he knew the truth, he was horrified by the answer.

"I'm positive she happened to overhear me give you Wymon's advice. Taken out of context, his words would have dealt her a fierce blow and turned her inside out. As you said tonight, you didn't recognize your sister. Neither did I."

He threw down his napkin and jumped up from the table. "I've got to find her at the MGM Grand and explain. Carrying this kind of pain has already caused her serious damage. She needs to know the whole truth so she can give the performances of her life out in the arena." He reached for his own set of car keys.

"I couldn't agree more. She's hurting bad, Toly. You go. I'll clean up here."

Toly grabbed his cowboy hat and lightweight jacket, then flew out of the rig to the car. He was surprised he wasn't pulled over by the police while he made his way through heavy traffic to the hotel at top speed. His mind kept replaying the words she'd overheard. He cringed to realize what he'd said about those rodeo beauty queen types. *They're in love with their own image. The dude who's hooked is doomed to be an afterthought.*

He pulled in to the short-term parking area. The first hour was free. He had no idea how long he would be there and kept the ticket to pay later. Once inside the hotel festively decorated for Christmas, he saw that the

WPRA party was meeting in the Vista room on the second level and went upstairs.

Men weren't part of this exclusive crowd of women who were the best barrel racers in the world. From the doorway Toly took in the dressed-up finalists who mingled and chatted with organizers and sponsors. Nikki blew everyone away. She stood talking to several of the finalists he recognized. He found her so breathtaking, he wondered if he would ever get it back. Earlier tonight when she'd walked in the kitchen, her beauty had almost caused him to pass out.

Toly had no idea how long she would stay at the party, but it didn't matter. He planted himself by the entrance to wait for her. Photographers took pictures, but she ignored them and moved around the room. He got the distinct impression she couldn't wait to leave and had only put in an appearance because it was expected.

That was fine with Toly, who couldn't wait to get her alone so they could have a long talk. Another ten minutes and it turned out his instincts had been right. She was the first woman to move away from the crowd and head out the main doors. When she walked past him without seeing him, he called her name.

She turned her head. "Toly?" Her expression changed to one of pure fear. "What's wrong? Has something happened to Mills?"

He hadn't seen that coming. The twins had a special bond of love and were close, but he'd just witnessed for himself *how* close. She would never have expected to see Toly here. Naturally her shock was genuine and it touched him how much she cared for her brother.

But it also caused something to twist in his gut because of the painful reason for seeking her out. She shouldn't have to deal with anything but the coming events out in the arena.

"Mills is fine, but I'm not. We have to talk."

Her jaw hardened. "Not tonight. I'm tired."

"It has to be tonight, but not here," he insisted. "We can do it in your rig or at your hotel."

He could see the pulse throbbing at the base of her creamy throat. "What will you do if I don't cooperate? Tie me up like one of your Corriente steers and haul me off?"

Her sarcasm came as a surprise. "If I have to. It's up to you if you don't want a scene."

Color swept into her cheeks. She started walking. He followed her all the way out of the hotel to her car in the parking lot where she sustained a barrage of whistles from every male in sight. When she unlocked it and got in, he climbed in the passenger side.

"How did you get here?" she blurted.

"I drove our rental car."

"Tell me where it is and I'll take you to it."

"I'll worry about it later."

She turned on the engine. "You don't trust me not to take off and leave you standing there?"

"Frankly no. Not in your state of mind."

"What state is that?" She wheeled around before finding the exit.

"The one that brought you close to clipping the end of that car when you turned too fast just now."

She pressed on the accelerator. "There's no way I'm letting you in my hotel room."

"That's fine with me. As you know I'm allergic to them and much prefer our rigs."

Even having to weave through heavy traffic, it didn't

take her long to reach the RV park. She wound around to her rig and parked behind it. He got out and reached the trailer door before she did.

The interior of the Dobson rig was every bit as luxurious and comfortable as his. Mills had told him their parents had invested in it for their children several years ago. It was a damn shame they were no longer alive.

He took off his hat and removed his jacket, putting both on the love seat next to him. She disappeared to her bedroom and came out a minute later without her hat.

"I've already told you I'm exhausted." She sat down opposite him. "Please say what you have to say so I can get to bed."

He learned forward with his hands on his thighs. "During dinner, it was obvious to me you overheard Mills and me talking in your family's den on Friday night. I'm sorry you only heard part of it, the part that offended you. For that I'm deeply sorry and want to apologize."

She crossed her long, elegant legs. "There's no need. You didn't know I was outside the door and you're entitled to your own opinion. I was about to say good-night to you, but I heard you talking and—"

"And you found out enough to—"

"To know your opinion of my kind is held by most of the male population," she interrupted him.

Toly sucked in his breath. "You know that's not true and you're wrong, Nikki. What you heard was an opinion voiced by my oldest brother, Wymon, years ago when I started competing in the rodeo. He'd been hurt by the woman he'd thought loved him and hoped to marry. In his pain, he gave me advice so I wouldn't get destroyed.

"That speech you heard was *his* speech, not mine. I was trying to comfort your brother who's been knocked sideways by Denise. To be honest, I was hurt for him that she chose to break up with him this close to Finals. Of course, it's none of my business and I'm sure the timing wasn't planned, but he has suffered and it has affected his performance."

Nikki averted her eyes.

"By the time you left for the MGM Grand, I realized you had to have heard enough of my conversation with Mills to infuriate you. In fact, it shows great character that you didn't tell me to go to hell to my face before leaving the rig."

"I came close," she admitted.

He smiled. "I knew that. It's why I took after you and wouldn't let you get away from me before I was able to explain what you overheard. The last thing I want is to see you thrown off during the competition because of the cruel remarks you attributed to my feelings. You couldn't be more wrong, Nikki. In my opinion, no other woman comes close to you in any way, shape or form."

She laughed sadly. "You don't have to go overboard."

"Actually I do." No matter how friendly the three of them had been over the last year, Nikki didn't have a clue how he really felt about her. "What's vital to me is that you believe me. I won't rest until I know I have your forgiveness."

Her luminous gray gaze lifted to his. "Of course. I'm afraid I'm the one who needs to ask forgiveness. It proves how much damage can be done by only hearing part of a conversation I wasn't privy to. My reaction does me no credit, especially when you were trying to help my brother. Let's be honest. Neither you nor Mills had any idea I'd come home."

That sounded like the Nikki who'd taken up space in his heart.

"When we left the dealership, I'd hoped the three of us would all head back to the ranch together. But you were still being swarmed by your fans and Mills decided not to wait for you."

"I was surprised how many people came by to meet us." She got to her feet. "I'm thirsty. Would you like a cola? I think it's all we've got."

Toly wouldn't have cared what it was. She was speaking to him again. "I'd love one."

Nikki went into the kitchen and brought back two cans from the fridge. "I'm sorry I was so rude during dinner, Toly. It's my loss that I turned down your home-made biscuits."

"They're my one claim to fame."

"I happen to know that's not true. You're the one who cooked dinner, not Mills. He would never have thought to add pieces of tangerines and walnuts to the salad, or add cheese to the potatoes."

So she'd noticed. "Will you let me take you to dinner tomorrow after the vet checks our horses? Spending time on your ranch, I know how much you like pasta. I thought we'd enjoy some Mediterranean food at Todd English's Olives in the Bellagio Hotel. It'll be my way of apologizing to you in style."

Her eyes smiled at him. "I'd be a fool to turn down an offer like that. You're on."

"Good. You've made my night."

On his way to the hotel earlier, he'd felt like the bottom had dropped out of his life. He could hardly credit the change in the situation since clearing up a misunderstanding that could have done a great deal of harm to all of them.

"As soon as we finish our drinks, I'll drive you back to the parking lot to get your car."

He wished she didn't have to go. "Can't you just stay here and we'll drive to your hotel in the morning?"

"No. I've got an early breakfast with some of the marketers I can't miss. I would rather get back to the hotel tonight. Mills should be coming inside any minute so he can go to bed. It'll be easy to drop you off on my way."

"Then I'm ready to leave when you are." He stood up and put his empty can in the wastebasket.

She left hers on the counter and went back to the bedroom for her things. Before long they were on their way.

"We haven't had a chance to talk privately about Denise. Do you have any idea why she broke it off with Mills? I don't mean to pry. If you don't feel comfortable telling me, I understand."

"I wish I knew." That sounded honest. "She hasn't called me since they stopped seeing each other."

"Would you like to hear Mills's theory?"

"Yes!" she cried. "We usually share everything, but not about this. I've been worried sick about him."

"He thinks she's so jealous of you, she can't be around you anymore. Since you and your brother are so close, it forced her to call things off."

"What?"

"I was shocked too."

"That *couldn't* be the reason, Toly!"

"I don't want to think it, either. He has accepted it's

over, but it's sad that she did it so close to the competition."

"I thought so too, but decided there had to be another reason she's not telling anyone. You can tell my brother it's not because of me. I don't think it's about him, either. I know she cared for him a lot and is the sweetest, kindest girl in the world."

"That's what he thought."

"He can still think it! Something's not right. We became close friends. One of these days we'll learn the truth. For her to call him and tell him she couldn't see him anymore means something traumatic had to have happened. But I know it's killing Mills. He's never cared for another girl like this."

"He'll feel better knowing you believe in her."

"I do." They'd reached the MGM Grand. "Where are you parked?"

Toly gave her directions. She stopped in front of his car. He turned to her. "Thank you for giving me the chance to talk to you."

"I'm glad you insisted. I have to admit I was hurt. It's a lesson I've needed to learn so I'll never let anything like this happen again."

"You were pretty scary at dinner. Mills looked green."

"Don't remind me. I'm ashamed of acting like a woman scorned."

Toly burst into laughter. "To be honest, you not only fascinated me, you were dead-on about my lack of talents."

She shook her head, causing her flouncy black hair to swish across her shoulders. "I didn't mean it."

"I believe you, but it's true. I've been so obsessed

with the rodeo, when it's all over I'm going to have to work at becoming a participating member of the human race again."

"That makes two of us. We have to be terribly boring to people who've never been around horses and never want to be."

Now was the perfect time to ask her a question Mills hadn't been able to answer. "Your brother told me you were in a relationship a while back that didn't work out. He's been worried about you. I guess that's the nature of being twins."

He heard her soft chuckle. "We do far too much thinking about each other and try to solve each other's problems. It's worse since our parents died. A psychiatrist would tell us it's not healthy, but we don't know any other way."

"My brothers and I aren't so different, even if we aren't twins. Our father's death changed our lives too."

"Tell me what happened."

He'd never shared this with anyone outside of his family, but it felt good talking to her about it. "I'll never forget. My dad had taken me hunting up in the Sapphire Mountains. We'd camped out for a couple of nights and I'd never felt closer to him.

"He'd been a rodeo champion and knew how much I loved the sport. During our talks he encouraged me to go for it if that's what was important to me. I could earn money to pay for my college and enjoy the sport at the same time. I loved him for being so understanding. On our way down the mountain, he suddenly fell over. Blood poured out of his head. I knew immediately he'd been shot."

"Oh no, Toly! How horrible."

"It was the worst thing I ever lived through."

"I know how you felt. We got the call from the police that our parents had been killed in a head-on crash. The pain of knowing they're gone and you're absolutely helpless to do anything about it is unreal."

Toly nodded. "Exactly. I called my brothers and they came with the sheriff. There was nothing to do for Dad. He'd died immediately. One bullet had wiped out his life. The authorities investigated and discovered it had been a freak accident by another hunter. It changed our lives."

"Oh, how I know that. I'm so sorry for your loss, Toly."

"I feel the same about yours."

"You can tell Mills that Ted Bayliss is long gone from my life with no lingering regrets. It wouldn't have worked. But if my brother hears that from you, he'll believe it. I don't know if you've figured it out yet, but you're more or less the final word with him. I'll reveal one more secret in case you weren't aware. The great Toly Clayton was always his idol."

So many revelations at one time had made Toly's night, particularly the knowledge that she was no longer hung up on the man who, according to Mills, she'd come close to marrying.

The way he was feeling right now, he was ready to rope the steers lined up for the next ten nights at unheard-of speeds. Talk about leaping tall buildings in a single bound—

He got out of the car. "Thanks for bringing me back. I'll follow you to your hotel to make sure you get there safely. Looking like you do, you need a bodyguard."

"That's heady talk." She flashed him a smile that sent

his pulse skyrocketing before he shut the door and got into his car. During dinner he never expected to see a smile like that from her again.

Toly turned on the engine and followed her all the way to the Cyclades Hotel. He waited while she parked her car in the lot. After finding a space nearby, he got out of his to walk her to the entrance.

"You don't have to do this, Toly."

Yes, he did. She looked like a miracle of femininity. He wanted to be with her as long as possible. "I feel like it."

"Thank you," she said when they reached the doors.

"Good night, Nikki. Don't forget dinner tomorrow. I'll see you after the vet leaves the stalls."

"Sounds good." There was a moment of hesitation before she turned to walk inside. He wondered if she'd wanted to invite him to her room to talk some more, but had controlled the impulse.

Toly walked back to his car, determined that there were going to be lots of talks over the next ten nights, either in her hotel room or his rig. Tonight they'd achieved détente. This was just the beginning.

Nikki got through her next busy day in a daze because she knew she'd be seeing Toly for dinner. So much had been going on in her head after she'd gone to bed, she hadn't fallen asleep for a long time. The old adage about love and hate being two sides of the same coin had taken on new meaning.

Last night she'd left for the MGM Grand so upset, she couldn't imagine calming down. While she'd attended the party, she'd realized what a pathetic fool she'd been to let that anger go on any longer. Wasn't it the truth that eavesdroppers never heard good of themselves.

Before she left the room, she'd decided that tomorrow she would concentrate on improving her skills. How else to come in with the shortest time possible around the barrels every night? Nothing else was important.

Then she'd seen Toly outside the Vista room entrance and her anger had spiraled, almost sending her into shock. Yet once they'd ended up in her rig and he'd explained the situation that had turned her inside out in the first place, everything changed. By the time he'd walked her to the front entrance of her hotel, she hadn't wanted him to go. Faster than she could believe, Toly had become the most important man in her universe.

After the vet had checked out all their horses, Toly had told her he'd be by her hotel at six and meet her in the foyer. From there they'd drive over to the Bellagio.

Though she willed her heart to behave, it still thudded out of control when she saw him walk through the hotel doors at six. He wore a tan Western suit with a cream shirt and a gold-and-silver bolo tie with gold cords.

Toly's handsome features and hard-muscled physique made him striking in a way that prevented Nikki from noticing anyone else. His light green eyes roved over her features. It was crazy how her breathing quickened.

"You're right on time." She could smell the soap he'd used in the shower.

"I've been waiting for tonight and you look sensational. Let's go."

He cupped her elbow and walked her outside to his car. Nikki was glad she'd bought the black skirt and black short Western jacket with the colored red embroidery and fringed sleeves. It had been worth the steep price to evoke a compliment from him.

Toly had booked their table in advance at Todd English's Olives. Once they reached the Bellagio, they weren't kept waiting long. Throughout their dinner of succulent beef carpaccio and ricotta ravioli, he hardly kept his eyes off of her. She had a difficult time not staring at him too.

"Do you know what Mills is doing this evening? He didn't answer my text."

"He met up with friends after doing some shopping."

It wasn't like her brother not to answer. The poor guy wasn't acting himself, but she knew Denise was the reason why. "I did my shopping in Great Falls."

"I think he left it until now so he can walk off his nerves."

"I'm sure you're right. Everyone has their own way of coping before competition."

"Well, I don't know about you, but being out to dinner with the most beautiful woman in the restaurant has made me forget everything else."

She smiled. "Flattering as that is, I don't buy it. For the last hour I've noticed you flexing your right hand off and on during our meal. If I didn't know better, I'd think you were imagining yourself on your horse, waiting for the gate to open while you figured out how best to rope your steer."

His eyes narrowed. "Only a pro like yourself would catch me out."

"I've watched my brother long enough to know he goes through roping scenarios in his head, even when he's talking to me. He gets this vacant look."

Toly laughed. "I know it well. Are you ready to order dessert?"

"Not tonight. I need a good sleep and the extra sugar will keep me awake."

"I'm passing on it too. Shall we go?" He signaled the waiter for the bill, and they left. "Tomorrow's our big day," Toly murmured as they made their way back to her hotel.

"Don't I know it. I want to thank you for getting me through tonight. The dinner was delicious."

"The pleasure has been mine." He parked the car and took her arm to walk her inside. His touch sent a current of electricity through her body. Their eyes met one more time. "I'll be cooking dinner again at four thirty tomorrow. Why don't you join me and Mills before we head on over to the Mack Center? Before you say no, just keep in mind it's a great relaxer for me."

"When I have the time, it is for me too. Thank you, Toly. I'll come if I can leave my last scheduled party soon enough. Good night."

She turned and headed toward the other end of the foyer. Though she didn't look around, she could feel his gaze on her. It gave her the kind of delicious shakes she'd heard about all her life, but had never experienced until now.

Nikki was in love with him and knew it. That's why it had almost destroyed her to hear what he'd told Mills in private. Yet somehow she had to handle her emotions while she was facing the most challenging moments in her career as a professional barrel racer.

Being in love with her brother's roping partner had heightened the stakes. When she reached her hotel room, she found she was breathless reliving the events of the evening with him. *Toly, Toly.*

Chapter 4

After Toly returned to the RV park, he grabbed some horse treats out of his rig and walked over to the barn where he found Mills inspecting his favorite horse. His friend barely acknowledged him. Toly stood near the stall. "What's wrong with Atlas? The vet already checked out our horses today."

Mills lifted his head. "He's fine. Where were you tonight?"

He frowned. "I took Nikki to dinner as my way of apologizing to her. Didn't you get my text?"

"Nope."

"That's strange." Toly pulled out his phone and checked it. "Damn! I wrote it, but didn't press Send. Here. Take a look."

"Forget it. I believe you."

"Did you and the guys go to dinner?"

He nodded.

Toly gave his own horses a pat down before he walked over to Mills who was settling his other horse Dusty for the night. "Want to tell me what's going on with you?"

Mills looked at him hard. "My sister wouldn't have gone to dinner with you if she weren't interested."

His head jerked back. Where had that come from? "She agreed to go because she knew I felt terrible about what happened. It was my way of making it up to her."

"No." He walked out of the stall. "She went because she wanted to."

He felt as if he'd been gut-punched. "I thought you were glad I drove to the MGM Grand to talk to her."

"I was, and I'm thankful she was able to forgive you because that's the kind of person she is. Maybe too forgiving."

Whoa. "Mills? What's going on with you? Since when was it wrong for me to ask her to dinner? Talk to me!"

"I'm not saying it was wrong. But because it's *you*—the cowboy who can have any girl he wants at any time and walk away until the next one comes along—I'm worried. My sister isn't that kind."

A prickling of anger started at the back of Toly's neck. "You mean she's not like the groupies. Don't you think I know that? I've never gone out of my way to attract her attention."

"I know. That's the hell of it. You're a magnet. That Amanda Fleming you met during the last rodeo? Lyle sent me some emails and said she's in Vegas and has emailed you more than once on our website. All you had to do was have one dinner with her, and she's back for more. But you and I both know you never plan to see her again."

Toly couldn't believe what he was hearing and it hurt like hell. "I had no idea you've resented me for such a long time."

He shook his head. "I don't resent you, Toly. Not at all. But I can see what's happening to my sister and I'm scared you're going to hurt her more than she's ever been hurt in her life."

"You honestly think I would do anything to cause her grief?"

"Not intentionally. The guy she fell in love with hurt her so badly, she's really fragile."

That wasn't the impression Nikki had given him. But he could see Mills was a mess right now. "Shall I uninvite her for dinner tomorrow afternoon before we all leave for the rodeo?"

Mills's eyes darkened. "You asked her?"

"Wasn't that the plan while we were here in Las Vegas? Eat our meals together before each event? Isn't that what we decided before we drove here? What's changed?"

Mills looked stone-faced. "Has she already accepted?"

"She said she'd come if she could get away in time from another party she'll be attending."

He looked down. "You can be sure she'll do whatever she has to do to be there, so it's already too late to tell her not to come."

Toly had to think fast. "We can send a message right now that dinner is off because you and I have been talking and need to go over to the center early tomorrow."

"No. You can't do that."

"Then what do you want me to do, Mills?"

"I wish the hell I knew."

"That's not a good enough answer. Talk to me."

Mills squinted at him. "I guess it's because Dad isn't around. He'd give her the kind of advice she needs. When I try to talk to her, she doesn't take me seriously."

"What advice is that?"

His jaw hardened. "That she needs to concentrate on her rodeo career before she gets involved with another man." He turned abruptly and strode out of the barn.

Ninety-nine percent of this reaction had to do with Denise's rejection. But the remaining 1 percent convinced him that Mills didn't want Toly to be that man. Was that because Mills didn't like him personally and didn't think he was good enough for Nikki? That thought hurt.

The two of them needed to work this out before too much more time passed. After saying good-night to his horses and giving them some treats they devoured in record time, he followed after Mills.

But when he knocked on the rig door, his friend didn't answer. At that point Toly walked to his own rig and phoned Wymon. To his relief his brother answered and they talked about everything.

"Sorry that my advice to you years ago has caused problems now."

"Ironic, isn't it, when it was such good advice for me back then?"

"Bro—I've known you've been in love with her this last year. Not in so many words, but I've recognized the signs. And Mom has moaned at the way you've spent so much time at their ranch to train."

Wymon understood a lot. He wasn't the older brother for nothing. "Yep."

"I'm sure Mills has sensed it."

"I realize that, but I don't know what to do. What a time for this to happen with the competition starting tomorrow!"

"Tonight he exploded with nerves and everything else. But *he's* got to be the one who figures that out, Toly. Not you. He knows you didn't do anything wrong. By morning he'll have cooled off and probably apologize. He's a good man."

"I *know* he is."

"If you want my advice, until you leave Las Vegas, be your friendly self to him and Nikki. Do what you always do and concentrate on winning that championship. Don't change anything. If Nikki can tell he's trying to come between the two of you, let *her* be the one who goes to her brother. No one will ever be able to reassure him the way she can."

Toly took a deep breath. "Thanks, Wymon. I needed to hear that."

"One more thing. I'm glad you've finally admitted you're in love. Be assured I won't tell anyone else. Good luck tomorrow night. We'll be watching you on TV. I'm counting on all three of you coming in first!"

During the early hours Thursday morning, Nikki's crew transported her horses to the Mack Center stalls. She worked with them before all the finalists met to rehearse for the arena parade that would take place that evening. Toly and Mills had the honor of carrying the Montana flags for their event. Laurie Rippon had won the right to hoist the Texas flag for the barrel racers.

With the rehearsal over, she left for the Cowboy Gifts Party, but didn't stay long. After going back to the hotel to shower and pack a bag, she drove to the RV park to join Mills and Toly for an early dinner in his rig. Once again she could smell food cooking when she walked inside. Toly was at the stove.

"Hi!"

His head turned. "Hi, yourself!"

"I noticed the car missing. Where's Mills?"

"His glove got a rip in it today during practice. He ran out to buy a new pair. I expect him back pretty soon."

She walked through and sat down at the kitchen table. He'd already made blueberry muffins and urged her to try one. After a first bite she ate the whole thing. "These are wonderful. I'm addicted already."

"Good. I've got a roast cooking with potatoes. It'll be done before long."

"There's no hurry. I haven't stopped all day. It feels good to sit."

"How was the Christmas party?"

"Wonderful, but crowded even if it was staged at the South Halls Center, or maybe because it was." She chuckled and eyed him covertly. "Have you had a chance to tell my brother about my thoughts where Denise is concerned?"

Toly poured them coffee and sat down. "Yes. He's reserving judgment, but I know it made him feel better to hear that you felt there was another explanation for why she broke up with him."

"I don't think anything could improve his spirits right now."

He studied her for a moment. "How about yours? Tonight we'll be posting our first scores. Are you ready to knock them dead?"

"Don't I wish, but I'm not worried about you and Mills. You've averaged number one going into Finals. I'm positive you're going to win the whole thing."

"*I'm* not." The fear that his hand might lose feeling at the wrong moment was haunting him more and more. "Did you check out Shay Carlson's last couple of scores? He got a 3.90 in Oklahoma. We're going to have to do better to win."

She moaned. "I hear what you're saying. I've got to beat Laurie Rippon. At the Austin rodeo I got a 13.57 on Bombshell. That was my best score this year, but Laurie turned in a 13.49 and is in the number one spot going into Finals. She's the one who makes me the most nervous."

"You can bet she's scared of you being in second place. So little separates the two of you."

"I know." She sighed.

"This is the hard part, isn't it? Anticipating the odds. Waiting for it to start."

"It's awful." She needed to stay busy. "I'll set the table." Nikki finished another muffin. "I really put my foot in it when I refused your biscuits the other night. You knew I was a fraud."

His eyes lit up in amusement, sending curling warmth through her. "But while you were making your point, no one could have topped your delivery. Did you say you were the number one debater in your high school?"

"Are you kidding?" She burst into laughter.

"You could have fooled me."

She knew when he was joshing her. Nikki tried to

remember the last time she'd had this much fun, but she couldn't.

He darted her glance. "Tell you what. Since your brother hasn't come yet, let's go in the living room to wait for him. I'm in the mood for cards. What's your game?"

This was going to be fun. "Anything."

"Is that right?" He sent her a wicked smile.

"Yep."

"I get to pick the penalties."

"I think we should take turns on that."

She felt his chuckle resonate inside her.

"How about a little music?" He turned on the radio to some soft rock and reached for a deck of cards before they sat down at the little table.

"I wonder how many cards games have been played on this?"

"Thousands," he said with a poker face.

Nikki shook her head. "That wouldn't surprise me."

He grinned. "How about pontoon?"

"Great! It's kind of like blackjack. I love it."

"Shall we say a set of twenty rounds to start? If I win, you'll have to dance with me. If you win, you'll have to dance with me."

That set Nikki off laughing and they played a fast, slap-down hysterical game. To her surprise she did win, but that didn't seem to bother Toly who pulled her out of the chair into his arms without giving her a chance to think about it. "Um. This is nice."

Nikki felt his words in every atom of her body. She'd never been this close to Toly's rock-hard physique and had been waiting secretly for this moment for a long time. It was a far cry from line dancing where there were separations in their togetherness. They were both tall and they fit together as if they were made for each other.

He smelled wonderful. Nikki loved the feel of his hard jaw against her cheek. It sent darts of awareness through her body. The temptation to turn her head and kiss his compelling mouth was killing her. Toly didn't let her go and she could have stayed in his arms all night.

"If you hadn't been involved with someone else, we could have relaxed like this before an event long before now," he whispered into her hair.

Her heart jumped to think he might have been thinking about her on a more intimate level over the last few months too. Still, he'd never let her know. They'd all been friends and she knew Toly kept his cards close to the chest. But the way she was feeling right now, he had to know she didn't want to be anywhere else.

They both heard a car door slam at the same time. "That'll be Mills," she murmured in silent protest. His arrival had saved her from making a fool of herself in a grand way.

She eased herself away from Toly and hurried back to the kitchen. He followed her. The time spent with him for the last hour had been a bit of heaven she hadn't wanted to end. Last night her anger had flowed like lava. Tonight she was mush in Toly's arms.

If her brother had seen them dancing together with no air separating them, it would have shocked him and she wouldn't have blamed him for that reaction.

Mills opened the door and came in the kitchen. "Hey, guys."

Nikki eyed her brother. "There you are! I heard you had to buy a new pair of gloves."

"Yep. One of them got ripped. I found a new flex knit kind that are thinner and easier to work with. Not so much bulk." He stood at the sink to wash his hands.

"Do you wear that kind too?" she asked Toly.

He sent her a slow smile, as if he too was remembering what was going on before Mills came in. "No. Since I'm the header, I have to have the heavier Kevlar glove for protection."

"I didn't realize. You learn something new every day." She turned to Mills. "We're glad you're back."

"Come and sit down, dude. Our dinner's in the oven waiting for you and we're starving."

"I got held up with a couple of friends."

"That's okay. You were gone longer than we thought, so we started a card game. Your sister beat me."

Toly took out the roast and put it on the table. Nikki could see he'd arranged potatoes and carrots around it and they'd cooked in the juice. Her own mother couldn't have done it better. "That looks scrumptious."

"I need a lot of protein along with carbs."

She'd witnessed that at dinner last night when she'd wished they could have spent all night together. "Don't we all, and plenty of snacks throughout the day."

It was fun to eat and talk shop with the top team roper cowboy on this year's circuit. With the kind of regimen they had to keep, there was nothing to explain. They could read each other's minds.

Besides not being completely in love with him, this was yet another reason she could never have married Ted. It would have meant giving up the world of horses.

Being with Toly like this let her know more than ever that being with a man like him was the life she wanted.

Toly slanted her a glance. "I was hoping the three of us could play another set of cards before we have to leave for the center."

"I'd like that too." She struggled to keep the throb out of her voice.

"It's too late," Mills muttered.

Well…that solved that.

Nikki's brother was being impossible. Trying to lighten the mood she said, "Tomorrow I'll cook dinner just to make it fair. You guys will eat in our rig. I can plan our meal a little earlier so we can play a game of pontoon before we leave for the arena."

Toly nodded. "I hope you meant that, because now that you've offered, I'm not going to let you out of it." His tone excited her. She saw a glint in Toly's eyes, thrilling her more than anything because it meant the feelings she was experiencing weren't only on her part.

"Mills?" she prodded him. "Does that sound good to you?"

"Sure."

Sure? He wasn't only depressed, he was downright rude. "I like to cook," she continued, "and it will give Toly a break. Maybe my brother will even volunteer to help me?" she said to get a reaction, but none was forthcoming. They settled down to eat and she passed Mills some blueberry muffins.

"Don't mind if I do." He took one and devoured it, but he was unusually quiet.

Nikki smiled at Toly. "You really are a great cook."

"At least I'm good for something."

Upset at Mills by now she said, "You two looked

great out there today carrying our flag. I've never been more proud." Her heart had swelled with pride to watch the two of them race into the arena like the champions they were. Tonight there'd be fireworks and ear-deafening cheers from the packed center.

"You didn't look so bad yourself," her brother finally murmured.

"Well thank you for the overwhelming compliment. On that note, I'm going to go in the bedroom and get ready before we drive over to the arena."

If any of them won a gold buckle tonight, they'd pick them up at the South Point Hotel. Every night after the Wrangler National Finals, the public could watch the Go-Round Buckle Presentations. She had no doubts Toly and Mills would come in the top winners, but a first-place win for her was iffy.

"Hurry—" her brother interjected. "Otherwise we'll be late for the parade. I'll drive us over."

She had it on the tip of her tongue to remind him *he* was the reason they needed to rush now. But she held back and noticed that Toly had already started to clean things up.

"Give me a minute to put on my gear and I'll meet you outside." Nikki had a special Western shirt to wear with fringe and the ProRodeo insignia. After running a brush through her hair and applying lipstick, she was ready.

On the way out of the trailer, she reached for her white cowboy hat and put it on. Toly held the door open for her. "If you don't know it yet, you take my breath away," he whispered.

Much as she wanted to believe it, she was afraid to, not after her brother had told her Toly was *the* ladies' man on the circuit and always had been. How many other women had he said that to over the years?

She hurried out to the car where Toly was already standing. In a low voice he said, "With your long legs, you should sit in front." On that note he opened the front passenger door for her. No woman could be immune to the smile he flashed at her. "I'll sprawl across the backseat. Shall we go?"

Nikki climbed in and fastened her seat belt while she contemplated his flirtatious comments that took her mind off the coming event. Toly had a way of completely disarming her.

They were off to the Mack Center where the crowds were just about impossible to get through. Mills had radar eyes and found an empty space behind the center where all the trailers were parked.

This is it, Nikki Dobson. It's what they'd all killed themselves for and dreamed of. She got out of the car and they made their way into the rear of the building.

When they reached the inside, the three of them had to part company. She lifted her eyes to them. "Good luck, you guys."

"The same to you," they called after her.

Her heart was in her throat as she hurried off to mount her horse and line up in the alley prior to the parade.

Tonight Nikki had decided to ride Sassy, her palomino. In her tan Western shirt, they matched. As her father had once said, this horse had shown sass from the beginning, prompting Nikki to give her that name. She was a showstopper and handled crowds and noise like a trooper. Not only that, she was fast and would explode down the alley into the arena.

Andy and Santos met her at the stalls. They had her horse saddled and bridled with her softest bit to prevent pain from the rein tension. She walked up to Sassy and pressed her face near her ear. "Tonight's the night we've been working for, my girl," she crooned. Her horse nickered. "I know you're going to give me your all."

She fed her a Pony Pop from her pocket and Sassy chomped away, causing the three of them to chuckle. It was time. She pulled her gloves from her pocket and mounted her horse. Sassy had been through this routine earlier in the day and knew what was coming.

Making a clicking sound, she led her horse through the aisle to the back of the center where everyone was lining up according to their event. Nikki passed several of her competitors. They all smiled and looked fabulous. She swallowed hard to think she'd reached this milestone.

She looked for Toly, but couldn't see him because his group would be entering the arena long before hers. The music had started and the announcer was welcoming everyone to the Wrangler National Finals Rodeo. Between the noise and the fireworks, in her opinion, there was no buildup or excitement like it anywhere in sports.

Nikki patted Sassy's neck and kept talking to her while they waited in place for their turn to come. She spotted Laurie up in front carrying the Texas flag. It was almost their turn. "Remember what we're here for," she whispered to Sassy. "There's no horse like you. Act like someone and show your stuff!"

Suddenly her group started to move and they took off down the alley. The thrill of it sent a rush through Nikki's body. As they poured into the arena, the announcer named each contestant.

"Here comes Nikki Dobson in second place from the Sweet Clover Ranch in Great Falls, Montana. She's the former Miss Rodeo Montana riding her palomino Sassy."

The crowd went crazy and Nikki had to admit this was one experience she was thankful she hadn't missed while living on this earth. She raced around to her spot and drew up next to Laurie. At her other side was Portia Landwell, the number three finalist from Nebraska. Before long, all hundred-plus finalists were on display.

She doubted any of the pageants during the Middle Ages with their knights and pennants were any more spectacular and colorful than the sight of these superb athletic national champions carrying their flags and decked out in all their Western finery. Nikki felt great pride to even be a part of this, no matter if she came in last at the end of the ten days.

As they left the arena the way they came in, she caught sight of Toly carrying the Montana flag and leading their group with Mills who also carried a flag. Toly was a magnificent sight wearing a black Western shirt and his black cowboy hat. As far as Nikki was concerned, the quintessential male rodeo performer from the Clayton Cattle Ranch left everyone else in the dust.

Tears smarted her eyes before it was her turn to leave and exit the arena with the speed of the wind. Sassy was in her glory. Nikki had endowed her horse with human feelings. Maybe it was silly, but she didn't care.

When she reached the stalls, the first person she saw was Toly. He was still mounted on Snapper, but minus his flag. Their eyes met for a quiet moment. She knew he was seeing the look of elation on her face that illuminated his own countenance. Joy radiated through her being that they were experiencing this once-in-a-lifetime moment together.

His event would take place before hers, but it wouldn't be long now. "Go get 'em, cowboy."

"I intend to," he answered in his deep, rich voice. "But I'll be back to watch you cut circles around those barrels with the precision of a surgeon." Then he was off to win what she felt sure was their first victory for tonight.

"Nikki?" Santos called to her. "Are you all right?"

She turned to look down at him. How could she possibly answer that question when her heart was so full of emotions? The only thing she could say was yes.

Taking a deep breath, she led her horse down the aisle and walked her around until it was time for her event. There were screens in the back so she could watch the other events. She said a special prayer when she saw Toly and Mills were up next. But she had to wait because the first-place winners had to compete last.

She couldn't move as she watched and listened as they flew out of their gates with the steer running between them. Toly threw a butterfly loop with lightning speed and Mills was right there to finish up. The crowd went wild when it was announced they took first. No surprise there. Toly did it in 3.7 seconds and Mills in 3.8.

Beyond thrilled for them, Nikki mounted her horse and got in line. Soon her event was announced. "You've got to fly like the wind, Sassy girl. Here we go!"

She made a clicking sound and they were off with her heart thudding. They shot down the alley and out into the arena. Her mind was on Toly's words to cut those precision circles. But as she went around the first barrel, she felt something was wrong and corrected too late, losing time.

As she rode home, she saw her score and knew it wasn't good enough to be first. In a few minutes she learned Portia had brought in the top score, with Nikki a disappointing second. This score kept her at her second-place average. Her thoughts flew to Sassy who'd lost time. It meant Nikki had done something wrong, not her horse. Nikki realized she'd been in too big a hurry.

The guys came to congratulate her. She kept a smile on her face as she congratulated them. "I couldn't outdo you."

"You will," Toly assured her. "This was only the first night."

Mills hugged her and told her the same thing.

Together they drove to the South Point Hotel. Nikki loved watching them receive their gold buckles to the ear-splitting applause of the audience. She told them that if they wanted to party, she'd take a taxi back to the RV park. Both of them declined, saying they were tired and the three of them drove back to their rigs.

Nikki jumped out of the car ahead of them, needing quiet time to understand how to fix what had gone wrong tonight so it wouldn't happen again. "I'm so proud of you two, but now I have to get back to my hotel. I need to get up early and exercise the horses before tomorrow night's event.

"Don't forget, you guys. My turn to fix dinner. Come at four!" She hugged her brother.

Toly followed her to her car. "We'll be there. If you want to talk now, I'll come to your hotel."

There was nothing Nikki wanted more than to be alone with him, but Mills was waiting for him in their car.

"Thank you, Toly, but I'd prefer to get back and just crash."

"That's a good plan too. I've done it many times. Blot tonight out of your mind and start again tomorrow. But if you want to talk to me earlier tomorrow, you know where to find me."

She nodded.

In an unexpected move, he kissed her cheek and walked away before she got in her car. The touch of his lips on her skin sent tingles of delight through her body. She was still feeling the effects after she got in bed an hour later. Nikki finally fell asleep, longing for the moment when she felt his mouth on hers.

Chapter 5

Toly knew Nikki had suffered a huge setback tonight. Second place would never satisfy her, but she'd put on such a great front while they'd been out celebrating, you would never have known it.

He couldn't fully enjoy his first-place win with Mills, knowing how disappointed she had to be. As for Mills, he'd been in a bad place for a long time. Now with his sister's second-place win, he would be worrying over her even more.

"I'm going to bed, Toly." No small talk from Mills tonight. That was just as well. Toly wasn't in the mood for it, either.

"I hear you. See you in the morning." He watched Mills walk to the Dobson rig until he disappeared.

Toly felt like he was in an impossible situation wanting to be a good friend to Mills without revealing what was in his heart about Nikki.

After reaching for his gold buckle, he locked the car with his set of keys and entered his own rig. As he walked back to his bedroom, he read the half a dozen texts from family and close friends who'd sent their congratulations. Hail to the conquering hero. His brother Roce's well-meant message rang hollow. At one time Roce had been his partner until he gave up the rodeo to start veterinarian school.

Never had Toly felt less jubilant, not when his soul was so torn and conflicted. His interest in Nikki was part of the reason Mills couldn't pull himself out of the blackness. But there was no way Toly could stop caring about her any more than he could stop the sun from rising in the morning.

He'd told her he'd wanted to drive to her hotel and talk to her face-to-face. He ached to comfort her. After being with her earlier and dancing with her, he realized that he needed her in his life on a constant basis. But she'd said she'd wanted to go home and crash.

Had she told him that because her brother would be aware of it? Since they couldn't be together tonight, his only choice was to do the next best thing. After showering, he got in bed and phoned the Cyclades Hotel. Toly had never asked for her cell phone number, so he had to go through the operator and hoped Nikki picked up. At least he could say good-night to her one more time.

"I'm sorry, sir, but Ms. Dobson isn't answering. Do you want to leave a message?"

He debated for a moment. Maybe she wasn't in her room yet. Maybe she *was,* and fighting off deep pain. But when he thought about it, the things he wanted to talk to her about needed to be said in person.

"No. Thank you."

Any conversation with her would have to take place tomorrow. In the morning he'd give Mills some space and go to the local gym he always frequented. He'd work out to strengthen his lower right arm until he felt like dropping. Afterward he'd run his horses through some light exercise while he waited for four o'clock to roll around.

Knowing he wouldn't be falling asleep anytime soon, he turned on the TV and watched an old *Indiana Jones* movie until he knew nothing more.

Funny how Nikki had been living to perform at Finals, yet as soon as she'd finished her late Friday morning workout with the horses at the center, she'd rushed to the store to buy groceries for their dinner. This was her night to cook for Toly and wanted it to be special. Knowing she'd be seeing him shortly helped put last night's second-place finish behind her. She knew what she had to do to come in first.

Meat loaf and scalloped potatoes were big hits with her brother at home. She was sure Toly would like everything. But she didn't have time to make yeast rolls, so she bought the kind that all you had to do was let the dough rise and then bake them.

While she was putting the potatoes together, she heard a knock on the trailer door. Nikki left what she was doing to answer it.

"Toly—" He stood there with a twenty-inch-tall Christmas tree covered in tiny ornaments and lights.

"Merry Christmas!"

She couldn't believe it. "What a surprise! You're early! We won't be eating for another hour."

"I know, but Mills is still outside putting Atlas

through some more training exercises. My horses have done enough for one day. After practicing some loops on the dummy steer set up in the RV park, I didn't have anything else to do and thought I'd come and bother you. Maybe play some more cards with you."

She smiled. "The champion team roper who won last night didn't have one thing to do?"

"Nope. I had such a great time at our dinner last night, I want it to continue." *So do I, Toly. So do I.* "That is if you'll let me in."

"Oh—sorry. Of course." She was so thrilled to see him, she wasn't thinking clearly. "Forgive me. Come in the kitchen with your Christmas cheer. You can put it on the end of the counter and plug it in."

He set it up easily and the lights went on. It touched her heart that he'd been so thoughtful. "I love it! Thank you!"

"You're very welcome."

"Want some coffee and a doughnut?" She'd picked up half a dozen of those too.

"Thank you, ma'am. It's just what this cowboy needs."

She hurried to pour him a cup and told him to sit down at the kitchen table. After placing a plate of doughnuts in front of him, she put the potatoes and meat loaf in the oven. Once she'd fixed coffee for herself she joined him and munched on a doughnut. As usual they devoured carbs to stay energized.

In his Western shirt and jeans, Toly was so hunky she couldn't believe he'd come over just to hang out with her. It was like a dream come true to have him all to herself before Mills showed up. The tree made it seem like this was their little home, filling her with happiness.

Nikki studied him for a minute. "I'm sure you're going to win the championship this year. What I want to know is, did Mills speak the truth when he told me you're really going to retire from the rodeo when this is over, no matter what?"

When he said yes, it was after a long silence.

That seemed odd to her. "Would you mind telling me why?"

He sat back in the chair, eyeing her over the rim of his coffee mug. "I'm needed on the ranch full-time."

She considered his answer. "Not that it isn't a good reason, but is it your only one for walking away from the sport that has put you on the map? You've got more great years ahead of you. I'm curious."

A thoughtful look crossed over Toly's arresting male features, as if he were considering what he wanted to tell her. She wondered what had caused his hesitation in the first place.

"You've been in this business a long time like me, Nikki. We both know where the rodeo is headed. Team roping is the most popular event among amateur participants. The fans relate to the sport better than anything else in rodeo.

"Yet off the top of my head I can think of four Professional Rodeo Cowboys Association rodeos around the country that offer a shootout-style performance outside of the PRCA that *exclude* team roping, and in most cases tie-down roping."

She nodded. "I'm very much aware of it. I've seen the same problem with barrel racing. It isn't always included unless the Women's Pro Rodeo Association is involved. You know, the traditionalist's view of rodeo. I find it interesting that team roping was only added as a Professional Rodeo Cowboy Association standard event in 2006. Though a casual fan might not notice the exclusion of an event, an active one will know the difference if it's not included."

"Exactly, Nikki. You take those elements away and you're weakening it. Shoot-out rodeos that eliminate those venues are becoming the new sensation, bringing in a bigger market, especially on television." He poured more coffee for them. "One of my rodeo friends, Buck Slidell, said the attendance at the Houston Livestock Show and Rodeo in March was down 16 percent from fourteen years ago."

"I heard it was because of cost-of-living expenses across the state, but that can't be the only reason."

"It's part of it, including higher gas and utilities prices," he stated. "In the end it means some families won't spend any extra money on the rodeo. The same problem has hit many states, and money isn't the only problem. Bad weather keeps people away. There are so many other activities like Friday night football and baseball, fans have to make a choice of where to go and it isn't always the rodeo."

Nikki stirred in her chair. "Not to mention complaints that the live entertainment at a lot of rodeos doesn't feature enough big singers and bands. Even bull riding, which is a fan favorite, can't fill the stands without the right musical acts. And I heard some of the guys complain in Austin that the rough stock events were fouled up by a mix of dairy calves with Angus. It was a mess. The list of problems goes on and on."

"But it's the team ropers and tie-down ropers I'm the most concerned about if they become a casualty in the shake-up. It's safe to say that no one in the industry understands or is aware of everything that is happening on every level. I know I'm not. For me, seeing the sport contested at the highest levels with the ropers and barrel racers is part of what keeps our dreams alive."

"For me too," she concurred.

"But the PRCA is trying to gain a new audience and push rodeo to a new level of television coverage. It's been tough the last few years with all the big rodeos wanting to limit some of the venues." He swallowed his second cup of coffee. "I hate to see that happen. Progress has a way of changing the dynamic in all the areas of the sport."

"I know."

"I've had the time of my life since I got into it. But I've decided it's time to get out before the fragmenting because of money and world market interests dilutes the whole scope of things."

She nodded, even though she felt there was still another reason he didn't care to divulge. "I've been thinking a lot about that since the talk I had with my brother. Ages ago we decided that after retirement we'd go into business together to run our own rodeo and perpetuate the events we love.

"Even three years ago I was sure a venture like that would be successful. But because the world is changing all the time, it's impossible to see into the future. Which means it's going to take more effort to keep it alive."

He reached across the table and grasped her hand. Her breath caught from the contact. "There will always be the rodeo, even with animal rights activists making their protests. We just have to be prepared to make accommodations and move with it."

Nikki heaved a sigh. "Except that I'm afraid I'm a

purist and want things to be like they were in the past. I know I sound like my grandparents. They hate cell phones and want life to go back to a slower pace. I've never been able to convince them that new advances in technology have transformed the world. They just look back at me with sad eyes because I don't understand."

Toly smiled before letting go of her hand. "Before my grandparents died, they expressed the same thing. I remember them telling me they felt sorry for me because I hadn't grown up in their world. It was the golden age to them, even with the Depression."

She laughed gently. "Now I find myself feeling the same way about what's happening with rodeo trends."

"But the rodeo will never go away, and we'll have our memories of this year's Finals to treasure."

Nikki was beginning to get teary-eyed because she'd never known this kind of happiness before. She'd always admired Toly from a distance. But because he shared her passion for the sport, she loved being able to talk to him intimately like this. To think this time would never come again brought her pain.

"You're right, Toly. And now I'd better get this show on the road if we expect to eat." She got up from the table to take their meal out of the oven and bake the rolls when she heard the door open. "That'll be Mills."

"I'll make sure."

She heard the two of them talking for a few minutes before her brother came into the kitchen. He looked around. "You've decorated for Christmas!"

"Toly brought it to us."

Instead of commenting, her brother flicked his gaze to her. "What can I do to help?"

"Set the table maybe?"

"Sure." He grabbed the remaining doughnut and demolished it before getting busy. "Something smells good. How come you've been cooking up a storm?"

"Because I like to cook. Toly needed a break. Maybe *you* will even volunteer one night. Hot dogs and chili?" But the minute the words came out, both she and Toly laughed knowing that would never happen.

Her brother didn't join in. "How long have you been here, Toly?"

Did she detect an edge? She guessed that his first-place win last night hadn't compensated for a broken heart.

"Long enough to bother your sister." For the last year they'd all enjoyed a good-natured camaraderie. It was so sad that Mills's unhappiness continued to stand out, making her uncomfortable.

"That's not true," she blurted. "He brought Christmas into the trailer. While we've been waiting for you, we've had a fascinating discussion about the future of the rodeo with its ups and downs. As Toly said, we just have to be prepared to move with it."

Mills put the cutlery and plates around. "Let's not spoil this year's competition by getting on that subject."

Oh dear. Her brother really was in pain and it wasn't about to go away. Thankfully Toly's phone rang, interrupting the conversation. When he picked up, he put it on speaker.

"You've called at the perfect time, Mom. I'm in the rig with Mills and Nikki. She's taking fantastic care of us. Tonight she made meat loaf and scalloped potatoes. We're just sitting down to eat before tonight's event."

His family took turns talking. Each brother sounded excited for them. His mother spoke at the end. "Congratulations on last night's scores. Good luck to all three of you tonight! We'll be watching you on TV. God bless."

Toly's little niece Libby shouted good luck, making them all laugh before they hung up.

Nikki smiled at Toly. "She sounds so cute! Do you have a picture of her?"

"I've got a bunch on my cell."

"While we eat I want to look at them."

Her dinner was a great success. She passed around the rolls. While everyone ate their fill, she looked through his photo gallery. "Oh, Toly, she's adorable."

"She's Eli's daughter from his first marriage."

"Is that her dog?"

"No. Daisy belongs to my brother Roce. He's the vet."

"I could use him here to find out what's wrong with Sassy." She scrolled to the next photo. "Oh—the dog only has three legs."

"It's a sad story. Daisy got caught in a bear trap, but she functions like any normal dog and is so devoted to my brother it's pathetic."

"How sweet. Ah…and there's another darling baby."

Toly nodded. "That's David, Eli and Brianna's son. They're so happy it's sickening." Nikki chuckled. "He was named after our father who died a few years ago."

It wasn't fair to lose parents so early in life. She kept on going through his photo collection, more and more aware of Mills's silence. "You have a lovely mother, and all you brothers bear a strong resemblance to each other. Their wives are beautiful."

"I agree."

She gave him back his phone and started to do the dishes. The guys helped and before long they were ready to leave for the Mack Center. After changing into her denim blue Western outfit for tonight, she unplugged the Christmas tree lights and hurried outside with her hat.

This time Toly said he would drive. She scrambled into the backseat, forcing her brother to get in front where he would have more leg room. On their way into town, Mills looked at her over his shoulder.

"I saw you working with Bombshell today."

"Yes. I'm riding her tonight. Usually Sassy is so stable. Maybe something's wrong with her, but after thinking it over, I've decided I came in too fast around that first barrel and didn't rate her properly. Not getting her into the right position lost me some time, so I practiced that technique with Bombshell. After I talked to Andy about it, I figured I'd give Sassy a rest and see if I can't get a win with Bombshell tonight."

When Mills didn't respond, Toly said, "I think you're smart to trade off. You've still got nine more nights to bring in the lowest scores. I'm going to switch horses too and ride Chaz tonight."

Nikki leaned forward and patted her brother's shoulder. "What about you?"

"I'm sticking with Atlas."

"He's a great horse." But her comment didn't prompt Mills to do any more talking.

They reached the center and walked inside. Toly smiled at her. "Here we go again. You don't need luck, but I'll wish it for you anyway."

"The same to the two of you." She looked at her brother before kissing his cheek. "Love you."

"Ditto."

Oh, Mills... When they headed for the stalls, she

took a different turn and walked out to the stands. The team roping event would be coming up soon. Nikki didn't want to miss it. For a little while she could pretend to be a spectator and melt into the crowd.

Her tension grew while she waited for the guys' event to start. Since they held first place in the standings, they wouldn't come out of the alley until last.

One by one the fifteen finalists took off. Up came Shay Carlson and his partner who were second in the standings. He was the roper Toly wanted to beat.

Nikki held her breath as they roped their steer. Shay did it in 3.8 seconds, his partner in 4.0. Those were the same scores they'd made last night. She'd been keeping tabs. Now it was Toly's turn.

The second their names were announced, the crowd went crazy. So did she. Crazy with excitement and love for him. The gates opened and Toly flew out on Chaz. Over the years she'd learned that the header set up the run. If he didn't get the steer turned, it was all over. Mills called Toly the quarterback of their team.

Her brother was right. She saw Toly line up the steer so perfectly, a 3.7 score flashed on the counter. *Yes!* To her relief Mills wrapped it up in 3.8. They won the night. Again!

Ecstatic at this point, she hurried back to get ready for her event. She entered Sassy's stall to show her some love and was rewarded with a nicker. "You have tonight off. Enjoy the rest."

She patted her, visited Duchess and walked around to Bombshell's stall where Andy was checking the saddle. He had her horse ready to ride and turned to her. "I have a feeling this is going to be your night."

"I hope so. Thanks for everything, Andy."

After mounting her horse, Nikki patted her neck. "How's my girl? You know what's going on and don't fool me. We had a good workout today and you're going to help me win tonight, right?"

Andy laughed when Bombshell nodded her head, as if she understood her words. Maybe she did, but the nodding was the endearing way this horse always greeted Nikki. The different personalities of her horses delighted her.

"Let's go for a walk and get ourselves ready." Andy patted the horse's rump as they moved out of the stall toward the alley. She could hear the roars from the crowd. The tie-down roping was just finishing up. Nikki got in line in front of Laurie to wait. Her heart was still pumping hard from her adrenaline rush after seeing Toly's score.

Suddenly the line was moving. Another few seconds and her name was announced. "Here's Nikki Dobson from Montana in second place, riding Bombshell tonight!" A roar went up from the crowd.

"Here we go, sweetie. Come on. Let's do it!"

Chapter 6

After the team roping event, Toly had worked his way through the crowd to the front row where he could watch the barrel racing. Mills followed him, still uncharacteristically silent. With another first place and another gold buckle, he'd hoped his friend would be more animated, but such wasn't the case.

They heard Nikki's name over the loudspeaker. Like a shot, she found her first target and circled the barrel so fast, her beautiful hair flew like a black banner beneath her white cowboy hat.

He couldn't believe his eyes as she rounded two more barrels on Bombshell. The only way to describe her action was poetry in motion, an old cliché that couldn't be improved upon. She sped toward the alley in a record time of 3.43 seconds. *Incredible!*

Her rival Laurie rode last, but she took a little bit too

much time around the first barrel and came in at 3.67. He let out a whoop of joy and turned to Mills. "She did it! Nikki won! Come on. Let's go back to the stalls to congratulate her."

Mills had become a man of few words, but when they saw Nikki, who'd just dismounted, he hurried toward her and gave her a long hug. Toly saw tears on her cheeks and hung back. This was a huge moment for brother and sister.

Andy and Santos were there to take care of her horses and gear. Pretty soon a couple of her competitors crowded around to congratulate her. Suddenly Nikki's gaze met Toly's. Her heart was in her eyes. For a moment it was as if everyone else had disappeared while they communed their joy in silence.

He took a step closer to her. "Are you ready to head for the victory celebration? It's your night."

"Yours, too," she said. "I watched you out in front and doubt anyone can beat you two now."

It meant everything to know she'd been there when she could have watched on one of the screens. Naturally he wanted to win the overall championship, but he wanted that same prize for her too. It had become of vital importance to him. He felt euphoric. "Come on. Let's go collect our gold buckles."

Mills said nothing as the three of them made their way out of the center to the car. Nikki climbed in the backseat. "Toby Keith is performing tonight, guys. I hope he sings 'I Wanna Talk about Me.' It's my favorite. Hilarious!"

On the way to the South Point, Toly sang the lines of the song with her pretty much off-key. How funny that he knew all the words too! It was such a unique song and both of them were laughing by the time they reached the hotel and went inside. The crowd went crazy over all the rodeo winners, and then came the entertainment.

Toby sang the song Nikki loved as part of his set. Throughout the number Toly kept looking at Nikki, who smiled back several times. It was a night he would treasure forever and knew the reason why. He was desperately in love with Nikki Dobson, the woman who was here while they shared this magical night together.

Before they decided to leave, Toly checked the text messages his family had sent him. On the way back to the RV park, he conveyed their congratulations to Mills and Nikki.

He was aware his friends didn't have their parents to revel in the excitement. But the lack of animation on Mills's face told him his partner was thinking about Denise. There wasn't a damn thing Toly could do about that, much as he wanted to.

Once he'd parked the car he looked at Nikki, knowing she would be leaving for the hotel. The three of them got out with their buckles and walked her to her car. With Mills there, Toly couldn't tell her all the things on his mind.

"Drive safely," he said. "Dinner in my rig tomorrow."

"I'll be on time."

Those words helped him keep his sanity until he could be alone. After she drove away, he turned to Mills. "We did good work tonight."

"Yep."

Just yep?

"See you in the morning." Without trying to talk to him further, Toly entered his rig. He would wait until Nikki got back to her hotel, and then he'd call her. But once inside, his phone rang. It was Lyle.

"Toly? You've received several thousand emails I've been trying to keep up with, including three more from Amanda Fleming. She's staying at the Excalibur Hotel and hopes you'll call her there."

He let out a sound of frustration because he'd forgotten about her. "Message received. I'll take care of it." They chatted for a moment before he hung up and called her hotel. To his dismay she answered the phone when the operator put his call through.

"At last!" she exclaimed. "I've been dying to talk to you. I was beginning to wonder if you ever saw my emails."

"Hi, Amanda. I'm flattered that you would keep trying to get through to me."

"I came all this way to watch you perform. Is there a night we can get together?"

He had to make a quick decision. "Tell you what. I don't have any nights open, but if it's convenient, I'll come over to your hotel in the morning and meet you in the coffee shop. It'll have to be early because my day is full. Shall we say eight thirty?"

"You're really that busy?" The disappointment in her voice was palpable.

"Afraid so. Tomorrow morning is the only free time I'll have while I'm in Las Vegas." He ought to tell her the truth now, but after taking her out for dinner a month ago following his rodeo event, he felt he had to explain in person.

"Okay, I'll look for you in the morning."

"Good. I'll see you then." He rang off and phoned Mills who answered on the third ring.

"What's up?"

Toly explained about Amanda and Lyle's phone call. "Do you want to drive me into town in the morning? I plan to tell her I'm not interested, and won't be longer than a half hour. Then we can head over to the center. Or I can come back for you."

Quiet reigned. "What time?"

"I told her I'd meet her in the coffee shop at eight thirty."

"I'll drive you."

"Thanks. See you in the morning."

Toly hung up.

He could hear all the things Mills hadn't said. Like, why in the hell did you have to pick on my sister for your latest conquest? The situation between Toly and his roping partner was growing more tense all the time.

Wymon's advice to act natural and be himself wasn't winning any points. At this juncture he knew Nikki had to be aware of her brother's attitude toward him. The time for talking to her about Mills's negative feelings was coming soon. This couldn't go on.

Nikki had just gotten dressed in jeans and a blouse when her cell phone rang. It was Mills. Curious why he'd be calling her at eight thirty on Saturday morning, she picked up. "Hi! What's going on with my brother?"

"Want a little company?"

She blinked. "Always. Where are you?"

"On my way to your room."

"You're kidding! I'll put the coffee on."

She hung up and opened the door for him before she fixed them their brew. A minute later he walked in and gave her a hug. They sat down in her little sitting room with their mugs. "To what do I owe the pleasure of your company this early in the morning?"

"I thought I'd hang out with my sister while I'm waiting for Toly." Her heart thumped harder just hearing his name.

"Why didn't he come with you?"

Her brother took a long swallow. "He's at the Excalibur having breakfast with a woman he met at the Omaha rodeo. I expect he'll call when he's ready for me to pick him up. I have no clue how long he'll be, if you know what I mean. In the meantime there's no point in waiting for him. Why don't you and I head on over to the center. It'll save you having to bring your own car while we exercise the horses."

Nikki almost choked on her coffee. *Toly was with someone else at this time of morning? Had he spent the night with her?* Pain darted through her so real she felt as if she'd been thrown from her horse and trampled by its hooves.

"Good idea." She forced a smile to hide the hurt. "Are you excited for tonight? I know I am. But I'm wondering which horse I should ride. What do you think?"

He smiled back, something she hadn't seen for a while. "Which one of your three horses will get their feelings hurt the most if you choose the other?"

She chuckled. "I might have known you'd say something like that. I guess I'll have to have a talk with them when we get over to the center and see which of them begs me the most."

Laughter broke from her brother. She hadn't heard that sound for quite a while. Nikki swallowed the last of her coffee. "Turn on the TV if you want while I finish getting ready."

While she was in the bathroom she heard his phone ring. Was it Toly, the cowboy her brother had told her charmed all the ladies on the circuit? The Sapphire Cowboy who'd crept into Nikki's heart without her even realizing it?

Had he told the woman he'd been with all night that she took his breath away? Of course he had, and probably too many other things she couldn't bear to think about. The hurt went too deep.

You have to gird up your loins, her dad used to say when he had a tough task ahead of him. That's what Nikki intended to do.

She put on lipstick and pulled her hair back in a long ponytail. Once she'd fastened it with an elastic, she was ready to face the pain of the day. She ought to be used to it by now because any real happiness didn't last long.

After putting on her cowboy hat, she walked into the sitting room with her purse, pretending she hadn't heard his phone ring. "I'm ready. If Toly should need a ride later, he can reach you at the center, right? Let's go."

Mills turned off the TV. His smile had disappeared. "Actually he did call and is ready to drive with us now."

"Great." She hadn't expected that to happen. They left the hotel for his car. She climbed in the back. "Before we go by for him, do we have time to go to a drive-through for a quickie breakfast?"

"Sure. I'm hungry too."

After they'd made that stop, they pulled up in front of the Excalibur. Nikki was just finishing her burrito when Toly walked up to the car and got in. "Thanks for picking me up."

Mills nodded and they took off.

Toly turned and looked over his shoulder at Nikki who smiled at him.

"We would have brought you breakfast, but I understand you already had it with a girlfriend this morning. Have you been holding out on us?" she teased.

"Not at all," he came back, totally composed. "When

we were in Omaha a month ago, we stayed one night at a hotel while I was having the rig serviced. A woman who worked at the hotel and had been to the rodeo asked me to join her for dinner there after our event. I shouldn't have accepted because I wasn't interested and never expected to see her again."

"I couldn't figure out why you did."

Nikki flinched at Mills's comment.

"Because she pushed and I decided to be nice. But it proved to be a mistake. Lyle informed me that she'd sent a lot of emails to our website. I didn't do anything about them until he said she was in Las Vegas. I was surprised to learn she was staying at the Excalibur.

"Lyle actually phoned me about it last night after I'd gone to my rig because she'd sent a bunch more and was becoming a nuisance. So I called the hotel and told her I'd meet her this morning for breakfast because it was all the time I could spare. Mills drove me over there. Once I sat down, I explained that I wasn't interested in a relationship with her, wished her well and left."

Nikki believed him and the relief of knowing the truth made her positively giddy. She couldn't help but wonder why her brother had led her to believe there might be something more to it, leaving it vague. That wasn't nice and it bothered her a lot.

To support Toly she said, "I've had a few guys send too many emails to my blog in the past. You try not to offend anyone, but when they go too far, you have to do something about it. Hey, Mills? Remember that guy from Idaho who turned up at our ranch to see me?"

"Yes," he muttered.

"I don't know how he dared seek me out. Thank

goodness Dad was there to threaten him with a lawsuit and a shotgun."

Toly's eyes danced as they studied her features. "Did it work?"

"I'll say."

"I wish I'd met your parents."

Her eyes smarted. "So do I."

Mills pulled around the back of the center and got out. He shut his door hard enough that she noticed. When she could get her brother alone, she was going to have a big talk with him. Denise or no Denise, his surliness couldn't be allowed to continue.

Toly walked Nikki inside. On the way to the stalls he grabbed her swinging ponytail and gave it a little tug. She flashed him a sideway glance. Anytime he touched her, she trembled.

"Forgive me. I couldn't resist."

"That I believe. You must have been a rascal when you were little."

His low laugh excited her as they moved to the stalls to put their horses through the paces.

An hour later Nikki dismounted Sassy and hugged her around the neck. "I'm going to ride you tonight and this time we'll get it right." As she was giving all three horses a treat, the guys came by for her and they walked back to the car.

"Mills? Drop me off at the hotel so I can change and get my car." They climbed inside and took off.

"We're having barbecued ribs tonight," Toly reminded her.

Tonight. She couldn't wait. "Those are my favorite. On the way to the RV park I'll pick up the makings for a yummy spinach salad and meet you guys at the rig later."

Toly flashed her a grin. "You and Popeye."

She'd forgotten about Popeye, the famous sailor man cartoon character who ate spinach to make himself strong. "It won't hurt to pack a little iron if we're going to win tonight, right?"

"Amen to that."

But Mills didn't say a word. That did it! She intended to confront him point-blank. He was beyond obnoxious.

A few minutes later he pulled up in front of her hotel. Toly got out and opened the rear door for her.

She thanked him. "See you guys around three."

"I'll be waiting," Toly murmured in an aside.

Her pulse was still racing as she hurried inside to get showered and changed for tonight's event.

Before long she drove her car to the supermarket for the needed ingredients, then headed for the RV park. But instead of going directly to Toly's rig, she walked to the other rig and unlocked the door, calling out to Mills from the entrance.

She could hear his radio playing. Not wanting to walk in on him unannounced when he wasn't expecting her, she phoned him. Pretty soon he answered. "Nikki?"

"Hi. I guess you couldn't hear me come in the rig. Are you decent?"

"Yes."

"We need to talk." She hung up and walked into the kitchen.

Her attractive brother had showered and wandered in wearing a T-shirt and sweats. "What's wrong?"

Nikki sat back in the chair and looked up at him. "Something has been wrong since Denise broke up with you. I've understood that pain, but a new element has been added to the mix that has turned you into someone I don't recognize. Your resentment of Toly since our arrival in Las Vegas has stunned me."

He wouldn't look at her. "What do you mean?"

"You know exactly what I'm saying. You've shown your dislike of him in a dozen ways. This morning you purposely led me to believe Toly had a girlfriend and might have stayed overnight with her. That was dishonest and cruel, both to him and to me. What has Toly ever done to you to make you behave this way?"

His head reared back and his eyes glittered. "So it's true. You've fallen in love with him."

It *was* truth time. "Even if I have, he knows nothing about it."

"The hell he doesn't! You're like all the other women who can't resist the great Toly Clayton. I thought you were different."

She studied him for a minute. "When did your hero worship of him turn to jealousy?"

His hands curled around the chair back. "I'm not jealous. I just don't want to watch him trample over your heart until he gets what he wants and then moves on."

Nikki couldn't believe what she was hearing and jumped to her feet. "Is that what he does? Do you have proof that he's a womanizer who has destroyed lives? He's incredibly attractive, so it's understandable the groupies can't leave him alone, but I've never heard anything like that about him, *except* from you."

Her brother had no comeback. She didn't think so.

"I know there are some cowboys on the rodeo circuit who have developed bad reputations. We girls are aware of the ones to avoid while we're traveling around. To date, Toly's name has never been mentioned except in glowing terms. When he apologized to me that night at the MGM Grand, he admitted that he liked the girls when he first started doing rodeo. But his brother's advice made him wise up fast."

She took a deep breath. "I think you need to analyze what's going on inside of you and decide if you're going to let this anger against Toly rob you of a championship. I love you, Mills, but I don't like what has happened to you. Unless you know Toly has a past prison record or a mistress I don't know about, then I don't want to see you act this way again!" She had the impression he was frightened about something. But what?

Nikki got out of there before she said too much. She had to stop at her car for the groceries before entering Toly's rig. The aroma of the ribs filled the air, making her mouth water.

"Toly?"

"I'll be with you in a minute," he called out from the rear. "Make yourself at home."

It was beginning to feel like she lived there. With Toly in the next room, all was right with her world. She washed her hands and got busy putting the salad together. While she was tossing it with the special avocado dressing, she felt a pair of strong male hands grip her waist from behind and give her a squeeze. A gasp escaped her lips and she almost melted on the spot.

"Sorry if I startled you," he whispered into her hair. Nikki could tell he'd just come from the shower. "I couldn't resist. You have no idea how wonderful you smell."

She could say the same thing to him. What would he do if she turned around and threw her arms around his neck? But before she acted on the impulse, they heard a noise and Mills walked into the kitchen.

Nikki quickly put the salad on the table while Toly took the ribs out of the oven and placed them on the table. That's when she saw him reach for a smaller pan on the lower rack. "You made corn bread? Before Finals are over, you're going to spoil us all rotten."

"That's the idea. I, for one, don't want any of this to end." They sat down at the set table and started to eat.

Neither did Nikki who could only marvel over the food. "I have to amend my judgment of your cooking skills. I don't know how I could have accused you of only knowing how to make coffee when it's clear you could open your own restaurant."

He chuckled and they both ignored the elephant in the room. "I have an idea for tomorrow. Why don't we take the horses out in the desert and ride with no one else around. I think it will be good for all of us to get away for part of a day."

Toly must have been reading her mind. Being around Mills was making them all stir-crazy. "I think that's a fabulous idea."

Of course her brother said nothing. His foul mood hadn't disappeared, but she wasn't going to let him ruin it for her. When she looked at Toly, he flashed her a covert glance.

"I'm glad you said that. We'll stop for fast food on our way back to the center and be there in time for our events."

"Perfect."

"I'm not sure it's a good idea."

Nikki stared at her brother. Here they went again. "Why not?"

"Too much exercise isn't the best thing while we're competing."

She counted to ten. "We'll just walk them. Nothing strenuous. They'll love getting out. So will I."

"I've been thinking about something else," Toly interjected. No doubt he could sense Mills was on the verge of forcing the issue. "What do you say that the day after Finals, we take a helicopter tour of the Grand Canyon before we head home? It only takes four hours and we'll fly over Hoover Dam."

Nikki's heart pounded with sickening speed. *Yes, yes, yes.* She'd done it before as one of the perks when she'd won last year's Miss Rodeo Montana title, but to see it with Toly would be an entirely different story.

"Let's plan on it," she said, so excited about that possibility, she didn't care how her brother was acting. Toly couldn't help but be aware of her brother's continued resentment, but he handled it in a way that made her love him more. He had a maturity anyone would admire.

Once their meal was over, Mills said he was going to his rig to change clothes before they left for the center. *Hooray!*

Nikki watched him go and turned to Toly while she cleared the table. "I'm sorry my brother didn't thank you for dinner. It was fantastic."

"Don't worry about it. We all deal with heartache differently."

"It's no excuse to be rude, especially not to you."

His gaze met hers. "One day he'll get past this."

"Maybe." She loaded the dishwasher. "But will we?"

Toly's laugh filled the interior of the rig and permeated her heart. When it subsided he said, "We *have* to get past it if we want to be number one tonight! My money is on you, Nikki."

"That goes both ways." I love you, Toly. *I love you.*

Chapter 7

Once they reached the center and parted company, Toly bridled his horse and reached for his Western saddle with its special double rigging. He'd affixed a rubber wrap around the horn to keep the rope dally from slipping when he left the gate.

Checking all the equipment, he saddled Chaz and walked him over to talk to Mills. "So you're going to ride Dusty tonight?"

He jerked his head around. "Yeah. Is that all right with you?"

"I was just making conversation." Toly mounted his horse. "Whatever bad feelings you have about me, can you let go of them long enough while we get through this event? I'll see you at the box."

Tomorrow when he took Nikki riding, he planned to tell her he wanted to be with her all the time. If she felt the same way, then did she have any ideas on how to treat Mills for the next week? He would abide by her decision until they left Las Vegas. After that, he would pursue her because she had fast become the woman he intended to marry. He knew in his soul she was the one.

Toly reached the area to watch as each set of team ropers awaited their turn. When the second-place team got ready, Mills drew up next to him. Soon it was time for them to enter the boxes. Toly was right-handed and walked Chaz in the left one. Mills entered the right box.

The steer had been moved into the chute between them, its horns wrapped for protection. The taut barrier rope ran in front of Toly's box and fastened to an easily released rope on the neck of the steer. It was used to make sure the steer got a head start.

Because he was the header, Toly needed to work with a softer rope that had more elasticity to snag the steer around the horns or the neck. Mills's rope had to be stiffer to rope the hind legs.

As always, Toly said a little prayer for their horses and their safety. These days he included Nikki in his prayer, then called for the steer. But as he was testing his own rope, he experienced that dreaded loss of feeling in his hand and wrist. *Dear God, no.*

A cold sweat broke out on his body. It was too late to do anything about it.

The roar of the crowd was deafening as the assistant opened the chute and the steer ran the length of the barrier rope. Immediately the gate opened and Toly took off, but he couldn't do the wraps of the rope around the saddle horn, called the dally. Without being able to execute that critical move, he couldn't turn Chaz to the left so the steer would follow.

Now that his lower arm had gone slack, the rope rested across his inner elbow. He had to hurl it using the strength from his upper arm and shoulder as the doctor had suggested, and hope it caught a steer horn, one of the three legal catches.

This threw Mills off. He had to make a blind throw, dallying tightly, but Toly couldn't maneuver his horse to face him or the steer. His partner did his best to immobilize it and stretch out its hind legs. But he only nabbed one leg.

When the official waved his flag, Toly's gut told him they'd lost valuable time plus gained a five second penalty because Mills didn't rope both legs. The crowd noise reflected their disappointment. Sure enough their score had been low enough that they probably netted third or fourth place when the scores were averaged. Depending on the scores of the other finalists, their number one standing was now in jeopardy.

In a lightning move he made a grab of the reins with his left hand and turned Chaz around so they could ride out of the arena and down the alley. Once he reached the stall, he dismounted on a run, hiding his right hand under his left arm. Until the feeling came back, he had no strength and it hung lifeless.

He patted his horse's neck. "Sorry, buddy. You did great out there." After signaling one of the attendants to take care of Chaz, he slipped out the back of the center past other contestants getting ready for the bull riding. Toly needed time to recover alone and hurried out to the car. Maybe Mills hadn't seen him leave yet.

He climbed in the backseat and began massaging his lower arm and hand, willing some feeling to come back. His shoulder ached like crazy. For all he knew he'd done some damage there with that throw. This was one time he wouldn't be able to see Nikki perform.

For this to happen in the middle of Finals, it meant a whole new change of tactics. Toly wasn't left-handed, but from now on he was going to have to train using his left hand if they expected to win. Over the years he'd thrown ropes with both hands. But the tricky part had to do with the dally. He needed to work on wrapping it with the hand that wasn't used to doing that maneuver.

It meant no trip to the desert tomorrow. He would train most of the day.

Since they'd planned to pick up fast food afterward, neither he nor Nikki would be cooking tomorrow. No expectations. That was good. While deep in thought, the front driver's door opened. Mills's head appeared. "Toly?"

"Yeah."

"Why didn't you wait for me?" He climbed behind the wheel and looked around at him.

"I…needed to be alone. You go back and watch Nikki."

"Not yet. It's my fault this happened tonight."

Toly's head reared. For once Mills was acting very subdued. "What in the hell are you talking about?"

"It's true. I've been such an ass, I'm surprised you didn't quit on me long before now. I have no right, but I'm going to ask you to forgive me for the way I've carried on about you and Nikki. She called me out earlier." Toly decided his older brother was some kind of a prophet. "I know I've been a jerk, and it put you off your game."

"It's not your fault, Mills. I swear it."

"Nevertheless things are going to change starting right now."

The sincerity in his voice sounded real enough, making Toly feel guilty that he hadn't shared his neuropathy condition with Mills. But he still didn't want him to know the truth until he'd done some training tomorrow. He imagined his doctor would be surprised if he knew what had happened tonight.

If he thought he could get through the rest of the events using his left hand, then he had to find out. Otherwise they would have to withdraw from competition and that would kill Mills. Toly was determined that for his partner's sake, he would move heaven and earth not to let that happen. Nikki's brother deserved and needed to be a national champion.

For the first time in his life, something was more important to Toly than winning. In this last year he'd met the love of his life. Losing the national championship would mean nothing to him personally if he couldn't have a future with Nikki Dobson.

"The only thing important about tonight is for one of us to be there for Nikki. I'll be fine. See you two in a little while. If she wins tonight, you'll have to take her to the South Point to pick up her gold buckle. I'll ask you to drop me off at the RV park on the way. Don't worry. I'll tell her I strained the muscles in my upper arm and shoulder. We don't want her to worry. Now go, or you'll miss her event!"

"We still need to talk, Toly. I've been too protective of her."

"If I had a sister, I'm sure I'd be the same way and probably worse, but we'll hash it out later. Before you go, I want you to know you saved the night with your throw. You got one of the legs, thank heaven, or we'd have ended up with the lowest score of the night and be finished. That's why you're the number one heeler on this year's circuit. Congratulations."

"You managed to snag a horn, Toly. I don't know how you did it. We're still alive."

"Yep. Now get out of here so Nikki will know we're cheering for her."

"I'm going."

After he shut the door, Toly leaned back against the seat. Some feeling had started entering his arm again. The weakness never lasted long, but tonight it cost them. He couldn't allow it to happen again.

Until they returned to the car, he went over the new strategy in his mind. He didn't dare switch boxes with Mills tomorrow night. He'd have to use his left arm to throw and make it work, though it would be harder. He would practice using his left arm before going to the arena.

"Toly?" he heard Nikki call to him some time later before she even opened the front passenger door. Once inside she leaned over the seat to look at him. The fear in her fabulous gray eyes for him was a revelation. It reminded him of the night he'd sought her out at the MGM Grand and she'd been worried about Mills. Things had changed drastically since that night.

"Are you all right? Please don't let one higher score change anything for you. You'll still average out first because of all your wins."

Could any woman be more beautiful, inside and out? "I'm fine, Nikki. All I need to know is, did you win another gold buckle tonight?"

"She did! You should have seen her sashay around those barrels!" Mills spoke up after opening his door. He sounded elated, but it couldn't match Toly's excitement for her.

Mills started the car and they left for the RV park. Before she could ask, Toly said, "Much as I'd like to see you get your buckle tonight, I've asked your brother to take me to the rig. My shoulder is hurting. I need to put an ice pack on it and get a good night's sleep. That will solve the problem, but I'm afraid it means a ride out on the desert tomorrow is out for me."

"Don't worry about that, Toly. You need to take care of yourself. We'll stay around and make sure you don't starve."

"I don't want you waiting on me. Tomorrow I'll be exercising my horses, but thank you for the thought. Hey, Mills—who did the fastest time tonight?"

"Luis Mondego and Kip Jackson from South Dakota. Clay's team came in second. We were third."

Toly swallowed hard. At least they'd stayed in the top three tonight. There was still a chance for them depending on how well his practice went tomorrow. By late afternoon he would know if he had to tell Mills the bad news or not.

"Thanks for bringing me back first." They'd pulled up to Toly's rig. He got out. His right hand was functioning well enough again that no one could tell what had happened. He stared at Nikki through her open window. "I'd love to go to the hotel tonight. Be assured I'll be there all the rest of the nights."

"Thank you, but I'm not concerned about me." The tremor in her voice got to his heart. "Take care of that shoulder, Toly. We'll see you tomorrow. If you need anything, call no matter the time."

Oh, Nikki. Was he ever going to take her up on that offer when this was all over.

Despite her latest win, Nikki awakened early Sunday morning, having spent a restless night at her hotel. Toly's hurt shoulder had to have caused him a lot of pain for him to go straight back to the rig. He would never ask for help, but she didn't care. They'd been living in and out of each other's pockets for a while now and she wanted to do what she could for him.

After washing her hair, she got ready for the day and put on the clothes she would wear in her event tonight. Once she'd exercised her horses, she drove to the RV park with some food from a deli she liked. Why not surprise him with a meal? Hopefully his shoulder would be much better.

Nikki didn't see anyone around when she parked her car behind the Dobson rig. She left the food in the car and walked over to the barn to find Toly. Snapper was gone, but Chaz was in his stall. Hmm. She didn't know how long he would be running his horse through the motions.

Finally she walked back to her car and put the food in the fridge of their trailer while she waited for him. The Christmas tree drew her gaze and she turned on the lights. It added a festive air she loved.

Unfortunately she didn't have Toly's cell phone number, so she called her brother. Mills wouldn't be happy about it, but she was long past worrying about his feelings.

To her disappointment it went through to his voice mail. She left a message for him to call or text her back with Toly's phone number. With her horses stalled at the center, she couldn't ride out to find Toly. Instead she walked to the barn again, hoping he might have come back, but no such luck.

As she wheeled around to leave one more time, he suddenly appeared at the entrance to the stall on foot, pulling the lead on Snapper. A coil of rope hung from the saddle horn. With that sore shoulder, she wondered if he'd been able to get in much practice.

His eyes played over her, making her senses come alive. "I've been thinking about you all day. To find you here couldn't be a better gift."

"I've been hoping you would come back," she said in a breathless voice. "I brought us a meal."

So fast she couldn't believe it, he dropped the lead and drew her into his arms. "Last night I didn't get to congratulate you the way I wanted. For a year I've wanted to kiss you. Now I'm going to do it, ready or not."

"Toly," she whispered his name, melting against his rock-hard body while he covered her mouth with his own. Nikki had never known a feeling like this in her life and came close to fainting from the desire he aroused in her as they began devouring each other. She'd dreamed of being with him, but no dream produced this kind of ecstasy. With his hands roaming over her back and hips, she'd turned wanton, craving his love.

"You're so beautiful, I don't believe you're real." He buried his face in her hair. "I've needed to feel you like this forever."

She twined her arms around his neck. "I wanted you to kiss me while we were dancing."

"Only then?" he teased before kissing each feature of her face. "There were reasons I didn't. Reasons we need to talk about, but right now I can't think."

Once again they gave each other one hungry kiss after another and she felt her passion bursting out of control. She had no idea when they would have come up for air if a couple of riders hadn't come down the aisle and were nearing Snapper's stall.

Toly moaned before easing Nikki away from him. His peridot-colored eyes held a glaze. She could tell he was out of breath too. The people were getting closer. She moved out of Toly's way so he could bring his horse inside the stall.

Once the people had passed, he pressed her against the wall. "Let me take care of Snapper," he murmured against her lips, "then we'll go back to my trailer." He gave her another long, hard kiss.

"I'll help you."

Together they removed the gear and made certain he had hay and water. Toly's shoulder didn't seem to be bothering him as much now, thank goodness.

"Let's go." He put his arm around her shoulders and they walked back to the rigs. The sensation of their bodies brushing against each other was another new exciting experience she never wanted to end.

"I put the food in our rig. I'll get it and come over to yours."

"That's a good idea. Mills went out with friends a little while ago, but he'll be back soon. Until he gets here I have things to say to you in private."

She felt an urgency coming from him apart from his wanting to be alone with her. What was it about? After retrieving their meal, she took the sack and the Christmas tree to his rig. He'd left the door unlocked. She went inside and locked it again. When she reached the kitchen, she plugged the Christmas lights in, then warmed up the Chinese takeout in his microwave.

He walked in from the other end of the trailer wearing a blue-and-white-plaid shirt. His sensational physique made him look good in anything. "Mmm. All it takes around here is a woman's touch. Christmas and Chinese. It smells delicious."

"I hope you're hungry. I bought a little bit of everything."

"Just the way I like it. How lucky am I to be waited on by a woman like you."

She darted him a sideway glance while she fixed their plates. "What do you mean?" Her curiosity was getting the best of her.

He fixed coffee for them. "Exactly what I said. There's not another woman like you on the planet. I'm not just talking about your gorgeous looks. Let's face it. No woman compares to you."

Heat swarmed her cheeks. "*Toly*—"

"It's true. But I'm also talking about what you're like on the inside. I've seen how kind you are to the foreman on your ranch, to everyone while you've been on the circuit. The crew thinks you walk on water. I've also witnessed the deep love you have for your brother."

Nikki put their plates on the table and sat down with him. "Brothers are pretty special. You would know all about that." They started eating.

He nodded. "That's why we need to talk about Mills. You're the only person who can advise me what to do."

"If you're talking about his being so r—"

"I'm not." He cut her off gently before she could finish. "This has to do with something much more serious."

"I knew it," she whispered.

"What do you think you know?"

"I'm guessing you've found out why Denise broke up with him."

"No, Nikki. I'm afraid I'm as in the dark about that as the two of you."

She stopped eating. "Now you're making me nervous."

"I don't mean to do that. Just hear me out."

A minute ago he'd said intimate things to her that any woman in love would want to hear from the man she adored. Yet Nikki had the awful premonition he was about to tell her something that was going to turn her world upside down. She wanted to run out of there, but the pained look in his eyes held her spellbound.

"I'm listening."

Toly hated what he had to tell Nikki, but she deserved to know the whole truth. He especially hated it that he had to say anything when she had an event tonight and needed all her powers of concentration.

"A month before Denise broke off with Mills, I had an incident while I was training that I didn't tell him or anyone about. Instead I went to our family doctor who referred me to a neurologist in Missoula."

Nikki's gray eyes darkened with what he knew was fear.

"To make a long story short, I have a neuropathy in my lower right arm and hand. It's a nerve that is affected by the tissue around it and causes temporary paralysis. The doctor said that all the years of roping must have aggravated it and that it could come on at any time."

"I just can't believe this would happen to you."

"No one is exempt from the unexpected. Twice during practice in the last two months my hand and lower arm went slack so I couldn't grip the dally. But Mills didn't pick up on it.

"My fear of upsetting your brother was so great, I decided to say nothing and hoped we could get through Finals before it happened again. To my horror, when I was in the block last night testing the rope, my hand and arm went slack. My worst nightmare had happened. It came on so fast I was stunned."

"So that's why you struggled!" Nikki cried. "Oh, Toly—how awful for you." She shook her head.

"But not just for me. For Mills too. If he weren't such an expert heeler, he couldn't have pulled off snagging at least one of the steer's hind legs. Now I have a serious dilemma. After seeing the doctor in the beginning, I could have told your brother everything, but I didn't because I didn't want us to drop out."

"Of course you didn't!"

"We were both going for the championship and the last thing I wanted was to tell him the bad news. He's worked so hard and has been living for this. But I have to be honest. Last night was a moment I'll never forget. I had to call for the steer and see it through, not knowing the outcome. You saw what happened. I had to use all the force of my shoulder and upper arm to throw the rope."

"Then it's a miracle you caught the steer around the horn."

"I agree, and another miracle that Mills was able to rope one of its hind legs to win us a third place and give us a fighting chance."

"How soon did you tell him what happened?"

He stared at her for a few seconds. "I haven't told him anything."

Her eyes searched his. "What does he think went wrong?"

"That I just made a bad toss and hurt my shoulder."

"You *did* hurt it. How does it feel today?"

"It's all right."

Nikki moaned. "No, it's not." She got up from the table and paced for a minute. "Tell me more about your condition. Can it be fixed?"

"Possibly with surgery, but there's no real guarantee." He didn't want to talk about the disease. Not until the rodeo was over.

She grabbed on to the counter. "So *that's* why you said that once Finals were over, you were giving up the rodeo for good."

"Yes. Otherwise Mills and I could go on the circuit again next season. But as you've gathered, my rodeo days are over. Of course he can team up with another roper going for the championship and enjoy several more years doing it."

"Oh. Toly—" Tears had filled her eyes. "I'm so, so sorry for you."

"Don't be, Nikki. I've had a run most guys only dream of doing. It's your brother I'm concerned about now and that's where you come in."

"What do you mean?"

"For one thing, he feels that my mistake last night was partially his fault because he's been uncommunicative lately. He's afraid it threw me off. You have no idea how guilty that makes me feel because it's not the truth. I told him he was wrong in his supposition and hoped he believed me, but I'm not sure he did.

"That's why I think I should tell him about my condition when he comes back to the rig. He deserves to know the truth. But if he doesn't have faith in me at this point, then we'll be forced to meet with the officials and withdraw before tonight's event."

Her face lost a little color. "To know what's wrong with you and withdraw now would kill him."

"You think I don't know that?" Toly got up from the table and walked over to her, putting his hands on her upper arms. He rubbed them gently. "You're his sister. I'm aware how much you two love each other, so I'm begging you to tell me what I should do."

She put a hand on his chest. "Are these episodes coming more often?"

"Last night was my third one in the last ten weeks."

He heard her take a quick breath. "Are you in pain after one of them?"

Toly loved her so terribly, he couldn't help giving her a brief kiss. "No. It's very strange. Once it's over, you'd never know it had happened or could happen again. There's no warning. Nothing."

"So it's possible you'll be free of them for the rest of the rodeo?"

"Yes. That's what I was banking on while we drove down here from Great Falls in the rig. But he has the right to know that if we go in the arena again tonight, the same thing could happen to me. We might not be so lucky and could end up in last place. That would dash our chances to win the championship."

She closed her eyes in obvious pain.

"Out of desperation, I went out this morning to practice on the dummy using my left arm and hand. The trick is to wrap the dally fast enough, but it's incredibly hard when I haven't done it that way before. Though my left-hand grip is strong, I've never used my left arm for team roping."

"But you *could* do it?" He heard hope in her question.

"Yes. I can try. You must understand it's very iffy. I'd have to race out of the box and hope my effort is good enough to come in with a decent score. So… I have a choice to make."

Nikki's groan revealed her torment.

"Either I tell Mills the truth now and see if he'd rather withdraw or try to beat the odds of another episode coming on during competition. The alternative would be to tell him nothing and I'll bungle through the next seven nights using my left arm, hoping he won't notice."

"He'll eventually find out, don't you think?"

"I don't know. While he's in the arena, he'll be living in the moment so completely that by the time we meet up at the stalls after the event, he won't realize what I did if I get another episode. But if he does notice, then I'll have to come clean. The point is, I can't change midstream. Once I'm in the box, I have to be set. Help me, Nikki," he begged.

Before she could make a sound, her cell phone rang. Nikki pulled it out of her pocket. Toly let go of her and stepped away. She looked up at him. "It's Mills. His timing couldn't be worse. When you weren't here earlier, I went to the barn to find you, but you were out on Snapper. So I called him and left a message for him to get back to me with your phone number."

Toly leaned against the counter. "He's going to want to know why you were asking him for it."

"I'll tell him I brought Chinese food for all of us and couldn't find either one of you."

"That sounds reasonable."

She phoned Mills and put him on speakerphone.

"Nikki? What's going on? Why do you want to speak to Toly?"

"I brought food for all of us and I'm afraid it'll go to waste."

"He's out exercising Snapper and will be back before long. I'm on way to the RV park right now. See you in a minute."

Toly heard the click and she hung up. "He still didn't give you my number."

"No. I'd better unlock the door." She dashed off and came back. "When he walks in, I'll tell him you returned and asked me to bring the food here while you iced your shoulder."

"That explanation ought to work. But before he gets here, I need to know what you want me to tell him."

Nikki grabbed the chair and unconsciously threw her head back, sending her glossy black hair sprawling across her shoulders. "We need the proverbial wisdom of Solomon, you know?"

Everything she said and did enamored him more. "That's why I've put this on you, because I trust you with my life. So does your brother."

Her eyes took on a haunted cast. "You give me far too much credit."

"What pains me most is that you have to carry this burden while you're facing another event tonight. It isn't fair while you're on your way to winning the national barrel racing championship."

He could hear her mind working. "You're honestly willing to try using your left arm?"

"That's why I've spent all day practicing instead of taking you out to the desert for a ride."

She straightened. "Then we can't let your sacrifice go to waste."

He let out the breath he didn't know he was holding. "Thank God you said that."

Toly would have reached for her, but they heard the car pull up. He sat back down at the table and ate one of the jumbo fried shrimps just as Mills walked in the kitchen.

Nikki flicked him a glance. "Come and sit. Toly got here a minute ago and was starving. I bet you are too. Let me serve you." She put a plate in front of him and served everyone coffee.

"Thanks. I love *char siu*."

"I know." He seemed to be in a better mood. She didn't know the reason why, but she was grateful for the slightest improvement.

"How's the shoulder, Toly?"

"Not bad at all."

"That's good. I've been going over the numbers. Last night's third place didn't ruin our standings. Most of the ropings will pay out over two hundred thousand dollars to the team roping winner. Along with your winnings, Nikki, we could really get going on our future ideas for the rodeo."

The shine in Mills's eyes told Toly the right decision had been made to risk everything and stay with the rodeo. His gaze fused with Nikki's. They communed in silence while he promised to do everything in his power to make them come out on top.

Mills finished off the rest of the food, then got to his feet. "I'm going to the rig to change clothes for tonight. Thanks for dinner. See you out at the car in a few minutes."

Toly was surprised he'd left the two of them alone. "While I'm thinking about it, we should have exchanged phone numbers months ago. Let's do it now." She immediately pulled out her phone and they shared numbers to program. He'd wanted to do that forever.

When they'd finished, she started clearing the table while he got up and filled the dishwasher. "Why didn't you just ask me for my number?"

He eyed her directly. "The truth?"

"What do you think?"

"Because once your brother and I decided to hook up, he let me know right away you were off-limits, so I didn't dare go against his wishes."

A delicate frown broke out on her face. "He actually told you that?"

Toly nodded. "But not in those exact words. I figured he was being so protective of you because you'd lost your parents and he was watching out for you. He also told me you were going through a very bad time after breaking up with the man you almost married."

"I can't believe he told you all that. It's embarrassing."

"He loves you. I got the hint and did my best to honor his wishes. After all, he and I had a mission to get to Finals and I didn't want to upset him by chasing after his beautiful sister. Don't you know you've left a trail of male bodies behind that you could line up around the arena at least a dozen times?"

"That's not true!" She really wasn't aware of her effect on a man.

He laughed. "You'd have to live in my world. I can name a couple of dozen guys who'd like to get to know you and have personally asked for my help because you're Mills's sister. Little do they know they'd have to get past me."

He loved the way she blushed. "You wanted to get to know me?"

"Do you really have to ask me that question? The minute we were introduced, I felt like I was in free fall."

"I don't believe it." But he saw a small smile break the corners of her mouth.

"Lady?" he whispered, afraid Mills might suddenly come back in. "You have no idea of what I've been through trying to get close to you without breaking your brother's set of commandments. Did you never wonder why we trained so much on your ranch?"

"That was your idea?"

"Yes."

"Toly—I wish I'd known."

"Well, you know it now. My mom hasn't been happy about it, I can tell you. She's complained for the last year that she's hardly seen me. It's your fault."

Nikki put away the leftovers while Toly finished filling the dishwasher. There was little to do, which was good. "Why don't we gather our things and go out to the car to wait for him. I want to discuss something with you."

Nikki nodded. Before long they were ready to leave, grabbing their gloves and Stetsons. She unplugged the Christmas tree lights and they hurried out to the car. He helped her in the front passenger side before climbing in the backseat. She turned around to look at him. "What's on your mind?"

"I've been thinking about last night. On a good night it only takes three seconds or less to throw the rope and set up the steer for Mills. If I get in the box while I'm waiting and don't feel that change in my arm and hand before the gate opens, maybe I should go for it with my right arm."

He waited to hear what she would say.

"That's a judgment call only you can make. I believe in you, Toly, and I'll be praying for you." The moment her touching sentiments permeated his being, the other door opened and Mills climbed behind the wheel.

On the way to the center, Toly pondered her words. They reminded him of a seminal moment in his past. He'd been in high school at the time. One weekend after going to the rodeo in Missoula with his dad and brothers, he told them he was going to be a national rodeo champion one day. His father, a former rodeo celebrity, had smiled into his eyes and said those exact words to him.

To think that ten years later, Toly and Mills were on the cusp of fulfilling that dream. This opportunity would never come for him again.

I have to make it happen for both of us, no matter what.

He looked at Nikki. What would he do if she weren't here believing in him? She'd become his whole world.

Chapter 8

As soon as they reached the center, the guys took off, leaving Nikki to make her way through the stands to the front where she could watch the team roping event. The place was filled to overflowing every night. As usual the atmosphere of the crowd was electric.

But Nikki felt distanced from everything because she was dying for Toly. Tonight he would have to make a split-second decision once he was in the box. His event would be coming up soon. The pressure on him had to be unimaginable because whatever he did would affect Mills too.

The roar from the steer wrestling event was pretty deafening. But when it came time for the team roping— clearly the fan favorite—everyone was on their feet and the noise was earsplitting.

As the fifteen teams came roaring out of the gates

two at a time, she started counting down. Toly's would be third to last. The scores were all over the place from 4.0 to 4.8, but there was only one set she cared about.

"Toly Clayton and Mills Dobson are up next. We'll see if our top winners coming into Finals can top last night's third-place score."

Nikki could hardly breathe as the steer charged out of the chute. She could see Toly with the rope. It was in his *right* hand. He'd made his decision. "Please, please be all right, Toly."

He shot out of the gate and roped the two horns almost instantly in his ocean wave loop. Mills followed with a superb throw that tied up both hind legs. Their speed and precision caused the audience to thunder their approval and give them a standing ovation. Their time: 3.7 and 3.8. Nikki thought she was going to burst for joy. She heard the announcer say, "No one's going to beat those scores tonight."

No they wouldn't!

As the next team was announced, Nikki hurried through the crowd to the stalls in the back so she could get ready for her event.

Santos wore a huge smile when he saw her coming. "It's a great night, Nikki."

"I'll say it is." He'd been there to get Sassy bridled and saddled. She gave him a hug, but was embarrassed because tears were streaming down her cheeks.

She hugged her horse around the neck. "He did it. He did it," she sobbed.

"Are you all right?"

She turned at Santos's voice and laughed, brushing the moisture from her face. "I'm just so happy."

"We all are. Now let's see you pull another score that will make you even more famous than you already are."

"Keep that bull coming, Santos. I love it." She mounted her horse, hardly knowing what she was doing. "Come on, Sassy girl. Let's get out there. I want to wow Toly. What do you say?"

Sassy neighed.

Nikki laughed in delight. "Nobody believes you understand me, but I know differently. Tonight is really important."

She passed her competitors and took her place at the end of the line. One by one the girls exploded down the alley. Nikki watched the screen. Several finalists missed their barrels and one took a nasty fall. Sobered by what she'd seen, she drew on her powers of concentration the way Toly had done earlier tonight.

Soon it was her turn. She rode low over Sassy the way she did in practice on the ranch. "Let's do it again," she urged her horse. They sailed around the barrels, cutting them close with no penalties. Then she rode her horse home, praising her all the way. Her time flashed on the scoreboard: 13.39!

"We did it!" she cried to Sassy.

The crowd went ballistic and she heard the announcer say she'd set a record tonight. When she rode to the stall, the guys and crew were there to greet her, but she only had eyes for Toly. His eyes gleamed like gemstones.

She wanted to fall right into his arms, but it was her brother who helped her off her horse and gave her a long hug. "You broke a record, Nikki. Tonight we're going to celebrate the night away."

Nikki hadn't seen Mills in such high spirits since

before Denise broke up with him. But all her thoughts were on Toly, who'd fought through his dilemma and his brave gamble had earned them another first-place win. She wanted to show him how she felt, but it would have to wait until they were alone.

They walked out to the car and left the parking area. But her spirits plunged when Toly asked Mills to drive him back to the RV park first. "My arm and shoulder need ice. Do you mind bringing my gold buckle back to the rig after you and Nikki have picked them up? I'd love to be there and honor you two for your brilliant performances, but I need some painkillers."

"That's our number one priority, isn't it, Nikki?"

"Absolutely."

Mills kept talking. "We've got to get you in the same shape you were in tonight. Everything came together like magic for all of us."

"It *was* magic." Toly's comment made her shiver.

"We can do it again, right, Nikki?" Her brother was in high form. She could only hope they had another night like tonight.

But for the moment she wished the situation were different and Toly wanted her with him. Mills could have brought back their buckles while she stayed at the rig with Toly so she could help take care of him. But she didn't have that right. Maybe he preferred to be alone.

Too soon they reached the RV park. Mills pulled up to Toly's rig. After he got out, his glance included both of them. "Go enjoy yourselves and have fun. A night like this is to be treasured. See you guys tomorrow."

"Take care of yourself, bud."

The door closed and they drove back to town. But for Nikki the rest of the night was a blur and she couldn't wait to get back to her hotel where she could give in to her emotions.

She put her buckle on the dresser with the other buckles. Naturally, part of her was ecstatic about the great scores the three of them had received tonight. But the major part of her needed to give in to the tears she'd been holding back since Toly had told her about his neuropathy.

Before she got ready for bed, she looked up his condition on her laptop, wanting to know all about it. While she was doing some research, her cell phone rang. At eleven at night it could only be her brother, or maybe one of the crew if an emergency had developed. She reached for it and checked the caller ID. The name she saw shocked her to the core.

Denise!

Nikki couldn't believe it and clicked on. "Is it really you?"

"Yes," she said in a halting voice. "I'm surprised you even picked up when you could see I was calling. Y-you have every right to hate me." The stammer told Nikki a lot.

"I could never do that. You've been one of my closest friends."

"Until I ruined everything."

"Whatever you did, I have to believe it was for a very important reason. I'm just surprised you've chosen now to get in touch with me."

"I couldn't put off phoning you any longer. To be truthful, I flew into Las Vegas on the eighth and have been staying at the Mirage Hotel so I could be at the arena every night."

A gasp escaped Nikki's lips. "You've been here the whole time?"

"Yes, and I've watched all the events from a front row seat at the center. Tonight your performance was so spectacular, I wanted to shout to everyone that you were my friend. Honestly, Nikki, I've never been so proud of anyone as I was of you tonight. I caught it all on my phone.

"When I got back to my hotel, I knew I wouldn't be able to go to sleep until I talked to you and let you know how much I've missed you."

Nikki's eyes stung from her tears. A lump had lodged in her throat. Denise hadn't mentioned Mills, but right now she didn't care. It was enough to hear her friend's voice again. "I've missed you too. You'll never know how much I've needed you to confide in."

She could hear sniffling. "Tell me about it. I know you must be exhausted and need your sleep. Would it be possible for us to meet tomorrow morning? I *have* to talk to you, Nikki."

The desperation in her voice convinced Nikki that her friend was going to tell her why she'd broken up with Mills. But Nikki wanted to drive over to Toly's rig as soon as she got up to make sure he was all right before she did anything else.

"Denise? I have an idea. Are you in bed?"

"No."

"Why don't you drive over to the Cyclades Hotel right now. Bring a bag so you can stay all night in the other bedroom."

"You mean it?" she cried.

"I've been wanting to talk to you too. Let's not put it off any longer."

"I'll come as soon as I can."

Nikki gave her the number of her suite. "I'll be waiting for you."

"You don't know what this means to me."

"I think I do. Nothing's been the same for me since you broke up with my brother."

"Thank you for being the best friend who ever lived."

Nikki heard the click before she hung up.

Talk about a red-letter night…

Tonight Nikki would get answers. She was so excited, she called kitchen services and ordered some club sandwiches and colas to be brought to her room. This would probably last half the night and they would need food.

She closed her laptop and put it in the drawer. Next she changed into her blue sweats to get comfortable. After putting on lipstick and brushing her hair, she heard a knock. "Room service."

Nikki grabbed some cash from her purse and ran to the door to get their dinner tray. Once the waiter was gone, she set it on the coffee table in the sitting room and opened one of the sodas. She didn't have to wait long until she heard another knock on the door. Without hesitation she ran to open it.

There stood her beautiful friend with her long blonde hair and those chocolate-brown eyes that had blown her brother away. "It's so good to see you, Denise!" she cried before they hugged. "Come in."

After an early Monday morning practice on Snapper, practicing his roping on a dummy, Toly entered his rig and poured himself a cup of coffee. He checked his phone and saw that one of his brothers had called, so he phoned him back.

"Roce?"

"Hey, bro—the way you took down that steer last night left us all breathless. What a score! Congratulations!"

"Thanks." Coming from the brother he'd roped with before Mills had become his partner meant the world to him.

"We all agreed that Dad had to be watching."

His throat constricted. "I'd like to think so."

"Our family expects a repeat performance tonight. Then you'll be halfway there. We're all set to fly out on Saturday."

"I'm looking forward to seeing everyone."

But Toly knew he and Mills wouldn't be duplicating last night's score. Because of his fear over having another episode, he'd overdone it wrapping the dally tightly and had strained his arm. He'd paid the price to get a big win. Tonight he would have to rely on his left arm to do the work.

"Hey—are you all right?"

He gripped the phone tighter. "Couldn't be better."

"That's good. You seem a little subdued."

"I was out practicing before I called you."

"Maybe you're overdoing it. You need to chill for a while."

He sipped his coffee. "That's exactly what I have in mind."

"I have to tell you I'm impressed with Mills."

"He's the best."

"Is he around? I'd like to tell him what a great job he and his knockout sister did out there last night."

Just the mention of Nikki tripled his heartbeat. "Sorry. Mills took off for the center to work with Dusty before tonight's performance. He'll be back later and I'll pass on what you said to both of them. How's Mom?"

"Excited to see you win the championship."

At the moment Toly couldn't imagine getting through six more nights with top scores. "What about your other half?"

"We're happier than I ever thought possible."

"That's great, Roce. Give her and everyone my love. We'll talk again soon."

"Go get 'em tonight, champ!"

No sooner had they hung up than he heard a knock on the door. It couldn't be Mills or he would have just walked in. Maybe it was one of the crew checking in over something to do with the horses. He put down his empty mug and walked through to open it.

"Nikki—"

There she was in all her glory, wearing jeans and a Western blouse her figure did wonders for. Her anxious gray eyes took a detailed inventory of him. "I had to find out how you are. Can I come in?"

"What do *you* think. But first I need this." He pulled her close with his left arm, shutting the door with his boot. Then he covered her mouth with his own. He found her so delectable, his hunger for her spiraled out of control.

"I'm sorry I got carried away," he whispered against her lips minutes later.

"If you noticed, I wasn't complaining."

He loved this woman and wanted to take her back to his bedroom, never to come out again. "Let's go in the living room where we can be comfortable." He reached for her hand and drew her with him till they reached the couch.

"I think I willed you here," he murmured, pulling her down on his lap. In the process, he forgot about his right arm. The pain caused him to let out a slight groan, but she heard it and moved off him.

"Your arm is bad."

He flashed her a smile. "It's fine if I don't try to do something I shouldn't."

She stared into his eyes. "You overdid it last night."

"You're right, which means I'll be using my left arm tonight. This time I won't have a choice."

"Your performance made history, Toly. It's on all the sports talk shows today. I heard that the betting in Las Vegas is heavy on you and Mills for the overall championship." She gripped his left hand. "When I saw the rope in your right hand and knew what you were going to do, I prayed so hard that horrid weakness wouldn't strike."

"Your prayer reached the right person." He kissed her again, long and slowly before lifting his mouth from hers. "Mills came over early this morning and told me they praised you at the gold buckle ceremony last night. He got you on his phone and let me see his video." He cupped the side of her face. "You deserved every accolade. I'm sorry I couldn't be there."

She kissed his jaw. "I'm glad you were here taking care of yourself. That's all that matters to me. Let me get the ice pack for you."

"I'll apply it later if I need it."

"If you're sure. How about some more painkillers?"

"Not yet."

"Do you want me to fix you something to eat?"

"I won't be hungry for another hour. Now tell me what's going on with you."

"What do you mean?"

"We've been together a lot lately and I sense you've got something on your mind."

She averted her eyes. "You must be psychic."

"I wouldn't go that far." He kissed her again. "But I want to know what it is before I die of curiosity. Remember we have another event tonight. I'd like to be there."

A gentle laugh escaped. Then she quieted down. "Denise called me last night."

Denise?

Unbelievable.

He pulled her close with his left arm. "That *is* news. Tell me everything."

"She's been in Las Vegas since the eighth and has come to the center every night. I couldn't believe it."

"Where's she staying?"

"At the Mirage. When I found that out, I asked her to drive over to my hotel and spend the night. It was so wonderful to see her again. I'm afraid we talked until three in the morning."

He played with her gorgeous black hair. "That must have been some conversation."

"It was." Nikki turned so she could look at him. He saw those heavenly eyes fill with moisture. "She never wanted to hurt Mills. She's terribly in love with him. It's the kind that will never go away."

He cocked his head. "But?"

"The day before she broke up with him, she came home from work and discovered she had a visitor at her door. It was Johnny Rayburn, the guy she'd known long before she ever met Mills. They'd met in college and dated. She didn't know until he'd asked her to marry him that he'd signed up to go in the military and make it his career.

"Though she loved him, that news came as a shock. It was the last life she wanted. I'm afraid Denise is a lot like me. We're both homebodies and love our ranch life. She couldn't handle the thought of living in other parts of the world as a soldier's wife, of being away from her family and her horses. She knew it wouldn't work and ended their relationship."

Toly frowned. "Did Mills know all about this?"

"Of course. She didn't meet my brother until two years later. If you recall, they were crazy about each other from the first moment they met."

He nodded. "I remember."

Nikki took a deep breath. "She never thought she'd see Johnny again. But there he was on her doorstep five weeks ago, out of uniform with a prosthetic where his hand had been."

Whoa.

"Johnny told her he was working at his father's insurance firm and found out she wasn't married. He admitted he was still in love with her and hoped that now he was home and out of the military for good, she would consider going out with him again."

"Good grief." Toly got up from the couch.

"Good grief is right," Nikki said. "As you can imagine, Denise was torn apart to see what had happened to Johnny. But she was in love with Mills and didn't have those kinds of feelings for Johnny anymore. Naturally, to see him like that broke her heart.

"He asked her to go out with him so they could talk.

When she explained that she was in love with someone else, he asked if she was engaged to this other man, if she was planning to marry him. That put Denise on the spot because Mills had never discussed marriage with her. She told him no, but hoped it would happen in the future."

Toly rubbed the back of his neck. "So Johnny figured all was fair and he prevailed on her, knowing she'd loved him once and would feel sorry for him. He wanted a fighting chance now that he was home and not going anywhere."

"Yes." Nikki flashed him a glance. "Like I said. You're psychic."

"No. I was just putting myself in that poor dude's place. I'm not sure I wouldn't have done the same thing under those circumstances. Knowing the way Mills feels about her, it's not hard to understand why this wounded veteran would want to win back the woman he'd loved."

"Denise *is* a wonderful person. Of course she had no intention of getting back together with Johnny, but she felt she needed to tread carefully and find a way to let him down. She sensed Johnny was fragile. When he told her he had PTSD and was getting therapy, that did it for her.

"Since Mills was so caught up facing Finals, she thought it might be better if he didn't have to worry about her. In the end she decided to stop seeing him until she got through to Johnny without hurting him too badly."

Toly shook his head. "I still don't understand that kind of thinking, but maybe it's because I'm not a woman. To me it's so simple. Just tell Mills what she was doing—he would have understood."

"Maybe. But she wasn't as secure with Mills because he'd never discussed a future with her."

"Not in all the time they'd been dating?"

"No. It's his insecurity. Denise's fears were real. What if he didn't have marriage in mind with her? What if she'd told him everything and he'd started fearing that maybe she was still in love with Johnny deep down? What if the news threw him off enough to affect his performance?"

"That's crazy, Nikki. How could she not have realized how adversely it would affect him by ending it with him and offering no explanation?"

"But he didn't give her enough to go on."

Toly shook his head. "I'm trying to understand."

"So am I. Since she knew she needed time to make Johnny realize he needed to move on with his life, she thought it would be better if Mills didn't know anything about it until you two had gone through Finals. She admits now it was probably the wrong thing to do and regrets it with all her heart."

"I take it Johnny hasn't given up."

"No." Nikki got to her feet. "Denise finally found the courage to end it with him. Since she'd already blocked out her vacation time at work, she flew to Las Vegas to watch Mills and be here when it was all over so they could talk. Denise loves him so much, Toly, and she's in torment."

"Has she asked you to intercede?"

"No. Not at all. She called me because we're friends and she wanted me to know the truth. As for Johnny, she can only hope that one day he'll realize he needs to find someone else to love."

"Do you *want* to do something about it?"

"I don't dare. If I told Mills the truth now, his first

reaction would be one of anger. I'm afraid this has to be worked out between the two of them after Finals are over. What I don't understand is why my brother has never told her he wants to marry her."

"Probably because having worked with him all year, I've discovered he wants more money in the bank and his ducks all lined up when he proposes. Your dad was a great role model, you know."

"But she doesn't care about that!"

"Haven't you noticed he has a more protective side to his nature since the death of your parents?"

She nodded. "It's all so complicated when it didn't need to be."

"I couldn't agree more. But we have to face the fact that she has hurt him, even if it was for the best of reasons."

"You're right."

He studied her features for a moment. "Why don't you and I go out for lunch at a drive-through? You'll have to take us since you have the only car."

Her face lit up in a smile. "I was just going to suggest it. Do you think you should take a pain pill first?"

"No. I'm okay as long as I don't wrap both my arms around you the way I want to. But I'll need another kiss before we go anywhere. Come here to me, you gorgeous creature."

"Toly—"

Holding and kissing her had become an addiction. The last thing he cared about was food or anything else. Nikki had become his whole world. After mocking his brothers who caved after meeting the right women, he now understood. But he needed to get her out of there, and tore his lips from hers before he forgot everything else.

"Come on." He gripped her hand and they headed outside to her car.

"How did it go wrapping the dally with your left hand this morning?" she asked while driving them to Buck's Fast Food for hamburgers and shakes.

"Not that great."

"But you'll do it well enough to stay on top. I know you will."

"Your faith in me is humbling."

"You had to be in the stands and watch what you did last night to convince me you can do anything. I wish there was something I could do to help."

"With you championing me, I don't want for anything else."

"Liar," she teased. "I think it's time to get you back to the rig. Your eyelids are getting heavy so I'm going to drop you off after we get our grub, and leave you to get a good nap with some ice and a pill. Hopefully you'll be revived for tonight. For once I'm going to drive to the center and meet you there."

What he wanted was to nap with her. But both of them knew it wouldn't be a good idea whether Mills was around or not.

When they returned to the rig, he leaned toward her. "Thanks for lunch, but most of all for your company. I needed you today, Nikki. You'll never know how much." He cupped her neck so he could give her a thorough kiss. "You're going to get another first tonight. I can feel it in my bones. Drive carefully and I'll see you later."

"I can hardly bear to leave you, Toly," she said and wrapped her arms around his neck to kiss him again. "Promise me you'll stay safe."

The throb in her voice was like music to his ears.

Chapter 9

Toly got out of the car and waved her off. A minute later Mills walked inside the rig. "I passed Nikki on the way in."

"She came by and took me to Buck's. We would have brought a burger back for you, but didn't know when we'd see you."

"Don't worry about that. How are you doing?"

"Good." He took another pain pill and pulled the ice bag out of the fridge. "I'm going to baby my arm until we leave for the center. Nikki says she'll meet us there."

"Hmm. That's a first for her. I would have thought she'd cook up a storm today."

He followed Toly to his bedroom where he lay down on top of the mattress. "She might have, but I told her not to bother because I'm going to sleep for a while."

"Good idea. Can I get you anything else?"

"No, thanks. How did your practice go?"

"I exercised both horses. I think I'll ride Dusty again."

"They're both winners. You can't go wrong."

"Wouldn't it be great if we could pull the same score tonight?"

Toly closed his eyes. "It would be miraculous."

"I know, but you can't help a guy from dreaming."

"Nope."

"You're obviously tired. I'll go over to my rig and phone you when it's time to leave for the center."

"I'd appreciate that."

After his partner left, he rearranged his pillows to get more comfortable, but nothing could take away his guilt for not telling him about Denise. The woman Mills loved would be out in the crowd tonight watching him.

Toly went through the conversation with Nikki in his mind and decided she'd been right. This was a situation only Mills and Denise could solve. Right now Toly had his own crisis to get through. He'd done the figures in his head. If they got a third place tonight, they were still in contention for a first place overall. That is if Shay didn't do something extraordinary, which he could.

But during the rest of the nights they would have to get some seconds and firsts. If he rested his right arm for three more events, then the last two nights he would use it again. Of course that depended on his not having another episode. Toly never knew when they would come. He was living with a virtual time bomb and his poor partner knew nothing about it.

Here Toly was questioning Denise's judgment when his own was in question. Why didn't he tell Mills about his neuropathy? Nikki didn't think it was wise to tell him, either. So one way or another, all three of them were guilty of keeping Mills in the dark.

Toly tried to put himself in his partner's shoes, but that didn't work. At one point he dozed off, and then his cell phone rang. When he looked at his watch, he couldn't believe it was time to leave for the center.

In a few minutes he'd changed clothes. After grabbing his gloves and hat, he joined Mills at the car. They took off and his partner chatted all the way about scores and what they had to do. Toly knew exactly what they had to do. He needed his left arm and hand to deliver a score that rated in the top three of the night.

To his disappointment he didn't see Nikki at the stalls. She was probably with Denise. Mills was surprised because his sister had always been there to cheer him on.

They walked to their stalls and got ready for their event. Andy had already prepared their horses. All Toly had to do was mount Snapper. When they were ready, they rode to the boxes to wait for their turn.

There'd only been two times in his life Toly had known real fear. One was when his father had been accidentally shot. The other was the night he heard Wymon had been kidnapped and almost killed. Tonight represented a third time that also involved a life-and-death situation.

But the stakes were different. As much as Toly would love to win the championship, he knew his partner needed it more. Everything in Mills's life depended on it. The Dobson twins didn't have family supporting them; their parents were gone. They needed money to keep the ranch going. They both could stand to revel in that moment of glory, vindicating all those years of hard work and dedication to the sport they loved.

Toly gripped the reins with his right hand and walked Snapper into the box. The steer between him and Mills was a wily one, anxious to get out. Toly flicked his partner a glance and knew the exact moment Mills saw he was going out there to rope with his left arm.

His body went cold because Mills would have figured out Toly's right arm couldn't do the job. Hell and hell.

It was time to call for the steer.

The chute opened. Toly had never prayed so hard in his life. He raced after the steer, roping him around the head, and then he wrapped the dally as hard and fast as he could to turn it. Mills roped those hind legs on cue and they left the arena with a 4.0, 4.2 score and hoped it meant a decent ranking.

They rode back to the stalls and dismounted. Mills eventually walked over to him. "I didn't realize your right arm was hurting so badly."

"Sorry I couldn't pull through for us tonight. I'm hoping I'll be able to use it tomorrow night."

"Santos said we came in second. We've still held on to our first-place average."

No thanks to Toly. "That's the best news tonight. You were sensational out there, Mills. Come on. Let's go watch Nikki knock them dead."

Not only was Toly madly in love, he was so proud of her he didn't know how to contain it. Earlier this evening she'd kissed the daylights out of him. A man could die for a kiss like that, but he was shockingly alive and ready for more.

Nikki and Denise hugged each other the moment the announcer came over the loudspeaker proclaiming that Toly and her brother still held the overall lead.

"I'll call you when I'm back in my room and let you know the way is clear so you can come over again."

"Can't wait. Good luck out there, Nikki. There's no one who can touch you."

"Oh, yes there is, but thanks for being my friend."

Taking her leave, she hurried through the stands to the stalls where Santos waited for her with Bombshell. He gave her the thumbs-up when she mounted her horse. "All bets are on you, Nikki."

"Thanks, Santos. That means everything."

She left the stall and walked her horse along the aisle. Five more nights and she would never go through this glorious experience again with Toly. Whatever the future held, she would treasure this moment forever.

While the finalists were gathering, she chatted with a few of them on her way to the end of the line. Tension was building. Nikki could feel it with the girls. They all wanted to win the championship. No one wanted it more than she did, but she wanted the guys to come out on top too. The three of them were in this together.

Nikki leaned forward to pat her horse's neck. "Remember how we went around the practice barrels this afternoon? Let's do it again."

Close to her turn now, the adrenaline surged through her veins, giving her a sense of empowerment. It was heady stuff.

"Up next is Nikki Dobson of the Sweet Clover Ranch in Great Falls, Montana. This rodeo queen has gained the lead. Let's see what she can do tonight on Bombshell!"

Her smart horse knew what to do, opening up her stride to enter the arena. After slowing her down around the first barrel with her inside rein, Nikki raised both to give Bombshell the freedom to accelerate in a straight line for the second barrel.

She entered the pocket in an arc and then headed for the third barrel. This one was always tricky. Nikki knew to pick up Bombshell's shoulder using her rein and leg. Once she'd moved her over and collected at the same time, she could finish with a tight turn and run home with power.

The roar from the audience was electric as she rode out of the arena with a 13.60, almost as good as last night. Once again her prayers had been answered. This time when she rode to her stall it was Toly, not her brother, who helped her down with his left arm and gave her a hug.

"I've decided you're a new kind of superhero," he whispered. "You're blowing the place up."

"I think you already did that a little while ago," she whispered back. If there was such a state of too much happiness, this was it.

"Way to go." Mills gave her a huge hug while Santos took care of her horse. "Let's go celebrate."

Mindful of Toly's sore arm, she looked up at him. "Why don't you guys call it a night and take care of that sore arm." They wouldn't be getting gold buckles tonight. "I'll go to the South Point and then I'll drive on back to the hotel. I really am bushed."

Mills frowned. "You don't want me there?"

"Of course, but maybe Toly will need some waiting on, and I'll only be at the South Point long enough to pick up my buckle. We'll have our own celebration to-morrow when I drive out to fix you guys waffles and sausage. How's that?"

Toly flashed her a heart-stopping grin. "That sounds perfect to me."

She knew he was hurting. "Good. Then it's a date."

Without hesitation she took off for her car, not wanting to get detained by Mills. He could tell something was going on. He had radar like Toly's. She decided it was a team roper thing because they'd had to work in harmony for so long.

An hour later she left the South Point having collected her buckle and pulled out her phone to call Denise. "I'll be at the Cyclades in a few minutes. Come over as soon as you can. I'll leave the door open."

"Thanks. You did it again tonight, Nikki. You really are on your way to the championship. I get gooseflesh just thinking about it."

So did Nikki.

On Tuesday morning the guys were so hungry, Nikki made another batch of waffles. She was relieved to see Toly had a good appetite and looked rested. She'd bought fresh strawberries from the market on her way over to his rig. They disappeared along with the sausage.

Mills poured more coffee for them. "Are you going to ride Bombshell again tonight?"

"No. She needs a rest. Sassy is ready for another go. I'm going to set up the practice barrels and work with her later today. What about you?"

"Dusty's doing great. I'll stick with him tonight. What about you, Toly?"

"I'll ride Snapper again."

Nikki eyed him. "How's the pain this morning?"

"Not nearly as bad as yesterday."

"That's wonderful, but, more than ever, you need to rest that arm. After I've gone over to the center to practice, I'll come back with dinner before we leave for tonight's events."

"You're spoiling us rotten." She caught Toly's smile just as his phone rang. When he answered, she could tell it was his family calling. She got up to clear the table and get the dishes done. The lighted Christmas tree reminded her that her favorite holiday was coming up soon. Once Finals were over she had a lot of shopping to do.

Denise planned to go with her while they were still in Las Vegas. Both of them wanted to find the perfect gifts for the men they loved. Since it appeared his family wanted to talk ranch business and would be on the phone awhile, she waved goodbye to Mills and left the rig.

He surprised her by following her out to her car. "Before you leave, there's something I want to talk to you about."

Her pulse quickened. Could he have possibly found out that Denise was there? She knew Toly wouldn't have told him.

"What is it?"

"Something's different about Toly."

Uh-oh. "Really?" She got in the driver's seat, but that didn't deter Mills.

He climbed in the front passenger side and shut the door. "I don't think he's telling me everything about his arm. What do you know that I don't?"

Heat warmed her cheeks. "Why are you asking me that?"

"Because I can tell you're really worried about him."

"No more than I would be about you."

"Come on, Nikki. It's me you're talking to. Night before last my heart went to my throat when I saw the way he threw the rope. Last night I could hardly breathe when I saw him use his left arm. He's never trained with it. But I can't get him to talk to me about it. I know *you* know the truth and I'm not letting you drive away until you level with me."

Nikki shuddered, realizing she had to put him out of his misery. Otherwise he wouldn't be able to perform at his best for the rest of the rodeo. But when she told him the truth, she feared he would feel so badly about Toly, it would affect him in a worse way.

What to do…

Forgive me, Toly. My brother needs an explanation.

She turned to face him. "All right. I'll tell you the truth." For the next little while Nikki told him about Toly's neuropathy. "He's had three episodes since he was diagnosed. Two happened during practice before you drove to Las Vegas. But the third one came on when he was in the box two nights ago."

Mills shook his head, but he'd lowered it so she couldn't see his expression.

"He's been going through excruciating torment to keep the news from you because he wants you guys to win the national championship. He feared that if he told you, it might make you want to pull out, which was the last thing he wanted. Yesterday he practiced throwing the rope with his left arm and it paid off because you got a second place last night."

Silence followed her comments.

"When did he tell you?" he finally asked in a deceptively quiet voice.

"The afternoon I brought the Chinese food for you. He said he needed my advice about something. I had no idea. When I learned about his condition, you can't imagine how heartbroken I was, not only for him but for you!"

"Did he swear you to secrecy?"

"No. It wasn't like that. Toly was torn apart and wanted me to tell him if he should tell you the truth, knowing you might decide to withdraw from the competition. He said he would abide by my decision because he trusted me with his life. Toly also said that he knew you trusted me more than anyone else in the world."

Mills lifted his dark head. "So *you* influenced him not to tell me?"

"After he told me he would start training with his left arm in order to stay in the competition, I knew in my heart and soul he didn't want to give up. I didn't want him to give up, either, so that's why he didn't tell you."

A grimace marred her brother's good-looking features. "I see. Interesting, isn't it, that he couldn't tell me, the guy he asked to partner with him for an entire year? We would have talked it over and discussed strategies. Instead, he decided I would have just given up everything we'd worked for because he had no faith in me."

"Yes, he does—" she cried, but he wasn't listening.

"No, Nikki. He came to you." She felt him trembling. "I find that the worst form of betrayal. When I get out of the car, I'm going back to his rig to tell him he can go to hell."

"Mills—you don't mean that. I know you're angry. But please, please be angry with me, not him. He was ready to be honest with you. I'm the one who made the final decision."

"Which means you have no faith in me."

By now *she* was trembling in frustration. "You're wrong, Mills. As Mom and Dad told me many times, you were born with an exceptionally compassionate nature and a pure heart."

"That's bull."

"You know it isn't because they told you that to your face when you didn't want our dog to be put down. I was there, remember?"

He lowered his head.

"I can point out dozens of other times too, especially after our parents died. You were there for me, comforting me like a guardian angel. I happen to know it's a fact that if Toly had come right out and told you what was wrong, you would have been totally heartbroken for him."

A strange sound escaped his lips.

"Don't shake your head. I know you, Mills. You would have put his welfare and pain above yours and let go of your dream to win a championship because you're selfless."

She could tell he was restless and ready to get out of the car. Nikki had to make one last attempt to reach him.

"Toly recognizes those traits in you. Have you forgotten he could have chosen any heeler in the country to work with him on this year's circuit? To think that he asked you to be his partner should tell you how much he respects and admires you, not just your horsemanship. Promise me you'll consider everything I've said before you tell him to go to hell."

Nikki's words resonated in the interior of the car before he got out. At least he didn't slam the door. Hopefully that meant something. This was a new situation for all of them. If she'd made matters worse, she guessed she'd find out soon enough.

As much as she'd have liked to warn Toly with a phone call, she didn't dare in case Mills had already gone in the rig to confront him. He'd know in a second if she was on the phone to him. But she could send him a text before she turned on the engine and drove away.

Toly had just gotten off the phone after talking ranch business with his brother Eli, when he saw that Nikki had just texted him. He'd hoped that she would have stayed with him. But she had another event tonight and no doubt wanted to get in some practice before she came back with their meal. He checked to see what she'd sent.

Sorry. Mills knows about your neuropathy. My fault.

No sooner had he taken a deep breath than he heard the distinctive knock on the door.

"Come on in!"

Mills walked through to the kitchen.

Toly eyed him over his coffee cup. "What are you doing back here? I thought you were headed for the center."

When Mills was upset, his hard jaw gave him a fierce look. He was loaded for bear. Apparently he'd suspected something wasn't right and had broken Nikki down. Toly wasn't sorry. It was time he knew the truth.

"When were you going to tell me about your disease?"

"Only one person besides my doctor knows about it, so I take it Nikki has told you everything."

"You're damn right. Thanks for trusting the guy you've been training and competing with for the last year. You're some friend, Toly Clayton."

"For just a minute, would you try to put yourself in my place?"

"No, Toly. That argument doesn't hold water. This issue goes far beyond winning the rodeo. I thought we were closer than friends." The pain Toly could hear in Mills's voice cut him like shards of glass. "You know. Brothers."

He swallowed hard. "That's the way I've felt about you for a long time."

"The hell you have! I don't think you know the meaning of the word." His gray eyes looked suspiciously bright. "Funny, isn't it, that all this time I was worried you would break Nikki's heart because you couldn't settle on one woman, and you've done an almighty job of breaking mine."

Toly knew there was no reasoning with him right now. Maybe Mills would never be able to get over it or forgive him. To try to make things better would be futile until he'd had time to absorb what he'd learned. All Toly knew at this point was that Mills wasn't the only one with a broken heart.

"Damn you, Toly," his voice grated before he flew out of the rig, slamming the door behind him.

A groan came out of Toly. There wasn't anything he could do. In Mills's state, no one could know where he'd gone or how he would deal with his pain. Toly didn't suppose even Nikki knew how to solve this one. Not yet anyway.

Before he did anything else, he sent her a text.

Mills delivered his message and hit his target dead center. He's not in good shape, but I'm thankful he heard it from you, the one person he loves and knows he can count on. I'm living till I see you this afternoon. T.

On his way out the door to do some practice throws on the dummy steer, he saw the car and was surprised. That meant Mills could be in his rig, or exercising Dusty in the RV park arena, or had even gone for a run.

No matter what, right now Toly needed to carry out his routine for today. His right arm was still too sore to use tonight. Tomorrow night it ought to be okay, but then he had to worry if his condition would act up on him at the wrong moment. This was agony.

Once he reached the barn, he grabbed the rope he needed and walked out in back to throw loops with his left hand. He didn't see any sign of Mills. An hour later he went back to the rig, popped some painkillers and took another nap.

When he awakened he saw that Lyle had left him a text congratulating him on their wins. He also asked him to take a look at the email he'd sent him. Amanda Fleming had made a post on the blog that Toly ought to see.

His anger flared. Amanda again?

Toly put the laptop on the kitchen table and opened the message.

For all you fans, I have news. Toly Clayton is a two-faced jerk. I ought to know. After being with me a month ago, the creep only had ten minutes for a cup of coffee after I traveled all the way to Las Vegas to be with him. I wonder how many women have ended up being dumped by him after loading them with promises. Is it because Nikki Dobson has him hog-tied? They show up together every night at the South Point. Does she know what he's been doing out on the circuit when he's on his own? Wouldn't she be shocked to know what he was doing with me?

I know a lot of people would like to know my story. In fact, I know a number of magazines that would pay a lot of money for an exclusive from me with the reigning cowboy in Las Vegas. I even have pictures.

Toly didn't give her post two thoughts before he picked up his phone and called Lyle.

"You've read it?"

"Yes. If I weren't leaving the rodeo forever, I'd hire an attorney and sue her for slander. But she's not worth the trouble. By the weekend my career will be over and the website will no longer be online. She'll have to pick on some other dude and rant elsewhere."

"What?"

"Yep. But don't tell a soul, and don't count out Mills who has several years yet and will hook up with another header."

"But, Toly—"

"That's my exclusive, Lyle," he interrupted him. "I'll call you again this weekend and you can go rogue with it once I'm back in Montana on the ranch."

"You're really giving it up?"

"I am. Thanks for all you've done. I'll be in touch soon."

"Wow. I can't believe it."

"You want to know what I can't believe? That someone like Ms. Fleming is that desperate for attention. I can almost feel sorry for her. Isn't it sad how many of them are out there?"

He hung up the phone. This had been Toly's lucky day with Amanda lining up behind Mills. Just wait until tonight when Toly's left arm let him down. The only light he could see in his life was Nikki. Where in heaven was she?

Chapter 10

"Knock, Knock!"

Nikki—

Toly hurried over to the door to let her in. Her arms were loaded with their dinner, but all he could see were her pain-filled eyes above the sacks. She walked through to the kitchen and put them down on the counter. He was right there to pull her into his arms and they clung to each other.

"Forgive me for telling him, Toly."

He covered her face with kisses. "Mills had to be told."

"I wouldn't have, but when he followed me out to the car earlier, he'd figured out that something was going on and demanded to know what it was. I couldn't hold back any longer."

"Shh," he murmured, sealing her words with another

long, hungry kiss. "If I made a mistake by not telling him immediately, it's too late now."

"You and I made it together, Toly. If I know my brother, this won't cause him to give up even if right now he wants to. Come on. Let's eat before we have to drive over to the center."

She was his rock. He held her for a moment longer before lifting his head. "Something smells good."

"I picked up meat pies with potatoes and gravy at the deli." She eased away and emptied the sacks. "Here's some mint brownies for an hors d'oeuvre if you need one right now." She put their food on the table and they sat down.

"How did you know I've been craving one?"

Nikki grinned. "I'm psychic when it comes to your appetite." Her glance fell on the open laptop. "More fan mail?"

"It's a post Lyle sent to me from an ex-fan."

"Uh-oh. Do I dare read it?"

"Only if you want to."

"I'm glad I got rid of my website," Nikki said before settling down to look at it. She read a couple of lines. "This is the woman you had coffee with the other morning."

"The very one."

"Ooh. She's mad." Nikki scrolled further. "There's nothing about the rodeo here."

Their eyes met. His held amusement. "Of course not."

She ended up reading the whole thing. "Surely this groupie knows you could go after her with a lawsuit, but she's probably disappeared already and you'd never find her."

Toly ruffled his dark blond head unconsciously. "I'd never want to." She loved it when he mussed it. The man was so striking, it didn't surprise her he'd received a post like that one on his blog. No one could match Toly.

He shut the laptop and leaned over to give her a deep kiss. "Mmm. You taste like mint."

Nikki chuckled. "So do you. How's your arm?"

"It's not too sore right now."

"Thank goodness."

They dug into their Chinese food. She kept hoping Mills might get in touch with her. But after knowing about his conversation with Toly, the news had enlarged the pit in her stomach. At the end of their meal her phone rang. She checked the caller ID before flicking him a glance.

"It's Mills." She picked up and put it on speaker. "Hey—where are you?" She was holding her breath.

"I'm at the center and will see you there."

"Great." She heard the click before she could say anything else.

Toly stared at her. "At least he's planning to compete tonight."

"Yes. I *know* he's going to get over this. We just have to give him more time and believe he'll move past this."

He shook his head. "I wish I had your faith. I couldn't have inflicted more damage if I'd shot him in the back. This on top of Denise's rejection is as bad as it gets."

She cleared the table. "Maybe the anger beneath these tumultuous feelings will help him get through the rest of the competition."

"That's one interesting way of looking at it." He put his left arm around her waist and drew her against his body. "Thank God you're here, Nikki," he spoke into her hair. "I couldn't get through this without you."

Nikki's hands slid up his chest to cup his chiseled face. "I feel the same way. We're in this together, and we'll see it through." For the first time since coming to Las Vegas, she took the initiative and kissed him with all the longing that had built up inside of her. Their bodies tried to merge.

His hungry response robbed her of breath. "I need you, Nikki Dobson," he said in a husky voice. "I wish to heaven we didn't have to leave for the center."

"But we do," she half moaned the words and eased away. "I'll finish the dishes when I bring you back later. Gather your things and we'll go."

On the drive to the center, Nikki felt that somewhere along the way they'd charted a new course. He might be a team roper, but the header and the barrel racer had become a team, bound by invisible cords over their love for Mills and all that this grueling year of hard work and sacrifice represented.

Nikki pulled in back of the center and they made their way to the stalls. One of the events had started and the noise of the crowd was unreal. Andy had Snapper bridled and saddled. "Mills said to tell you he'd meet you in the alley."

"Thanks, Andy. You and Santos do great work."

But beneath his Stetson, Toly flashed her a worried, silent message that tugged on her emotions. "It'll be fine," she whispered. "God bless you tonight."

"I already asked Him to bless you."

"Toly." Her voice caught.

He led Snapper out of the stall and mounted him. There was no more magnificent sight than Toly astride his horse dressed in his black Western shirt and jeans, the epitome of male beauty.

After he disappeared, she made her way through the stands to the place where Denise was waiting for her and they hugged. It meant everything that the woman who'd become her dear friend was here to talk to.

Last night she'd confided in Denise about Toly's condition. "Unfortunately today I had to tell Mills about Toly's neuropathy. He knew something was wrong. Toly and I had agreed not to tell him until the rodeo was over, but it didn't work out that way."

"Oh no—"

"It was horrible. He felt completely betrayed and looked like he'd lost his best friend. In a way it was almost as bad as the way he looked when he told me you'd broken up with him. My brother can't take much more. Neither can Toly," she whispered. "He's been living a nightmare since that episode the other night."

Suddenly the team roping was announced. They looked at each other without having to say a word. A bad night tonight could cause the guys to slip from their first-place standing and there'd be no coming back from it.

One by one the teams raced out of their gates, racking up a lot of times between 4.6 and 4.4, but as the announcer said, "The time to beat is 4.2. Here come our first-place winners from Montana, Toly Clayton and Mills Dobson! Can they do it again?" The crowd went crazy with everyone on their feet.

"I'm going to jump out of my skin."

Nikki looked at her friend. "You're not the only one." With her eyes glued to the box, she waited for them to race out. *Come on, Toly. You can do it, you can do it.*

Suddenly the gates lifted and he exploded into the arena. Nikki watched in wonder as he threw a perfect loop with his left arm that caught the steer around the horns. Mills snagged its legs in one swift throw. It all happened so fast and was over before she could take another breath.

Denise grabbed her and they both broke down in tears. "They got a 4.0 and 4.2. They did it!"

Another miracle for Toly.

Nikki sent up a prayer of thanksgiving that her brother had channeled his anger and hurt in a way that got them through another night. If they kept this up, they were on track to win it all.

"Oh boy. Now it's my turn."

"I'm not worried about you, Nikki."

She turned to Denise. "You don't know how glad I am that you're here. I'll call you tonight when I get back to the hotel. See you later."

Her adrenaline was working overtime as she hurried through the stands to the stalls to get ready for her event. "Hey, Santos. Looks like you've got my Sassy all ready."

"Yep. She's perkier than usual tonight. You can't tell me horses aren't like people. She's excited to get out there and show her stuff."

Santos spoke Nikki's language. "Is that true?" She rubbed Sassy's forelock. "You want to get out there and show off? Well, so do I. Let's do it."

After thanking Santos, she mounted her horse and walked her back past her competition. Now that Toly and Mills had accomplished another winning performance, Nikki could concentrate on what she had to do tonight.

She patted Sassy's neck. "You do seem a little friskier than usual. We had a good practice session earlier today and you know what's ahead." The wait seemed like forever before it was her turn to take off. "Here we go, Sassy."

From the moment they started down the alley, they seemed to go like the wind. Sassy circled both barrels with finesse. Now for the final one. But Nikki could tell her horse was going too fast. When she tried to square up around the third barrel, Sassy's right leg slid in reaction and sent them both banging into it.

Nikki was thrown to the ground and felt pain shoot up through her right leg when she tried to get to her feet. Nausea took over. She fell back and lay there for a few minutes while she waited for the ringing in her ears to stop. Voices were talking all around her. Someone started to examine her.

"Lie still, Ms. Dobson."

"But my horse— How's Sassy?"

"She's fine and being taken care of."

The Justin Sports Medicine Team had been the official health care provider for the PRCA for years. Nikki had seen them run to assist everyone who was hurt during an event, but she'd never dreamed she'd be the one who needed help.

Hot tears trickled out of her eyes. "I can't believe this has happened." One fatal slip and all her dreams had gone up in smoke.

"You're going to be fine too. Just let us do the work. We're going to stabilize you and get you to the hospital." By now they were taking her vital signs, but her head was still spinning.

"Nikki—" That was Mills's voice. Where was Toly? "I'm here. You're not alone."

Within seconds she was being transported out of the arena to a waiting ambulance. Once they'd helped her inside, she saw that her brother had come in and sat down beside her. He held her cowboy hat in his hand. His eyes were filled with tears while the attendants hooked up an IV and checked her vital signs again.

"Don't feel bad for me, Mills. It's life and we all take the risk when we get in the arena."

He shook his head. "This should never have happened to you."

"Sassy lost her footing. She was in extra high spirits after my workout with her today. I could feel it, but it doesn't matter now. How are you?"

"Don't worry about me."

"But I do, and you know it. Surely you realize Toly never wanted to hurt you."

"Let's not talk about that right now."

"All right. Do you have any idea how proud I am that you and Toly got a first-place win tonight? You'll never know how happy I am about that. Where is Toly?"

"He's gone to the South Point to pick up our buckles. He'll come to the hospital once the ceremony is over. We're both devastated for you. How's the pain?"

"We've given her something," the medic murmured.

"I'm floating right now."

"That's good."

"My car—"

"I'll take care of it later. You relax."

Her eyes closed. "Okay."

She had no sense of time. When they arrived at the hospital she was taken into the ER and sent up for a

CT scan. When next she opened her eyes, it was after eleven. Mills stood against the curtain on the other side of the bed.

"Ms. Dobson? I'm Dr. Hall, the orthopedic surgeon on duty tonight. Your scan tells me you have a fractured fibula below the knee, but you won't require surgery."

"I'm thankful for that."

"I've told your brother that I'm going to put a cast on you and you'll have to wear it for six weeks. Barring any unforeseen circumstances, it should heal without problems and your leg will be as good as new. Knowing what a famous barrel racer you are, I suspect you'll be back on your horse competing again in no time."

No. There'd be no more competitions.

"Thank you, Doctor."

"The hospital is buzzing that there's a celebrity on-site from the Mack Center." He smiled. "A beautiful one, I might add."

"Your bedside manner is delightful."

He chuckled. "Okay. Let's get this done and we'll put you in a private room tonight."

Nikki was surprised how fast he applied the cast. "It's a blessing to be given such amazing care."

"It's been a pleasure. A nurse will come in and the orderlies will be here shortly to wheel you upstairs. I'll be by in the morning to check on you. We'll talk then about how to handle your crutches and what to expect after you go home."

"Thank you so much," she whispered.

She heard Mills chat with him for a minute before the doctor left the cubicle. Then he walked over to her side. "I'm thankful you didn't have to undergo surgery."

"Me too."

"The crew has texted me several times wanting to know how you are. They've promised to take expert care of your horses."

"I already know they will."

"Toly texted me too. He's on his way back from the hotel. I told him to check with the front desk about which room you're going to be put in."

"Good. I need to congratulate him on your win tonight." Her heart pounded extra hard. Even if she knew she looked terrible, she was living for the moment when she saw him again.

The nurse swept in. "Ms. Dobson? You've already been on the ten o'clock news."

"You mean my spectacular fall."

"Accidents happen, even to the most famous barrel racer in Las Vegas. Are you ready to be taken to your room?"

"Yes."

"You'll be moved shortly."

Mills leaned over to kiss her forehead. "I'll bring the bags with your clothes."

"What about my phone?"

"I've got it in my pocket."

"What would I do without you? I love you, Mills."

"Ditto. When I saw Sassy's leg slide like that, I almost went into cardiac arrest."

"I could tell she was taking that last turn too fast. Sassy was overly excited tonight."

"That's because she loves you and wanted to make you proud."

"I thought you didn't believe she had human feelings."

"Tonight's accident has made a believer out of me."

"Then let me make a believer out of you where Toly is concerned. Remember that he was afraid to let you down by telling you about his neuropathy, especially after what happened with Denise. Through thick and thin he's been your truest loyal friend every step of the way. In your heart you have to know that."

As they were talking, the curtain was swept back. The orderlies had come to transport her on the gurney. She gripped the handrails during the journey. It felt strange to be moving while she was still feeling the effects of the painkillers. Nikki didn't like it and hoped she wouldn't have to take any more.

They got out on the third floor. Mills walked at her side while they wheeled her down the hall past the nursing station to room 314. No sooner had she been put in the hospital bed than a new nurse walked in the room carrying a vase of glorious white and yellow daisies. The colors were so different from the red Christmas poinsettias she'd seen everywhere at this time of year that they came as a lovely surprise.

"Flowers already? How beautiful!"

"You must have an admirer, Ms. Dobson." She put it on the side table. "I'm Lynette. How are you feeling?"

"I'm not feeling much of anything."

"That means your medication is working." She checked Nikki's vital signs and made notations on the computer. "I'll be back."

Mills had been putting her clothes in the closet. She looked over at him. "Is there a card with those flowers? Are they from Toly?"

"I'll check." He walked over and pulled a little envelope off the pick. "Here you go."

"Do you mind reading it to me?"

"Sure." He pulled out the card. "Dear Nikki, may these flowers put spring back in your heart. Love, a friend."

Mills's mouth tightened. "I don't know why Toly didn't sign his name."

"It's not from him."

"How do you know?"

"He would have written a *T* on the card." She was positive they were from Denise. It was something her friend would have written. Nikki had an idea she was there at the hospital, waiting until she could visit her alone. But Nikki didn't want her brother to know the woman who'd broken his heart was nearby. Not yet.

A little white lie wouldn't come amiss. "I'm pretty sure they're from Jules McGinnis at the WPRA. That was very kind of her to send them."

When the door opened again, she held her breath because she hoped it would be Toly. But it was the nurse again, compounding her disappointment. This time she was holding a straw cowboy hat with a small floral arrangement nestled on the crown.

"You're a very popular person, Ms. Dobson."

She placed it right in her lap. Nikki handed Mills the card to read.

"Love, Laurie Rippon and all the gals."

Nikki bit her lip. "She's going to win the championship now. It was very kind of her to do this. It shows she's a champion inside and out."

She looked down and saw the names of all the finalists written around the brim with the words "National Finals Rodeo." One of the girls must have brought it to the hospital, maybe Laurie herself.

Nikki broke down in tears. Mills picked it up and

studied the signatures. "There's a reason you were chosen as Miss Congeniality a year ago when you won
the Miss Rodeo Montana Pageant." His voice sounded
husky with emotion.

Just then the nurse came in one more time with a
vase of pink roses and baby's breath. A ribbon that said
WPRA was fastened to it.

Mills showed it to her before putting it on a side
table. "I'm still wondering who your *friend* is since
it wasn't from Jules McGinnis." He put the hat on the
other stand in the room. "A secret admirer maybe?"

"I have no idea." She smiled at him. "Mills? Could
you find the nurse and ask her if I can have a soda or
something?"

"Sure. Be right back."

Toly left the South Point at a quarter to eleven and
hurried back to his rig to gather a few things before he
took off for the hospital. En route he talked with his
family, all of whom were thrilled for him, yet horrified for Nikki. Several of his close friends texted their
congratulations.

At ten to midnight, Toly left the Flower Festival shop
on the Strip. He carried a vase of Spanish Dream—
large, brilliant red roses—protected with floral paper,
and got in the car. He'd already called the hospital and
couldn't get there fast enough. The operator told him
Nikki had been taken to room 314.

Without wasting any time, he pulled into visitor
parking and hurried inside to the main elevators. At
the third-floor nursing station he checked to make sure
he could visit Nikki. "We were both competing in the
rodeo tonight. I couldn't get here any sooner."

One of the nurses said, "She's asleep, but you can peek in and deliver your flowers."

"Thanks. Is her brother here?"

"Yes. But he's down at the cafeteria getting a bite to eat."

Glad he'd be able to see her alone, Toly walked down the hall and opened the door to the dimly lit room. His beautiful Nikki lay on her back with the IV still attached to her hand. Her flowing black hair was splayed across the pillow. Hard to believe her right leg, now elevated, was encased in a cast from the knee down. A light sheet covered part of her gorgeous body.

He'd often thought she could play the role of Sleeping Beauty, but never more so than right now. Unfortunately, he didn't dare kiss her awake. She needed her sleep after the horrendous shock dealt to her.

With as much care as possible he put the flowers on the hospital tray table placed against the wall. He removed the paper around the roses. Their strong scent would fill the room before long. When she awakened, they were the first thing he wanted her to see.

Toly put his cowboy hat on a chair and sat down in the leather one. This was the first moment he'd had to relax since leaving his rig before the rodeo. Her fall had shaken him to the foundations. He extended his long legs, crossed them at the ankles and rested his head.

Nikki hadn't stirred. He began to think she'd stay asleep unless the nurse came in during the night to check her vital signs and woke her up. Just as he was reliving the scene in his head when he saw her horse slide into the barrel, he heard her voice.

"Mills?"

He got out of the chair and walked over to the side of the bed. "No. It's me."

"Toly—" Her voice throbbed. "I've been hoping you'd come."

"Did you honestly think I wouldn't?" He lowered his mouth to give hers a warm kiss. "What I want to know is, if this had to happen, why did it have to happen to you?"

"I thought the same thing when you told me about your neuropathy. But nothing has held you back. You're still on top."

"The only thing that matters to me is that you're all right so I can tell you how much I love you. Do you hear me?"

Chapter 11

Nikki's body started to tremble. "You…love me?"

"How could you possibly doubt it?"

She shook her head. "I don't. I don't. Oh, Toly—I love you, too. You just don't know how much. It seems like I've been waiting to hear you say that to me forever."

He kissed her again. "You know why I haven't, but I can't worry over how Mills feels about it any longer. I've been in love with you for an entire year."

"We've both been in pain. So many times I've been on the verge of blurting my love for you."

He covered her face with kisses. "Tonight I came close to death watching you slam into the barrel. Nikki—if I'd lost you, I couldn't have gone on living."

"You'll never lose me. It could never happen. You know I adore you. There isn't anything I wouldn't do for you. I love you heart and soul, Toly Clayton."

"Enough to marry me?"

She looked into his eyes. "Say that again."

"Will you marry me? Be my wife? Be the mother of our children one day?"

"Yes, my love!" she cried, trying to sit up, but he gently pushed her back.

"Even if I have this condition that might not clear up with surgery?"

"Surely you don't have to ask me that. Whatever you have to face, we'll do it together. I can't imagine a future without you, Toly. Ever since the rodeo started, I've been dreading the day it was over. I'm so used to being with you all the time, I want it to go on forever. I need you desperately."

"I've longed to hear those words from you." He reached in his pocket and pulled out a ring. "I had this made up for you months ago even though we haven't dated officially. I'm glad your IV is in your right hand, because this belongs on your left. I'm sorry I couldn't have asked your father for his blessing so I could marry you." He felt for her hand and slid it on her ring finger.

"Will you turn on the light so I can see?"

Toly rushed to do her bidding. She looked at the pear-shaped gray gemstone mounted in white gold. Her breath caught. "I've never seen anything so exquisite in my life."

"I have. But a person has to be able to look into your eyes. They're this exact color and pure as enchanted pools."

"Darling—" Her voice shook. "Where did you ever find a stone like this?"

"You once referred to me as the Sapphire Cowboy. There's a reason for that. My family owns a sapphire mine in the Sapphire Mountains on our ranch. My mother has run the Clayton Sapphire Shop for a long time."

"Your mom is a jeweler?"

"At first it was a hobby, but she turned it into a real business. People came from all over to buy her sapphires."

"How fascinating!"

"We boys thought so too. One area called Gem Mountain produced over 180 million carats of sapphires for over 120 years. Before WWII people dug for the large stones, and the fragments were used for watch bearings in Switzerland. Later the rock hounds came to sift through them.

"Ages ago I looked in some of her velvet pouches and found the stone you're wearing. It's large, four carats, and exactly the color of your eyes. I had her mount it in white gold because I fell in love with your eyes along with everything else about you. The sapphires come in many colors. When you meet my three sisters-in-law, you'll see they each wear a sapphire engagement ring that matches their eyes."

"I can't wait to look at them and get acquainted with your whole family!"

"They're all going to love you."

"Is this really happening to me, or am I dreaming because of the medication?"

"I don't know. I've been taking painkillers too, but it all seemed real to me when I kissed you just now. What do *you* think?"

"I think I'm so in love, I'm delirious," she said as her brother came in the door.

"Whoops. I guess I'm interrupting something."

"No—" she called to Mills. "Toly and I have something important to tell you. Come on in."

His eyes took in the roses on the hospital tray table. "I guess you do. I take it the latest vase of roses is from you, Toly."

She blinked. "What roses?"

"These." Her brother picked up the vase and brought it over to the bed so Nikki could see them.

A gasp escaped her lips. "Oh, Toly—how gorgeous!"

"These Spanish roses are the same color as the embroidery on that black jacket you wore to dinner with me last week. You were stunning."

That was a magical night. She tore her eyes from Toly to look at her brother. "Tonight he asked me to marry him. Look at the engagement ring he gave me. It's a gray sapphire from his mother's sapphire shop on the ranch."

Mills looked closer. "Wow. Broken legs and engagement rings all in one night have left me spinning."

"Me too. Can I have a hug?"

Her brother went around the other side of the bed and gave her one. She could tell Mills was having a rough time taking it all in. "So, who are the daisies from?" he whispered.

She sucked in her breath. "I have no idea," she lied, "but right now I'm too happy to worry about anything. Thank you for being here for me, Mills. I love you."

"I love you too. If this makes you happy, then I'm happy for you."

"Goodness!" sounded an unfamiliar voice. The nurse had just walked in. "It's the middle of the night. You gentlemen will have to leave."

Toly leaned over to give her one more kiss. "Get

some sleep. We'll see you tomorrow after we get in some practice. Then we can stay with you until we have to drive over to the center. How does that sound, sweetheart?"

Sweetheart. He'd never called her that before. "I can't wait to see you."

"Good night." Mills kissed her cheek. She watched them leave the room, still incredulous that she wasn't dreaming.

"Well," the nurse said after checking her vital signs. "What's been going on here?"

"The man I love proposed to me tonight. He gave me this sapphire ring."

The nurse took hold of her hand. "How absolutely beautiful. You're a lucky woman to be engaged to that gorgeous blond hunk. Some women have all the luck. Kind of makes you forget your broken leg, right?"

Yes. She'd forgotten everything the moment Toly had told her he loved her and wanted to marry her.

"Get your sleep now."

"I will. Thank you."

"Nikki?"

Wednesday morning she looked up from the bed. "Denise—I'm so thrilled you're here. The doctor just left and they took out my IV. Now we've got time to talk before the guys come to the hospital."

Denise ran over and hugged her. "Let me see your ring."

She held out her hand and her friend squealed. "Toly was right. It matches your eyes. When I saw your accident, I never dreamed I'd see you looking this happy, Mrs. Clayton-to-be."

"*Mrs. Clayton*. To be his wife is the greatest wish of my life. I'm so happy, it's hard to contain. Forgive me for talking about myself. Thanks again for the beautiful daisies, Denise. Yours were the first flowers I received."

"I'm glad you liked them." She wandered over to the pink roses. "Who sent these?"

"Mills. They were delivered early this morning."

Her eyes grew misty. "How lovely." She kept moving. "There's no question who the red roses are from."

"No."

Denise picked up the straw cowboy hat. "What a wonderful gift to remember being in the rodeo. You'll treasure this forever."

"I know I will."

Finally, Denise pulled up a chair next to her and sat down. "Will you be released later to go back to the hotel? I'll drive you."

"Thanks for the offer, but no. The doctor is keeping me in the hospital until tomorrow so the therapist can work with me and my new crutches. It's probably for the best. Mills will be spared a night of fussing about me since the guys have another event tonight. I'm glad they won't be worrying about me.

"Besides, I'm such a klutz. The doctor joked that they put a cast on their patients and then send them home where a lot more damage is done by falling because they can't manage their crutches."

Her friend laughed and nodded. "That would be me for sure."

Nikki heard the sadness in her voice. "Denise? I've given everything a lot of thought and I think you should let Mills know you're here. He's so unhappy it breaks my heart."

"I'm afraid it will upset him too much."

"I disagree. So much has happened in the last twelve hours, I think to see you again would be the kind of relief he needs. Toly and I have each other. Now that he's asked me to marry him, I'm sure Mills is feeling more isolated than ever, emotionally."

"You don't know how worried I am about making everything worse."

"But how much worse can it be since you're not together now? Why not stay right here with me? I'll be getting a call from them soon. When I know the time they're coming, you can go down to the cafeteria. As soon as Mills walks in, I'll tell him you've come and are waiting for him. He can make up his own mind if he wants to talk to you or not. But nothing's going to happen if you don't make the first move."

"You're right. I'll think about it."

But not two minutes after she'd said those words, they heard a tap on the door. "Nikki?"

Her brother's voice. He hadn't phoned. "You're here!"

"Yep." He walked in her room without Toly.

Denise jumped up from the chair, white-faced. "Mills—"

The look on his face was a study in pure shock. "I don't believe it." But Nikki saw no anger, for which she was grateful. By now he had to realize the daisies were from Denise.

"I—I've been in Las Vegas since the eighth so I could watch your events." Her voice faltered. "I told Nikki I came so I could talk to you. At first I thought it would be better if I waited until Finals were over. But we've been talking and I decided to be here when you came in. Would you be willing to come to my hotel? I'm staying at the Mirage. We can talk there in private."

Mills's face was masklike. "Why would I do that?"

"Because it's a matter of life and death."

Whoa. *Did you hear that, brother dear?*

The love in her fabulous brown eyes would melt any man on the spot. But not Mills. Maybe too much damage had been done. When he didn't say anything, Denise suddenly rushed out of the room.

Nikki girded up her courage. "Are you honestly going to let her go before you find out what she wanted? It took guts for her to come to Las Vegas, let alone face you."

He stood there with his hands on his hips. "What has she told you?"

"Everything." There was no point in lying.

"What is it about you?" he almost hissed the question.

"I don't understand what you mean."

"My own partner went to you about his neuropathy, not to me. The woman I wanted to marry broke it off, and now she shows up here to talk to you about it."

"Don't play dumb with me, Mills. With the national championship at stake, if you'd been the one diagnosed with that condition, you would have done everything in your power to hide it from Toly in order not to let him down. As for Denise, she's in love with you. Always has been."

"How can you say that?"

"If you'll give her time to explain, you'll get answers to all your questions. Before you throw away your chance for a lifetime of happiness, just remember one thing. You never told her you were in love with her, that you wanted a future with her. A man can assume all he wants, but a woman needs to hear those words."

She paused, then said, "I was around Toly for a whole year, but I had to wait until tonight, after getting a broken leg no less, to hear them from Toly's lips for the first time."

His dark brows met in a frown. "Come on, Nikki. It was written all over him from the beginning."

"Really? I was hard-pressed to believe that after you warned me a year ago against Toly who was *the* ladies' man on the circuit and left broken hearts all over the country. For months I feared he was trying to charm me like he did the other cowgirls in his life. Amanda Fleming was a case in point."

She watched him swallow hard. Good. Maybe she was getting to him. "Have you seen Toly this morning?"

"I drove him to the center so he could pick up your rental car and use it. He's doing a few practice throws on the dummy before he comes. How soon are you being released? I'm here to take you back to the hotel."

"I can't go until tomorrow."

"Why? Is something wrong?"

"No. I have an appointment with the therapist to show me how to use crutches. The doctor will release me tomorrow morning. I'll have to watch tonight's event on TV. Do you want to stay and have lunch with me? I can ask them to bring you a tray."

"Do you want company?"

Well, well, well. That question was a dead giveaway. If Denise hadn't been the first sight he saw when he walked in, he would have sat down with Nikki and started a game of cards with her that would have lasted for hours.

"To be honest, I want to sleep. I didn't get enough last night. But thank you for offering to stay with me."

"If you're sure."

She yawned. "I'm positive."

"Then I'll be back later."

Want to bet? "Love you."

The second he left the room, she reached for her phone and called Toly. It was pure heaven to have the right. He picked up on the second ring. "Sweetheart?"

Heart attack. "How are you?"

"I woke up to a day like no other. I'm coming to get my fiancée and make you comfortable in my rig for the duration."

She couldn't stop smiling. "Mills was just here and offered to drive me to the hotel, but I can't leave until tomorrow. The therapist is going to help me learn how to walk with crutches."

A moan of protest escaped. "I'm so disappointed, but it's probably the best idea."

"I'm sure it is, but I'd rather be with you and never let you out of my sight."

"Amen. I love you, Nikki. I still can't believe you're going to marry me. We have a lot of plans to make."

"I know. I can't wait."

"How do you think Mills is taking the news?"

"I haven't had a chance to find out yet."

"Why?"

"When he walked in this morning, Denise was here."

"Dare I ask how that went?"

"She asked him to go to her hotel so they could talk." In the next breath, she told Toly about Mills's reaction. "He left just now instead of staying with me. We both know where he has gone. It's anyone's guess what will happen."

"Thank heaven she's come at last. He's been needing this in the worst way."

"I know. Denise was afraid it would throw him off his stride, but she loves him and knew it was time to tell him the truth."

"I guess we'll find out how things went if he shows up at the center tonight."

"He'll be there. But in what condition we can only guess."

"I'm putting my money on Denise getting through to him."

"So am I!" she cried. "How long will it take you to get here?"

"Ten minutes."

"Hurry."

"Sweetheart, before we hang up I need to talk to you about something."

Nikki's heart was listening. "What is it?"

"I don't know what's going to happen in the arena from here on out."

"No one knows, Toly. My accident taught me it's all a risk."

"Your spirit has taught me you're a champion's champion. But if it looks like Mills and I won't come out on top, it's him I'm worried about. I've never told you, but I've learned to love him like a brother."

With that admission, Nikki broke down sobbing quietly.

"Sweetheart?"

She cleared her throat. "He loves you too. I once told you that he worshipped you as a mentor. But over this last year I've seen that you've become like a brother to him and he hasn't wanted to share you with me. It's very sweet, really."

"Nikki...thank you for telling me that. I'll be there soon. We'll get my mother on the phone and give her our news. I'm her baby boy, the one she has worried about the most. I have a feeling our engagement isn't going to come as a surprise, not when I've spent every moment I could to be near you. She'll be overjoyed."

That was the word all right.

"See you in a minute."

Toly left the hospital early after eating dinner with Nikki. Their call to his mother couldn't have come at a better time for his fiancée who needed the love of her parents. His mother welcomed her to the Clayton family with tears in her voice. Nikki's reaction had him leaving for the center walking on air.

Andy had saddled and bridled Snapper for him. "Have you seen Mills?"

"Not yet. Santos has Dusty ready for him."

He nodded. "I'm going to take Snapper for a walk. When Mills gets here, tell him I'll meet him near the boxes."

"Sure. How's Nikki? Her horses are missing her."

"Don't we know it. She's coming along just great. Do you want to hear a piece of news before anyone else tells you?"

"Of course."

"I asked Nikki to marry me. You and Santos will be invited to the wedding."

"Hallelujah! You're one lucky dude." Andy threw his arms around him, giving him a bear hug. Pain shot through Toly's upper right arm and shoulder, reminding him of his mortal weakness. Fortunately, he would be roping with his left arm tonight.

Toly pulled out a Pony Pop to feed Snapper. The memory of Nikki tossing him one that time in the barn came to mind. So much had happened in the last week, he was reeling.

When his horse had chomped it down, he mounted him and started walking him through the various contestants getting ready for their events. He was proud and thrilled to have made it this far, but whatever results transpired in the next few nights, he had the prize he wanted above all else. Nikki would be his forever. Beside her, any award or honor faded into insignificance.

The finalists for the team roping were starting to gather. In a minute he saw his partner ride toward him, filling him with relief. "Here we go again."

Toly couldn't tell from his demeanor how it had gone with Denise. "I'll try to do my best, Mills."

"Don't you think I know that?" Right now there was no way to say things right. They got in line. "I guess you told the crew you're getting married."

"Andy wanted to know how Nikki was getting along and it just came out. We called my mother and told her before I left the hospital. But I've made a big mistake I'd like to apologize for."

"What's that?"

"I should have asked your permission before I proposed to her."

"That's bull. I'm not her father."

"No. But you are her beloved brother. Last night when I saw her lying in that hospital bed with her leg in the cast, I lost it and everything came out."

The line started to move. Their turn was coming up fast.

"I have no right to complain when that proposal turned her life around last night."

His heart was heavy. "*Mills—*"

"We're up!"

Their names had been announced over the loudspeaker. Again Toly faced the box, this time with Nikki's declared love buoying him up. But his body could only do so much. For Mills's sake, he prayed there was another win in him. He glanced at his partner, then called for the steer.

No matter how many times he chased it, the experience was never the same. Tonight he used a Spanish flash loop and pulled a half head, which meant one horn and the nose. It was still legal, but not pretty. Good old Mills tied up the hind legs with expertise and they rode out of there.

The score to beat was 4.3. Toly matched it, but it was far from perfection. Mills came in at 4.4. The crowd went wild because they'd maintained their average. Somebody upstairs was still listening.

He rode back to the stalls. Mills wasn't far behind. But after he'd dismounted, he saw that his partner had disappeared, cheating him out of the chance to praise him.

Nikki had already texted him her congratulations and her love. After he got in her car, he phoned to tell her he was on his way to the hospital.

"Toly? More than anything in the world, I want you to come. But Mills just phoned me and said he has to talk to me alone."

He smothered a moan. "I understand. He's been in turmoil."

"I don't know how long he'll stay after he gets here, but—"

"Sweetheart, don't worry about it. He obviously needs you now. I'm going to head back to the rig. Call me after he leaves, no matter how late it is."

"I promise. You were spectacular out there."

"Thanks, but 4.3 won't win a championship."

"It did for tonight. Keep the faith."

"I love you, Nikki."

Toly stayed up, talking to his brothers, but by one o'clock her call hadn't come. Whatever was going on was serious. He flopped on the couch and waited before falling into oblivion.

Nikki stared at her brother who'd just walked into her hospital room. "Mills—what are you doing here this late?" She'd hoped he would be with Denise right now.

"I need to talk to you and hoped you wouldn't be asleep."

"I'm wide-awake. Come and sit by me."

He drew a chair up to the side of the bed. "I've been talking to Denise and told her I don't want to see her anymore. She won't be coming to the hospital."

A groan came out of Nikki.

"She told me about Johnny Rayburn coming back from war without a hand. It put a horrifying picture in my head. I could understand her compassion for him. But I don't get why she couldn't have talked it over with me instead of just breaking up with me."

"Do you remember the conversation you and I had earlier?"

"What do you mean?"

"About Toly who didn't propose until last night?

Until he said the words, I didn't know how he truly felt. You thought of course it was obvious, but I'll say it again. I knew he was interested, but it wasn't obvious to me that he wanted to make a lifetime commitment to me and marry me. There's a difference between being someone's girlfriend and being *the* woman for all time."

"But—"

"No buts, Mills. Denise reacted exactly the way I would have acted. She needed to know you wanted her to be your wife. Without that reassurance she had to deal with Johnny the best way she could. His PTSD was a huge factor. She believed she was doing the right thing to give you your freedom while she helped let Johnny down gently. How did she know what your plans would be once the rodeo was over? What if you met another woman in the meantime?"

"That's crazy!"

"To you, because you knew you loved her. But not to her. She came to Las Vegas because she loves you and wanted to support you. It took a lot of courage. If you want to know the truth, I admire her for letting you go instead of clinging to you when you didn't make your intentions clear. There's nothing more pathetic than a woman or a man who hangs on hoping and hoping for something that might never happen.

"She's the real deal, Mills, and beautiful inside and out. Of course it's your decision. Now if you don't mind, I love you dearly, but that last medication has made me so sleepy I can't keep my eyes open."

"Sorry I've kept you up this late." He got out of the chair and kissed her cheek.

"Don't ever be sorry. See you tomorrow."

Chapter 12

When Thursday morning came, Toly was surprised to discover he'd slept on the couch all night. The call from Nikki had never come. He got up and wandered in the kitchen to get himself a cup of coffee before he phoned her.

His laptop was open and he discovered he'd received a message from his neurologist. Toly opened it.

Dear Mr. Clayton—
I told you I would get back to you when I'd done more research on your condition. The doctors in Paris just let me know that they don't feel ready to perform surgery on you before summer. Probably July.

In the meantime, I'm corresponding with another team of doctors at the Mayo Clinic. Again their timetable is probably June at the earliest. I've sent both groups your medical history and they'll contact me with further information as we get closer to those dates.

If you've had another episode since visiting my office, I'd like you to call me as soon as you can.

I'll ask my receptionist to put you through immediately.

Dr. Moore.

The doctor had left his phone number.

Toly frowned, deciding to make the call now. Within two minutes they were connected.

"Mr. Clayton—"

"Hello, Dr. Moore. You said to call if I'd had another episode, which I did a couple of nights ago during the competition. Is that alarming?"

"In the same hand?"

"Yes."

"Nowhere else?"

"No."

"It's not alarming, but it shows your rope throwing is aggravating your condition and the surgery can't come too soon."

"I realize that, but I want to know why you keep asking me if I have symptoms somewhere else."

"I don't think you're going to, but some patients develop problems in their feet too. You have a unique case. All the readouts on you lead me to believe that with the surgery, you shouldn't have more problems."

He gripped the phone tighter. "If I do, just tell me one thing. Is my disease fatal?"

"No, Mr. Clayton. People with this condition live out their life span like anyone else. It's not life threatening. The last thing I want is for you to sink into a depression over it or let it affect your ranching or personal life in any way."

Toly was reading between the lines. "You're talking about women."

"Yes. You can expect to live a fulfilled life with a wife and children. You're in your twenties and in excellent physical health and shape. With the exercise you get, you're doing all the right things. Any future progression of this condition, if there is any, is still too many years away to even think about.

"I've been following your rodeo competition and have learned that you and your partner are still in the lead to win the overall championship. I have every confidence that you'll maintain it to the end. You have a warrior's spirit. The best of luck to you and stay in touch."

After they hung up Toly realized the earliest he could do anything about his condition would be summer. But right now he had Nikki on his mind. After a quick shower, he needed to get over to the hospital. She'd be going home today. He couldn't wait!

Nikki gripped her cell phone tighter. "Denise? What did you say?" She could hardly hear her friend for the tears.

"Mills came to the hotel last evening. I can't get into it, but he asked me not to visit or call you. I'm going back to Great Falls today."

Her words brought pain to Nikki, who'd hoped they had worked things out. "I really thought he could forgive you. Under the circumstances, I'll call you after I know you're home. I love you, Denise."

"I love you too."

Just then Toly's tall, rock-hard body walked into her hospital room. Never did she need him more.

"Sweetheart," he cried softly when he saw her wet cheeks and put out his left arm to hug her. "What's happened?"

Nikki buried her face against his chest. "Mills went to see Denise yesterday and it didn't go well. She's leaving on the next plane and has been told not to call or visit me."

Toly ran his hands through her hair. "I can't say I'm surprised. Mills has made himself scarce."

"I can't believe it."

"What can't you believe?"

Another voice had sounded. It was her orthopedic surgeon. She hadn't realized he'd walked in. "Next year I expect to see you back in Las Vegas again to finish what you started."

"That's not why I'm crying." She gave a sad laugh and brushed the moisture off her face. "Doctor? This is my fiancé, Toly Clayton."

They shook hands before Toly sat down to give her doctor room to check her out. "I'm releasing you this morning. How did it go with the therapist?"

"I had no idea how hard it is to use crutches, but with practice I'm sure I'll get the hang of it."

"You will. I'm aware you'd like to go to the center to watch your brother and fiancé perform for the rest of the rodeo, but I would caution you to stay down in your hotel and keep your leg elevated until you fly home."

"But, Doctor—I can't stay away on the last night."

"You can watch everything on TV."

"But if they win the overall, I want to see them receive their award at the South Point Hotel afterward."

"Then I suggest you have a bodyguard to help protect

you so you're not accidentally knocked down. I don't want to see you in here again." He said it with a smile, but she knew he meant it.

He turned to Toly. "I take it you're driving her to the hotel?" He nodded. "Then I'll ask the nurse to come in with the wheelchair and the instructions I'm sending with you. When you get back home, you'll want to contact an orthopedic surgeon there to do any follow-up and remove your cast."

"Thank you so much. You've all been wonderful."

"That's nice to hear. I'm sorry you couldn't finish your brilliant run for the barrel championship. I'm sure you would have won it." He turned to Toly. "Good luck to you. Everyone's betting on you and your partner."

"Thank you, Doctor. No one's more precious to me than Nikki. I'm very grateful to you."

After he walked out, Toly gave her a quick kiss on the lips. "I'm going to carry all your flowers down to the car, then I'll come back for you."

"Toly? Wait. The doctor had to warn me, but I plan to be out there for your performances."

He shook his head. "No you're not. He was right. There's so much pandemonium, it'll be more difficult with crutches. I'll need the peace of mind knowing you're at the hotel. By the way, I plan to spend the rest of my nights in your hotel room.

"Before we left for Las Vegas, I had this dream of being your roommate and luring you into loving me. What I didn't envision was being your nurse, but I'll take it because I'm madly in love with you."

Nikki found out over the next few days that no man could have been a sweeter more tender lover who hadn't made love to her completely yet, let alone a better nurse.

The first thing she'd noticed when he'd brought her to the hotel was her little Christmas tree lit up.

He was so wonderful and waited on her hand and foot. They played cards. He brought her the chocolate marshmallow ice cream she craved and virtually showered her with the kind of love she could never have imagined.

The downside of all this was Mill's absence, except to show up at the center in time for the team roping event both evenings. After two scores that put them in second place, they'd tied with Shay's team for first place in the overalls. Tonight one of the teams would pull ahead to be the grand champions.

Toly put on a tough front, but she knew deep in his heart how devastated he was for Mills and the crisis he was going through. There could be no joy when the two of them were both worried sick about him and Denise.

Too soon they finished eating dinner and she was propped on the couch with her leg extended. Toly was about to leave for the center one last time. She gripped his hands and looked up at him. "I want to be there. My heart is with you and Mills."

"I know that. It's why I can go out there tonight, whatever happens."

"Has your family arrived yet?"

"Yes."

"*Toly*—" She sat up to embrace him, kissing him with all the urgency of her soul.

"I'll be back."

The minute he walked out the door, she burst into tears. Nikki was an emotional mess. She quickly turned on the TV with the remote to watch the lead-up to the rodeo. Anything to keep her from going crazy.

It was so surreal to be there trapped in a cast instead of being at that arena to get ready for her event.

It was so awful to think her brother was in terrible turmoil because of a broken heart.

It was so unbelievable that Toly had a strange neuropathy that had forced him to throw with his left arm, never knowing what would happen.

It was torture not to be able to be there tonight for the man she adored.

It killed her that her parents weren't alive to lean on, that Toly's father wasn't alive to cheer him on.

Nikki's list of pain kept growing until the rodeo actually started. She sat back to watch the events. But her heart was thudding too fast when it came time for the team roping.

She'd never heard such noise coming from the arena and couldn't seem to calm down. There was a tie between Toly and Shay. But because Toly and Mills had come in to the events with the overall lead, they would ride last with Shay and his partner just ahead of them.

So far the time to beat tonight was 3.8. Shay tore out of the gate and they snagged the steer with a 3.6, 3.8. Now it was Toly's turn. The crowd noise level went up. She didn't think she could watch.

Thump, thump. Thump, thump went the beat of her heart. The camera panned to Mills wearing his steely look. Then it settled on Toly in the box. There he was holding the rope in his right hand, the ultimate cowboy in every sense of the word. Though she knew his upper arm and shoulder still pained him a great deal, he was going for it.

Oh please, please. With everything that had gone wrong, make this one moment right. No episode tonight.

The gray sapphire on her finger reminded Nikki she already had her prize. Now it was their turn.

Out came the steer. Almost immediately the horns had been caught and before she knew it, the hind legs were sweetly tied up. She heard the announcer.

"Toly Clayton and Mills Dobson have just swept this year's Wrangler Team Roping Championship in an epic 3.2, 3.4 win."

In her joy, Nikki jumped up from the couch, forgetting all about her leg and lost her balance. Thank heaven she fell backward. She laughed because the doctor had been right and she hadn't even been using her crutches.

She grabbed her phone to send a text.

Darling Toly. Words can't express. Just wait till you come back later.

Nikki sent another one to Mills.

Dearest brother. There's no one like you. Tonight I'm positive the folks in heaven are rejoicing with me.

Their year of hard, grueling work, of exhausting travel over thousands of miles on the circuit, was over. She couldn't comprehend it as she waited for the barrel racing.

For once it was pure pleasure to watch each finalist fly into the arena. They were fabulous. All of them. She thought about the hat they'd signed and would never forget. Just as she'd imagined, Laurie Rippon rode out last and won the championship with a 13.48. No one deserved it more. She sent her a text congratulating her.

With it was finally over, she got up with the aid of

her crutches to get herself a cola from the minifridge. It would be several hours yet before Toly and Mills would be able to leave for the South Point. She had no idea of her brother's plans, but she couldn't worry about that right now. Nikki needed to throw her arms around Toly and never let him go.

To her surprise, she heard a knock on the door and knew it couldn't be Denise. Since she was already up, she hobbled to the door with her crutches and opened it.

"Mills—" He wasn't alone. "Denise—"

Nikki knew what this meant. In the next breath she grabbed them. They did a three-way hug, crutches included. She started to sob for happiness and couldn't stop. "Now all my dreams have come true."

"So have mine." Denise had broken down too. "Want to see what Mills gave me before tonight's event?" She put out her left hand where a diamond ring sparkled on her finger.

Nikki looked at her brother, who wore an ecstatic smile. "You told me Denise needed to know how I felt about her. I took your advice, but the truth is I've been carrying it around for months."

"Now he tells us!" Nikki cried. "I'm so happy for you two, I want to race around the arena and shout it to the world that my favorite people are in love and going to get married. Come all the way in and sit down. I want to hear everything.

"Does Toly know?" she asked after they got settled.

He shook his head.

"He's going to die when he finds out."

Mills had pulled Denise onto his lap. "We know he's coming to get you. We thought we'd surprise him when we show up at the South Point for the medal ceremony."

"This is the best news in the world. Here I was in despair because I could picture you at the airport taking off."

"She almost did. I had to race to get there in time."

Denise looked radiant. "I waited before leaving to hear the scores for him and Toly. While I was sitting in the lounge before we boarded, I heard Mills call out, "You can't leave, Denise! I've got something for you!"

"You're kidding—how romantic!"

"It was. He ran up to me and in front of everyone got down on one knee and proposed. I couldn't believe it until he slid this ring on my finger. All the people in the lounge clapped."

"Who wouldn't? I wish I had pictures. Let me take some now with my phone." Nikki pulled it out of her pocket and snapped half a dozen in succession. "Come on. One big kiss for posterity. Toly will want to see it."

Her normally reserved brother reached around and gave his fiancée a kiss to die for. Nikki made a video of it while she hooted and hollered.

When he finally let her go, he turned to Nikki. "Thank you for making me see reason."

Tears rolled down Denise's cheeks. "Thank you for being the best friend a girl ever had."

"What a night for celebrating!"

Denise nodded. "Speaking of that, we need to get back to my hotel so I can change before we drive over to the South Point." She slid off his lap.

Mills walked over to hug Nikki. "We'll see you there in a little while."

"Most definitely."

Not two minutes after they left, she heard a loud rap

on her hotel room door. That was odd. "Yes?" she called out. "Who is it?"

"Toly gave us a card key." *Us?* "Can we come in?"

"Yes," she said in a hesitant voice.

The door opened and in walked his three hunky brothers she'd only seen on his cell phone gallery. They wore his smile and all had inherited the Clayton charm and fabulous looks.

"I'm Wymon." The dark-haired one spoke first. "Our brother was right about his fiancée. You *are* gorgeous. By the way, this is Roce and that's Eli. According to Toly, the doctor said you would need a bodyguard if you wanted to see the ceremony in person. So the three of us have come to do the job. Our mom is already at the South Point with Toly and they're waiting for us."

"Oh my gosh." Thank goodness she'd done her makeup and had changed into her outfit so she'd be ready when he came.

"I'm glad you're ready because we don't want to miss anything."

Since Toly had loved the black outfit with the red embroidery, Nikki had chosen to wear it. She kept on the sandal she was wearing.

The one named Roce whistled. "You're on time too. Our bro is a lucky man."

"He says he belongs to the best family on earth and can't wait to help all of you on the ranch."

Eli, the dark-brown-haired brother, grinned at her. "That's when we're all going to get tired of hearing about the beautiful rodeo queen he was determined to rope for himself. But it looks like you roped him. Want me to carry your bag?"

She laughed. "Would you?"

"I'd be honored."

The next twenty minutes became a blur as they helped her out to a limo and escorted her to the South Point. As usual, the place was packed, but since it was the last night of Finals, there was an energy she'd never felt before.

They cleared the way for her to the front where she suddenly saw Toly sitting with his mother, their heads close together while they talked. Her heart did a thunderclap to see him decked out in his Western gear and Stetson.

Roce walked ahead and alerted Toly, who jumped up and turned around. Like in a dream, he moved toward her, his green eyes ablaze with joy and light. For tonight their win had changed him. She didn't see any sadness. He came close and swept her and her crutches into his arms—even if he was hurting—and kissed her in front of everyone.

"I love you, Toly. I love you."

Wymon patted his shoulder. "Come on, bro. We're all due on stage."

"Let's go, sweetheart."

"What do you mean?"

"You're coming with us."

Before she could think, the whole Clayton clan helped her go up onstage with him. But nothing could have shocked Toly more than to see Mills and Denise waiting for them. He had his arm around her and they both glowed.

Toly whispered, "If I'm having a hallucination, don't bring me out of it."

"It's no hallucination. Mills stopped her from leaving town. I'm sure he'll tell you the details later, but just before your brothers came to pick me up, Mills brought Denise to the hotel. They're getting married. Wouldn't it be exciting if we made it a double wedding?"

Mills walked over and hugged Toly hard. "Forgive me for everything."

"I will if you'll forgive me. After all, we're brothers."

"Yes, we are," Mills said with tears in his eyes.

Then Toly squeezed her waist. "Come on, sweetheart. We have to sit down so our award ceremony can begin. Then we're on our own."

After saying goodbye to Mills, who was flying back to Great Falls with Denise on Sunday morning, Toly loaded Nikki into his rig with her bags. He planned to drive her home, driving straight through so they could be alone. The crew had the job of returning the rental cars and taking all four horses back in the Dobson rig.

Toly knew Nikki wondered why they weren't flying too. But he needed time to tell her something. He dreaded it. Depending on her reaction, there might not be a wedding, after all.

She insisted on sitting in front next to him while he drove. Fortunately she could bend her leg. They'd stopped to stock up on snacks and drinks. Hard to believe they'd never driven in one of their rigs together on their way to a rodeo on the circuit. They could have done when they'd both been featured at different venues. But Mills had set the boundaries.

Now there were no boundaries. But a new hard cruel fact had arisen that could change everything in an instant. As the sun went down, it started to snow. The time seemed right to tell her what was on his mind. If they ran into a blizzard, then he'd stop at a lay-by until it stopped.

She smiled at him. "This is so cozy. I've had dreams about living with you in this rig."

She didn't know the half of it. "Nikki?"

"What is it, darling?"

"I have something important to tell you before you go to bed."

"I'm not ready for that yet."

"But you need to rest your leg."

"Obviously you've got something important on your mind."

"I need you to think about something hard. After I've taken you home, I'll be driving to the ranch. I won't call you until you've had a few days to deal with it."

"Deal with what? You're scaring me."

"If it weren't scary, we wouldn't be having this discussion."

"I don't know you like this, Toly!"

"I'm sorry, sweetheart. I don't know how to do this any other way."

He could hear her struggling. "Go on."

"I need to tell you everything about my neuropathy." For the next fifteen minutes he laid it out for her, sparing her nothing. She had to understand what could happen to his legs and feet, arches and toes. In time he might even have difficulty breathing or swallowing.

"This condition can affect your sense of touch, how you feel pain and temperature. One of the symptoms is a weakening of muscle strength. Another symptom might be losing your balance. It could be hard to do things that require coordination. I might get to the point that it would affect my walking, let alone fastening buttons."

"Stop! I've heard enough. The only thing I know is that you have a problem in your right hand and lower arm."

"But it could get worse, "Toly murmured. She shook her head. "I'm not going to listen."

"Please hear me out. The doctor told me I'd live out the years given to me, but at what price? I don't want a wife who has to push me around in a wheelchair. Last night I realized I shouldn't have proposed to you, but I love you too much. You don't want to marry a man who is already becoming an invalid."

"That's ridiculous, Toly. I won't listen."

"I was wrong to give you that ring. You shouldn't have to be tied to a man in my condition."

"Are you asking me to give it back?"

"I made a mistake. Now I'm begging you to sleep on this for a few days while you allow the reality of what I've said to sink in."

He heard her sharp intake of breath. "I don't need a few days. I can't believe the great Toly Clayton, the cowboy who was crowned king of the headers last night is ready to throw in the towel today. Am I even talking to the same person?"

"Nikki—"

"I don't want to hear another word." She reached for her crutches and stood up. "I'm going to bed. In the morning I want you to stop at the nearest airport and I'll fly the rest of the way home. Considering that you could be falling apart anytime now, I'm surprised you wanted to drive me at all."

She tossed the ring at him and hobbled away faster than he could have imagined. Dear God. What had he done?

* * *

"Toly? Are you awake yet? Solana, the housekeeper, tried to get you to come down to breakfast, but she said you didn't answer."

He rolled over and sat up. "I was awake all night and barely got to sleep. I don't feel like talking right now."

"I'm not the person who wants to talk to you, but if that's the way you feel, then I'll send her away."

Could it possibly be Nikki? After what he'd said to turn her inside out, he never thought to see her again.

"Wait, Mom—" But she didn't answer back.

Like lightning he jumped out of bed, pulled on a pair of jeans and a T-shirt. Then raced out of the room and down the stairs to the living room. The traditional tall Christmas tree with its multicolored lights dominated the interior. Its glow illuminated his former fiancée standing in front of a wall of family pictures, using her crutches for support. She was a breathtaking sight in a Western Levi's skirt and cherry-red sweater.

"Nikki?"

She turned and eyed him with a laser-like glance that was discomfiting. "I've been looking at everyone, all ages and sizes. After reading online, I understand that your condition is inherited, but I don't see one of your relatives who's in a wheelchair."

"Listen, I—"

"No. You listen. As I recall you told me to go home and think about this for a few days while I dealt with it. The question is, have *you* dealt with it? You look perfectly healthy to me right now. I don't see you weaving or wobbling on your feet. You even had enough strength to close the fly on your jeans before you flew down here like you were coming out of the alley."

He shook his head. "I can't believe you just said that."

"I do have a brother, you know, and I couldn't believe all that drivel you told me in the rig." She handled her crutches with amazing dexterity and walked right up to him. "Where's my ring?"

"Upstairs."

"I'd like you to put it on me again."

Toly had never been so humbled in his life. "Sweetheart, I—"

"I think you ought to stop talking and go get it. That is, if you can, or have you lost feeling in your feet?"

"It isn't funny, Nikki."

"No, it isn't. So let's have all the fun we can before I have the joy of wheeling you around. You know— a wedding, a wedding *night*! A honeymoon? I called your doctor.

"After talking to him, maybe we can plan a late one after you're operated on in Paris. I'd much rather go there than the Mayo Clinic. You and I have lived an inbred life in our horsey world. It's time we found out why everyone says that if you haven't been to France, you haven't lived."

"Would you be willing to live in the rig until our ranch house is built?"

"I've been planning on it. Denise will be moving into the ranch house with Mills. I told you before, the rig felt like our home while we were in Las Vegas."

"I was never happier in my life than being there with you. Just so you know, Mom gave me a piece of land up the road. She and Dad talked about it before he died. It's the perfect spot to build our ranch house. But with the snow, it probably won't be ready until late spring."

"I don't care how long it takes."

"After Christmas we'll hire an architect."

"I was thinking the four of us could get married two weeks from today, if that's all right with your family. We'll do a reception here and another one in Great Falls."

He nodded. "I'll be right back."

Solving the problem of levitation for all time, he flew through the house and up the stairs to get her ring out of his dresser drawer. On the way down, he almost ran over his mother at the landing.

She cupped his face in her hands. "That woman is pure gold and more valuable than all the gold buckles you ever won." He'd finally told his mother about his neuropathy.

His eyes smarted. "I know." He hugged her hard before hurrying into the living room. Nikki stood near the tree, balancing on her crutches with her right arm while she extended her left hand.

He walked over and slid the ring home. "Thank heaven for you," he murmured against her lips and rocked her in his arms for a long, long time. The crutches fell to the floor, but they didn't care.

Chapter 13

Nikki grabbed the playing cards and looked up at Toly from her side of the bed wearing only a sheet. Since their church wedding in Stevensville, they'd spent the last three days and nights in the rig decorated for Christmas by her new sisters-in-law. They'd put up a fabulous Christmas tree and had hung garlands that stretched from one end of the rig to the other.

Potted red poinsettias had been placed around his bedroom that had become their bedroom. The whole rig smelled of pine and Nikki was so in love, she never wanted to leave it or his arms.

"You're a cheater, Mr. Clayton, but I can't figure out how you do it."

"So you've noticed I have another skill besides cooking, Mrs. Clayton."

"You're fishing for compliments again. Are you ready for a post Christmas present?"

"You've showered me with too many."

"This one is different and my personal favorite. You'll have to get out of bed. It's up on the top shelf of the closet in the hallway."

"I didn't know that."

"I had a hard time trying to figure out where to keep it out of sight until now."

He kissed a certain spot. "I'll be right back."

Nikki watched her gorgeous husband pull on the bottom half of his sweats and leave the room for a minute. When he returned, he had to remove the Christmas wrapping from the fourteen-by-eighteen framed photograph.

She heard him suck in his breath. "*Nikki—* Where? How? When did you take this picture?"

"Last summer while you were out in the corral with Snapper practicing some throws, I was upstairs and saw you out the window. It was hot. You took off your shirt and had just dipped your Stetson in the rain barrel before putting it on your head. I thought you were the most amazing male specimen I'd ever seen in my life.

"Without hesitation I reached for my camera and took a dozen pictures of you. After having them developed, I decided I loved this one best. The art studio enlarged it to this size and I had it made up in black and white. The silver-and-black frame with the clear glass cover looks perfect with it. Did you see the plaque at the bottom?"

He looked down. In a husky voice he said, "The Sapphire Cowboy."

"Yup. One day our children will regard this as a great

treasure to cherish forever. I know I do. If you'll notice, the white gold band on my ring finger makes the perfect frame for my gray sapphire, another treasure."

Toly rested the photograph against the wall. "Just a minute. I'll be right back."

What was he up to?

In a minute he came back and handed her a gift of approximately the same size. "It's your turn."

Excited, she undid the wrapping and there was one of her posters. The kind she'd given out at the dealership in Great Falls before they'd left for Las Vegas. It was in glorious color and framed in a light oak color.

"Oh, Toly—"

He smiled. "I grabbed one when you weren't looking and planned to hang it in the tack room on the ranch. But everything has changed since then and I wanted us to have it. There's a plaque at the bottom."

She couldn't believe it and looked down. My Sweet Clover Sweetheart.

Her eyes filled with tears. "I can't believe it."

He put both pictures against the far wall and got back in bed. "Consider this an after Merry Christmas gift, my love. Now why don't we call it a night."

"I thought you'd never suggest it," she teased.

"You little hussy." He turned off the lamp at the side of the bed and leaned over her. "I don't know how it's possible, but my hunger for you just keeps growing."

He started devouring her. They made love again. She never wanted it to stop. Each time he touched her, it thrilled her so much she moaned in ecstasy. Amazing how her cast didn't interfere with the pleasure they brought to each other.

In the middle of the night Nikki awoke, wishing he

weren't asleep. She caressed the dusting of hair on his chest. He was such a beautiful man and almost too wonderful to be real. She'd known him for a year and couldn't believe she'd been lucky enough to have married him.

"I heard that sigh," he murmured, kissing her throat. "You're awake."

"Yes. It sounded serious."

"It was. I think I love you too much."

"Then we suffer from the same condition." He plunged his hands in her hair. "I've been worried you'd wake up before now and tell me you need a day away from me."

Nikki laughed and slid halfway on top of him. "I've been worried what your family will think. We haven't gone outside once."

"We're in the middle of a blizzard right now."

"Still—"

His deep chuckle permeated her body. "With three brothers who are crazy about their wives, you know exactly what they're thinking."

"It's kind of embarrassing."

"It's kind of wonderful to be this much in love, sweetheart. I still can't believe you wanted to marry me knowing what could be ahead of me."

"We're not going to talk about that. Neither of us knows what the future will hold. Do you remember when we both got excited about riding in the rodeo? We didn't think about the risk. It was too much fun doing something we were good at."

"I remember. I was obsessed."

"So was I. It didn't matter what we had to go through. We loved it so much we kept going back for more. That's how I feel about our marriage. Every day, every night is a great adventure. I never want to miss a moment of it, darling."

"We're not going to."

"No we're not. So let's not use birth control. I want to get pregnant with your baby as soon as we can. I'm jealous of your sisters-in-law and can't wait to have an adorable little boy or girl like Libby."

"You mean it?"

"Oh, Toly. I can't wait to fill those bedrooms we're going to have designed for our new house. Wouldn't it be fantastic if we had children who love the rodeo too?"

"What if they don't?"

"It doesn't matter because you're going to make the most terrific father. You had a wonderful role model."

"He was the best." Toly kissed her with tenderness. "So were your parents."

"You never knew them."

"No. But I know you. You're my favorite person in the world. Mills comes in a close second."

"What a beautiful thing for you to say. I'm crazy about your family too." She kissed his mouth. "Love me again, Toly."

He began kissing her back with growing desire. "I thought you'd never ask."

* * * * *

Amanda Renee was raised in the northeast and now wiggles her toes in the warm coastal Carolina sands. Her career began when she was discovered through Harlequin's So You Think You Can Write contest. When not creating stories about love and laughter, she enjoys the company of her schnoodle, Duffy, as well as camping, playing guitar and piano, photography, and anything involving animals. You can visit her at amandarenee.com.

Books by Amanda Renee

Harlequin Western Romance

Saddle Ridge, Montana

The Lawman's Rebel Bride
A Snowbound Cowboy Christmas
Wrangling Cupid's Cowboy
The Bull Rider's Baby Bombshell

Harlequin American Romance

Welcome to Ramblewood

Betting on Texas
Home to the Cowboy
Blame It on the Rodeo
A Texan for Hire
Back to Texas
Mistletoe Rodeo
The Trouble with Cowgirls
A Bull Rider's Pride
Twins for Christmas

Visit the Author Profile page at Harlequin.com for more titles.

A SNOWBOUND COWBOY CHRISTMAS

Amanda Renee

To my editor, Johanna Raisanen:

Thank you for your invaluable
guidance on this book!

Chapter 1

"I'm not selling you my ranch."

Emma Sheridan's skin prickled beneath her down parka at the sound of the voice behind her. She'd recognize it anywhere. *Dylan Slade.* They'd only met face-to-face once during the summer and had three or four brief phone conversations since, but his masculine resonance was impossible to forget. He was every man's cowboy and every woman's fantasy. Okay, maybe not every woman's, but he had snuck into her dreams a time or ten. Then again, it could just be her pregnancy hormones talking.

Emma handed her credit card to the front desk clerk at the Silver Bells Guest Ranch, and then turned to face Dylan. "Mr. Slade." Her breath caught at the realization he stood less than an arm's length away. "Please accept my sincerest sympathies. I only knew your Uncle Jax for a year, but he was a wonderful man with a generous heart."

"That he was." Dylan tugged off his work gloves and unzipped his whiskey-colored rancher jacket. "I appreciate your condolences, but it doesn't explain why you're here. We received your company's floral arrangement."

Emma cringed. She hated the customary funeral-home flowers her firm had sent. They were cold and impersonal. She'd mailed Dylan a hand-written card as well, but he didn't bother to mention it. Then again, why would he? Her visit wasn't to relay condolences in person. It was business. Business she needed to settle before her baby was born. She glanced up at him. His dark, well-worn cowboy hat shielded his eyes more than she'd have preferred. It made reading him difficult, which she assumed was intentional.

"I thought if we could talk—"

"You'd what? Change my mind? I'm not selling the ranch." He shrugged out of his coat as he strode past her, revealing faded snug Wranglers that fit him better than any pair of jeans had a right to. Inwardly, she groaned, relieved when he walked behind the lodge's rustic cedar-log front desk.

"You're all set, Ms. Sheridan." The check-in clerk slid her room key across the marred wood surface. An actual key. Her plans for the ranch included multiple guest-service agents and the latest digital room-entry technology. A guest's Bluetooth-enabled smartphone would become their room key via a downloadable app. "I'll have someone bring up your bags. Please help yourself to the complimentary snack bar in the dining room."

"Why are you staying here?" Dylan tilted back his hat, revealing an errant lock of chestnut-brown hair.

There was no mistaking his scowl now. "My decision isn't up for debate."

"You never heard my final proposal. At least hear me out." Emma shifted uncomfortably in her too-tight rubber duck boots. The shoes were far from fashionable, but they were snow-friendly and easy to slip on. At least, they had been before she boarded her red-eye flight from Chicago to Saddle Ridge in northwestern Montana. Now she'd need a crowbar to pry them off. "Besides, Jax told me he hadn't booked any reservations after December in anticipation of closing this deal on January 2. It doesn't look like people are waiting in line for you to reopen, so what's the harm in discussing it?" A sharp internal kick to her ribs caused Emma to inhale. Her daughter had been super active today and the nerve-racking drive in the snow from the airport hadn't helped matters any. She had read that her unborn baby could sense her emotions and today definitely confirmed it. The doctor had told her it was safe to make the trip, but he had also warned it would be her last until after the baby was born. "I have to sit down."

As much as she wanted—correction, *needed*—to discuss the agreement Jax had made to sell the guest ranch, her feet had reached their limit. She tottered toward the lodge's great room. At thirty-two weeks pregnant, she envied the women who radiated in the pre-baby hormonal glow and managed to survive the entire nine months in a blissfully beautiful state of impending motherhood. She'd trade an ounce of their exuberance for her swollen feet and ankles, not to mention the other parts of her body that had seen better days.

"Are you all right?" Dylan's closeness startled her again. "Would you like a bottle of water?" He guided her by the arm to the most comfortable-looking chair she'd ever seen. "You look terrible."

Emma laughed, dropping her handbag at her feet. "You really shouldn't say that to a woman." She unfastened her jacket, not bothering to remove it as she sank into the burnished leather chair near the massive granite fireplace. *Oh, this is heaven.* She'd definitely need help to get up, but she'd worry about that later.

"You're pregnant." Dylan's deep blue eyes grew large as he stared at her protruding belly. "I had no idea."

Feeling exposed, Emma struggled to pull her parka closed over her fisherman-knit sweater. Of course, now she was sitting on half of the coat, which made the task impossible.

"Eight months." Emma rested her hands protectively on her stomach. "It's a girl, but I haven't chosen a name yet. I'm surprised your uncle didn't tell you." Jax had instinctively known, even though she hadn't begun to show when they'd spoken. He'd said her panicked smile gave it away. Well, that on top of the morning sickness and the constant heartburn she'd had during her visit.

Dylan shook his head. "My uncle may have been somewhat eccentric and unfiltered at times, but he wasn't a gossiping man. Not that your pregnancy is gossip."

That wasn't altogether true. The fact that her boyfriend of six months had ditched her the second he found out she was pregnant had made for great watercooler gossip around the office. Especially since her job as a commercial real estate analyst hinged on her ability to fly anywhere in the world at a moment's notice. That ended with this trip.

She traveled as many as twenty days a month and

while her job paid well, it didn't afford her the luxury of a nanny to accompany her and care for her baby while she was scouting resort locations or meeting with clients and investors. Once her daughter was born, she would be unable to meet the travel requirements her job demanded. She had two options: accept a lesser position with less pay or get the acquisitions director promotion she'd been vying for and work solely from their Chicago corporate offices. Acquiring the Silver Bells Ranch almost guaranteed that promotion. She refused to give up now.

"Water would be great. Thank you." His exit gave her a chance to compose herself a little better and get out of her suffocating coat. The full-length parka was overkill for mid-December, but she wasn't taking any chances. Plus, wearing it beat trying to stuff it into another piece of luggage. By the time she freed herself from its confines, Dylan had returned and she was perspiring profusely.

"Are you sure you're okay?" He handed her the bottle.

Emma twisted the cap off and took a long swallow. "I'm fine, thank you. It's just the warmth of the fireplace and this monstrosity of a coat."

Standing in front of her silhouetted by the midmorning sun filtering in through the floor-to-ceiling windows, Dylan epitomized tall, dark and sexy.

"Good. Then go home. I'm not selling."

And obstinate to the core. Emma had already decided she liked Dylan much better when he didn't speak. Unfortunately, getting him to sell his ranch was why she was there. She refused to leave until he did.

Dylan hadn't even grieved yet for the man he had loved as a father. Jax had been in perfect health, which made his sudden heart attack even more shocking. He had wanted to hold on to the ranch and bring in a new business partner, but no one wanted to invest in an aging ranch. Not even his own brothers. A part of him wondered if the bickering he and Jax had done over the sale had contributed to his uncle's death. Now Silver Bells was his and he had to prove to himself that he'd been right to keep it all along.

Without steady revenue, he had to rely on what was left of his savings to float the business. Jax had stopped taking reservations months ago and Emma was right... no one was beating down their door to get in. They hadn't been for more than a year—and the instant the ranch had taken a downturn, she had swooped in and offered to buy it.

Emma bordered between a vixen and a cherub. Her intelligence coupled with her persistence had hooked Jax from their first meeting. At five and a half feet, she wasn't overly tall or bombshell curvaceous. Instead, the brunette had a wicked grin that usually ended in a friendly wink. She exuded charm along with a street-savvy wit that left those around her intoxicated by her performance. And it was a performance designed to lull potential sellers into a euphoric sense of *everything would be wonderful* once they closed the deal. She was a brilliant saleswoman and Dylan understood why she was so successful, but he could also see right through her.

Today, her perfectly manicured facade had a crack in it. But that crack made her appear more natural and she wore it well, despite her obvious discomfort. She winced for the second time since her arrival. The ranch should be the least of her concerns, and she had to be the least of his. He didn't have the patience to deal with a pushy pregnant woman, let alone one who should be relaxing at home choosing baby names.

"Isn't your husband worried about you?"

"Thanks for the concern, but I'm not married, attached or otherwise. It's just me and the butter bean."

"Butter bean? That's what you call your kid?"

Emma rubbed her belly and smiled up at him. Any man worth his salt could get lost in her bourbon-colored eyes if he wasn't careful. Good thing he'd sworn off women with kids years ago.

"I have craved butter beans since the beginning of my pregnancy. That's how I found out I was expecting. A friend jokingly asked if I was pregnant. Biggest surprise of my life."

"And the father?" Dylan held up his hands. "No, I'm sorry. That's none of my business."

"It's no secret. He left two seconds after I told him." She tilted her chin up defiantly. "I had his parental rights terminated shortly thereafter. He didn't fight it and my baby is better off this way. I'd never force my daughter on a man who wants nothing to do with her."

"I give you a lot of credit." It pained him whenever he heard a man had relinquished his paternal rights to a child. Dylan had wanted kids and a family more than anything. He'd lived that dream, and then he lost it after he'd partnered with Jax on Silver Bells. His ex-wife had warned him she wouldn't like living on a ranch. Stubbornly, he thought he'd change her mind. Lauren had tried her best, but living in an outdated log cabin away from her family and friends proved to be too much. She packed up his two step-kids and moved back to Bozeman. No way would he raise another man's child again. It was too heartbreaking when it didn't work out.

Lauren and the kids leaving, coupled with his father's death a few months later, damn near broke him. From then on, he devoted every waking hour to the ranch. He and Jax had updated what they could afford to, and the Silver Bells did great until more guest ranches cropped up nearby. They couldn't compete with the new.

"It's all good," she said.

Her robotic response told him otherwise, but he couldn't allow that to matter. Dylan squatted next to her chair and rested a hand on her arm. He immediately regretted the close contact, even though her bulky sweater separated her skin from his palm. It was bad enough her almond-scented shampoo left him wanting to bury his face in the long silky strands. He found this vulnerable side of Emma endearing when he knew to avoid her. She was off-limits in far too many ways.

"I admire your strength and fortitude to see this deal come to fruition but, Emma, it won't happen. I went along with my uncle because he owned the majority stake in the business. I didn't have a choice then. There are a few options I'm mulling over, but selling to you isn't on the list." Dylan stood and walked to the windows overlooking the ranch. "This is a guest ranch where people come to be cowboys and cowgirls for a week or two. It will never be the luxurious five-star spa resort you want to turn it into."

"Um, excuse me. Some help over here," Emma called behind him.

He turned to find her struggling to stand and couldn't help but laugh a little. She was cute when she was vulnerable. He closed the distance between them and offered both his hands. Their eyes met as he pulled her to her feet and inadvertently against his body.

"Sorry," he mumbled before stepping back.

A tinge of pink flooded her cheeks as she smoothed her sweater. "Would you rather turn your employees out on the street?"

The woman didn't miss a beat. "You and my uncle already have." Dylan headed toward the front desk, sensing her close behind him. "Some already left to secure work somewhere else. When my uncle announced that the ranch would close its doors on January 1, many of our employees began searching for work elsewhere. Some found positions, while others planned on staying until the end. I've already told them Silver Bells isn't closing, and I'll do whatever I can to keep them employed here. We have families living on the ranch. Did my uncle tell you that? And some of my employees worked on my father's ranch before his death. I've known many of these people my entire life."

Emma shook her head. "I didn't know."

"I can't tell you how many marriages have taken place amongst the Silver Bells employees. We have another in a few days, don't we, Sandy?" Dylan wrapped his arm around a dining-room server who had been passing by. "Sandy's the one getting married. Her fiancé, Luke, is a ranch hand here." Dylan continued into the kitchen. "Hopefully this won't be the last wedding. Many babies have been born here, too. Some of the kids raised on Silver Bells are raising families of their own on the ranch and you want to take that away. I can't understand why my uncle agreed to any of it. I just thank God he hadn't finalized anything."

"We were scheduled to in fifteen days." Emma lifted

her chin. "And your employees can reapply once the renovations are completed."

Sandy scoffed at her statement. "Your company refused to guarantee us employment. You can't expect us to go without any income or health insurance for six months."

"Many of the people working here live paycheck-to-paycheck," Dylan said over his shoulder as he walked to the pantry. His father had taught him to treat his employees like family and the thought of them suffering aggravated him further. He needed distance from Emma before he said something he'd regret.

"I'm sure we can work something out." She followed him, unrelenting. "Maybe a severance package."

"To cover six months? I highly doubt that." He hoisted a case of water onto his shoulder and faced her. "Listen. I'm not going to change my mind. So please, catch the first flight out of here because you're wasting your time pursuing this further. If you'll excuse me, I have a lot to do since we're shorthanded."

"Uh, Dylan? She's not going anywhere," Sandy said from the kitchen doorway. "Harlan just called. They closed all the roads because of this storm and we're expecting another foot of snow by tomorrow morning."

"You've got to be kidding me." But he knew she wasn't. His brother was a deputy sheriff and he would have heard the news directly from the Department of Transportation. "We're snowed in?"

"And here I thought Montana laughed in the face of snow." Emma stared at him with a confident smile and her arms folded above her baby bump. "The roads wouldn't be an issue if we owned the property."

Dylan set the water on the stainless-steel counter. "I

have news for you. Saddle Ridge is a small town and we don't have the equipment to plow roads as fast as Chicago or even Kalispell and Whitefish."

"That's why we planned on donating two new snow-plows to the town, ensuring the roads leading to the resort would be kept clear."

"It's a ranch. Not a resort." A fact she needed to get through her head. "And who is going to pay for the manpower to run those plows?"

"It's only two plows, Dylan." She toddled over to the counter and leaned against it, looking more tired than before. "We're talking about two drivers, four if they are running two shifts. I doubt it will bankrupt the town. They're getting new equipment and they are thrilled with the idea."

"Thrilled? You've already spoken with them?" Of course she had. He didn't think there was anything business-related she had overlooked, except the human side of the equation.

"Months ago. Your uncle even went with me to my Department of Transportation meeting. I assumed you knew."

"No. No, I didn't." He wondered what else he didn't know about the sale. "It doesn't matter now. The deal is off."

"Well, since it doesn't appear I'm leaving anytime soon, why don't we talk about that?"

"I hope you enjoy your stay, Ms. Sheridan, but I assure you, we will never have that conversation." The last thing Dylan needed was to be snowbound with the woman determined to take his ranch. Hell would freeze over before he'd let that happen.

Chapter 2

Emma couldn't believe her luck. If mother nature hadn't intervened, she was certain Dylan would have tossed her off the ranch. The storm hadn't been a surprise. She had been carefully watching the weather since last night, hoping the airline wouldn't cancel her flight. As much as she needed a reason to stay on the ranch, the snowed-in part made her nervous. She hadn't had any complications with her pregnancy, but she still wanted access to a hospital in case something did happen. Back home in Chicago, her apartment was six blocks from the hospital. The steady stream of sirens and medevac helicopters had become second nature to her. Most of the time she didn't hear them.

She glanced around the small room. It had seen better decades, but it was clean and tidy. Leaving her bags by the door, she took her laptop case and purse to the small round table by the window. Despite the hardness of the chair, she was happy to sit down again. After prying off her shoes, she propped up her feet on the chair across from her and set up her computer. She wanted to get as much work done as possible in case the lodge lost power. And judging by the looks of the place, the possibility was very real.

She typed a quick text message to her boss.

Made it to Silver Bells. Bad storm. Having hard time getting cell service. Hope this message gets through. Will try calling again later.

Providing no one from her office called the lodge directly, which she doubted they would, her white lie would go unnoticed. She pressed send, shut off her phone and tossed it on the table. Between yesterday's conference calls with their investors on the project and this morning's call from her boss when she landed, she'd had all the pressure she could stand. She needed time to work on her strategy. The ranch was still grieving Jax's death and there was a fine line between being aggressive and being obnoxious. Judging by Sandy's reaction to her in the dining room, her presence wasn't a welcome one. And she totally understood where they were coming from. Dylan wanted to protect his livelihood and she wanted to protect hers.

Her daughter thumped against her lower left rib. "Easy, butter bean. You're going to leave your mommy black and blue before you're born." Emma rubbed her belly. "We'll be home soon. Once I close this deal and get my promotion, your future will be secure and I can spend the rest of my pregnancy shopping for your arrival. I can't wait to meet you."

Despite the discomfort, her pregnancy had already gone faster than she had imagined. A little too fast, considering all she had to do. There were only eight weeks left and she hadn't even started working on the nursery. She had no one to rely on except herself. Until this deal closed, she couldn't afford to ease up. Raising a baby alone was hard enough. It was even harder in a big city, and she refused to let her daughter down.

She had managed to pick up a few outfits during her business trips. Traveling hadn't given her much of a chance to shop, but she loved the idea of buying her daughter dresses from all over the world. It was something she wouldn't be able to do once she got her promotion. She had mixed emotions about not traveling anymore. As much as she loved it, she found it exhausting.

Making plans with friends had become a rare luxury over the years. She'd lost touch with many of them and looked forward to reconnecting with them once she had a more normal schedule. Many had families of their own and play dates with her daughter beat traipsing across the globe any day. But unless she got to work now, none of that would happen. She focused her attention on her laptop screen and began reviewing her notes.

An hour later, Emma stood and stretched. Her skin felt grimy from the flight and she wanted to slip into something less bulky and hot. She peeked into the bathroom. It wasn't lavish by any means, but it was spotless. And that suited her just fine.

Emma had just finished showering and dressing when she heard a knock on her room door. She opened it, startled to see Dylan holding a miniature decorated Christmas tree.

"This is a surprise." Emma had heard of waving the white flag, but never waving a Christmas tree. None-theless, she appreciated the effort. "How sweet!"

"All of our guests get a tree during the holidays. Normally they are in the room before they arrive, but since we hadn't booked this room before your unex-pected visit, we hadn't bothered. Everyone deserves a little Christmas cheer."

Even her. He hadn't said the words, but they were certainly implied. So much for assuming he had done something just for her. Not that it mattered.

"Thank you." Emma took the tree from him and sat it on the worn oak dresser. "I'm hoping to be home by Christmas. You don't really think we'll still be snowed in then, do you? That's a week away." Not that she had any big plans. Her mother always said it was a kids' holiday and once she became an adult, they didn't do much to celebrate it. However, she still didn't want to spend her rare day off stuck in No-Man's-Land, Mon-tana with the Grinch.

"I certainly hope not. But it has been unusually cold this year and this is our second snow storm of the season. Let's not even think about the possibility. I'm sure you'll be back home before you know it. Anyway, that thing lights up." Dylan crossed the room like he owned the place—which he did—and eased between her and the tree. The slight brush of his body against hers caused the hair on the back of her neck to stand on end. Of course, he probably wouldn't have touched her if her belly hadn't been in the way. She had never felt more unattractive in her life. He wiggled the dresser from the wall to access the outlet and bent over, allowing her the perfect view of his backside. At least that brought a smile to her face.

"There you go." He moved the dresser back into place and admired the tree as if he'd been the one to invent the electric light. "Now you're all set."

Dylan tilted back his hat. "I don't know if anyone had the chance to tell you our meal schedule around here. Breakfast runs from six to eight, lunch is at noon and dinner at six. Breakfast and lunch are buffets and we serve dinner family-style, where everyone eats together. Although I'm sure you already know what our lodge has to offer. While it's not sushi and escargot, I assure you it's stick-to-your-ribs good food."

"Great." Emma had never been fond of the whole meat-and-potatoes thing. After wining and dining corporate clients in some of the finest restaurants in the world, her taste buds had been spoiled. She tried to muster some enthusiasm. "I look forward to it." She was already hungry and at this point, she couldn't afford to be picky.

"I notified the staff that you may have some extra needs." Dylan jammed his hands into his pockets and glanced around the room. Was it possible that Mr. Surly was nervous being alone with a pregnant woman? Emma privately laughed at the thought. "We're not a fancy resort with a twenty-four-hour kitchen, but our head chef said he'd make you some pre-prepared snacks that you will be able to heat up very quickly in the microwave down there. Just tell him your preferences. I know it's not the greatest, but we haven't had too many pregnant guests stay here. We're a little unprepared. I'm sure pre-baby vacations were part of your luxury resort spa, weren't they?"

"They were." Emma would give anything for a little pampering. "I appreciate the extra effort you're making on my behalf, but it's not necessary. I don't want to put anybody out."

"You're not putting us out." There was no disguising Dylan's double meaning. "The staff is good about keeping the walkways clear at all times, but I've asked them to be vigilant with the ice melt. So, if you do go outside, you won't slip and fall. They will continually recheck it during the day, especially in the mornings."

"Thank you." Emma thought about her company's plans for the ranch. It included heated walkways, ensuring guests could safely walk from one area of the resort to the other.

He tugged his hat down low, shielding his eyes. "I'm just being hospitable. After all, this is a guest ranch and you're a guest." He turned his back to her and strode to the open door. "Let my staff know if you need anything."

Before she could respond further, he was gone. Despite his gruffness, she found his gesture endearing. Not that he'd ever admit to it being more than his job. Because they both knew he could have sent anyone up with a tree or forgotten about it altogether. Either way, she was there to convince him to sell the ranch, not make friends.

Dylan kicked himself for going to her room. The only reason he had was because she'd looked exhausted earlier and he wanted to make sure she was all right. That was his job as the ranch owner. He could've insisted an employee drop off the tree and report back to him. The thought had crossed his mind, but he vetoed it because Emma had managed to make quite a few enemies on the ranch. It was hard enough adjusting to life without Jax. Everyone had begun to breathe again when he told them he wasn't selling Silver Bells. Now her presence brought up myriad speculations. He'd spent the better part of an hour reassuring everyone he hadn't changed his mind. He didn't have extra time for that, but he'd had to make the time. Instead, he needed to focus on finding another investor in the ranch if he wanted to keep rooves over his employees' heads. It irked him that Emma was there. Now he felt responsible for her while they were snowed in and she was one more aggravation he didn't need.

It was almost noon when Dylan hopped on one of the ranch's snowmobiles and headed toward the stables. Nothing cured a man's worries like honest hard work. He shut the engine off in front of the first building. With almost a hundred horses in residence, they had four separate stables in a row with the last building reserved mostly for maintenance. The weathered barn siding had faded to a light gray over the years. They needed updating along with the rest of the ranch. Dylan had tried to allocate money equally between the horses and the lodge, but there just wasn't enough to go around.

When you didn't have a whole lot of money, it meant you always had work to do. Considering they were short-staffed after many of their employees had decided to leave when Jax announced the ranch's imminent closing, Dylan had been pulling double duty. But he needed the distraction of extra work now more than anything.

One of the stables still hadn't been mucked thanks to

Wes once again skipping out on work. In hindsight, he should've fired his brother a long time ago, but Dylan and Jax had been the only ranch around willing to put up with his extensive bull-riding schedule. He'd thought after the World Finals that Wes would have returned to work full-time again. He'd been mistaken. At least his brother had the courtesy to send him a text message and say he wasn't coming in. He didn't even know where the man was sleeping anymore. He had a cabin on the ranch, but he rarely stayed in it.

He couldn't blame Wes for not wanting to stick around. Their family had fractured the moment their father had died. Correction, had been killed. His brother, Ryder, had confessed to running over their father after a drunken argument. Four and a half years later and it still didn't make sense to him. Ryder and their father had always had a great relationship. He had never seen them argue let alone get into a drunken brawl. It didn't matter now. Dylan had been forced to accept it. He just wished it hadn't destroyed the rest of his family. He still couldn't bring himself to visit his brother in prison.

His mother had sold the family ranch and moved to California shortly after the funeral. She'd remarried a year ago and had no plans of returning. His other brother, Garrett, had moved to Wyoming with his wife years earlier and Wes devoted ninety-nine percent of his time to bull riding. That left only Dylan and Harlan in Saddle Ridge. Jax had become a second father to them both. And now he was gone, too.

Dylan reached into his back pocket for his work gloves and realized he'd left them in his truck. He grabbed a spare pair from the tack room and set off in search of the wheelbarrow. He'd already fed the horses that morning. Normally the stalls were empty this time of day, but he'd kept the horses inside when he'd seen the weather report. Mucking stalls when you had to continually move horses around was a pain in the ass. Between that, repairing some tack, ordering supplies and a second attempt at fixing one of their ranch trucks, it would be well past sunset before he finished for the day. Good. That's what he wanted. No—it's what he needed.

Over the past six months, Dylan felt like what was left of his family had splintered even further. After Harlan and his ex-wife had split up, whenever he was on late-night patrol as deputy sheriff, Dylan used to babysit his daughter, Ivy. Now that Harlan had married Belle, she watched Ivy when he wasn't home. There were still rare instances when they both had work or were in desperate need of a date night, but it wasn't like it used to be. He missed spending time with his niece. Combined with many of his friends leaving the ranch and Jax's death, he had never felt more alone.

Dylan snatched a shovel from the wall bracket and swung open a stall door. He jammed it into the soiled hay and tossed it into the wheelbarrow. By the time he reached the last stall in the first stable, he no longer felt the cold. Hay and manure replaced the sweet scent of Emma's hair. A blister had begun to form between his thumb and index finger and he welcomed the ache. If only it would replace the one that had settled deep within his heart.

Five years ago, he had been a man-with-a-plan. He had bought into Silver Bells with the best of intentions. Jax had owned the ranch for three decades and it made a solid income. But he'd had plans to make it better. Together, they were going to create the biggest and best family guest ranch in the state of Montana. His ex, Lauren, had told him repeatedly that she didn't want to live on a ranch. She wanted to stay in her modern home with sheetrock walls, not rough-hewn cedar logs. She wanted neighbors and a two-car garage, not hundreds of acres for a backyard. And the horses… She'd warned him she wasn't an animal person, yet he had pushed and pushed until finally she'd pushed back and left.

In hindsight, they couldn't have been more opposites of each other. It's what had attracted him to her in the first place. She wasn't a big city girl like Emma, but she was definitely suburbia. Dylan had made a name for himself training horses and he had set aside every penny he'd made, earning interest. When he'd met Lauren, she'd been divorced for a solid two years already. She had two kids—a boy and a girl, ages three and five. Sweet as the day was long. He loved those kids as if they were his own. And they loved him enough to call him dad. It made her leaving that much harder.

Maybe it wouldn't have been so bad if their marriage had started on a ranch. If he had let her know from the beginning that this was the life he wanted. Instead, he had moved into her traditional four-bedroom home in Bozeman. The city was touristy, rugged and quaint all in the same breath. He had found work but felt suffocated living in their cookie-cutter housing development. The only time he had felt at home during their marriage was when he was working on someone else's ranch. So, when Jax had presented him with the opportunity to partner in Silver Bells, he jumped on it.

Lauren had followed him faithfully, despite her protests. The day they sold her house, she bawled like he'd never seen before. That had been his first sign they may not last. Dylan hadn't touched any of the money from that sale. His conscience wouldn't allow him to. That decision had given Lauren the financial freedom to leave.

The kids had been seven and nine when they moved to the ranch. They had been excited at first, but had quickly grown bored of ranch life when they realized they couldn't run down the street to play with their friends. Lauren missed her book club and Board of Education administration position. She'd accepted an office job in town, but she couldn't relate to the other women and their laid-back country lifestyle. The connection just wasn't there.

She had stuck it out for a year. An actual year to the day. And then that was it. He hadn't tried to stop her when she left. There had been no point. She was better off without him. Happier, at least. And the last he'd heard, she had married a Bozeman businessman and had returned to living in a cookie-cutter housing development with manicured lawns and white vinyl fences.

He didn't blame her. He blamed himself. He'd made her believe he was somebody other than he was. It didn't make losing her and the kids any easier. Since he hadn't legally adopted the children, he had no claim to them. He'd been their father for four years and he missed it as much today as he had when she'd left.

"I don't think I've ever seen a real live cowboy at work."

Emma's voice startled him and he almost impaled himself on the shovel.

"Somebody has to do it around here since you ran off my men." Dylan blew out a hard breath. "I didn't mean that."

"Yeah, you kind of did. But I get it. No harm, no f—What is that smell?"

"Manure."

"Does it always stink so bad?"

Dylan started laughing so hard he had to brace himself against the stall door. "It's pretty rank, but I think it might smell stronger because you're pregnant. But don't throw up in this stall, I just finished cleaning it."

"I'm way past the morning-sickness stage. Thank God," she mumbled while trying to hold her breath.

A gentleman would have offered to walk away from the manure-filled wheelbarrow so she could breathe again, but he wasn't feeling very gentlemanly. Maybe she would hate the smell enough and wait for him in the stable office until he could find someone to drive her back to the lodge.

"What can I do for you, Emma?" He purposely walked close to her as he passed so she could get a good whiff of him, knowing he wasn't playing very fair. "How did you get out here, anyway?"

"Your brother gave me a ride."

"Wes is here?" Dylan tugged off his gloves and yanked his phone out of his pocket. "That son of a—He should be the one doing this, not me. Did he come in with you?"

Emma shook her head. "No. He's plowing the ranch roads. I don't think he plans on working in the stables right now."

At least his brother had decided to work after all. "I love how I own the ranch and I'm the one doing the grunt work. So, I guess now you're stuck out here with me. I don't have time to drive you back and I certainly don't have time to entertain you."

"I'm not asking you to entertain me."

"Why are you out here, Emma?"

"Kindly lose the attitude. I realize I'm not your favorite person. All I'm asking for is a couple hours of your time to hear my proposal."

"You have a lot of nerve, sweetheart." He couldn't believe her attitude. "I know all about your plans for the ranch."

"No, Dylan, you don't. You think you do, but you don't. How do I know? Because I never pitched them to you, and Jax told me you didn't want to listen to him. You might feel differently if we talked about it."

"As you can already see, I don't have a couple hours to spare." Dylan tossed his shovel on top of the wheelbarrow and began pushing it down the stable corridor. "Honestly, I'm finding your insistence insulting."

"I—I never meant to offend you." Emma backed away from him and straight into one of the open stall doors.

"Be careful." He sighed. "Listen, I know you're just doing your job. I apologize for my attitude. You being here is bringing up some memories I would rather have kept in the past. And before you ask, no, I don't want to talk about them."

"Is this about your ex-wife?"

Dylan abruptly released the handles of the wheelbarrow, almost causing it to tip over. "How the hell do you know about that?"

"Jax told me your wife and kids left because you moved them out here and that's a big reason why you didn't want to sell the ranch."

"You're half-right. My wife and *her* kids. And there's more to my not wanting to sell than that. Here I thought my uncle wasn't much of a gossip. Turns out I was wrong."

"Jax cared for you very much. Part of his reason for selling was so you could have your freedom again."

Dylan tugged off his gloves. "Well, doesn't that just beat all? This ranch was my freedom. My home. By taking it away from me, he was taking away the last breath I had. Did he really say that to you?"

Emma nodded slowly, closing the distance between them. "He thought if you had a fresh start on your own ranch without the debt and problems of this place hanging over your head that you'd be able to move on."

Dylan recoiled at her words. "Oh, you're good."

"I don't understand."

"Your job is to convince me to sell and you're using the information my uncle told you against me." He had known she was a shrewd businesswoman; he hadn't known she'd take it this far. "I already know my uncle's final wish was to sell this place. Doesn't mean I'm going to honor it, and your charms will not convince me otherwise."

"You want to be mad at me for being here? Go right ahead. You want to be mad that Jax died? Do it. Let it out. Scream, shout, kick something. It's okay to be mad at the past. But please don't insult me in the process."

Emma stormed out of the stables, leaving him alone with nothing but a pile of manure.

"The nerve of that man," Emma grumbled to herself as she traipsed down the freshly-plowed road toward the lodge. She could just about make out the roof of the building from where she stood. At least there was a lull in the storm and it had stopped snowing. While the exercise felt good, her feet were beginning to ache and her fingers were cold. She reached inside her pocket for her phone. Maybe if she called the lodge, somebody could come get her.

She pulled off a glove with her teeth and began to scroll through her contacts when she heard an engine coming up behind her. She stepped off the road and into a pile of cold, wet snow that instantly seeped down into her duck boot moccasins. After she'd let out a few choice curse words, the snowmobile stopped in front of her and cut the engine.

Dylan.

"I don't want to talk to you." Emma stomped onto the path in a vain attempt to shake the snow from her shoes. She only succeeded in shaking it farther down toward her toes.

"I don't want to talk to you either, but I'm not going to allow you to freeze out here. You were crazy to think you could walk back to the lodge in this weather."

Emma wanted to ignore him, but she was too cold and no amount of pride was worth freezing over. "I was just calling the lodge to have someone come and get me."

"I'm your somebody. Hop on."

"Hop on where?" While the snowmobile was a decent size, there was no way her and her belly would fit behind him. At least not without her holding on to him for dear life.

Dylan scooted forward to make more room. "Get on. I'll go slow, I promise."

Emma raked her hands down her face. She had never been snowmobiling in her life and she didn't think her doctor back home in Chicago would approve of this little outdoor activity. She climbed on behind him and gripped his hips.

"Wrap your arms around me," Dylan said over his shoulder.

"I can't. My stomach is in the way," Emma muttered.

She didn't hear or see Dylan laughing, but she felt his body reverberating against hers. She smacked his arm. "It's not funny. You try being pregnant."

"I'm sorry." He continued to laugh. "Can you hold on to my shoulders?"

Emma slid her hands up his back, relishing the solid muscle beneath her palms. "I can handle that."

"Apparently." Dylan arched against her as she squeezed his shoulders.

"You stink." His odor was probably her only saving grace. If he had smelled musky and manly, she might not have been able to control herself. And she wouldn't have been able to blame it on her pregnancy hormones.

By the time they reached the lodge, she needed another change of clothes. She didn't want to sit down to dinner smelling like… Dylan. She wanted to make a graceful escape from the back of the snowmobile—unfortunately getting on was easier than getting off. The story of her pregnancy.

After Dylan's assistance, she managed to break free of him. "Thank you for the ride." She headed into the lodge. She may have been grateful for the ride, but she was still mad at him.

"Emma, wait."

She didn't bother to stop. She'd had enough of Dylan Slade for one day.

Chapter 3

Emma hadn't realized she'd slept through dinner until she heard a soft knock at the door. If her stomach hadn't been grumbling, she would've ignored it. She couldn't deal with another minute of Dylan this evening. She checked the peephole, surprised to see Sandy standing in the hallway holding a tray.

She unlocked the door and eased it open. "I'm sorry, I fell asleep."

"That's okay. I figured that's what happened so I brought you dinner. May I come in?" Emma stepped aside as the petite brunette entered the room and set the tray on the small table near the window. "I wanted to apologize for the way I spoke to you earlier. I'm a little frazzled with my Christmas Day wedding coming up. It's no excuse, though."

"Believe me, I realize I'm the enemy. We're on opposite sides. It's cool. I do hope you have the wedding of your dreams."

"Thanks." Sandy tucked a piece of hair behind her ear that had worked its way loose from her French braid. "There's a little bit of everything on here. If you want more, just ring downstairs. I see Dylan brought you up the Christmas tree. I know he's a little gruff on the outside, but he really is a big teddy bear once you get to know him."

"Somehow I don't think anyone's going to mistake Dylan for a squishable stuffed animal anytime soon."

"Then I guess you won't mind me telling you he was the one who fixed your tray." Sandy winked as she walked into the hallway. "I live here in the lodge. Extension 307. Call me if you need anything."

"Thanks, I will." Emma closed the door.

Dylan fixed her tray? She eyed it warily. "I wonder what he did to it."

She lifted the plate to remove the plastic wrap and found a folded note.

I'm sorry for earlier.
Dylan.

Well, that was unexpected. The smell of fried chicken, mashed potatoes and gravy got the best of her. And then she saw them…butter beans. *He remembered.* There was also a huge slab of chocolate cake, macaroni and cheese and a slice of meatloaf. Classic comfort food. She'd never desired it until this very moment. And she planned to eat every ounce of it or explode trying.

Halfway through her meal, her text-message tone

sounded from the other side of the table. She'd forgotten to turn her phone back off after calling her best friend, Jennie, to help forget her argument with Dylan. She wanted to ignore it, but she was already full anyway. She reached for her phone and tapped the screen to see a message from her boss.

Conference call tomorrow. 1 p.m. Chicago time. Want update.

Her boss had a penchant for caveman text messaging and emails. She didn't know if she was supposed to call him or he was supposed to call her. Either way, it wouldn't be a good conversation. At least it gave her the morning to prepare for it. She would have preferred to wait until after Dylan heard her proposal, if she could ever convince him to give her half a chance. Maybe her boss could offer some insight on how to change Dylan's mind, although that felt as if she were admitting she didn't have any ideas of her own.

Emma would have preferred staying in her room for the rest of the night, but she didn't think Silver Bells had tray pick up, especially since they didn't offer room service. While she was down there, she'd find out about laundry service or the use of a washing machine and dryer.

Carrying her tray down a flight of stairs proved to be more precarious than she'd anticipated. She couldn't wait for her center of gravity to be back where it belonged. By the time she reached the kitchen, she'd broken out into a cold sweat. Thankfully, she hadn't made a scene by dropping the tray along the way.

A group of around twenty people had gathered near

the fireplace while someone played guitar and sang "Jingle Bell Rock." She loved that song. It had always put her in a festive holiday mood. She walked toward the small crowd, singing along until she caught a glimpse of who was playing. Dylan. Of course, it had to be Dylan.

A slow easy grin settled over his face as his eyes met hers. He continued to sing, and for a moment, everyone else disappeared. When the song ended, their applause jolted her back to reality. Good thing it was only a fantasy, because the last thing she wanted was to be alone with Dylan again. They'd kissed and made up and that was good enough for her. *Kissed?* No! She could not think about kissing Dylan Slade.

Absolutely not.

Not going to happen.

Not even in her dreams.

Okay, so she had kissed him in her dreams once before. But that was then and this was now.

He began playing Brooks & Dunn's "Hangin' 'Round the Mistletoe," which sounded dangerously sexy when Dylan sang it. He had a great voice. It didn't help that he still hadn't broken eye contact. She wanted to look away first, but she couldn't will herself to do so. That was until she noticed everyone else was staring at her. Great. Now she felt even more self-conscious. And then she realized why she was the center of attention. Hanging above her head was none other than a sprig of mistletoe. Double crap!

Dylan ended the song to a round of applause. He placed the house guitar back on the stand where anyone was welcome to play it. Emma had latched herself on to two other female guests, probably to avoid him. And who could blame her.

The three of them disappeared, leaving him to wonder if he would see Emma again tonight. Dylan attempted to mingle with the ranch's guests. They didn't have a full house, but they had managed to fill almost a dozen rooms. Instead of making small talk or thinking about Emma, he needed to focus on finding a new investor. The road closures meant the kids living on the ranch wouldn't have school. He'd bribe them to muck the stalls tomorrow if his brother didn't show up for work again. There was no point in saying anything to Wes, because he never stayed around long enough for it to matter. That didn't mean the responsibility of the horses was going away anytime soon.

He still couldn't get what Emma had told him about Jax out of his head. Had his uncle truly believed selling the ranch was in Dylan's best interest? It would have been different if Lauren had left a few months ago. Then maybe he could have salvaged his marriage. In the end, it probably would have only been a temporary bandage. Sometimes you couldn't fix what wasn't meant to be.

When Emma reappeared, he could have sworn his heart quickened. But that was impossible, unless it was out of aggravation. A part of him wanted to find out what else Jax had said to her about him, but the other part figured he was better off not knowing. Sandy and Luke interrupted his thoughts when they carried out two large trays of s'mores fixings and told the guests to grab their jackets and follow them outside.

A fire was already burning in the stone fire pit behind the lodge. A light snow continued to fall as flames danced between him and Emma while Sandy showed her how to make the melted chocolate, toasted marshmallow and graham cracker sandwich. For someone as worldly as he thought she was, he found it funny that she had never made s'mores before. Then again, she was a city girl.

At least Sandy had apologized for earlier. Which is what he had hoped she would do when he asked her to bring Emma a tray of food. It was one thing for him to be annoyed she was there, but she was a guest and his employees needed to respect that.

"Oh, my God! These are amazing!" Emma happily squealed. Sandy placed her reindeer antlers headband on Emma's head as Luke stuck another marshmallow on the end of her stick.

Dylan felt like a kid looking through the window of a birthday party he hadn't been invited to. He wanted to share in their laughter. Dylan shook the thought from his brain. In a few days, he would never see or speak to Emma again. Good. So why did that thought bother him? She had her life in the big city and he had his in rural Montana. And if there was one thing he knew for sure, the two didn't mix.

"Thank you for dinner." Emma managed to startle him once again.

"You really need to stop sneaking up on people."

"What people? And you were looking right at me." Emma shook her head. "I won't take up any of your time. I just wanted to say thank you for your apology and I accept."

Dylan tried not to laugh at the bells jingling on her antlers as she spoke. "I'm taking some of the guests on a snowcat tour of the ranch in a little while. I have room for one more if you care to join us?"

"Is that the giant red boxy-looking vehicle with the tracks I saw near the stables earlier?"

"Yep. We give tours a couple times a day. We're just coming off a new moon, and if it was a clear night, you'd be able to see a million stars. And every once in a while, we're able to see the northern lights. Because of the snow and the low visibility, we're just driving around the ranch tonight."

"I'd love to go, but I don't think I can get my butt up into that thing."

"There are steps in the back. It's easy and perfectly safe. We don't go fast at all."

"Sure, sounds like fun. It will be another first for me."

"Like s'mores?" Dylan envisioned Emma having a running checklist of things she had to accomplish in life.

"Hey now, not everyone grew up around campfires." *Jingle, jingle.*

"Fair enough. We'll leave here at ten. The tour is about an hour."

"Great, I look forward to it." She gave him a slight wink as she smiled. That was the Emma smile he remembered the first day they met. It had transfixed him even then. He needed to get it out of his head and fast before he found himself agreeing to her ideas as Jax had.

Once Dylan began loading everyone into the snow-cat, he realized they had booked more people than he had thought. By the time Emma made it outside, the only place left for her to sit was up front next to him. He had wanted to be hospitable, not have her inches away from him in the cab of his favorite diesel toy.

"I thought you said there were steps." Emma said as he helped her climb onto the track and into the cab, already regretting her close proximity.

"That's when I thought fewer people were coming along tonight." Dylan made a mental note to double-check future reservations before offering to take her along anyplace else. He closed her door and hopped into the driver's side.

"Where's the steering wheel?" Emma asked once she settled in her seat.

"There isn't one." Dylan laughed. He had asked Jax the same question when he first learned how to drive the vehicle. His uncle had picked it up used at auction for a ridiculously low price. They couldn't have afforded it any other way. The tours were a nice package addition to offer their guests. Newer ranches might be sprouting up around them, but they didn't have snowcat tours. And they didn't have the acreage that Silver Bells had.

Dylan started the engine and gripped both control sticks. "Almost every part of a snowcat is controlled by hydraulics. When I turn left, the right track speeds up and pushes the vehicle to the left. Same thing if we're turning right."

"I don't see a brake pedal." Emma leaned toward him to get a better look, giving him an inadvertent chance to smell her hair. There it was again. Almonds.

"It doesn't have that, either. Snowcats are super heavy. By letting off the gas or pulling back on the control sticks, it slows to a stop. It does have a parking brake, though, if that makes you feel any better."

"I'm surprised how warm it is in here. I expected to freeze."

"These vehicles are designed for subzero temperatures. Even the windshield is heated to prevent icing. Providing there's diesel to power it, you'll stay nice and warm in this thing."

Emma continued to ask questions until they reached the far side of the ranch, overlooking the town of Saddle Ridge.

"This is normally where I let everyone out to walk around and take some night photography shots. Since the snow is so light, I'm going to check in the back to see if anyone wants to get out."

"I could stand to get out and walk around a little. I think I'm wearing every item of clothing I brought with me. I'm about ready to roast."

"Just let me make sure the snow is hard-packed enough. I don't want to chance you falling."

Dylan unloaded his passengers out of the back door of the snowcat before returning to Emma. He needed a few minutes of distance to catch his breath. He had never had a woman in his cab before, let alone one who smelled as intoxicating as she did. He didn't know what she bathed in, but it wasn't the lodge's complimentary body wash.

After his nerves had cooled, he tested the ground near Emma's door and cleared the snow off the tracks so she could exit safely. When he climbed up to open her door, he saw she was sound asleep through the window. He didn't have the heart to wake her. In hindsight, he probably should've waited until tomorrow to ask her to come out with them. He had assumed she traveled all night judging by the time she had arrived. Sandy told him she had fallen asleep before dinner. The woman was exhausted and sleeping for two. A fact he needed to keep reminding himself of.

* * *

Emma woke to the sound of Dylan climbing in next to her. The question was, what was he climbing into? Considering she was sitting upright, they weren't in bed together. Although she could have sworn she had been dreaming just that a few minutes ago. She rubbed her eyes and forced herself to open them. Darkness surrounded them.

She reached out in front of her and met the hard steel of the snowcat. "You've got to be kidding me." She attempted to straighten her spine. "Did I fall asleep on your tour?"

"Technically, no. We were already stopped when you fell asleep."

Emma checked her watch and then realized she'd forgotten to put it on today. "How long was I out?"

"Maybe a half hour. I told everyone you decided to stay inside because it was so cold. This probably wasn't a good idea after the day you've had." Dylan shifted to face her. "You need your sleep. At least you can stay in bed tomorrow." He started the snowcat.

"Not quite. I have a conference call with my boss in the afternoon that I need to prepare for. I don't suppose you could help a girl out and listen to my proposal before then?" Emma hadn't given up hope yet.

Warmth quickly faded from Dylan's face. "I don't think so."

"You know I had to ask."

"I wish you wouldn't. You could have yourself a nice little vacation while we're snowed in if you would just accept that I'm not selling you the ranch."

"And I wish it were that simple. Since we're talking

about being snowed in, what happens if a guest has a medical emergency?"

Dylan pushed both control sticks forward as the snowcat began to move. "We've had it happen before. We take the snowcat to the nearest paved road and the ambulance or sheriff's department meets us there. If need be, we can drive this straight to the hospital, but we can't drive it down Main Street at will."

At least there was a way to get to the hospital. Emma shifted uncomfortably in her seat. She wished her daughter would settle down for the night. Then again, she probably sensed the movement despite the snowcat's relatively smooth ride on the freshly fallen snow.

By the time they reached the lodge, the snow had begun falling heavily again. She'd be glad to get back to her room and into bed. She'd start fresh in the morning. And brace herself for the onslaught of her boss.

Dylan hesitated after he helped her out of the snowcat. For a brief moment, she thought he might agree to hear her proposal in the morning.

"Get a good night's sleep. Do you need me to get someone to help you to your room?"

"Um, no. Thank you." So much for wishful thinking. She'd try again in the morning. She'd come too far to give up now.

Chapter 4

Emma showered, dressed and got downstairs by seven the following morning, eager to eat breakfast and try to persuade Dylan to hear her proposal one last time before her conference call. She had glanced out the window earlier but only saw a sea of white through the darkness. That was all she saw last night before she went to bed, too. It was still snowing. She'd only been on the ranch for one day and she was already homesick. It was one thing to travel and have places to go and see. The prospect of being confined on the ranch for the next few days was less exciting than watching water drip from a faucet.

Her stomach grumbled and the scent of fresh baked muffins beckoned her to the dining area. She knew the ranch had a breakfast buffet, but she hadn't expected one this large. And there they were...a basket of glorious golden blueberry muffins. She snatched one before she even picked up a plate. Unable to wait until she sat down, she bit into the streusel-covered top. Heaven couldn't have created a better muffin.

"Oh, my God, French toast!" *Carbs!* Her body craved them like no tomorrow. She piled four slices on her plate and doused them in real maple syrup. Not the artificial stuff. She would kill for a cup of regular coffee, but settled for a small carton of orange juice, instead. *Sugar!* Her body craved that, too. Her mother would die if she saw what she had eaten over the past twenty-four hours. Emma didn't care. She knew pregnancy wasn't a free pass to eat whatever she wanted, but sometimes you just had to make an exception. She just hoped they didn't bring out pancakes because then somebody would have to roll her out the door.

"Good morning." Sandy greeted her at the table. "I didn't expect to see you up this early. I saw you drooling over the coffee. Would you like a cup of decaf? I brewed a pot a few minutes ago."

"No thank you. It gives me cotton mouth and just makes me crave the real thing that much more." Emma unwrapped her silverware from her napkin and began cutting into her French toast. "Please give my compliments to the chef on those muffins. They are amazing. I haven't tried anything else yet, but I'm sure it will be as good, if not better than it smells."

"You really like the muffins?" Sandy beamed. "I made them. And Melinda made the French toast. I don't know if you met her or not last night. She's another server here." Sandy looked around the room. "She's the tall blonde over by the kitchen door. The one that looks like she should be modeling for *Sports Illustrated* instead of working on a ranch. Rhonda's also on kitchen duty this morning because the staff still couldn't make it in due to the road closures. She's the one with the reddish-purple updo next to Melinda. The chefs don't live on the ranch like we do."

"You made this?" Emma waved her fork. "Did you also make last night's dinner?"

"We sure did. We're all cross-trained here. I love cooking so it's always a treat for me to cook for everyone." Sandy grabbed a heated syrup pitcher from the buffet and set it in front of her. "Here, in case you want some more."

"This is incredible. You should move into the kitchen instead of serving."

"I had planned to, but then Jax said he was selling the ranch." Sandy grimaced. "But now that it's not for sale, I'll have that chance again. Unless you changed Dylan's mind last night."

"No chance of that." Guilt crept into Emma's heart. The woman had dreams and aspirations and she was there to take them away. Wonderful. "Any word on how much snow we had overnight?"

"Eight inches. Not quite the foot they had expected. Normally we don't see this type of accumulation until late January or early February. But it has been known to happen."

"So I guess you're still stuck with me." Emma tried to smile. The snow worked in her favor at the moment, but unless she could change Dylan's mind, she'd go stir-crazy on the ranch.

"We're all in this together. Don't worry. We have plenty of provisions and the lodge has generators in case we lose power. Dylan's brother Harlan is a deputy

sheriff in town so he'll keep us updated on the roads."
Sandy pulled out a chair next to her and sat down. "You
and Dylan looked awfully cozy in the cab of the snowcat when you pulled out of here last night."

Emma wiped at her mouth, no longer hungry. "As
cozy as two people can get when the driver has both of
his hands full steering a multi-ton vehicle across the
snow. Believe me when I tell you, Dylan has no plans
to sell this place. He won't even discuss it."

"I already knew that. I thought maybe there was a
romance brewing between you two."

She pushed her plate aside. "You are out of your
mind. Don't take this the wrong way, but this lifestyle
isn't for me. I'm used to having every amenity available at a moment's notice. We have road closures, but
never like this. At least not where I live in Chicago. I'm
blocks away from the hospital so they clear those roads
first. This is very—"

"Calming, if you allow it to be."

Emma covered her mouth for fear she might burst out
laughing. The Montana wilderness was not calming to
her. It was terrifying in more than one way.

"Maybe he'll take you out for a private sleigh ride
today." Sandy nibbled her bottom lip. "Can you just
imagine?"

Emma had never been the hopeless-romantic type.
Even romantic was questionable. She'd read the fairy
tales and had hoped her Prince Charming would sweep
her off her feet one day. Then she had gotten knocked
up and her boyfriend walked out on her. So much for
romance. And hopeless? Yeah, she was feeling pretty
hopeless right now, considering she couldn't even convince Dylan to listen to her.

"I think you're super excited about your wedding and you're trying to play matchmaker. You're conveniently forgetting I'm carrying another man's baby."

"But I overheard you tell Dylan that he wasn't in your life."

"That's right, he's not."

"Then what's the problem? Dylan loves kids. He still misses the ones he lost when Lauren divorced him. And you challenge each other."

"How do you know that?" Emma jabbed her fork into a piece of French toast. It would be a shame to let it go to waste. "I've only been here for a day."

"I see the way you look at each other. And the way he sang to you last night." Sandy fanned herself with her hand. "Now that was hot."

"It was a Christmas song, not a love song," Emma protested.

"But you were standing under the mistletoe."

"An unfortunate misstep on my part. It's not like he came over and kissed me afterward."

"And what if I had?" Dylan said from behind her.

Emma froze. Mouth-open, fork-in-hand, syrup-dripping froze. Now, she was going to die.

Dylan knew he wasn't playing fair. Then again, Emma hadn't played fair since the day they had met.

"I'll give you two a little privacy." Sandy stood and held out her chair for him.

Before he even had a chance to sit, Emma rose. "I should be going, too."

"Going where? The ranch is snowed in."

Emma's pinky grazed his. It was innocent and intimate in the same breath. And dammit if it hadn't left him wanting more. He moved his chair a few inches farther away from hers before he sat down.

"Did you change your mind about hearing my proposal?"

"No." He shook his head. "But I would like to pick your brain."

Emma's eyes widened. "About the ranch? Dylan, I have a conference call this afternoon and I have to explain how I can't convince you to give me a few hours of your time. Yet, you want to pick my brain, as you put it, over the ranch. Yeah, um, I'm sorry. That's not going to happen."

"You seem to be awfully stressed over one phone call. Stay and have breakfast with me. I insist." Dylan picked up her dish. "Let me get you a hot plate of food. You can meet some of my people and relax for an hour."

"No offense, but being near you is anything but relaxing. Especially when you're pushing your own agenda."

"I haven't asked much of you, but you're asking me to give up my entire life. Honestly, I didn't think having breakfast with me and my employees was that big of a deal." Dylan forced himself to remain polite. "Don't worry, they won't tell you their life stories. I just thought it would be nice if you met some of Silver Bells' extended family. The ranch wasn't just my uncle. It's all of us together."

"Okay." Emma sat down. "I'll stay."

"Oh-kay." The way she agreed with him seemed off. He half-expected her to bolt before he returned to the table. "I'll be right back."

By the time he reached the buffet, many of the guests were in line ahead of him. When the ranch had been fully operational, they'd had a separate employee buf-fet two hours earlier. They had combined them when there wasn't enough of either group for a full buffet. At least it made the massive dining room appear much less empty.

He checked the table a few times to make sure Emma was still there. She had her head buried in that phone of hers. A part of him wished the snowstorm would take out the internet, but then he wouldn't be able to make his own inquiries to save the ranch. He'd spent half the night online researching potential investors. He'd even sent out a few feeler emails, but this wasn't his forte.

With Christmas less than a week away, he figured most people wouldn't want to be bothered discussing a business deal this size. He wondered if one partner would even be enough. He might need to form his own investment group. But who would want to finance a sinking ship?

Dylan stopped a few of his ranch hands' wives in line and directed them to the large round table where Emma sat. By the time he arrived, it was almost full and she was happily chatting about babies. Perfect. She was forming a connection with them. That was exactly what he had hoped for.

"The women want to teach me how to knit." Emma frowned as he placed a fresh plate in front of her and took a seat.

"What's wrong with knitting?" Most of the women he knew did it. Wasn't that the in thing? Not that he was up-to-date on women's hobbies but, based on bits of conversations he'd overheard around the ranch, many of his female employees were involved in some sort of crafting.

"I can barely sew a button on a shirt, let alone intricately weave yarn into clothing."

"So make a simple blanket. Create something special for your daughter that she'll hand down to her own daughter someday."

"I hadn't expected you to be the sentimental type."

"I'm sentimental about a lot of things." Dylan forked a mouthful of scrambled eggs.

"I know, I know. This ranch being one of them."

"I'm attached to this ranch because I live on it and my employees depend on it. But I wouldn't say it's a sentimental attachment. The homestead my family lost after my father died…that was a sentimental attachment. I hope to one day buy it back if the current owner ever decides to sell."

"I'm sorry, I didn't know."

"No need to apologize. It's no secret around here. My brother Ryder killed my father. He was sentenced to ten years in prison, half of which he's already served. I'm the oldest of five. I've always looked after everyone else. I feel the responsibility to have a place where people can work and make an honest living. I wanted Ryder to have that option once he got out of jail—if there's anything left to salvage of our relationship—but now that may not be possible if the ranch continues on a downward spiral."

"And you want me to help you?"

Dylan nodded. "You've met some of these people. This isn't just my home. It's theirs, too. I don't want them to have to start over. I could handle it. Many of them can't."

Emma looked down at her hands. "I didn't realize how difficult this has been for you."

Her eyes met his and for the first time, he believed her. "No, you didn't."

Emma tensed. "At least we have that much in common. I don't think you understand how difficult this has been for me, either."

As much as he could use Emma's expertise on how to entice potential investors, asking her to do so would violate her ethics. It was a shame they had such opposite goals. Their combined determination would have made them a great team.

It was nine o'clock before Emma waddled away from the table. Somewhere during that time, she had amassed the phone numbers of ranch women willing to share all the secrets of child-rearing, or so they said. Melinda had a six-month-old of her own and had generously offered to teach her the basics of bathing and changing an infant. Emma wasn't sure she was ready for the hands-on approach just yet. She still had the child-care class to take at the hospital back home. She had thought she would have two more months to prepare for actual infant holding. The thought terrified her more and more each day. Especially since she had never held a baby... ever.

When noon rolled around—one o'clock Chicago time—Emma's stomach began to churn. Either the baby was pressing her nausea button or her nerves about the conference call were getting the best of her. She was halfway to her room when her phone rang.

Crap! It was a video call. Not what she had expected. "Hello."

"Emma." Charlie's face appeared on the screen. "I'm

here with Rob and Don. We need an update on the Silver Bells acquisition."

"I haven't made any progress yet. I—"

"You've been there for a day and you've done nothing?" Charlie scowled.

"The ranch is snowed in and Dylan's had his hands full dealing with that. I've barely seen him," she fibbed. "I'm sure I'll have a chance once things calm down around here."

Emma sat on a bench in the hallway, dreading Charlie's response.

"Okay, getting snowed in may be a good thing." Don's face popped into the screen. "That will give you some time to work on…" He shuffled some papers. "Dylan, is it?"

"Yes." She'd just said his name two seconds ago. So much for her home team being on top of things.

Charlie's brows furrowed. "Emma, are you sure you can handle this?"

"You need to find something to use against this Dylan person," Rob said before she had a chance to respond to Charlie. "Convince him to sell at any cost."

Emma fought the retort that was on the tip of her tongue. She refused to play dirty.

"I don't need to remind you what's at stake, do I?" Charlie leaned in, his face filled the entire screen like an ominous presence. "If you can't close this deal then I'm afraid you're not ready for the acquisitions director promotion. Why don't I send Don up to assist you?"

Emma couldn't believe what she was hearing. She didn't need Don's help. "The roads are closed. You can't get here. Nobody can get here."

"I'm sure somebody around there must rent snow-mobiles," Don snipped.

Snowmobiles. Of course, he would think of that. "I'm sure they do. But thanks, anyway. I'm fine on my own."

"Emma, close this deal before you leave there. We have too many long-standing investors counting on this."

Emma stood and felt lightheaded. She gripped the corner of the wall and sat down. "I'm trying, Charlie. Believe me, I'm evaluating every available option."

"Okay, then. We'll talk more later. Take care of that baby of yours." And then the screen went blank.

"Merry Christmas to you, as— Dylan! How long have you been standing there?"

Mr. Pick-Your-Brain leaned languidly against the wall opposite her.

"Long enough to see that conversation made your blood boil."

"You know it's not nice to eavesdrop."

"You're having a conference call in the middle of the hallway in my lodge. It's kind of impossible not to overhear."

Yeah, okay that was true. For some reason, face-to-face conference calls with men in her hotel room creeped her out. "Now you understand my pressure?"

"Let me ask you something." Dylan settled next to her on the bench, the length of his thigh touching hers. "Why do you put up with it? Can't you find another job where they appreciate your talents? That was a whole lot of ridicule for a short conversation."

"Then I would be admitting defeat." Emma wouldn't dream of quitting her job. Not after the six years of her life she'd devoted to the commercial real estate acquisitions firm. "It was the first place I worked for when I got out of college. I literally started at the bottom as an intern and worked my way up. I've accomplished quite a bit for someone who's only twenty-eight. My goal was to make acquisitions director before I turned thirty. The problem is, that position rarely opens. The last acquisitions director had been there for twenty years. It's available because he retired. This is my chance. Probably my only chance to advance."

"But I'm not willing to sell."

"I know but—" Emma doubled forward. The pain below her ribs felt like someone had shoved an ice pick through her body. "Dylan, help me! Something's wrong with my baby. Oh, God, please!"

Chapter 5

The urgency in her voice told him something was really wrong. He lifted her into his arms. "I've got you." Dylan carried her down the stairs and into the lobby. "Sandy!" he shouted toward the dining room. "I need to get Emma to the hospital. Stay with her while I get the snowcat."

"Oh, my God, it hurts." Emma sobbed as he lowered her into the lobby chair. "Please hurry, Dylan. Don't let me lose my baby."

"I won't." He promised as he ran out the front door. He pulled his keys from his pocket and jumped on his snowmobile. His hands shook as he found the right key. Jamming it into the ignition, he started the machine and tore off toward the stables. From a distance he could see the layer of snow on the snowcat's windshield and he prayed it hadn't iced over. There wasn't time to wait for it to defrost.

The snowmobile skidded to a stop alongside the snowcat's tracks. He snatched the keys from the ignition and fumbled for the one to open the door. Then he hopped onto the track and swiped at the windshield. It was all powder, thank God. He unlocked the door, swung it wide and climbed into the driver's seat. The diesel turned over without hesitation. His snowcat may be old, but it was reliable.

When he reached the lodge's entrance, he couldn't be sure how much time had passed. One second seemed too long. He felt something had been off with Emma since she had arrived and his instincts had been correct.

Dylan parked outside the entrance and raced inside for her. Tears streamed down her face as he lifted her back into his arms. He tightened his grip on her and stepped into the cold. A bitter wind stung his cheeks as he tucked her closer to his body.

Sandy ran ahead of them and opened the passenger door. "Here's her bag. Rhonda went to her room and got it. And I called Harlan," she panted. "He's going to meet you at the intersection of South Fork and Anderson. He said the roads to the hospital are plowed from there."

"Thank you." He eased Emma onto the seat and gently fastened her seat belt across her lap. "The hospital isn't far." He closed the door, looked skyward and silently prayed Jax was looking down on them.

Dylan paced the hospital waiting area. A wiser man would have dropped Emma off and been done with the situation. Unfortunately, he had this inexplicable need to remain close by in case she needed him, even though the logical part of his brain reassured him she wouldn't. Sure, he wanted to be certain she was all right, but he had zero connection to this woman and her child outside of their nonexistent sale of the ranch.

Okay, so that wasn't altogether true. He'd been physically attracted to Emma from the moment they'd met. He just had a strong distaste for her endgame. But his attraction to her began and ended there. There certainly wasn't an emotional attachment. Yet he couldn't force himself to walk out the hospital's doors.

"Mr. Sheridan." A nurse in bright pink scrubs approached him. "Both momma and baby are stable. The doctor is about to begin the ultrasound, so if you will follow me, I will take you to her."

Mr. Sheridan? The woman assumed he was Emma's husband. He opened his mouth to correct her but ended up saying the opposite of what he'd intended. "Great, thank you."

The walk down the hospital corridor seemed endless. With each step, the voice inside his head begged him to run in the opposite direction. But his body refused to obey. He needed to see for himself that Emma and the baby were fine.

He halted in the doorway of the room when he saw her reclined on a bed, wearing a hiked-up hospital gown to expose her bare belly and nothing more than a sheet covering her lap and legs. Two wide bands stretched around her abdomen and held what Dylan assumed were fetal monitors of some sort in place. Emma's attention was transfixed on the screen attached to her stomach as the sound of a heartbeat reverberated throughout the otherwise quiet room.

"Your daughter still sounds strong and healthy." The doctor looked up from the monitor's printout. "Your blood pressure is my primary concern. It's more elevated than I would prefer." The woman glanced in his direction. "Is this the baby's father?" she asked.

Emma held out her hand to him. "Please, come in." Despite her weak smile, fear emanated from her delicate features. Even if he wanted to, he couldn't leave now. Any desire to escape had faded and he didn't understand why. He crossed the room to her bed. Her fingers entwined with his, gripping his hand tightly. "Dylan's a friend," she said as her eyes met his. "Right? At least for today."

They had been sworn enemies since the beginning, but even he refused to deny her when she needed someone most. He scanned the numerous machines connected to her body. "Are you in labor?"

She squeezed her eyes shut and dug her fingers into his flesh as the doctor returned her attention to the printout. "Easy, Emma, it's almost over. She's experiencing Braxton-Hicks contractions. It's false labor, but we'll continue to monitor her overnight. Let's begin your ultrasound."

"I should leave." As soon as he uttered the words, he realized he hadn't meant them. He didn't know if it was because he wanted to see for himself that the baby was okay or if his strong desire to stay was out of curiosity. He'd never been involved in any pregnancy aside from his brother Harlan's wife, Belle, who was almost in the middle of her second trimester. He'd seen an ultrasound photo, but that was the extent of it. When she didn't release his hand after the contraction subsided, it unnerved him even more. The ultrasound didn't scare him. The situation did. He didn't want to get close to Emma or her baby, because he had no intention of ever forming an attachment to another man's kid again. Losing his stepchildren had almost destroyed him and he refused to be a two-time fool.

Emma averted her eyes. "I want you to stay." Her voice no more than a whisper.

"Okay." Dylan relented. He reached for the chair near the bed and pulled it closer.

"This will feel cold at first." The doctor squeezed a tube of clear gel on Emma's abdomen and spread it with the ultrasound probe. Various shades of white and grey danced across the screen until an image of the baby appeared. "There's your daughter."

"My little butter bean." Emma smiled through her tears. "Is she really all right?"

The doctor continued to move the probe. "I don't see any abnormalities. She's exactly where she should be at thirty-two weeks."

Dylan fought the urge to wipe away her tears. He looked from the screen to Emma's belly and back again. That tiny person was growing inside of her. He'd seen plenty of horse ultrasounds, but this was different. This was…far too intimate for her to share with him. She needed her mother or her best friends by her side. Not someone who hadn't been very nice to her.

"We'll perform another one tomorrow, but I'm fairly confident there won't be any change. I'm more concerned about your blood pressure and the possibility of preeclampsia. Your baby is healthy and strong, and I need you to be healthy and strong so you can carry her at least another six weeks." She handed the probe to another woman in pink. "Tricia is going to get a good ultrasound photo for you. I want you to rest tonight. I know that's difficult to do in a hospital. We'll leave your fetal monitors on as a precaution, so if there's anything out of the ordinary they will alert us right away. Again, Emma, the signs point to Braxton-Hicks and not pre-term labor. Try to get some sleep and I'll check on you in the morning." The doctor squeezed her other hand.

"Thank you," Emma said as the woman left the room. She readjusted her gown and pressed the bed's remote until she sat more upright. "And thank you for staying here with me even though you didn't have to." She smiled up at Dylan. "I didn't want to go through this alone."

"Don't mention it." Dylan stood, breaking physical contact with Emma. He jammed his hands in his pockets to prevent touching her again. "I should get going and let you sleep."

"As if I could sleep now. Besides, it's not even two o'clock." She stared at the photo Tricia handed her. "Believe me, I am anything but tired. Stay with me for a little while longer. Help distract my mind from all of this."

Two o'clock? One hour had felt like twelve. "What would you like to talk about?" He didn't know how to idly chitchat with a pregnant woman. He sat on the edge of the chair, braced for a quick exit. He'd already crossed too many lines this evening. "Baby names? You mentioned earlier that you haven't chosen one yet. Do you have any in mind?" Dylan couldn't believe what he was saying. He sounded like his mother. Now, there was a woman who would have been right at home discussing babies with Emma. If only she hadn't moved to California, he could have called and asked her to trade places with him. For both his and Emma's sake.

"I haven't even had a chance to buy a baby name book yet." A tinge of pink rose to her cheeks. "I've been busting my butt to close this deal before I go on maternity leave."

"There is no deal, Emma. I know the ranch is in trouble, but I'll find a way to save it. Selling is not an option. Your vision for it doesn't mesh with mine."

"Can you hand me my bag over there?"

Dylan retrieved the large leather purse from the windowsill. Emma dug inside of it and removed a small black tablet. "Let me show you my plans for Silver Bells."

"You have got to be kidding me. You're in the hospital, supposedly concerned about your baby and you're still trying to convince me to sell. No wonder your blood pressure is so high. Instead of fixating on my ranch, you should download a baby name book on that thing." Dylan returned the chair he had been sitting on to its original place against the wall. "I think it's time for me to call it a night."

"I am concerned about my baby. That's why I came to Montana."

"That doesn't make any sense."

"Once I have this baby, I won't be able to travel for work any longer. I can't afford a nanny to fly around the world with me. My job pays for my expenses only. Not a companion's. I don't have a husband or anyone else at home to leave my child with while I go on business trips. Besides, I plan to nurse my daughter. I can't be gone twenty days a month and do that. I'm on my own. I shouldn't even be telling you any of this, but maybe you'll understand if I do." Emma took a deep breath before continuing. "The promotion I told you about earlier isn't something I want. It's something I need. Without it, I'll have to accept a lesser position. Living in Chicago is expensive enough. Even more so when you're a single mom. I need to secure my child's future and the only way I can do that is to convince you to sell. You only heard the initial proposal. Your uncle changed a lot of things. He told me you wouldn't give him the time of day when it came to discussing the plans. At least look at our final design. You might be surprised."

"I'm sorry. I sympathize with your situation, but I can't put your job security above my employees. Including myself. Regardless of what your plan is, you've already said there are no guarantees you would rehire my employees and even if there were, they would be out of work for months. That alone is why I won't hear you out. Change those parameters and then maybe I'd be willing to listen. But you're still asking me to give up a part of my family. Silver Bells was my uncle's ranch. A place I found a hell of a lot of serenity in during some really dark times."

"Your uncle was willing to give it up. And I'm sorry, but there is no way I can promise to take on a full staff while they're renovating the ranch. It doesn't fit into the timetable."

"Then you don't fit into mine. I'm sorry, Emma." Dylan noticed her blood pressure had increased since the doctor had left the room. "I'll return in the morning to see how you're doing. I wish you would take the doctor's advice and relax for the rest of the day. I don't know what the relationship is between you and your family, but maybe you should call them. Or a friend, at least. Let business rest for a while. I'll see you tomorrow."

Dylan awkwardly waved as he beelined for the door. Once out in the hallway, he questioned if he'd been too hard on her. He resisted the urge to peek back in her room to make sure she was okay. He'd already gotten far too involved. The gnawing at the pit of his stomach told him this was just the beginning.

Emma stared at the doorway, willing Dylan to return. She hadn't meant to run him off. While it was true she wanted to talk business, the truth was she didn't want to be alone. And while she needed to acquire the ranch to secure her promotion, Silver Bells happened to be the only subject they had in common.

Great job, Emma. You managed to run off another man. Not that Dylan Slade was of any consequence. Well, at least not outside of work. Although, if Paul had been half as attentive as Dylan had been today, they might still be together. She knew very little about his personal life, but Jax had made a point to mention on more than one occasion that Dylan was single. If he was as stubborn about everything else in his life as he was about the sale of the ranch, she could understand why. Regardless, the fact he had remained by her side spoke volumes to his integrity. She wouldn't mind a man like that in her life. She could do without the orneriness, though.

Emma wanted to remain calm, but the constant flutter in her belly made it impossible. Never mind the glare of the fetal monitor screen, the repeated squeeze of the blood-pressure cuff, the annoying pulse oximeter at the end of her finger and the two bands wrapped around her belly. They were constant reminders that things were not okay. While her pregnancy had been a surprise, she had adjusted rather quickly to the idea of being a mom despite her ex-good-for-nothing walking out on her.

She wanted to give her daughter the love and attention she hadn't received growing up. As far as her parents were concerned, she was surprised they had found time to conceive a child since they sure hadn't had time to raise one. Not that she'd had a difficult life, because hers had been rather charmed. At least from the outside looking in.

Nannies had raised her until she went away to boarding school. She'd traveled the world on vacations and had even spent a semester at sea aboard a luxury cruise liner. But there was a price for being away from home most of her childhood. She never felt a bond with her parents. Her baby wasn't even born and she felt more of a bond with her daughter than she'd ever felt with her own mother. When she had spent time with them, they'd been far from affectionate. She had received more attention from her nannies and she refused to ever play a secondary role to a stand-in mom.

Her mother was an appellate court judge and her father was a neurosurgeon. Their work tended to come above needless hugs or petty playtime. They had groomed Emma to succeed, and she craved that success. But only so she could become a hands-on mother and be able to make enough money to raise her daughter more conventionally.

Emma pulled her phone from her bag and scrolled through the contacts. She hadn't even told her parents she was going to Montana. Not that they expected her to keep them apprised of her travel schedule. She tapped the screen and waited for them to answer. After the fifth ring, she just about gave up when she heard her mother's voice.

"Hi, Mom. I just wanted to let you know I'm in the hospital."

"You're having the baby?" Kate Sheridan asked. "Is it that time already?"

Emma sighed. She envied the women whose mothers had their due date circled on the calendar and counted down week by week with them. "Hopefully not for another eight weeks. The doctor will be happy with six, though. I'm in Montana on business and I started having contractions. Turns out they were only Braxton-Hicks, but they're keeping me in the hospital overnight because my blood pressure is elevated. They want to rule out preeclampsia."

"You're keeping your weight down, aren't you?" Kate asked. Her mother was obsessed with other people's weight. They could be the most beautiful people in the world, but heaven forbid they carried an extra five pounds. Her mother always had to point it out.

"I'm doing fine. Thank you for asking, though." Emma huffed. "And yes, I'm keeping my weight down." As long as she didn't count the food she'd eaten in the last twenty-four hours.

"Emma, if you called to argue, I don't have time for it."

"I thought you would be concerned." The hint of a contraction warned her to remain calm. "My mistake."

"You had some false labor pains. It's common. I'm glad you're okay, but it's nothing to get upset over. I'm assuming you're there to wrap up that ranch deal."

Emma exhaled slowly. "I'm trying to, but the owner doesn't want to sell."

"I don't know what you're going to do, then. You need this promotion."

"I will figure it out." She ground her back teeth together.

"I'm sure you will. You always do. You're a strong woman, Emma. Don't forget that."

Amazingly enough, when Emma had found out she was pregnant, her parents hadn't gotten upset. She'd expected them to chastise her, but they said they had faith in her ability to raise a child without a partner to lean on. They also made it clear that their parents hadn't helped them and they expected her to stand on her own if she was determined to keep her child. At least her mother thought she was strong, because today she felt anything but.

"Thank you, Mom. I have some notes to review since I can't do much of anything else right now. I will give you a call if anything changes. I should be released tomorrow."

"Okay. Get to work."

"Bye, Mom."

Emma rested her head against the pillow and closed her eyes. She didn't know what she had expected from that conversation, but some concern or comforting words would have been nice. Another twinge from deep within her body jolted her upright. She quickly checked the numerous screens next to the bed, not exactly sure what she was looking for. No bells and alarms went off. That was a good sign. The cuff around her arm tightened. She checked the monitor over her left shoulder. 135/80. It wasn't great but it was still better than the 140/90 it had read when she was admitted.

"Easy, butter bean." She needed to choose a name for her daughter. Calling her a vegetable, however sweetly intended, no longer felt right. She didn't even have a birthing plan. Or a crib. Or a car seat. Or anything. She kept meaning to sign up for the prepared childbirth and infant care classes the hospital offered in Chicago but hadn't found the time yet. Jennie had offered to go with her for support. Considering they only held the classes once a month, she needed to make it a priority.

Emma opened the web browser on her tablet and registered for the next available classes. Her first and second Saturdays of the new year were officially booked. At least she felt she'd accomplished something for her daughter.

She pressed the call button and asked for something to drink. The doctor said her baby was strong and healthy, and she intended to keep her that way. If that meant temporary bed rest then so be it. It would give her the opportunity to reformulate her plan of attack on Dylan Slade. She needed to find a way to make things work for them both. She couldn't give him what he wanted. She couldn't guarantee jobs and she couldn't promise employment for the next six months.

Her decisions affected many people regardless of what she did or didn't do. In the end, some people would lose their jobs. There was no avoiding it. It weighed on her conscience with each acquisition, but it was business and she couldn't allow her personal feelings to get in the way.

Chapter 6

"You've got to be kidding me." It was two in the morning and Dylan added another outstanding invoice to the growing mound beside him. Sleep had evaded him as he pored over the ranch's financial records in his uncle's office. He'd uncovered more debts Jax had hidden from him. Maybe hidden wasn't fair. But they were debts Dylan hadn't known about. "What are you doing to me Jax?"

His uncle had handled most of the business affairs while he oversaw the management and maintenance of the many ranch buildings, including the lodge, private guest cabins and stables, along with the ranch's 730 acres and almost a hundred horses.

Dylan had gone to the lodge office to get Emma out of his head. He thought if he searched hard enough, he'd uncover an overlooked bank account or discover some way to keep the ranch and send her packing. The farther she was from him, the better. His heart had grown restless ever since she stepped foot on Silver Bells putting him in a dangerous and vulnerable position. And those were two words he refused to entertain.

The increased debt meant the money he had in savings wouldn't carry the ranch for as long as he'd anticipated. He was in more trouble than he thought. There had to be a way out. He just hadn't found it yet. He sighed heavily and removed another unmarked folder from one of many file boxes next to the desk. It was either this or call everyone they'd done business with over the years and ask if the ranch owed them money. At this point, he didn't know which would be easier.

By the time Dylan entered the stables later that morning, he had already downed two pots of coffee and was no closer to a solution.

Regardless of how many times he said he wouldn't sell Emma's company the ranch, if he didn't come up with alternative financing soon, he feared he would have to sell to someone. But it wouldn't be Emma. They wanted to destroy the place he loved.

Garrett and his two kids were visiting for Christmas and Dylan debated about asking his brother one more time if he'd consider buying into the ranch. He'd asked him a year ago, when Jax first started his rumblings about selling the ranch, but Garrett said he didn't want to uproot the kids. It had been almost three years since his sister-in-law Rebecca had died from cancer and his brother had thrown himself into managing her parents' cattle ranch in Wyoming.

Every time they spoke on the phone, Garrett sounded wearier of living under their roof. He had said numerous times he felt like they were living in a constant state of depression. Maybe he'd reconsider this time. The only thing stopping Dylan was his conscience. Did he really want to be responsible for his brother sinking his savings into a ranch that may not turn around when he had two kids to support?

"Hey, man," Wes said from behind Dylan's desk as he entered his office. "I expected you here an hour ago."

"And I expected you not to show up for work again." Dylan crossed the room and hitched his thumb signaling for Wes to get up. "I was at the lodge going through Jax's less-than-stellar filing system."

"Find anything to help you?" Wes grabbed his coffee and a notepad before standing.

"Nope." Dylan rubbed his morning stubble. He should shave before visiting Emma at the hospital. Then again, it wasn't like he had to impress her. "What are you working on?" Dylan angled his head to read the notes tucked under Wes's arm as he walked by.

"Just working out some dates." Wes pushed up his hat. "A rodeo school in Ramblewood, Texas, offered me a teaching position during my last competition. I called them yesterday and accepted. I'm going to head down there on the second. The job will still allow me to compete and I'll be doing what I love most. Bull riding."

"That soon, huh?" Dylan hated losing another employee, not that Wes was around much. But even more so, he hated losing his brother. "It sounds like a great opportunity, but are you sure this is what you want?"

"Staying is too hard." Wes shook his head. "Even harder now that Jax is gone. There are too many reminders here. Every time I drive into town I keep thinking I see Dad's truck or Mom coming out of a store. It's been five years and I still hear people talking behind my back about Ryder. Garrett had the right idea. He got far away from Saddle Ridge. I need that clean break. I want to spend one last Christmas with you guys, and then I'm out."

His brother's words felt like a fist to the gut. "One last Christmas? You're not planning to come home ever again?"

"Don't you get it?" Deep lines creased Wes's forehead. "Saddle Ridge isn't home anymore. Ryder destroyed that. I have tried, Lord help me, I've tried, but I can't do this anymore. I need to be some place where every corner doesn't hold a memory of what once was. I'm tired of looking backwards."

"Yeah, I get it." Out of the five brothers, Wes had taken their father's death the hardest, not counting the guilt Ryder had to live with. "If you ever change your mind, the door here is always open."

Wes laughed under his breath. "Providing you still have a door to keep open."

"Ain't that the truth." Dylan sat down behind his desk. "If you can think of any potential investors, let me know. I'd ask you, but I already know the answer."

"Sell."

"What?"

Wes took the last swig of his coffee and tossed the cup in the trash. "Sell this place and start over someplace else. Come to Texas with me. You can do this same thing down there, only without the snow."

"I can't give up."

"You can't or you won't?" Wes strode to the office door. "Just remember, wherever I am, my door's always open, too."

Dylan leaned back in his chair and pinched the bridge of his nose. He wished letting go was as easy for him as it was for Wes. It would make his life a hell of a lot easier.

Two hours later, Dylan arrived at the hospital to check on Emma. She'd been at the forefront of his mind all morning. Despite their temporary truce, he needed to continually remind himself who he was dealing with. The woman wanted to destroy the place that had become his sanctuary. The Silver Bells Ranch wasn't intended to be a five-star couples-only luxury resort with yoga and mud baths. The only mud you'd find here was on the bottom of your boots and chances were it wasn't mud. His ranch was a chuck wagon, line dancing, horse-riding-in-the-Montana-mountains experience. That's what people wanted. At least, they had until other guest ranches had cropped up in the Saddle Ridge area. Now Silver Bells had to compete with the new. He needed to find a way to keep the ranch open without going further in debt. Time was ticking down and all income would officially end in two weeks. If the ranch went under that meant the last five years of his life had been for naught.

He had lost everything he loved most when he invested in the ranch and had devoted every waking hour since to forget Lauren and the kids. He had succeeded up until now. Emma's presence reminded him how much he still wanted a family. At thirty-five, his chances grew slimmer each day. Especially when he didn't have the time to meet someone or go out on a date.

He envied the families Garrett and Harlan had created. Granted, he wasn't the only Slade sibling without kids. His brother Wes was adamantly against them while his other brother Ryder still had five and a half years left on his ten-year prison sentence.

"I have to be able to travel." Dylan heard Emma say as he approached her hospital room. "Once I wrap up my business here, I have a job to get back to. I can't stay in Montana until New Year's Day. You just mean I can't fly, right?"

"No travel at all. Definitely no planes from this point forward. Trains are too dangerous because medical care isn't immediately available if you need it. The same with driving, although the likelihood of a hospital being close by is greater. I don't want you in a seated position for that long. Light exercise is the best thing for you. I will give you a list of what you can and can't do. I'm releasing you from the hospital, but you're not out of the woods yet. Providing there are no further issues during the next two weeks, the train would be your safest bet because you can get up and move around. But not now."

Dylan removed his hat and raked his hand through his hair. He couldn't handle Emma on his ranch for another two weeks. She'd drive him insane.

He cleared his throat loudly to announce his presence before entering the room. "How's the patient this morning?" He didn't want to let on he had overheard their conversation. "You look better." Her color had returned to a delicate pink porcelain compared to the borderline red she had exhibited yesterday. Her blood pressure monitor registered 125/80. Definite improvement there.

"The doctor just told me I can't travel for two weeks." A nurse unfastened one of Emma's belly bands.

Dylan swallowed hard. "Um, is that really necessary?"

The doctor's eyes narrowed at his question. "For the sake of my patient and her unborn child, yes. Yes, it is." She redirected her attention to Emma. "You can choose to do what you want, but I strongly advise you to stay put. Your contractions went on longer than we had anticipated last night. We received your records from your obstetrician in Chicago. After conferring with him, we feel it's best if you stay where I can monitor you closely. I'll get your discharge papers ready and I'll be in to see you before you leave."

"I don't know what I'm going to do." Emma shifted so the nurse could remove the second belly band and fetal monitor. "This was only supposed to be a two- or three-day trip. My doctor told me I could fly up to thirty-four weeks. So much for that."

Dylan's mind raced in a million directions. As much as he didn't want to get involved, he couldn't possibly turn her out in the cold with only six days until Christmas.

"You're welcome to stay at the ranch for as long as you need."

"I appreciate that. I promise not to be too much trouble."

Dylan wasn't so sure about that. "No more arguing with me over the ranch, though. It just upsets both of us."

The nurse stopped unhooking Emma from her various monitors and regarded him briefly before continuing. Dylan had tried to sound as sympathetic yet firm as possible without coming across as an insensitive jerk. Apparently, he failed at sensitivity.

Emma mumbled a halfhearted okay before easing out of the opposite side of the bed. Dylan averted his eyes just as she realized he had been privy to her pink cotton-clad bottom thanks to the open-backed gown. He had to hand it to her…she was in fine shape at eight months pregnant.

She gripped at her gown. "I can't wait to get into my own clothes. Make that a change of clothes." She grabbed the sweater and leggings she had worn yesterday from a chair and padded toward the bathroom in her thin hospital slippers. "I'll be out in a minute." She began to close the door and then hesitated. "Are the roads open or did you take the snowcat halfway here again?"

"They're open."

"Then would you mind giving me a ride to the ranch?"

"You don't even have to ask."

"Thank you." She smiled sweetly before closing the door. Now that was a smile he could get used to. Not that he wanted to get used to her smile, because Emma wasn't going to be in town long enough for him to get attached to it. She was there for two weeks only.

"I'm going to run down to the cafeteria," Dylan said to the nurse. "That should give her time to do what she needs to do before we go home. I mean back to the ranch. We don't live together."

Dylan groaned. He couldn't escape the room fast enough. He half walked, half ran down the corridor, desperate to distance himself from all things Emma.

Two weeks. He didn't know how he'd survive two weeks and the holidays near her every day. Sure, he could make a point of avoiding her, but even he wasn't that heartless. Maybe he could convince his sister-in-law, Belle, to spend some time with Emma. They could talk babies and pregnancy.

Dylan's mind was racing by the time he reached the cafeteria. He wanted Emma and her baby off his ranch, but the image of the ultrasound had been burned in his brain. Scared as she may be, Emma was far from weak. He had a suspicion she just hadn't realized her own strength. It wasn't his job to point it out or steer her in the right direction. And it certainly wasn't his place to build her daughter a rocking horse, yet he had found himself sketching one repeatedly on his notepad last night. He'd taken up woodworking in high school and had always found the hobby relaxing. He hadn't thought of building anything child-related since Lauren had packed up her kids and left.

He poured a cup of coffee and sighed. The next two weeks couldn't go by fast enough.

Climbing into the passenger side of Dylan's lifted pickup truck was no easy feat in her condition, even with Dylan's assistance. Emma wasn't a big fan of lifted trucks, or any truck for that matter. What was it about boys and their toys? She couldn't even fathom getting a child fastened in a car seat in one of these contraptions. But then, she guessed that was the point. What man wanted to be bothered toting an infant around town? Sure, it looked well and good on television, but most of the men she worked with drove sports cars they had purchased with their yearly bonuses and she guaranteed they were car-seat free. They were in a league she had worked hard to join for the last six years. Unless she closed this deal, it would be forever out of her reach.

But how could she convince Dylan to see things her way when he had refused to discuss it further?

"She's only eighteen weeks along, but I'm sure she'd love to get together with you."

"Huh?" Emma stared at him.

"You didn't hear a word I said, did you?"

"No, I'm sorry. My mind was…elsewhere."

"I was talking about my sister-in-law, Belle. She's eighteen weeks pregnant and I'm sure she would love to meet you." Dylan steered the truck out of the hospital parking lot. "She and Harlan live on the other side of town. Maybe we can even go over there if you're up to it. She runs an animal rescue center if you're into that sort of thing."

"Like a dog shelter?"

"No like a farm animal sanctuary. She takes in animals that were injured or born with deformities. Some have suffered ill-treatment or have been rescued from backyard butchers. Any animal in need of a safe forever home can live out their life at Belle's Forever Ranch. They even have a cow named Cash—after Johnny Cash—who will be fitted with a prosthesis shortly, since he had a lower leg amputation this past summer. She does have a few Great Pyrenees watchdogs, though. They protect the center from predators."

"I didn't know places like that existed."

"You need to get out of the city more."

"I will have you know I've traveled the world over numerous times. It's just that most of my destinations are—how should I phrase it—a little more exclusive." Dylan winced at her description and she immediately regretted her poor choice of words. "Not that Saddle Ridge isn't exclusive."

"No, I get it. Saddle Ridge is a small town. So, I have to ask, why are you so interested in my property when places like Aspen and Lake Tahoe fit the lifestyle you're promoting?"

"Price and acreage for one. Saddle Ridge has the same outdoor attractions the well-known resort areas have. We've been looking to acquire a large ranch away from the usual travel destinations but not completely off the beaten path. We want to take full advantage of northwestern Montana's year-round activities without sacrificing an ounce of luxury. I get that you're against my vision, but people can enjoy the rugged outdoors and still be pampered once they return to the resort. It's like outfitting a bunkhouse with cots versus feather beds. What you're sleeping on doesn't make it any less of a bunkhouse."

"It does when you're gutting the interior and exterior of the bunkhouse and then hanging a sign on the door that says yoga retreat."

"Nobody wants to gut Silver Bells. But even you must admit, it needs some serious updating. And I know you've put a lot of time, money and effort into the place. Your uncle told me everything you've done and what you have accomplished is great. But turning this ranch around is bigger than that. It costs much more money than you have. I want to preserve the log cabins, but they need renovations. Especially the bathrooms, along with all the bathrooms in the lodge. And we have many plans for that building. A state-of-the-art kitchen along with new energy-efficient windows throughout. The heating system needs an upgrade and the guest rooms need new furnishings. That's just the beginning. We want to bring the buildings back to life, not cover them up. I've done a solid year of market research and our capital partners have signed off on our ideas. We have the resources to create a beautiful resort experience, if you'll let us."

Emma wanted to say more, but already feared she'd said too much. She had agreed not to mention the sale again, at least not until she found another angle to work.

"Say I agree to your terms," Dylan began, giving her a glimmer of hope. "What are the chances of your acquisitions firm or another of your investors buying more properties in Saddle Ridge with the idea of capitalizing on your luxury spa resort? As it stands now, Saddle Ridge is a very affordable place to live. If your investors begin buying smaller mom-and-pop stores to set up high-end boutiques that will push our local businessmen and women out, which would eventually raise the median real estate prices, then the town becomes unaffordable for those who live here now. Austin, Charleston, Nashville are prime examples, never mind Aspen itself."

The man clearly did his homework. "I can't say that hasn't happened in the past and there's always that possibility. But with the increased home prices and business sales comes an influx of cash to those who sell."

"You're under the assumption it's about money. I know a lot of people here who would stay regardless of what they were offered. That and the fact we like our sleepy town just the way it is."

"If that's the case, then why are you so concerned?"

"Because there's an equal amount that would sell. My uncle was one of them." Emma watched Dylan's knuckles turn white as he gripped the steering wheel tighter. "What about my horses? What are your plans for them?" He braked at a red light and faced her. "I know Jax had them written into the sale, despite my protests."

"Some would remain here, but others would most likely be sold."

"To who? Sold to other local ranches or sold for slaughter? And what would you do with the horses that remained during your six-month renovation?"

"They wouldn't be left to fend for themselves, Dylan. They would have caretakers assigned to them. Most likely people who are already working on your ranch. Or you, if that's what you want. We can write it into the contract." Emma hadn't expected a barrage of questions on the way back. "As for selling the horses, I can't imagine they would be sold for slaughter."

"Then you have a lot to learn about the horse industry." Dylan held up his hand to stop her from saying anything further as he stepped on the accelerator. "I said I wasn't going to do this and I won't debate it further. It doesn't matter what your answer is, I'm not selling."

Emma remained silent for the remainder of the short drive, chastising herself for once again blowing her opportunity to change Dylan's mind. His questions were valid and had piqued her curiosity. She hadn't thought about who the horses would be sold to before. Now she wondered herself.

By the time they reached the ranch, Emma was barely able to keep her eyes open. She hadn't slept much last night courtesy of the butter bean. Tired as she was, the massive Christmas tree at the front entrance of the Silver Bells lodge snapped her awake.

"Oh, how pretty!" Large silver bell ornaments glistened in the morning sun on the two-story tree. "How did you get it up and decorated so fast?"

Dylan cut the engine and silently stared at her as if she had two heads.

"What? Am I not supposed to ask questions, now?"

"No, you can ask whatever you'd like."

"Then what's the problem? Don't you like Christmas?" she asked.

Dylan laughed. "I love Christmas. I'm just surprised you didn't notice that blue spruce yesterday or during your previous visits to the ranch. It's been growing in that very spot probably since before you were born. We always decorate it on the first of December."

How could she have missed a giant Christmas tree? How could she have missed the tree period since it was a permanent fixture?

Dylan hopped out of the truck and held the passenger door open for her. "Maybe you need to slow down a little and appreciate what's in front of you instead of trying to change what you never really saw in the first place." He held out his hand to help her step down onto the pavement. "Humor me for a second. Do your new plans for the ranch include this tree? Or was it eliminated from the architectural drawings?"

Emma shook her head. "I don't remember seeing it on any of the sketches. I can only assume it was removed to showcase the lodge's facade instead of hiding it."

"Is that how you see it right now? A tree covering up a building?"

"No." Emma's palm seared against his. "It's the most beautiful Christmas tree I've ever seen. And I've seen Christmas all over the world. I get what you're saying. It does enhance the place. It doesn't detract from it. I'm ashamed to admit I hadn't noticed it before."

"Then it would be fair to say you may have over-looked other parts of the ranch as well?"

Emma released his hand. "Possibly, but you can't dis-regard all my suggestions because I overlooked a tree. Based on what your uncle told me, even you've admit-ted the ranch needs more updates than you can afford."

"You still don't get it, do you?" Dylan held open the lodge entrance door for her. "If you can miss some-thing as big as a tree, you're running in the wrong gear. I know Saddle Ridge isn't where you had planned to spend Christmas. Since you're stuck here, take the time to get to know some of my employees. Now that the roads are open, go in to town and meet people. Go baby shopping. You can send things back to Chicago after the holiday. You're surrounded by the Swan Range and Mission Mountains. Enjoy the scenery and focus on your daughter. I'm sure your job will understand when you tell them you're laid up for medical reasons. And we have Wi-Fi so it's not like you're cut off from the outside world."

Emma closed her eyes. She already dreaded telling Charlie about her travel restrictions. Knowing him, he'd see it as another advantage. And if she returned to Chi-cago after two weeks without a contract in hand, she'd be lucky to still have any job at the firm.

"Thank you for yesterday, this morning and in ad-vance for the next two weeks." She dug in her bag for her room key.

Emma didn't wait for him to respond. She was in desperate need of a shower and a change of clothes. She wound her way past the numerous poinsettia plants sur-rounding the front desk and then looked up and saw the enormous Christmas wreath hanging from the second-floor balcony and the garland draped along the railing on either side of it. *Could she have been that blind?* She wanted to believe Dylan was playing a colossal joke on her. As much as she wanted to think it wasn't her fault, he was right.

She had been laser focused on acquiring Silver Bells. What was wrong with that, though? So she was career-oriented. She had goals she wanted to obtain for her and her daughter. Financial security was everything. She had two weeks to come up with an alternate plan and she'd stop at nothing to succeed. Her daughter's future depended on it.

Chapter 7

Outside of lunch, Emma spent much of the day in her room napping. Now she was wide awake and probably would be for the rest of the night. An hour ago, Dylan had phoned her room to check up on her. She wondered why he had made the call himself instead of asking the front desk to do it, then she figured after he'd seen her at her worst, the formality of their relationship had gone out the window.

To her surprise, he asked if she would be interested in going on a group sleigh ride, and even warned that if she did, she had to either ride up front with him or Wes, because the seats had already been reserved by couples. After Sandy had mentioned sleigh riding yesterday, she didn't care where she rode as long as she got to go. She had never thought she'd have the opportunity to ride in an open sleigh and refused to pass up the chance.

The crisp sting of cold Montana air against her cheeks couldn't quell her excitement. The landscape was majestic once she took the time to appreciate it. Last night's snow had heavily blanketed the trees. The below-freezing temperatures had created a thin ice-covered crust on top of the snow, creating a diamond-like sparkle. And when the winds gently blew, the horizon exploded in a magical dance of glistening elegance. She thought she had stepped into a photograph. Mother Nature had outdone herself.

Dylan and Wes approached their group wearing bright red snow pants and heavy black boots. Their red parkas hung open revealing red suspenders over white thermal shirts. Santa wished he looked that sexy. They led two teams of palomino-colored Belgian draft horses pulling two large red sleighs. Actual sleighs, like in the Christmas song! Emma practically bounced up and down like a little kid.

When Sandy had mentioned sleigh riding yesterday, she thought she was joking. Today at lunch Emma had asked what horse breeds the ranch owned. Dylan's question about who they would be sold to after the sale still bothered her and she wanted to learn all she could about the magnificent animals.

It puzzled Emma why Silver Bells wasn't advertising sleigh rides and snowcat tours. After scouring their website again, she finally found mention of both tour packages at the end of the booking page. Both items needed to be front and center. From a tourist's standpoint, those activities would have drawn her in. But there was no mention of either in their brochures, which were sparse and outdated. They didn't even mention Wi-Fi. It baffled her and explained why the new competition had gobbled up their customers. She'd love to see the ranch's marketing budget.

"Okay, momma-to-be. You get to board first." A sexy cowboy Santa jarred her back to reality. "Do you want to ride with me or my brother?" Dylan asked.

"I guess you," Emma answered wondering how he would have reacted if she had said Wes.

Dylan guided her to the first row of the sleigh. He had lined the front seat with layers of faux fur blankets to keep her warm while the rest of the rows only had a wool blanket. He had expected her to choose him and it made her feel like a princess in one of those Hallmark movies. Okay, so Dylan was no Prince Charming, and she had never seen a pregnant princess in a fairytale, but she allowed herself the fantasy for a few minutes. Work be damned, she was going to enjoy every second of her sleigh ride.

Dylan slid in beside her. The length of his strong, muscular body pressed against her side as he picked up the reins and clucked his tongue. The sound of sleigh bells jingled as the horses plodded through the snow with ease. She never imagined herself riding in a horse-drawn sleigh through the Montana wilderness. Okay, so it wasn't exactly the wild here on the ranch, but close enough to it.

"I don't think I've seen anyone smile that big before," Dylan said.

"You have no idea." Emma looked behind her to see if the other passengers were as excited as she was. Some of them came close, but she owned it. "I've wanted to do this since I was old enough to know what a horse-drawn sleigh was. It's near the top of my bucket list."

"I knew it. I knew you had a list." Dylan laughed.

"Doesn't everybody?"

Dylan shrugged. "I don't."

"Sure you do. It doesn't have to be written down to be a bucket list." Emma nudged him playfully with her elbow. "Come on, what's something you absolutely must do before you die?"

"Raise a family."

And in the frigid cold of the Montana winter, Emma melted.

Emma's enthusiasm was contagious. Even he found himself in a better mood than he'd been in all day. "Why don't you lead us off in *Jingle Bells*?"

"Me?" She laughed heartily. "I don't sing. At least not very well."

"The horses don't mind and neither do I." He playfully nudged her arm. "Entertain us."

For someone who didn't sing, she didn't take much coaxing. She belted out the song at the top of her lungs and then actually looked surprised when the rest of the group joined in. Within minutes, their sleigh was out-singing his brother's.

He sighed at the realization these moments with his brother were about to end. He'd miss Wes once he moved. One more loss to add to the list. Regardless of how he felt, he couldn't fault him for wanting to move on with his life.

In a way, he was beginning to understand what Jax had meant when he told Emma one of the reason's he was selling was so Dylan could move on from Lauren and the kids. His uncle didn't realize he had made that transition years ago. A part of him wondered if Jax sensed he was going to die. Was that what drove him to sell the place Dylan always assumed he had loved more than life? If the sale had happened first, Dylan would have had money without any responsibilities. But Jax had failed to realize that the responsibility of the ranch made him happy. Now more than ever, he wanted to keep Silver Bells in memory of his uncle. Maybe listening to Emma's presentation would give him ideas on how to save the ranch.

After an hour-and-a-half long sleigh ride, Dylan and Wes dropped their guests off in front of the lodge. Sandy had warm apple cider, hot chocolate and cookies waiting for the guests while Dylan and Wes finished tending to their teams.

After they had joined everyone at the lodge, Wes disappeared within minutes. Probably with whatever single woman was available. His brother believed in loving and leaving them fast before either of them got attached. Dylan on the other hand, hadn't been with anyone since Lauren.

He set out in search of Emma, hoping the ride hadn't been too much for her. Although, by the looks of things, she'd had the time of her life. And that's what he wanted her to experience every day.

He found her sitting in the same chair by the fireplace that he had helped her out of only two days prior. This time, she was holding Melinda's infant daughter in her arms. He couldn't imagine another woman looking more beautiful or natural holding a baby than Emma Slade.

Sheridan!

Her last name was Sheridan. Dylan couldn't believe his subconscious gave her his last name. Sure, he was attracted to Emma and had even enjoyed getting to know her better over the past few days, but that's where it ended. He had too much going on in his life even to consider marriage to anyone. Especially when he had zero claim to her child.

No.

Definitely not.

Dylan shook his head. He and Emma weren't anything other than two people thrown together by happenstance. If she hadn't been after the ranch, neither one of them would have ever given the other a second look. Okay, so he would have looked. But she wouldn't have.

"Do you have a tick or something?" Luke interrupted his thoughts.

"What? No. Why?" Dylan stared at the man.

"You're shaking your head like the dogs do when something's biting at them." Luke looked from Dylan to Emma and back again.

"Oh. Now it makes sense."

"What makes sense?" Dylan felt his good mood beginning to slip away.

"Emma's caught your eye. Sandy told me there was some romance brewing between the two of you."

"Sandy needs to stop spreading rumors." Dylan rolled his eyes. "I assure you, there is nothing going on except genuine concern for her and her daughter. I thought she was losing that baby. I've never seen someone so scared in my entire life. Never mind how terrified I was. But they're safe now, and I'll make sure they continue to be safe for as long as she's here."

"Yep. You've got it bad, man." Luke slapped him on the back. "She looks pretty good holding that baby, doesn't she?"

Dylan took off his hat and whacked Luke with it. "I

do not have it bad for her." Suddenly the room felt hot and for a minute, he thought he might suffocate. He had no romantic feelings for Emma whatsoever. And he planned to keep it that way.

After her heart slowed to a normal rate, Emma began to enjoy holding Gabriella in her arms. She had always heard people say nothing smelled better than a baby. She couldn't fathom what they meant. She had always equated babies with smelly diapers and sour spit-up. Now she understood the meaning. Gabriella had a certain scent. It was like a new car scent for humans. It was innocent and clean.

And those tiny fingers! Gabriella wrapped her hand around Emma's index finger and didn't let go. She couldn't believe the amount of strength a six-month-old had. She was a bundle of perfection, making Emma even more excited to meet her own daughter. The next eight weeks would be agonizingly slow. And she still wasn't the least bit prepared.

Hopefully the doctor would clear her after the two weeks, but there weren't any guarantees. She wondered if she ordered baby items online if they would arrive at the ranch before she left for home due to the holidays. She couldn't have them sent to her apartment in Chicago because nobody was there to receive them. She could try shopping in town, not that she expected them to have anything that she needed.

She had handled her entire pregnancy poorly. She'd put everything baby-related on the back burner while she focused solely on her career. It hadn't mattered how many times she had sworn she wouldn't repeat her mother's patterns, because that was exactly what she had done.

She should have completed her daughter's nursery already. Her desk and bookcases along with boxes of client research files still filled the room. She couldn't move them until she figured out how to make an office fit elsewhere in the apartment. She needed to get rid of half of what she owned to make room for the baby's things. The office was a definite must, so either the living room or the dining area needed to go. Eating at a table was overrated, anyway.

None of it may matter, though. She'd have to move into a one-bedroom elsewhere if she didn't close this deal. The lower salary of her demoted position wouldn't cover her current rent.

Anxiety rapidly replaced Emma's short-lived baby joy.

"Are you all right?" Melinda asked.

"No. I'm not." Gabriella began to cry in her arms.

Melinda lifted the baby and gently rocked her. "It's okay. She's just picking up on your tension. You should be happy. You're about to have a baby."

"I don't know what I'm going to do."

"Talk to us." Sandy perched on the overstuffed arm of the chair. "Maybe we can help."

"I wish it were that simple." Emma filled in Melinda, Rhonda and Sandy about her apartment situation. She left out the part regarding the sale of the ranch. As far as they knew, the deal was off. They'd hate her if they found out she still intended to change Dylan's mind.

"I don't know much about Chicago, but I can tell you downsizing was the best thing I've ever done," Rhonda said. "I had an apartment before I started working here a few years ago. It was filled with more crap than I knew what to do with. I was juggling multiple jobs depending on the season. I was working non-stop to keep a roof over all my possessions. Then I realized they were possessing me. When Jax told me that room and board were part of my salary here, I hesitated to accept the job. I went home and took inventory of everything I owned. You know what? Ninety percent of it was stuff I could live without. I sold some of it, gave the rest away and moved in here. I have more money now, even though I make less cash because of the room and board. You might be surprised with what you can do without."

"I don't mean to sound harsh." Melinda continued to rock Gabriella, who had gone from crying to cooing. "But I'm a single mom living with an infant in one room that doesn't even have a kitchen in it. Is it ideal? No, but it's not impossible. Regardless whether you move or not, don't get hung up on having a separate office space or a separate baby space. Your daughter isn't going to care if she shares a room with you or if the walls are painted pink. Baby furniture can be ordered online and if you don't have anyone to put the crib together for you, buy from a local store and pay the extra charge for them to put it together or get a portable crib. I don't mean one of those fabric and mesh play yards, I mean a wooden portable crib on wheels. They fold open, set up in seconds and look like a real crib. You can wheel it right into your bedroom. If you're anything like me, you'll want your baby sleeping near you at night."

"One trip to Walmart and you'll be able to pick up all the necessities or you can order it all online and have it shipped," Sandy chimed in. "Melinda had a baby registry there."

They made it sound so logical. "I don't have a baby registry."

"Guess what we're doing after dinner?" Rhonda wrapped an arm around her shoulder. "You've got this, girl. Just remember, the simpler you keep things, the easier they are to change down the line."

A couple hours later, Emma had successfully filled out her baby registry with the womens' help. Even if no one purchased a single item, she had a list of everything she needed and could order it all with a few simple clicks.

Feeling more in control, Emma headed back to her room. She scanned the great room and dining area along the way, hoping to see Dylan. She still needed to convince him to sell, although now it felt like a betrayal to her newfound friends.

He'd kept his distance from her since they'd arrived back at the lodge. She had expected him to join her for dinner as he had during previous meals, but instead he fixed a plate and disappeared. It was as if a switch had flipped when he saw her holding Gabriella. Maybe he'd gotten a good dose of her soon-to-be reality. She couldn't fault him for it. Men didn't want to be bothered with pregnant women.

Two hours later, Dylan texted Emma to meet him in what used to be Jax's old office near the rear of the lodge and he'd listen to her proposal. She didn't even know he had her number. But it didn't matter. She finally had her chance and she refused to blow it.

He silently held the door for her as she entered. No hello, how are you? No greeting of any kind. She could understand him wanting to get down to business, but this bordered on rudeness.

"Are you ready to get started? You have an hour." All friendliness had vanished from his voice, leaving behind a cold detachment. She wondered if he'd have more warmth toward a total stranger.

"Did I upset you in some way?" Emma asked. There was no point in giving a presentation to a contentious audience. She already felt as if she was wasting both of their time.

"You've asked me for this repeatedly and I'm giving it to you. What's the problem?"

Emma sat her bag on the chair across from his desk. "You could at least be cordial." When he didn't respond, she almost turned around and walked out. A soft kick from her daughter reminded her how much rode on this presentation. "Where can I set up?"

They both looked around the room. Stacks of papers, folders and worn loose-leaf binders littered every hard surface. The office had been disorganized when she'd met Jax there, but not to this extent.

"What happened in here?" she asked.

"I did." Dylan grabbed an empty file box from the floor and began piling papers into it. He set it on top of a haphazard stack of folders. "My uncle's so-called filing system is getting the best of me." He faced her, making eye contact for the first time since she'd walked through the door. "Question… Did Jax disclose all of the ranch's debt during your negotiations?"

"Yes. It was part of our due diligence. I can email you the spreadsheet."

Dylan laughed. "A spreadsheet. That would have been nice to have had earlier. You'd think he'd have his own."

"He did. At least, I sent him mine for his approval."

Dylan sat down behind the desk. "I still haven't figured out how to access his email. I'd appreciate seeing what you have. I'm just glad my uncle had the foresight to make me the only heir to his estate or else I'd be scrambling to find a way to buy out my brothers. Jax had every scenario covered in the event of illness or death."

"I know." Emma unzipped her laptop case. "He didn't want to leave anything to chance."

"How would you know that?" The gruffness in his voice took her by surprise. She looked up to see him staring at her incredulously.

"That's part of what we do. We examine all contractual documentation, which is why the process takes so long." She set her computer on the desk. "Your uncle couldn't have sold the ranch without your shares. Why did you go along with it if you were that set against it? You could have bought him out."

Dylan reclined in his chair and regarded her silently before answering. Charlie did the same thing when she asked a question and it bugged the heck out of her. It was as if they were weighing what they should or shouldn't say around her.

"My family has gone through a lot of heartache and misery in recent years. Fighting my uncle would have torn it apart further. Neither of us could afford to buy the other out. The ranch was our life. Silver Bells is all we own after investing every penny we had into it."

Emma hadn't realized how tight Dylan's financial situation was, which made selling even more logical to her. "What were you planning to do after the ranch sold?"

"I hadn't committed to anything yet. My share of the sale would have been decent but not nearly enough to buy another guest ranch. I was interested in a place not far from here, but they had to come way down on the price. The day I made up my mind to buy it, someone else beat me to it with a full price offer. I couldn't counter at that point. Not that it matters anymore. I can float the ranch for only so long. And from the debts I discovered tonight, I won't be able to float it for as long as I thought. I'm curious to see how much debt your spreadsheet tells me I still haven't found."

"Is that why you're willing to listen to my proposal? Because of Jax's debt?" Emma hated being Dylan's last resort. Yes, she wanted him to sell, but because he saw a future and happiness elsewhere. Not because he didn't have any other choice.

"I looked at a few smaller places—around ten to fifteen acres at most—just to live on, but that will tie up my money in case I find a guest ranch I can afford. I had just begun to expand my search into Wyoming near my brother Garrett when Jax died." The leather chair creaked as he tilted it back and rocked. "It's ironic, isn't it? I'm the sole owner of a guest ranch—which is what I wanted— but I can't afford to update it. You already knew that, though. Just like you apparently know more about the ranch finances than I do. Hell, after what you told me yesterday, you may have even known Jax better than me."

Emma didn't like the undercurrent of the conversation. "There's no need to take this out on me." If Dylan wanted to vent, she'd listen, but she wasn't going to tolerate his anger when she had done nothing wrong. "I get that you're upset, but don't get mad at me because of your uncle's lack of communication."

Dylan placed both hands on the desk and slowly rose. "You're right. I'm sorry." He picked up her laptop and handed it to her. "I think we should table this presentation for another time. I'm discovering more than I had anticipated about a lot of things."

Emma jammed the computer into the case and slung the strap over her shoulder. "That's fine." She turned and reached for the door, leaving him to wallow in his misery.

"Nah, honey, I mean it. I really am sorry."

Emma sighed. She should keep going and not look back. After all, tomorrow was another day. Nope... Even channeling her inner Scarlett O'Hara wouldn't save her from his ornery Rhett Butler attitude.

She turned to face him. "We don't have to discuss work. If you want a shoulder to lean on, I'm available. We're stuck here together. Might as well make the best of it, right? I thought we were becoming friends."

"I don't want to be friends with you."

"Wow! You don't mince words, do you?"

"Nope."

"Well, I'm certainly not staying where I'm not wanted." He'd passed rudeness and gone straight to impertinent ass. Emma stormed out of his office and through the lodge, hoping nobody would see her. She'd been a fool to allow any man to get under her skin during her pregnancy. Romance wasn't an option. There wasn't room in her heart for anyone except her daughter, and she had already neglected her daughter's needs because of some tired old ranch. She'd jeopardized her and her baby's health in order to convince Dylan Slade to change his mind. No job was worth that risk.

Charlie had offered to send someone in her place twice and she had said no. If she had agreed and they succeeded in finalizing the paperwork, she still would have had a 50-50 chance of getting her promotion, since the majority of the work had been hers and they couldn't penalize her for being pregnant. Instead, she had balked at the idea of allowing anyone to help her because she didn't like their condescending attitude. She had learned a long time ago that in business there were times when swallowing your pride was necessary. This was one of them.

She jammed the key into the lock of her door. Tomorrow she would look into finding a new place to stay. Even if Dylan had listened to her presentation, it wouldn't have mattered. He'd made up his mind and she had made up hers. It was time to give up.

"You don't understand." Suddenly, Dylan was behind her and filled her doorway before she had a chance to shut the door.

Emma tossed her laptop case on the bed and faced him. "I understood you perfectly."

Dylan closed the distance between them in two long strides. "Being friends with you means not being able to touch you. Not being able to kiss you or hold you in my arms." He held her face in his hands. "Dammit woman, I lose my senses when I'm around you."

His mouth crashed down upon hers, claiming every bit of resolve she had left. She wanted to push him away and avoid the roller coaster of emotions that were certain to accompany this—whatever this was. Instead, she pulled him closer, tasted him deeper and allowed him to brand her with his kisses.

They broke apart and in between panted breaths he whispered, "I don't know you well enough to ask you to stay, but I know enough not to let you go. Not yet."

"This is crazy." Her hands splayed across his chest, wanting to push him away...knowing nothing good could come out of this. His fingers lightly trailed down her neck and shoulders until his arms wound around her, drawing her closer to him. "This can never work. *We* can never work."

Dylan eased her toward the bed. "I know we can't. That doesn't mean we can't enjoy the next two weeks together." He shifted her body, so he could sit on the edge of the bed while she stood in front of him. He lifted her hands and placed them on her belly. Covering them with his own, he smiled as he looked up at her. "Let's see where this takes us. Maybe it won't lead to anything more than a beautiful Christmas memory. Then again, maybe it will be the first of many Christmas memories."

Dylan said the words any woman would love to hear. Any woman who wasn't pregnant and didn't live sixteen hundred miles away. "Dylan, be realistic. I live in Chicago and I come with an eighteen-year commitment. A child is a surreal thought, even for me, and I'm the one who's pregnant. I can't imagine anyone wanting to take on that responsibility."

"It's not an unfamiliar responsibility to me. I've been a father before. And I would've continued being one if my marriage hadn't fallen apart. My father was a family man and he raised me to be the same way. Children don't scare me. But the thought of not having the chance to find out if there is more between us terrifies me. I realized that today."

"Is that why you disappeared after you saw me holding Gabriella?"

"Yes and no. That only confirmed it. It began to hit me this morning when I was driving to the hospital. I realized I couldn't wait to see you. And when the doctor said you had to stay in town for two weeks, I panicked. You were too close and I knew I'd be too tempted to see if we had a chance. And I was right. Between the sleigh ride and seeing you with a baby, I knew I had to find a way out. So I dove into my uncle's finances, hoping I could find a missing bank account or some way to make you leave and stay away for good. Then it hit me. I didn't want you to go."

"But I can't stay, either." Emma crossed the room to gain whatever space she could from him. She needed to think clearly and rationally and being near him clouded her judgment. "All we have are these two weeks, and then I'm gone. I won't change my mind, Dylan, just as you won't change your mind and sell me the ranch. Why did you ask me to give you my presentation tonight?"

"Because I wanted to steal your ideas and see if I could use them to find my own investors."

"Wow." Her heart sank into the pit of her stomach. "That's honest."

Dylan rose from the bed. "I'd never be anything but honest with you."

"But you're not being honest with yourself. So I'll have to be honest enough for the both of us." Emma willed herself to deny him. "I don't think I'm strong enough for a two-week fling with you. Not because I'm afraid I'll stay. I know I won't. I'm afraid my heart will shatter when I leave."

"Then let me hold it in the palm of my hand and keep it safe. Give us a chance."

Emma closed her eyes. Her heart told her to say yes while her brain screamed no!

No!

No!

"Yes, let's make a Christmas memory."

Chapter 8

The following morning Dylan stumbled into the kitchen and started a pot of coffee in the old stainless steel percolator. Modern had been a foreign concept to Jax. Even his old beat-up Jeep Wagoneer was over fifty years old. The thing ran beautifully though, so Dylan couldn't fault the man too much.

Jax had taken good care of everything he owned and Dylan wouldn't change much of the log home's rustic charm. The kitchen appliances could use some updating and the butcher-block countertop needed sanding and resealing. The custom handmade cabinets could stand refinishing, as could the floors. All things Dylan could easily handle. He'd change out some of the dated furniture, but the bones of the structure weren't that bad. At almost three thousand square feet, the house would be a great place to raise a family.

The sun wasn't even up and he already had a headache. He pulled out a chair and sat at the kitchen table, which had notes strewn across it. He hadn't meant to spend half the night in Emma's room, but after she had agreed to give them a chance, she offered to show him the ranch presentation. He didn't ask why, since he'd already admitted to wanting to use her ideas. He didn't know if it was her last ditch effort to change his mind and be able to honestly tell her boss she'd given it her all, or if she was trying to help him. Either way, he had listened to every word she said. While the majority of it went against the cowboy way of life, she had some solid ideas that he would have loved to work in to the ranch.

The state-of-the-art kitchen would allow the ranch to book weddings and other events. They handled some weddings here and there, but an outside vendor had catered most of them. Providing in-house catering along with an event planner would allow them to offer destination wedding packages.

He tried to hide his embarrassment when Emma pulled up their website. He knew it was outdated and he had talked to Jax a few times about having it redesigned. But after astronomical quotes, Jax had nixed the idea. It was on his current to-do list, but the ranch didn't have the extra thousands of dollars to spare. When Emma told him there were ways to have sites designed for free by college students trying to make a name for themselves, he realized he had options. She even took the time to show him other guest ranches and pointed out key features that drove business to their sites. By the time she was through, he understood why the business was struggling.

Dylan wasn't up on the latest technology. He'd spent most of his life outdoors, working with his hands and animals. Some of her ideas along with the keyless entry system she had mentioned were well out of his realm of expertise. He still couldn't figure out what the problem was with using a regular key. A lot less went wrong when you kept it simple.

When he left her room sometime after midnight, he hadn't told her his plans one way or the other. He knew she was disappointed with his silence, but at the time, he hadn't completely made up his mind. The more he thought about last night and the more notes he took, the more of a future he saw for Silver Bells. As a guest ranch, not a luxury spa.

His decision killed any chance Emma had at getting her promotion. That was a guilt he wasn't ready to face. He didn't want to string her along, either. Unless he could convince her to stay in Montana. But he wanted the decision to be her choice. He'd love to hire her as the lodge's manager, knowing the place would have a fighting chance with her on board. It had been a job both Dylan and Jax had shared and it needed one person's entire attention. He'd still need to find an investor or two, but that seemed more obtainable if she signed on.

Dylan poured a cup of coffee, laughing at the irony of the situation. Emma had come to Saddle Ridge to change his mind, now he had to find a way to change hers. That meant he had to remain on his best behavior and not only convince her to stay past New Year's Day, but to give their relationship the courtesy of acknowledging it could be more than a two-week fling. Dating Emma and her accepting the position didn't necessarily have to go hand-in-hand. But after she had agreed to give them a chance while she remained in town over the holidays, hope began to grow inside him. Not just for them as a couple, but for the ranch, as well. He had his work cut out for him. He wanted her to live in the very place she wanted to change.

A hard knock followed by his back door opening snapped him back to the present. Wes strode in still wearing yesterday's clothes. His brother grunted hello as he poured a cup of coffee and then flopped into a kitchen chair.

"Rough night?"

"Yeah." Wes flipped through Dylan's notes. "Still at it huh?"

Dylan joined him at the table. "I have some new ideas. I just need someone willing to invest in the ranch."

"So nothing I said yesterday convinced you to change your mind?" Wes asked.

"I can't walk away."

"Well, good luck, then." Wes sipped his coffee.

"Don't sound too enthusiastic." Dylan gathered up his paperwork and stacked it in the center of the table before his brother saw the sketches of the rocking horse.

"No, I mean it. I hope you do save Silver Bells. Just because I don't want to stay in Saddle Ridge doesn't mean I don't want you to be happy here. Speaking of happy, what's going on with you and the pregnant woman? Isn't she public enemy number one?"

"Not so much anymore. We have agreed to see where the next two weeks take us."

"You can't be serious?" Wes rocked his chair back onto two legs. "Man, you don't learn from your mistakes, do you?"

"What's that supposed to mean?"

"How is the situation any different from you and Lauren? Once again, you want a city girl with children to move on the ranch with you. How did that work out for you the first time?"

"Lauren wasn't a city girl and Emma has one kid. At least she will soon." Emma's situation was completely different from Lauren's, but he didn't feel the need to justify it to Wes.

"The fact Lauren wasn't a city girl should be even more of a red flag. Emma is way more city than Lauren and look how that turned out. Why do you want to put yourself through this again? These women don't want to live way out on an isolated ranch. Look what happened to Harlan and his first wife. Same thing."

"Molly had other issues going on, too. This place isn't isolated. We have people coming and going year round."

"Yep. Other people are coming and going from this place and you and Jax and everyone else who worked here never got off the ranch. You're proving my point. You're looking for any excuse to convince yourself that this will work." Wes rocked forward until all four chair legs were on the floor. "Hey, for your sake, I hope I'm wrong. Maybe she's a country girl at heart who likes the outdoors but just hasn't found a way to cut ties with Chicago. Either way, good luck. I need to head home and shower."

"Don't let me stop you." Dylan mentally tabulated the chances Wes was right about Emma. Was he making the same mistake?

"By the way, the reason I stopped in here this morning wasn't to harass you. Billy Johnson got into a bad snowmobile wreck. He might lose his leg. I spent most of the night in the hospital with his wife. I tried to call but couldn't reach you. Just thought you'd want to know since he used to work here. His family is going to need some extra support and I thought it would be nice if we took up a collection for him with it being Christmas. They are going to have it pretty rough. His new health insurance hasn't kicked in yet and he couldn't afford to continue paying on the old insurance without the ranch's percentage."

"Oh, man." Dylan's phone had died when he was with Emma. He'd put it on the charger last night but had forgotten to turn it back on. Billy had been their ranch manager. The man was in his midforties with a wife and four kids. He had hated losing him as an employee but understood his reasons for taking another offer and not wanting to wait and see if Dylan could save the ranch. They had talked at length and Dylan told him there would always be a place for him if he wanted to return. "I'll let everyone know about Billy. This is just another reason why I need to keep this place going."

"How would that have saved Billy?" Wes set his mug in the sink. "The accident wasn't related to his job."

"No, but he would have still had insurance. Those medical bills may wipe them out."

"Yeah, you're right. That does make a difference." Wes headed for the door. "Thanks for the coffee. I'll see you in a bit."

Dylan spread the notes across the table, more fired up than he had been fifteen minutes ago. He needed to create his own presentation to give to potential investors. It wouldn't be fancy or animated like Emma's had been, but he knew how to work a computer. In the end, only the facts mattered. He couldn't lose another employee or allow another person to go without health insurance. He refused to let anyone else suffer because of his and Jax's mismanagement. He had to right the wrong, and as guilty as he may feel for borrowing Emma's ideas, he had to push that aside. Too many families depended on him. Emma would understand. She had to.

Emma had never been happier to see a washing machine and dryer in her entire life. The ranch had an on-site mini laundromat and she had managed to wash a small load of whites and darks before breakfast. She planned to head into town later and check out the local shop situation. She didn't have high hopes for it, but it would be a new adventure just the same. Hopefully she could find some things to last her the next two weeks.

Emma tried to avoid maternity clothes. She couldn't see spending money on something she would only wear for a few months. She made a decent salary but it didn't allow her to spend her earnings foolishly. She had to watch every penny with the butter bean on the way. Granted, there were some things like underwear and pants that couldn't be avoided, but for the most part she had managed to wear loose fitting tops that she could get away with after she gave birth.

Her friend, Jennie, told her she'd probably get sick of those clothes by then. And she may be right. Her fisherman's knit sweater had lost its appeal a month ago. She needed to buy a pair or two of shoes in a bigger size. She felt larger than life over the past few days and she still had a little over seven and a half weeks to go.

The lodge employees were in a somber mood when she entered the dining area. The little talking she heard was hushed. She spotted Dylan and wondered if he had told them about her presentation last night. She scanned their faces. Could she live with uprooting so many people's lives?

"Good morning," Dylan greeted her.

"Is it?" Emma looked around. "What's going on?"

"I just finished telling them that a former employee got into a terrible accident last night. He may lose his leg. Four kids, a wife and no insurance."

"Oh, that's awful." Emma sensed some blame behind his words. "Did he leave recently?"

Dylan nodded. "Shortly after Jax told him we were selling the ranch. The accident had nothing to do with that. Not having insurance sure did, though."

"I'm sorry he and his family are suffering." Emma wondered if any of her new friends blamed her the way Dylan did. "Please let me know if there's anything I can do."

"We're taking up a collection to help pay their bills. We've decided to adopt the family for Christmas. We will head into town later and go grocery shopping for them, buy gifts for the kids, decorate and do everything we can to make their life as normal as possible during this time. It would be great if you joined us."

Emma nodded, unable to speak. Helping the family was the very least she could do. She would talk to Charlie later and see if the firm would donate to the family. She had closed dozens of similar deals and had never witnessed the fallout on such a personal level. Whether it was an apartment building they were turning into condominiums or a strip mall they were turning into a mega center, her firm negatively affected many lives while making their investors richer. She'd always known that and had been a willing participant. But this time she was witnessing it firsthand, and it really hit home. Now that she was getting to know many of the people here better, turning the ranch into a luxury resort spa didn't seem that wonderful, anymore. Of course, that had been Dylan's plan when he had asked her to spend time with his employees. She'd been played to a certain extent, but she was okay with it. It had opened her eyes. Emma had been eager to get off the ranch so she could gain the advantage and push Dylan to sell. Now, not so much.

"About last night…" Dylan began.

"Is this personal or business?"

"Business first."

Emma shook her head. "I don't want to talk business right now. It hardly seems appropriate and I don't want anyone to know what we have discussed. I know what your answer is going to be, and that's fine."

"Well, that's not quite what I wanted to talk about, but it can wait."

They stood staring at each other halfway between the tables and the empty buffet line. When Dylan didn't continue to the personal side of the conversation, she shrugged and made her way to the French toast. Which reminded her of France and the baby name book she had downloaded.

She had always been partial to French names for some reason. She'd only been to Paris once, but had visited the French countryside many times on business. Her favorite place had been the small picturesque town of Vienne along the Rhone River. Vienne Sheridan had a nice ring to it. But she wondered if too many people would mistake it for Vienna or Vivian?

Emma checked to see if Dylan had followed her to the line. He was on the phone, walking toward the front of the lodge. Maybe he had already eaten. She fixed her plate and sat quietly at a table by herself. A few of the other employees remained clustered by the fireplace, but most had already scattered. She ate in uncomfortable silence and then made her way back to her room.

Her job demanded that she follow through with everything she came to Saddle Ridge for. Work should come first, but the weather had warmed a few degrees and Emma wanted to take full advantage of what the ranch had to offer—what she could do in her condition, anyway. *So why don't you?* The doctor had told her to get light exercise and Dylan had told her to get out and meet people. After being confined to a hospital room for eighteen hours, the last thing she wanted to do was stay cooped up in her room. Emma added a few more layers to her outfit and headed out the door. Work could wait. At least a few more hours.

Snowshoeing was at the top of her list.

After borrowing a pair of boots from Sandy, another employee fitted her in a pair of wide deck shoes and helped her snap her feet into the bindings. She slipped on her jacket and gloves, made sure she had her phone and headed outside.

The slight mountain breeze didn't help cool her body, still trembling from Dylan's kiss last night. She hadn't known she could be kissed like that. She could only imagine what making love to him would feel like. No. That's the last thing she needed to do. Making love to Dylan Slade was off-limits, not to mention unprofessional. Not that kissing was professional, either.

Emma started to laugh. She didn't know which was funnier, the idea Dylan would want to make love to her while she was pregnant or the actual act itself. At this stage, she didn't think she was capable of sex, although she had heard some wild stories.

She gripped her poles as she trudged through the

snow, willing sex from her brain. Despite her girth, she sank only a couple inches with each step. By the time the stables were in sight, she had worked up a slight sweat. She saw Dylan and another man heading into the second building. She stopped along one of the pasture fences and looked out over the hearty draft horse herd. They seemed to be enjoying the snow. She never knew horses could withstand such cold temperatures.

She made her way toward the second stables when she heard a man's voice.

"I know it's not what that commercial real estate firm offered you, but I can guarantee everyone immediate employment. My only condition is I need you to run the place. I've known you and Jax for a long time and I can't see the employees staying if you're not here."

"You've given me a lot to chew on." She heard Dylan say. "Are you sure you won't consider partnering with me instead of a full buyout?"

"I'm afraid not. I'd like to join the two ranches since they're next to one another. You have a lot of acreage now, but almost doubling the size would allow us to add to the amenities."

"I'm glad you reached out to me. I haven't decided anything yet, but I'll definitely let you know one way or the other."

"I look forward to hearing from you."

Emma attempted to turn around make a casual retreat, until she saw her massive snowshoe tracks in the snow. There was no hiding her presence. When the men didn't come out of the stables, she continued to the entrance and poked her head in. The building was empty.

"What are you doing out here?" Dylan said from behind her.

"Oh, hi." How did he do that? Emma attempted to remain calm. "I'm just getting my exercise."

"Are you sure snowshoeing is safe during your pregnancy?" he asked as they both watched a snowmobile drive out from behind the stables. Emma scrutinized his expression. So far, nothing screamed, *You were eavesdropping on my conversation.* Maybe she'd gotten away with it.

"Snowshoeing is a very safe sport for pregnant women. But rest assured, before I came out here, I double-checked the list the doctor gave me. Plus, I used to go snowshoeing all the time when I was in boarding school."

Dylan shook his head.

"What?" Emma asked.

"The whole boarding school thing. I don't understand why people have children if they plan on sending them away for most of their adolescent life."

She had asked herself that very same question when she was growing up. Yet she still felt the need to defend her parents' decision. "I had a great education. I learned to socialize and communicate with others well since I didn't have my parents to fall back on. Living away from home at an early age teaches you how to be strong. That being said, I have no intention of sending my daughter to boarding school, much to my parents' dismay. I want to be there for her every day she comes home from school. I want to help her with her homework, bake brownies for bake sales, go to her school recitals and be a member of that Parent-Teacher Association thing. I want my daughter to have a normal, healthy life. She'll be different from some of the kids because I'm a single mom, but I'm sure she won't be the only kid without two parents."

Dylan dug his boot into the hard-packed snow by the stables entrance. "Have you given last night's discussion any more thought?"

"The you-and-I part?" Emma tugged on his jacket, urging him to step closer. "Some. I don't know how much we can think about it without overthinking it. I wouldn't mind spending some time alone with you again, though."

"I'd like that, too." Dylan held her face in his gloved hands and kissed her softly. "How would you like to have dinner alone with me tonight at my uncle's house?" He released her face and slid his hands down her shoulders. "Before you say yes, I feel obligated to tell you I have an ulterior motive."

"You do, huh?" Emma wondered if he planned to mention the offer she had overheard.

"My uncle was a huge Christmas fan and he hadn't decorated his house before he died. I'd really like to cut down a tree and decorate it in his memory. But I don't want to do it alone. So if you'd be willing to give me a shoulder to lean on tonight, I'd appreciate it."

Tough-as-nails Dylan Slade had an even bigger heart than she'd imagined. "I'd be honored to lend you my shoulder."

"Great, I promise to make it fun. He would've wanted it that way." Dylan gave her a quick kiss on the lips before stepping away from her. "But I have a lot to get done before then. Can you meet me at the lodge entrance at six?"

"Most definitely. I should get back to my workout." Emma wanted to stay and ask him who the man on the snowmobile had been, but she thought better of it. She gripped her poles and plodded back to the lodge. She needed to call Charlie and tell him Dylan had another offer. A small part of her was relieved it was over, because there was no way he would accept her deal over the other one, if he sold at all. The new offer guaranteed employment. A bigger part of her was devastated she would lose her promotion. That meant even more changes to her life. Starting with moving into a smaller apartment. She'd call Charlie when she got back to the ranch. Maybe they could counter with something better. Dylan's kiss was good, but she wasn't ready to give up her dream just yet.

A few hours later, Emma had a new offer from Charlie and he expected her to present it tonight. She suggested looking into the neighboring ranch as a possible expansion project or a suitable replacement if Dylan continued to stand his ground. But she refused to discuss any of it with him tonight. Dylan wanted to honor his uncle's memory and that didn't leave any room for business. She would tell him about Charlie's pending donation to Billy's family so she could get their information. But the rest could wait until the following morning. Nobody would be any wiser. She may be an aggressive businesswoman but even she had her limits.

She wanted to be there for Dylan the way he had been there for her when she was in the hospital. It would be their first official Christmas memory. And maybe it would be the only one they would share, but it would be theirs.

Chapter 9

Dylan had just finished putting the chicken in the oven when it was time to pick up Emma from the lodge. A few of the Silver Bells' housekeeping staff had given the house a good cleaning from top to bottom earlier that day. His nerves were beginning to catch up to him as he gave everything one last perusal before heading out the door.

He pulled up to the lodge's entrance, driving Jax's red Wagoneer. It was the only vehicle he had that Emma wouldn't have to climb up in. Plus, for a car from 1967, it was a sweet ride. He especially loved the bench seats. They were perfect for getting a little closer to your date. Not that they had time to snuggle during the five-minute drive. But this did constitute a date. The first since Lauren. He was ready. And from the looks of her, so was Emma.

Dylan left the truck running as he hopped out and opened the door for her. "You look beautiful." He gave her a kiss on the cheek. "You didn't have to wait out here. I would have come in and gotten you."

"I wasn't outside for long." She eased onto the passenger seat. "I recognized Jax's truck from my visits and I wanted to avoid any more questions. It seems everyone on the ranch knows we are having dinner together."

Dylan closed her door and ran around to slide in beside her. "Sorry. I hadn't thought about that when I asked some of the employees to help me freshen up Jax's house."

"You didn't have to go through so much trouble for me."

He found it next to impossible to focus on his driving. Thank God it was a short trip because all he wanted to do was admire her. She looked different tonight. Not just more put together, but more serene. Her hair fell in soft brown waves around her shoulders. It took every ounce of strength not to run his fingers through them to find out if they felt as soft as they looked.

"Believe me, you wouldn't want to have seen my uncle's house before we tackled it."

"I love this truck." Emma glanced around the sparse red and charcoal interior. "Especially since I didn't need a stepladder to get into it."

He detected a hint of nervousness in her laughter. "It was Jax's pride and joy." He parked in front of the log home's expansive porch and helped her out. "I just thought of something. You've probably already seen the house."

Emma shook her head. "No, actually I haven't. I always met with your uncle at the lodge. We had figured all dwellings into our proposal, but since the house wasn't part of the guest quarters, I didn't feel it was necessary to traipse through it. We planned to use it as an on-site living quarters for our firm while the project was underway and then evaluate its use during that time."

Dylan held the door open for her as she entered. "I've always loved this house. The craftsmanship is impeccable for a place that's been around for almost a hundred years. It was the first structure on the property."

Emma's mouth gaped open at the two-story interior. "This isn't what I expected at all." She ran her hands over the smooth golden logs. "I thought it would be much darker inside. This is a surprise. A very pleasant surprise."

"The chinking needs some TLC here and there, but other than that it's move-in ready." Dylan helped her out of her coat. "I know I said this already, but you look beautiful tonight."

Emma beamed up at him. "I found this great store in town today and I treated myself to something new." She ran her hands over the feminine, pale-blue sweater. "I severely under packed, not anticipating the length of my stay. I actually found quite a few places in town that I liked. I was pleasantly surprised." She wandered toward the kitchen. "What smells so amazing?"

"Chicken parmesan." Dylan strode into the kitchen and turned on the burner for the pot of water he had waiting. "With a side of pasta. I hope that's okay. I forgot to ask you what you like to eat, but I've seen you eat chicken so I took the chance."

"It's perfect. I had no idea you could cook."

"I can't make anything too elaborate, but I do all

right. Between my mom and hanging around with some of the chefs here, I've picked up a few things."

Cooking for Emma suddenly became more intimate. Convincing her to stay in Montana had been his main goal, but with each passing hour, he wanted it more than he had realized.

"This is a massive kitchen. I didn't expect it to be so large for a place this old."

Emma stood at the sink and peered through the window. She looked more natural in the home than he had envisioned. His heart began to beat rapidly at the thought of raising a family with her on the ranch. Now that he had a definite way to stay on the land, he wanted to make plans for the future.

Dylan was glad he hadn't mentioned the lodge manager job to Emma earlier. Not that she had given him much of a chance. Barnaby's offer had been unexpected but not all that surprising. By combining the acreage of both ranches, they could offer more trail options and possibly even open a small downhill ski run since Barnaby's land extended into the mountains. It sounded great, but he hadn't decided to take him up on his offer yet. He still would rather maintain some ownership, but Barnaby wanted to buy the ranch outright. It was a solid plan to fall back on if he couldn't find a partner. He needed to be sure though, before he told his employees they didn't have to leave.

During the past few days, his vision had changed from saving the ranch to running the ranch with Emma by his side. The thought alone was crazy. But despite the absurdity, it felt damn right.

"It's been updated a time or two in its life. I'd like

to refinish the wood surfaces throughout the house and bring out the character of the grain."

"You can do all of that yourself?"

"Sure. Woodworking is a hobby of mine, plus my father was really handy and I learned how to build just about anything from him. This house would be a great place for a bunch of kids to run around in. We loved it as children, but Jax never married or had any of his own. Would you like something to drink?"

"Just water is fine." Emma sat at the kitchen table. "I can see kids here. It has what, three bedrooms?"

"Four. But my uncle used the smallest for a study." Dylan twisted open a bottle of water and poured it into a glass for Emma. "This place has always been a second home to me, but I never fully appreciated its craftsmanship until after he was gone. It seems strange without him here."

"I bet it does. I'm glad you have the memories to look back on."

"Cheers to the memories yet to come." Dylan held up his glass to hers. "I hope you like what I have planned for after dinner."

"I thought we were decorating the Christmas tree."

"We have to get it first." Tonight's anticipation built up in him like a kid on Christmas morning. He almost wanted to skip dinner and show Emma the surprise he had planned.

"Yeah, you mentioned something about cutting one down. Wouldn't it be easier to go into town and buy one? I saw Christmas trees for sale in front of the supermarket."

"Darlin', no self-respecting cowboy buys a Christmas tree. Trust me, you'll enjoy the experience."

* * *

When Dylan uncovered her eyes, she never in a million years expected to see a small white and silver sleigh harnessed to a lone Belgian.

"I feel like I've stepped into a storybook." Emma giggled as Dylan wrapped her in wool and faux fur blankets. "I can't believe this is how we're getting a Christmas tree."

"Aren't you glad we didn't go into town?"

"Absolutely!" None of her friends would ever believe she rode on a one-horse open sleigh, let alone one driven by a sexy cowboy after he'd cooked her the most incredible dinner she'd ever eaten. And that wasn't her pregnancy hormones talking, either. The man could seriously cook. The majority of her meals came from the freezer and involved her heating them in the microwave.

The pale light of the moon lit their path as their sleigh glided across the snow. Emma didn't think the smile would ever fade from her face after tonight. This moment was too perfect for words.

"I can't believe this is your life."

"What do you mean?" Dylan asked. He shifted slightly, causing more of his body to press against hers. Emma wanted to rest her head on his shoulders, but feared she'd miss something along the way if she did.

"You live in a winter wonderland. It's like *Doctor Zhivago* meets *Frozen*."

"As beautiful as the snow is, winter can also be harsh and cruel in these parts. You have to stay prepared all season and it is a long season."

"It's not like Chicago, though. We have dirty snow."

Dylan laughed. "Give it a few days and you'll see dirty snow here, too. Of course, fresh powder will probably fall on top of it within a day or two, but it does get dirty every now and then."

They stopped at the same spot they had the other night, only tonight they could see the town with its moonlit mountains magically rising behind it.

"This would be the perfect location for an outdoor wedding chapel. Can't you just picture it right here? With a few modifications to some of the more private cabins, this could be the quintessential wedding destination in all of Saddle Ridge. It would draw people in year round with that backdrop."

Dylan could picture it very easily with Emma by his side. "I don't remember an outdoor chapel in your proposal."

"It hadn't occurred to me until now. I was remembering the first time I came to Silver Bells to meet Jax. This was the first place he showed me. Of course, in my mind I saw dollars signs and ways to capitalize on the view. I had considered another lodge of sorts right here, taking advantage of the landscape, but no matter what I came up with, they all ruined the beauty of what drew me here in the first place. That's why there aren't any new structures in my proposal. After sitting here now and the other night, I see much more. This is God's country and what better way to celebrate that than with love and marriage. I totally get why you're so protective of this place."

Dylan wrapped his arm around her and tilted her chin toward him. "I think that's the best idea you've had yet."

His lips brushed hers, gently at first before becoming more demanding. She returned his hunger as desire coursed through her veins like venom seeking a beating heart. The fervent need to make love to a man she had just gotten to know a few days prior lustfully beckoned while mocking her sensibilities. Powerless against the seduction, yet more impatient with each breath she took, for the first time in her life, Emma wanted to completely surrender to another person...to Dylan.

"Emma," he gasped. "What are you doing to me?"

"Are you asking me to stop?" She ran her tongue over his bottom lip, daring him to take her higher than she'd ever been.

"Absolutely not. I just need to know if this is leading where I think it is."

"I don't want to stop or let go of this moment. It may be all we ever have. It may be more. Whatever it is, I want to share it with you...right here under the stars in the place you love more than life itself."

Emma knew her heart would never be the same after tonight. But she was recklessly willing to take a chance on the man she suddenly didn't want to live without. She longed to be a part of his hope for the future. To share in those dreams and help him realize them without limitations. Heaven help her, she wanted Dylan Slade, in every way.

Making love to Emma under the Montana night sky hadn't been on his evening itinerary. Unable to resist the woman who intrigued him more than any other had, he willingly gave her the piece of his heart he hadn't believed still existed. Each kiss had driven them deeper into complete abandon. And when they had finally broken apart, his desire for her grew stronger.

Swathed in layers of warmth, he began to believe the odds were turning in their favor. Between some of Emma's proposal ideas and the wedding chapel, a clearer vision for the ranch developed in his mind. But it wouldn't be complete without Emma. He wanted to finalize the plans before asking her to stay in Montana again. He needed to offer her more than just talk and concepts. Emma required stability for her and her daughter. He couldn't ask anything of her without it.

"I promised you a Christmas tree." Dylan kissed the top of Emma's head, relishing the feel of her body against his beneath the blankets.

"No, you said we'd cut down a tree. You promised tonight would be fun." Her voice was laced with seduction, commanding his body to attention. "You definitely kept your word." Emma straddled his lap, and for the second time that evening, he lost himself within her.

By the time they arrived back at the house with their tree in tow, Dylan could barely stand. Between the day's earlier tension and the sex, all he wanted to do was crawl in bed and sleep.

"I have to tend to the horse and sleigh." Dylan kissed her in the doorway. "Will you stay the night?"

Emma nodded, her eyes heavy with sleep.

"The bedroom is at the end of the hall. It's the only one on this floor." He wanted to lift her in his arms and carry her to bed, but he knew he'd never make it outside if he did. "I'll be back shortly."

She disappeared inside as he carried the tree onto the porch. Decorating could wait another day. Tonight, he wanted to hold Emma in his arms and forget the world around them.

After unhooking the sleigh and settling his horse down for the night, he climbed in beside her sleeping form. A soft breath escaped her lips with each exhale.

Not quite a snore but more of a wildcat purr. Not that he'd had the opportunity to lie down next to a wildcat. It was just the sound he imagined them having. And she had been a wildcat tonight. His wildcat.

He brushed the hair from her face and kissed her cheek goodnight. Yeah, he could definitely get used to sharing his life with Emma.

Emma awoke alone. *Had last night been a dream?* She looked around. No, she definitely wasn't in her room at the lodge. The faint sound of whisking came from the kitchen. Emma tossed on the sweatshirt she found on a chair next to the bed and padded down the hallway.

"Good morning, sleepyhead."

"Morning." She wrapped her arms around Dylan and snuggled against his chest. "What time is it, anyway?"

"Almost nine."

"Nine? What are you still doing here?" She looked up at him, loving the day-old scruff along his jawline. "Don't you have to work?"

"I've already been out and back. Wes is handling some things for me while I take the rest of the morning off. A little break is long overdue, considering I've been pulling my weight and his around here."

Charlie's voice nagged at her from the recesses of her mind. She didn't want to hear it. Not now when things were blissfully happy between her and Dylan. "Are you making French toast?"

"I am. I know it's your favorite." He kissed the top of her head.

Emma yawned and sat down at the table. "A woman could get easily spoiled this way."

Dylan smiled, but didn't ask her to stay as he had the other night. Not that she expected him to again. Although, it would be nice to hear. The thought had crossed her mind a few times during their evening. Moving to Montana would be ludicrous and bold, even for her. She took risks in business but rarely in her personal life. As much as she had grown to admire the ranch's beauty, she still couldn't see herself living there.

"After breakfast, I thought we'd decorate the tree. Unless you have other plans."

She did. She had a date with her credit card and a baby store she saw on her way back to the ranch yesterday. But shopping could wait a little while longer. So could telling Dylan about the new offer. "Um, sure."

He expertly flipped the toast in the pan with the flick of his wrist. "That wasn't the reaction I had expected."

"I need to tell you something. Two things actually, but I don't want it to break the mood."

Dylan shut the burner off on the stove and faced her. "You have my full attention."

The smile he'd worn seconds earlier had faded into seriousness. She inwardly groaned. "I had inquired about the horses, even though you asked me not to. The horses they didn't keep would have been sold at auction. I informed my office that was unacceptable and told them it was an absolute deal-breaker. They countered and said the horses would be excluded from the deal, allowing you to decide where they went."

"That's a significant contract change." Dylan turned the burner back on and continued cooking. "I appreciate the effort. I'm still not changing my mind, but I'm glad to hear they were open to it just the same."

"Okay, well that's the one I thought would upset you."

"I'm not upset at all. I'm disheartened that your company has a complete and blatant disregard for animals, but it doesn't surprise me. They may or may not know what goes on at horse auctions. Some choose to ignore it. I'm glad you didn't. Thank you." Dylan slid the toast on to a plate and set it before her. "What's the other thing you wanted to tell me?" He sat down across from her.

"Aren't you eating?" Emma asked.

"I already did, while you were sleeping." Dylan hopped up from the table, opened the microwave and removed a small bowl. "I almost forgot. I heated up some syrup for you."

"Thank you." Emma hated when people watched her eat, but breakfast smelled too good to resist. She took a mouthful and almost dropped her fork. "These are heaven. Is that cinnamon I'm tasting? And a hint of nutmeg?"

Dylan's smile lit the room. "Now that you know my secret ingredients, I'm going to have to find a way to keep you quiet." He winked. "There's a tablespoon of sugar in there, too and one other ingredient, but I'm not telling."

"That's not right." Emma playfully nudged him with her bare feet.

"Sure it is." Dylan caught her foot in his hands and began kneading it. There was nothing like an orgasmic foot massage while eating your favorite breakfast after a night of repeated sex on the back of a one-horse open sleigh…in the snow. Yep, she'd found heaven.

"God, that feels good." The man sure knew how to treat her like a queen. "The other thing was, I told my boss about your ex-employee who got injured. The firm would like to donate twenty-five thousand dollars to his family and I will need their contact information so we can set that up for them."

Dylan stopped massaging her foot.

"Okay, that wasn't the reaction I had expected." Emma tucked her feet under her chair. "What is it?" She already knew the answer because she'd felt the same way when Charlie told her the amount. It felt like a payoff of some sort. They wouldn't have needed to worry about medical bills if Emma and her company hadn't swooped in and tried to buy the ranch.

"I don't know how Billy's wife will react to the money." Dylan jumped up from the table again and poured a cup of coffee. "She was outspoken against Jax for a while. Billy had had to run interference between the two. He hadn't liked the situation, but he understood Jax owned the ranch and could do with it as he pleased. It was no different from other corporate buyouts. Only most of the time those people kept their jobs, or at least some did."

"I get it. I'm the enemy."

Dylan reached across the table for her. "No, you're not. You were doing your job."

Were doing? She was glad she held off on mentioning the offer until later. He might reconsider the enemy part. For now, or at least for the morning, Emma wanted to leave their responsibilities behind and get lost in a little Christmas spirit.

Chapter 10

Dylan hadn't expected to choke up while unboxing the Christmas ornaments. He hadn't realized how many his uncle had from Dylan's childhood. The realization his mother hadn't taken any of them with her to California surprised and upset him. Then again, she'd left town the day after his father's funeral. She'd put the ranch up for sale weeks later and that was when he and his brothers realized she never planned to return to Saddle Ridge.

"Some of these look really old." Emma carefully unwrapped a wad of tissue paper, revealing a delicate pale pink glass ornament.

"That was my grandmother's. No, wait. It was my great grandmother's on my mom's side." Dylan sighed. "I remember my mom hanging them high up on the tree when we were kids, for fear one of us would knock them off."

"Five boys must have been a handful." Emma rubbed her baby belly. "I'm still trying to grasp the concept of having one child, let alone that many."

"You'll do just fine." Dylan sat on the couch and reached out for her hand, pulling Emma onto his lap. "I have faith in you."

"I can't even choose a name. I thought I had one, but the more I say Vienne Sheridan, the more it sounds like a hotel in France."

Dylan couldn't help laughing. "It kind of does." She swatted him and attempted to squirm off his lap, but he wasn't letting her go. At least not any time soon. "You could always name her Montana."

"What would be the significance?" She reached for another wrapped ornament. "She wasn't conceived here and she won't be born here."

Dylan's heart dropped into his stomach like a bowling ball in a vacuum. Granted, they hadn't settled on anything permanent, or even discussed it further, but he'd thought she would have at least considered the possibility of moving to Montana if things progressed with their relationship. He realized they had only given it a two-week timeline, but even he had hoped it would last longer than that.

"I guess you've made up your mind."

Emma stilled. "About what?" She turned in his lap to face him. "Us?"

He nodded.

"Our two weeks have just begun. I don't think that's really fair to ask me. My home is in Chicago and so is everything I own. At some point, I have to go back. I may not have a definitive birthing plan, but my doctor and my parents are in Illinois, so yes, I intend to give birth on my home turf." Emma sat the ornament on the coffee table. "Does that bother you?"

"I don't know." Dylan eased her off him and onto the couch. "I guess it does. After last night and… I don't know. I kind of wanted to be there."

"For the birth?" Emma's brows rose. "Seriously?"

Dylan had never felt more like a fool. He had no business being anywhere near the delivery room, nor did he have any claim to her child. "It was a thought. A bad one, apparently."

She reached for his hand as tears trailed down her cheeks. "Dylan."

"Emma, what is it?" He knelt before her. "Don't cry, baby."

She struggled to regain her composure. "I never thought," she said between sniffles, "that another man would want to be there for my baby that way."

Now it was Dylan's turn to breathe a sigh of relief. "Honey, babies are the most innocent creatures on earth. Just because she was conceived with someone else doesn't mean I don't have the capacity to love her."

The realization of his words almost knocked him out cold. He reached for the coffee table behind him to steady himself. He had done the one thing he swore he'd never do again. He'd fully accepted another man's child, and he hadn't even met the butter bean yet.

"Are you okay?" Emma asked, concern etched across her face. "I think I need to get you some water." She rose from the couch.

Dylan grabbed hold of her hand before she could walk away. "I don't need water." He needed something much, much stronger. "The past twenty-four hours have caught me off-guard. Your presence in my life was a complete surprise. When I'm with you, I feel like a super hero one minute and a lovesick teenager the next. You've changed my life in ways I hadn't thought possible. You opened my heart after it had been welded shut. I've devoted so much time to this ranch, I had forgotten what living feels like."

"I don't know what to tell you beyond today." Emma remained standing. "I feel guilty in so many ways."

"Why?"

"I aggressively sought out this ranch and targeted your uncle. In the process, I disrupted your life along with everybody else's who works here. I ignored my own child's needs because of this deal. I should be working on a way to convince you to sell instead of being here decorating the Christmas tree. But the truth is, I would rather be here than any other place in the world."

"I feel the same way." Dylan stood to meet her.

"I've gone from workaholic to *I need a break* in a matter of days. And while I'm sure a lot of that had to do with my labor scare, there is a whole other side of me that's tired. I'm tired of the uncertainty and the stress. I'm tired of constantly trying to get ahead. And even though I've been trying to change your mind about the ranch over the past four days, there's been a sense of relief knowing you never will. There's also deep loss I still haven't wrapped my head around. By accepting your refusal to sell, I accept that I failed. And that failure directly affects my child. That's a hard pill to swallow. And while I'm learning to love it here, I don't think I can honestly say I'm ready to give up walking up and down three flights of stairs to get to my apartment. Or hailing a cab to buy groceries. Or listening to my neighbor's kid learn how to play the saxophone. I love Chicago. I love the noise, but I don't miss going into my office, or any of that stress. I love more about Saddle Ridge than I thought I would. And now I have a decision to make of my own. And it's a tough one because I fell hard for a cowboy."

"Really, you fell for me?" Dylan attempted to lighten the burden she carried with a bit of levity.

"Look, I realize I'm unmarried and pregnant and we just had sex on a sleigh, but I assure you, I don't make a habit out of sleeping around. I've had three relationships in my life, this being the third. I don't take anything that has happened between us lightly, but I have to ask myself repeatedly how much of it is real and how much are my hormones running in overdrive?"

"I'm real and what I feel for you is real. I know it's fast and unexpected but, honey, we can't ignore what's in front of us."

"You're right. I'm having a baby. There's no getting around it. I'd love a father for my child, but she doesn't need one to thrive. I'd love to have a man in my life to lean on when things get tough, but I can get along just fine without one. And I'd love to have somebody to grow old with and watch the butter bean grow up and have children of her own, but I can survive on my own."

"So what… You're resolved to be alone?"

"I'm not saying that at all. I'm saying for this to work I have to want you…not need you and I'm having a hard time distinguishing the two at the moment."

"I'm not." Dylan lifted her chin to him. "I want you because I'm attracted to you and I admire your strength and determination even when the odds are against you. And I need you because you've awoken me to the possibilities of tomorrow. Possibilities that only exist with you by my side. I could have asked Harlan to decorate the tree with me. He's one of the most sentimental men I know. We could have shared a beer or two and talked about old times, but I asked you. I needed the strength only you could provide."

"You don't even know me." Emma's voice was barely a whisper.

"I know enough." Dylan bent to taste her lips. Her body trembled beneath his touch as his fingers traveled down her arms and to her palms, entwining his hands with hers. He slowly lowered to his knees, and kissed her belly. "And I want to know you, butter bean. I want to see you grow up strong like your mother. She's a force to be reckoned with. Pay attention, little one. Follow your mom's lead and you can conquer the world."

Emma placed her hands on either side of his face, urging him to stand. "You sweet man. You sweet, sweet man."

Whatever beat ferociously deep within his heart was foreign to him. He'd experienced love before and it hadn't even come close. Whatever this was, he couldn't let it go without giving it everything he had. The calendar be damned. He refused to put a timeline on their relationship. However fast or whatever time they had meant nothing. All that mattered were Emma and her baby.

By the time Dylan had dropped her off at the ranch, it was well after noon. She managed to sneak in the side door without anyone seeing her. Doing the walk-of-shame wearing yesterday's clothes is always bad.

Doing the walk-of-shame when pregnant was the ultimate worst.

She fumbled with the key in the lock of her room, anxious to get it open before she had to explain her whereabouts. Once inside, she collapsed against the door. Dating took a lot out of a pregnant woman.

Emma smiled when she saw the Christmas tree on the dresser. She'd never look at one the same way again. After making love twice on the way to get a tree, followed by making love all morning under it, decking the halls now had a significantly new meaning.

She crossed the room to the bed, admiring the tiny outfits she'd purchased the day before while she was in town. They had been too precious to pack away last night. They were the first clothes she had purchased for...for... She needed a name.

Emma sat on the edge of the bed and held up a tiny red and white onesie. Technically, it was meant for Christmas, but her due date was February 11, just in time for Valentine's Day. Her daughter had to have something red to wear for the holiday. She'd blown whatever baby clothing budget she'd set. Amazingly, she didn't care.

Watching her finances was still important, but it was time to bend the rules a little. She'd been so rigid and laser focused on every detail in her life, she'd forgotten to enjoy her pregnancy. It felt good to let go. A little too good. She could really get used to living in Montana. The people, the views, the stress-free lifestyle... the lack of a job.

Reality check.

The funny thing was, the more Dylan talked about the ranch, the more she wanted to be a part of it. She had some money saved. It had originally been her job-loss contingency plan, then it morphed into the butter bean's college fund. While it was enough to carry her for a year in Chicago, it wasn't nearly enough to partner with Dylan.

Was that even an option? Every day she saw more and more possibilities for the ranch. In the same breath, with the increased proposal from her company, Dylan could have a bigger and better ranch. A place where all his employees could still work for him. But was it enough for him...and her? Silver Bells had begun to grow on her. Imagine that. The big city girl contemplating a move to the country. Her mother would die.

After a day of shopping, a stop by town hall to pull the plats on Silver Bells and the neighboring ranch, followed by a chocolate shake and an order of fries, Emma found her second wind to do more baby shopping. She saw a crib and dresser set she loved in a baby boutique, but it wasn't practical to buy and send back to Chicago. Even if she did wind up moving to Montana, it wouldn't be until after the baby was born. Until she had a steady income to move toward, she wasn't going anywhere.

She passed a toy store, and thought about Billy Johnson's four children who wouldn't have their father home for Christmas. Her budget could go hide under the covers because she was buying those kids some presents. By the time she pulled back into the ranch, her rental car was full. Front seat, backseat and the trunk. Granted, it wasn't a very big car, but she'd done some heavy damage to her credit card.

Sandy and Melinda helped bring her packages inside. Between the women working at the ranch and some of the female guests, they spent the rest of the afternoon sitting by the fire in the great room discussing babies, men and all the mistakes they'd made with both.

"How do you know when you've found the right man and he's worth taking a leap of faith with?" Emma asked the group of women.

"You mean, how do you know you've found the right cowboy?" Sandy then proceeded to tell everyone there was a Christmas romance brewing.

"I knew there had to be something going on when he insisted you ride up front in the snowcat," one of the guests said. "We could've made room for you in the back. It would have been a little tight, but there was room."

"He certainly is a fine specimen of a man," another said. "If I were thirty years younger and fifty pounds lighter, I'd be all over him. Emma, I'd be your biggest competition."

Everyone laughed until the man of the hour himself appeared.

"Wow, I'm so glad my employees are so fast at their jobs they have time to sit around and chat with our guests."

Emma hadn't wanted anyone to get in trouble. She'd done enough damage to the ranch as it was. "Hey now, they're just on break. They deserve a little relaxation after putting up with you for all these years."

"Yeah, don't be such a grouch." Sandy jabbed Dylan's arm. "You have a baby on the way. You should be happy."

"Sandy! I can't believe you said that." Emma turned to Dylan, pulling him into a quiet corner. "I swear I had nothing to do with that."

Dylan shrugged. "No worries. I've known Sandy since she was born. She likes to tease. That's how she landed Luke." The women's laughter reverberated behind them. "I see you did some shopping. Is this all for the baby?" He picked up a train set. "Don't you think you're getting a little ahead of yourself?"

"The pink and blue bags are for the butter bean. The rest are for the Johnson kids."

"Emma, that's a lot of stuff. You didn't have to do that."

"Yes, I did. And let's just leave it at that." Emma didn't want to rehash her guilt. She had enough of it to last a lifetime.

"How would you like to join me for dinner at Harlan and Belle's house tonight? You already know my brother, but I would like you to meet my sister-in-law. My brother Garrett and his two kids are coming in Christmas Eve. I thought it would be nice to spend some time with Belle and Harlan away from the ranch. Besides, I am sure you and Belle can spend hours talking baby."

"Taking me to your brother's house for dinner almost sounds official." Emma playfully winked at him.

"You're right, it does."

She laughed at his comment, only Dylan wasn't laughing with her. He looked painfully serious. Oh. My. God. He was making them official. Was she ready for that?

Chapter 11

Dylan hadn't been the least bit nervous about introducing Emma to his brother and sister-in-law until they turned off on to their ranch road. He knew his seven-year-old niece Ivy would like Emma. Ivy liked everyone. And Belle and Emma shared a common baby bond. It was Harlan he worried about, even though they had already met. And he hadn't been concerned up until his conversation with Wes yesterday morning. Granted, a lot had changed between him and Emma since then, but Wes's concern that Dylan was repeating old patterns bothered him. He didn't see any similarity between Emma and Lauren, but Wes had. Now he wondered if Harlan would, too.

Ivy greeted them before Emma had a chance to step out of the truck. "You're having a baby, just like Belle!" The little girl danced in front of them on the snow-packed drive. "Do you know if it's going to be a boy or girl?"

"It's a girl." Emma shared in Ivy's enthusiasm.

"Do you have a name yet?"

"Not yet. But I have to choose one soon."

"You could always name her Ivy." His niece grabbed hold of Emma's hand and led her through the back gate of his brother's white clapboard farmhouse. "Dad, Belle! Emma is having a baby!"

"Ivy, use your inside voice," Harlan warned from the top of the porch steps.

"But I'm outside," she protested.

Harlan rolled his eyes and stretched out his arm. "See what you have to look forward to? It's nice to see you under better circumstances. You look much better than the last time I saw you."

"Yeah, about that." Emma grimaced. "I'm sorry I screamed and cursed all the way to the hospital. I'm surprised I didn't shatter your eardrums."

"No worries. I've heard much worse. I'm just glad you're okay." Harlan slapped Dylan on the back. "Hey, man. You actually look a little more relaxed since I last saw you."

"Is Emma having your baby?" Ivy asked.

"Enough," Harlan warned again. "Why don't you take Elvis for a walk?

"Come on in." Harlan held the door open for them. "Belle will be down in a minute or two."

"Here I am." His sister-in-law pulled Emma into an all-encompassing hug. Dylan didn't know Emma well enough to know if she was the hug-everyone-you-meet type or not. Belle hadn't been until her pregnancy. "How far along are you?" Belle wrapped her arm around Emma's shoulder and steered her into the living room.

"Well, that's the last we'll see of them until dinner." Harlan opened the fridge and handed Dylan a beer. "What's going on? Wes told me you and your arch enemy have gotten pretty hot and heavy."

"I wouldn't say she's the enemy, anymore. I think we've come to an understanding." Dylan twisted the top off his beer and flicked the cap into the garbage can. "She knows I'm not going to sell."

"Does she?" Harlan asked.

"Yeah, why?"

Harlan shook his head. "It's nothing."

"No, if you have something to say, say it."

"Did you know Emma was in town today?" Harlan asked.

Dylan nodded. "She was buying things for the baby and Billy Johnson's kids."

"Okay." Harlan opened the oven door and peeked in. "Honey, you may want to check the lasagna. It's looking a little brown on top."

"I'll be right there," Belle called from the living room.

Dylan held up his arms. "You can't leave me hanging. What are you not telling me?"

"Get out of the way, you two." Belle swatted at them. "Pregnant woman coming through. This room isn't big enough for all of us and my belly."

Emma laughed from the doorway. "Wait until you reach thirty-three weeks. And I hear we get even bigger."

"I wouldn't mind so much if I didn't have to pee every two seconds."

"Really?" Harlan looked at Belle. "We're getting ready to eat and you're talking about your bathroom habits."

"What habits? I made a statement, that's all." Belle opened the oven and quickly closed it. "Okay, dinner's ready. Here." She thrust two potholders at Harlan's chest. "You can take it out."

"Did you know, I'm her new manservant?"

"And he's not too happy about it. The doctor doesn't want me around any animal urine so that means this one here has to clean up after all my little ones at the rescue center when my volunteers aren't available."

"I'm sorry, that cow is not little. Neither is your three-hundred pound pig."

Emma laughed at Belle and Harlan's banter, but Dylan couldn't help wondering what his brother wasn't telling him about Emma. She hadn't mentioned going anywhere else in town, not that he expected her to report to him. She was free to go where she wanted. Still, something was amiss and he was going to find out before they left tonight.

Emma couldn't figure out what had changed between the time they arrived and the time they sat down to eat. Dylan had barely said two words throughout their meal. He'd glanced at her a few times, almost questioningly. Their tension began to make her feel uncomfortable and she could see the uncertainty in Belle's face as she wondered what was going on, as well. She was fairly certain Dylan had bad-mouthed her in the past, but they were past that now, weren't they?

Dylan and Harlan retired into the living room after dinner while Emma helped Belle clean up the kitchen.

She had tried to hear what they were saying, but couldn't make out a word.

"Emma, please sit down. You don't have to help me. Your feet must be killing you at this stage."

"They were until I bought bigger boots. When I got here, I actually had to borrow somebody else's. No one told me my feet were going to get bigger during this whole process." Emma waved her hands in front of her belly. "And names. How do you choose a name for your child?"

"Tell me about it. How many names do you have on your list?" Belle asked. "I have hundreds and I can't manage to narrow them down. It doesn't help that we're waiting until the birth to find out the sex."

Emma shook her head. "I don't even have two."

Belle stared at her. "You have one name on your list? Doesn't that make it really easy then?"

"No, because I keep second-guessing it. I liked it and now I hate it, but I haven't come up with anything else."

"Whatever you do, don't ask Dylan for baby name advice. If he's anything like Harlan it will be something off-the-wall like Aloysius."

"Aloysius?"

Belle's brows furrowed. "It was some great-great uncle of theirs from way back when. Harlan said it was unusual enough to stand out and not worry about another kid in class having the same name."

"No doubt," Emma agreed. "Can I ask you something just between us?" Belle didn't owe Emma any loyalty, but she needed a logical explanation to explain Dylan's sudden mood change.

"Sure, go ahead."

"Dylan… Does he tend to—how should I put this?"

"Brood?"

Emma sagged against the counter. "Yes." She lowered her voice. "Exactly that."

"I've known him for almost my entire life, and the man he is today is much more jaded than he used to be. He tends to see the negative before the positive. It's my understanding you've already seen that side of him."

"That's an understatement." After the heartfelt talk he had with her stomach this morning, she had thought they had turned a new corner in their relationship. She still didn't know how to define it, although Dylan had hinted about making things official. Official as in dating. At least that's what she thought he meant. Because he couldn't possibly mean marriage. That was out of the question this early in the relationship. She didn't even know if they had a chance of dating past New Year's, let alone walk down the aisle. She didn't want to spend two seconds to say "I do" and then have to spend two years trying to say "I don't" in divorce court. At least that's what some of her coworkers had told her about their marriages.

"I'd like to tell you to take things day-by-day with him, but I know you two are pushing time. That is, unless you decide to move to Saddle Ridge."

"Let me get through this pregnancy first." Why did everyone make it sound so easy?

Emma filled Belle in on her Braxton-Hicks scare until Dylan and Harlan joined them. Dylan refused to make eye contact with her as they said their goodbyes. What could possibly have happened? At this point, it wasn't just frustrating, it was annoying the hell out of her.

"Thank you both for having me." Emma nodded to Harlan and gave Ivy and Belle a hug goodbye. "And don't forget to send me that vegetarian lasagna recipe. It was really good."

"I will." Belle called from the porch. "You two should drive around town and see the Christmas lights while you're out. Only four more days until Santa comes."

"I'd love to see the lights."

Dylan wordlessly held the car door open for her as she eased onto the seat. She was about to open her mouth to ask him if they could drive around for a while before heading back to the ranch when he closed the door. So much for that conversation.

Emma may be relatively new to town, but she knew her way around. The way they were heading home was definitely the most direct route and not to see any Christmas lights.

"Okay, Scrooge. Do you mind telling me what happened back there? You were fine when we arrived and then you weren't."

"Is there something you want to tell me?" he asked.

"Like what?"

"Like, I don't know, maybe how you went into town today and pulled the plats on my ranch and Barnaby Holcomb's. I can understand you pulling the plats on my land, although you should have them already. At least your office should. But Barnaby's? I'm sure he'll find out about that. This is a small town and news like that spreads faster than green grass through a goose."

Emma didn't know what to say. She clasped her hands on her belly and faced forward. If he could get this judgmental without discussing it with her then they had a problem.

"I guess it's true, then."

"You tell me. You seem to have already made up your mind."

"I had told you I wasn't going to sell. So why would you do that? It puts me in a really bad position."

"Because it's my job, Dylan. I spoke to Charlie earlier and he asked me to pull the plats on the Holcomb ranch so he could see the land survey. It doesn't matter if you were planning to sell or not. I'm not just answering to Charlie. I have to answer to a group of investors. If it goes south, I have to detail the reasons why and what I did to prevent it. Just be glad I'm the one here from my firm. They are already clamoring to take my place. You thought I pressured you? They would've swarmed like vultures around you."

"No, they wouldn't have. I would've thrown them off my ranch. Just like I—"

Emma snapped her head in his direction. "Just like you what? Should've done with me?"

"No. I was going to say just like I had tried to do with you." He tugged off his gloves and adjusted the heat. "I feel like a damned fool taking you to my brother's house and then hearing that."

Emma began to feel lightheaded. She inhaled deeply and exhaled slowly, trying her best not to raise her voice. "How do you think I feel knowing I sat at your brother's table and neither one of you trusted me?" The thought alone made her feel sick. "You both made me feel about as welcome as a skunk in church."

"How can we have a relationship if there isn't any trust?"

"We can't. So let's put it all out there." Emma fought against her seat belt in an attempt to gain more air. "You're only mad at me because if Barnaby Holcomb hears I pulled the plats on both lands he'll think I did it for you. And you don't want anything to jeopardize that offer, do you? Why didn't you tell me you received another bid on the ranch?"

"I knew it. How did you find out?" Dylan pulled into the supermarket parking lot and shifted the Wagoneer into Park. "I haven't even discussed that with anyone."

She unbuckled the blasted restraint and turned to him. "I overheard you and that man talking when I snowshoed out to the stables yesterday. Seriously, Dylan, if you don't want people listening in, I suggest you hold your meetings in a more private place like… oh, I don't know…maybe your house or your office. I waited over twenty-four hours for you to tell me about that offer and you haven't said a word. You probably still wouldn't have unless I brought it up."

"I didn't tell you because I haven't made a decision. It's a nice offer to fall back on, but it's not exactly what I had in mind. I would have preferred a partnership with Barnaby instead of relinquishing control of Silver Bells, but it was an all-or-nothing deal. I still have so many ideas for the ranch. I'm not ready to give it up."

"What if I said you could have your dream ranch?"

His icy laugh crackled between them. "Did I suddenly win a lottery I don't remember entering?"

"My firm has increased their offer by $100,000 and will guarantee employment for all current employees. While it won't be immediate employment at Silver Bells, we are willing to pay relocation fees if they want to work at one of our other investment groups resorts anywhere in the world."

"You're kidding, right?"

"Nope." Emma couldn't see how he could refuse the offer when it gave him the freedom to build whatever he wanted. "It would be a great opportunity for them. And you could buy your dream guest ranch here or elsewhere. You don't have to split the money with anyone and with the extra hundred grand, your options just increased exponentially. Imagine the possibilities."

"How can you preach to me about honesty? When were you planning to tell me this? After I told you about my offer?"

"My boss had asked me to tell you last night and get back to him today with your answer."

"So why didn't you?" Dylan rubbed the sleeve of his jacket against the fogged window.

"Because you invited me over for dinner and to decorate the Christmas tree in your uncle's memory. I wanted to honor him as well without ruining the moment with business."

Dylan's shoulders sagged and Emma believed she was finally getting through to him. "Fair enough. But I still don't understand why you pulled the plats. Oh, my God, they want Barnaby's ranch, too, don't they? Or was his a consolation prize in case I didn't sell?"

"It was a combination of both. If you don't sell and we present the investors with equally suitable land, the deal will remain intact. Just with different owners. And if you sold to us, we would try to purchase his land and expand the original design."

"And you would get your promotion."

"Yes, I would, but it wasn't about that."

"Whose idea was it to go after Barnaby's land? Yours or your boss's?" Dylan asked.

"I presented the idea and Charlie gave the go-ahead to pursue it." Emma swallowed and patted her belly. The butter bean was beginning to rock and roll inside her and Emma wasn't sure how much longer she could stand the pressure. "You should be happy. In the end, you're getting what you want. You never wanted to sell in the first place."

"This is about you being honest with me, Emma. At least now we know neither one of us has been completely honest with the other."

Emma waved her fingers at the car keys. "Hey, the butter bean's not too fond of our conversation. We need to get back to the ranch."

"Are you all right?" Dylan started the engine and shifted into gear before taking her hand. "Do you need me to drive you to the hospital?"

"No." She continued to breathe. "It's just Braxton-Hicks again. I know what it feels like this time around."

"If you're sure?"

"Just drive, Dylan." Why did men always have to argue when you needed them to do something? "You still haven't answered me. What about my offer? It's pretty substantial."

"You seriously want to talk about this now?"

"As long as we both stay calm, we might as well get this over with once and for all. You've heard my final offer. What's your final answer?"

"It was never about the money," Dylan said under his breath.

"No, I thought it was about your employees. We're offering them a tremendous opportunity, and you're refusing to give them the chance to even consider it. I could understand if after you had sat down with them, put it on the table and *they* said no. But for you to make that decision for them…" Emma shook her head. "That tells me this was about your stubborn pride from the beginning."

* * *

Dylan parked as close to the lodge's entrance as he possibly could. Before he could get out of the Wagoneer, Emma had opened her door and was testing her ability to stand.

"Here, let me help you to your room." Dylan gripped her firmly by the elbow.

"I'm fine." She shrugged out of his grasp. "Please just go home and leave me alone. You bring out the contractions in me. I've had enough for one night."

"I'll let Sandy know what's going on so she can check on you."

Emma swatted goodbye over her shoulder as if he were a mosquito she was trying to kill. "Don't call me, I'll call you."

He understood Emma's annoyance, considering he was once again the reason she was in this condition. Nonetheless, he watched her through the glass doors as she made her way up the stairs and to her room. He tugged his phone from his jacket pocket and punched in Sandy's number. He knew she was busy with her wedding plans, but he needed someone to check in on Emma during the night and there was no way she'd allow him anywhere near her. Which was fine by him. They needed some distance.

After speaking with Sandy, he called Melinda for good measure. And then he called Harlan to fill him in on the details. He loved his brother dearly, but Harlan may have overreacted a tad to the situation, which in turn had damaged Dylan's relationship with Emma. He couldn't blame his brother for being suspicious. It was his nature as an officer of the law to question everything, but neither one of them had had the facts. He couldn't fault Emma for doing her job. He may not like it, but it was her job and he had known that before they got involved. He couldn't expect her to put her livelihood behind his.

He'd been an ass. And a first-class one at that. He needed to make it up to her, and there was only one way he knew how. He unlocked the front door of the house, flicked on the lights and tore through the stacks of paperwork on the kitchen table until he found it. The drawing he had sketched of the rocking horse for Emma's baby. And on the back, a cradle. He may never have the opportunity to see the butter bean use them, but he wanted her to have something special that he had made with his own two hands.

Dylan ran back down the front porch stairs, almost wiping out in the process. He drove the Wagoneer farther down the road to his log cabin, and pulled around back near the woodshop. Christmas was in four days, technically three once midnight rolled around. Both were fairly basic designs, but he needed to start now, if he planned to have them finished by then. That is, if she didn't pack up and leave in the morning. There weren't many hotel-type places to stay in town. But Whitefish and Kalispell weren't far and he was sure they'd have vacancies available. Then he ran the risk of never seeing her again. And he couldn't bear the thought.

Dylan ran his hands over a couple pieces of mahogany he had set aside for a special project. He didn't know what could be more special than Emma's baby. He already missed the butter bean and they hadn't even met yet. Hopefully he'd still have that chance.

Chapter 12

Christmas Eve morning rolled around and Emma had managed to evade Dylan since their argument. He hadn't seen a single sign of her around the lodge and had even questioned Sandy if she was still staying there. Her rental hadn't moved from where she'd last parked it days ago. After Luke told him Emma had been avoiding the dining room because of him, he began eating at home so she could freely mingle with everyone else.

He understood and respected her reasons, but it was Christmas Eve. Nobody should be alone on Christmas Eve. His brother Garrett and his two children would be arriving soon. Harlan, Belle and Ivy were joining them for dinner and even Wes agreed to make an appearance. It was as close to complete as their family could get with Ryder being in jail and his mom in California with her new husband.

Bracing himself for an onslaught, he knocked lightly on Emma's door. When she didn't answer, he knocked again. Still no answer. He figured either she wasn't there or she had seen him through the peephole and refused to acknowledge him.

Unwilling to give up that easily, Dylan thought of the one thing that would get her to open the door. He took a few steps back and started to sing at the top of his lungs, "Oh what fun it is to ride in a one-horse open sleigh!"

He heard Emma fumble with the lock before swinging the door wide. "Are you crazy? Keep your voice down. The situation is bad enough. I don't need you telling everyone what we did."

"You mean that we made love on a sleigh under a moonlit sky. Sounds pretty romantic to me." Dylan scanned the length of her body, reassuring himself she was okay.

"Hey, cowboy, my eyes are up here."

"Can I come in?"

Emma stepped aside. "Why not? You own the place."

For someone who hadn't been out of the hotel for days, she'd certainly been busy. Neatly wrapped packages lined the wall next to the bed. Numerous pink and blue bags sat next to the bed along with new soft pink luggage.

"Where did you get all of this stuff?"

"I picked up a few things here and in Kalispell."

"But your car hasn't moved."

Emma's left brow rose. "What did you do, draw a chalk outline around it? I haven't been driving. I don't trust myself in case I get one of those Braxton-Hicks contractions again."

"Who's been your chauffeur?"

"Well, if you must know, yesterday I went into town with Melinda and Rhonda, and other days I called for car service. What is the big deal?"

Here, Dylan thought she'd been cooped up in a room avoiding him and she'd been out having a good time. Which was great for her, it just made him feel like a complete and total idiot.

"I didn't realize you were going out. I thought you were staying in your room because of me."

"Don't flatter yourself. No man is ever worth locking yourself in a room and pining over."

Emma certainly didn't keep her feelings to herself.

"I know you are still mad at me and I can't blame you. It's Christmas Eve, and I would like to invite you to celebrate with my family. They will all be here tonight and despite what happened with Harlan, who feels bad about the situation, I think you would have a good time with us. We are loud and fun, a little quirky, but most importantly we all believe there's always room for one more at the table. Besides, I have another reason for asking you."

Emma sat on the edge of the bed, looking as uncomfortable as the day was long. "What is your reason?"

"Jax used to play Santa for all the kids on the ranch. Since he's no longer here, I'm playing Santa, and I was hoping you would be my Mrs. Claus. I asked Sandy, but she's too busy getting ready for the wedding. Unless you're not up to it."

Emma seemed more pregnant than she had a few days ago. He'd always heard about women popping in the weeks leading up to the delivery, and he wondered if this was what they meant.

"Are you all right?"

"I'm just tired. I overdid it yesterday. What time do you need me to play Mrs. Claus?"

"Not until after dinner. I'm honoring the tradition and hosting it at Jax's house. We have more than enough food, especially since I didn't make it. The chefs here did. It's very casual and I would love to see you there."

Emma studied him for a second or two, making him think she'd say no. "Where am I supposed to find a Mrs. Claus costume?"

"Oh, we have one. The woman who used to play Mrs. Claus quit over the summer." Dylan held up his hands. "And before you ask, yes, you will fit into it. It's very loose fitting."

"Okay."

"Okay to which part?" Dylan wanted her to say yes to both, but his heart couldn't afford to get his hopes up. Just being in the same room with her knowing she despised him was agony.

"Both, if someone's willing to pick me up and drive me back."

"And by someone I am assuming you mean someone other than me."

Emma shifted on the bed so both of her legs were outstretched in front of her. "I will ride with you, providing you behave yourself."

It was a start, and he was thrilled to have the chance to try and set things right between them.

"I will pick you up out front around 4:30, if that's okay."

"Good, then I can nap until three." Emma rolled on to her side, and he longed to spoon her as he had the night of their sleigh ride. "Can you lock the door behind you, please?"

The sound of her breathing had changed from normal to deep before his hand reached the knob. She was already asleep. He allowed himself the pleasure of watching her for a few seconds before leaving. She was beautifully strong and fragile in the same breath, and he already missed her more than he should.

Emma awoke to the sound of her text message tone. It was Sunday so nobody from work should be bothering her. She reached for her phone and saw Dylan's name on the screen. Wasn't it enough that she had agreed to spend the evening with him and his family? She just hoped this time went better than the last. Besides, she'd already met three of the Slade men, she might as well make it an even four. She tapped the screen to display his message.

Just a friendly wake-up text since you hadn't set your alarm before you fell asleep.

Had she really fallen asleep while he was there? She replayed his visit in her mind, unable to remember him leaving. Well, that had been incredibly rude of her. Even Dylan didn't deserve that.

Dylan didn't deserve most of what she'd been dishing out. She hadn't been avoiding him because she was mad. A bit miffed, but not mad. She had kept her distance to maintain her sanity and protect her heart. She couldn't believe some of the things she'd done. Namely sleeping with a virtual stranger. But even more so, she couldn't believe some of the things she'd almost done. Like contemplating partnering with him on the ranch. She needed to have her head examined for all of the above. If she had been one of her friends, she'd be extremely worried about them. Which was why she hadn' filled Jennie in on any of the juicier Dylan details. He recklessness embarrassed her, but dammit if she didn' miss him.

Dressed and downstairs by half past four, she was surprised when Belle pulled in front of the lodge instead of Dylan. She tried telling herself it eliminated the pressure of being alone with him in the car, but even she couldn't deny the fact she was disappointed. Belle was great company, though and if she lived in town, they'd probably be fast friends.

Emma could hear little kids screeching from inside Jax's house the moment she stepped out of Belle's truck. At least hers was a relatively normal height off the ground.

"Are you ready for this?" Belle asked. "Because I'm not sure if I am."

"Why not?" Emma was surprised to see Belle hesitate at the front door. "This is my first Christmas with the Slades since I was a teenager. I haven't seen Garrett since my first wedding to Harlan, which was a no-go because he left me at the altar."

"Harlan left you at the altar? And you married him anyway?" And she thought she and Dylan had problems.

"I let him suffer for eight years before we tried it again. It's a long story. Remind me to tell you about it someday."

"Here I thought I was the only nervous one tonight." Emma peered through the window on the other side of the door. "I'll tell you what. You have my back and I'll have yours."

"You have a deal." The women shook on it before walking into the madhouse known as the Slade family Christmas.

"I'm glad you made it." Dylan kissed her lightly on the cheek. "I had my doubts you would show up."

"I'm curious to see how the other half lives."

"The other half?"

"My parents never did much for the holidays. Don't get me wrong, we had a good time and it was special, but it wasn't anything like this." She couldn't imagine children and pets running around her parents' townhouse, or people eating off paper plates and drinking out of red plastic cups. "We celebrated Christmas, but the tree went up and came down within a matter of days. When I was home for the holidays, it was just my parents and myself since I'm an only child."

"You don't have any other family?"

"I have family scattered across the country, but none that live in Illinois. My father moved there for his hospital residency and they never left. Then I came along."

"Thank God for small favors."

"Ha!" Emma laughed so hard, she thought the butter bean would make an appearance. "A week ago you thought I was the worst person on earth."

"I wouldn't exactly say the worst." Ivy ran between them followed by another little girl and boy. "That's Kacey and Bryce, my brother Garrett's two kids. Kacey's seven and Bryce is four. Let me introduce you."

Dylan hadn't seen Emma laugh since, well, ever. And when she did, she cried. Actual tears. Harlan had taken her aside shortly after her arrival and apologized for meddling in her business. Between the children's fascination with her and Belle's baby bellies and Ivy's dog Elvis's fixation on Emma's plate, the woman barely managed a mouthful here and there. None of it appeared to bother her. Except when it came time to sing *Jingle Bells*. Emma turned a brilliant red every time they sang the line "Oh what fun it is to ride in a one-horse open sleigh."

Their magical moonlight romp would forever remain their secret and their secret alone. Dylan couldn't imagine spending that moment with anyone other than Emma. It would forever remain his favorite memory of all time. He didn't think anything could possibly beat it.

When the children were busy playing near the large stone fireplace, Dylan motioned for Emma to follow him into the bedroom. He had both of their costumes hidden in the back of the closet for fear the little ones would stumble across them during a game of hide-and-seek. While he was sure Bryce still believed in Santa, he wasn't so sure he could fool Kacey and Ivy. Especially Ivy, since he spent the most time around her.

Dylan closed the door behind them, giving them a moment alone while they changed. "Um, I didn't think this part through." He turned and faced the corner. "You go ahead. I'll stay here and give you your privacy."

"I appreciate it, but it's not necessary. When you're pregnant, you lose your inhibitions about people seeing you in various stages of undress real quick. Besides, you're probably going to have to help me get these bloomer things on. I wasn't expecting this intricate of a costume."

Dylan faced Emma who had managed to get her head and one arm into Mrs. Claus's dress before realizing it had a zipper down the back. "Oh crap! Help me already."

"Stop flailing around like a catfish on a dock." Dylan lowered the zipper and eased the red and white apron dress over her curves. "See, that wasn't so bad."

"For you. Why do I have two pairs of bloomers? You just have to put on pants and a jacket."

"If I remember correctly, one pair of bloomers is shorter than the other to allow for the dress to pouf out."

"Oh, sure. That's just what I need. To look even pouffier than I already do." Emma eyed his bare abs as he tugged off his shirt. "Let me tell you something, Santa. You better shove a pillow or two under that jacket so I don't look like roly-poly Mrs. Claus."

Dylan stepped into the red velour pants and adjusted the suspenders. "I think you make a sexy Mrs. Claus." He braved a quick peck on her lips.

"I think you've been sipping too much eggnog." Emma attempted to step into the second pair of bloomers and almost fell onto the bed. "See, I told you."

Dylan picked the bloomers up off the floor and knelt before her. He widened one leg opening and held it out for her to step into before doing the same with the other. He eased the white cotton up her thighs before settling them on her hips. The costume may be corny, but the intimacy left him wanting more. The swell of her belly and breasts pressed against him, her lips inches from his own. He wanted to brand her with his mouth and claim her body and soul before she had a chance to leave him again.

"Santa?" A soft rap emanated from the other side of the door, interrupting the moment. "It's me, Belle. I have the naughty and nice list."

Dylan unlocked the door. Belle eased it open with one hand over her eyes. "Okay you two, put your clothes back on."

"Ha, ha. Very funny. I'll have you know I'm wearing two pairs of bloomers. Santa can't get through these."

"You wanna bet?" Dylan sidled up next to her until she swatted him away. "Hey, Belle, why do you look so frazzled? Are the kids getting the best of you?"

"There are so many of them."

"There's three," Emma laughed.

"Yes, but when they're together, it's like they multiply." Belle collapsed on the bed. "You two go without me. Tell everyone I'm guarding Santa's sleigh. They'll understand."

"Oh no you don't." Emma grabbed her hand and began pulling her off the bed. "You're not sending me in there without backup."

"Dylan's your backup. I'm pooped."

"Come on, Belle." He reached for her other hand. "Someone has to distract the kids while we sneak outside."

"Outside?" Emma and Belle said in unison.

"It's cold out there. You hadn't mentioned anything about going outside in my bloomers when I agreed to this."

"Okay, fine." One pregnant woman was enough, let alone two. "Belle, you just distract them and we'll pretend we came in from outside. When you're ready just say something like, *Do I hear Santa Claus?* And we'll take it from there."

They turned out the bedroom lights and waited in the darkness for Belle's signal. Even a white-haired wig and wire-rimmed glasses couldn't abate the feelings he had for Emma. He just hoped her jovial mood continued until tomorrow morning, because he had a special surprise planned for her and the butter bean.

"Did you hear that?" Belle said from the living room. "I think I heard reindeer on the roof. Who wants to run upstairs and check it out for me?"

"I will, I will," the kids shouted. They waited until they heard tiny footsteps on the staircase before emerging from the bedroom.

"Ho, ho, ho!" Dylan belted in his deepest voice as he and Emma walked toward the fireplace.

"We probably should've put the fire out before we did this. They're never going to believe we came down that thing." Emma squeezed beside him. "Ho, ho, ho!" She leaned closer and asked, "Mrs. Claus says, 'ho, ho, ho,' right?"

"Every time she catches Santa at the strip joint," Wes offered. "Be careful you don't set your bloomers on fire."

Belle started to laugh. "Then we can call you hotpants."

Emma stuck her tongue out.

"Who's been naughty and who's been nice?" Dylan chuckled in his best Santa impression.

"I swear to God," Emma said with a hiss. "If any of you say anything, I'll make sure there's a lump of coal in your stocking tomorrow morning."

At least they were all laughing when the kids clambered down the stairs. After twenty minutes of beard pulling, questions about reindeer poop and Elvis almost attacking his jingle bells, Dylan had enough Santa for the year.

Once they had changed and the kids were tucked

into their beds for the night, Dylan drove Emma back to the lodge and walked her to her door.

"Thank you for inviting me tonight. I really enjoyed spending time with your family."

"The pleasure was all mine. Thank you for letting this rift between us go for the holiday."

"Maybe peace on earth could spread past tomorrow." Emma looked up at him. "I would love to ask you in, but I'm afraid I don't have the strength or the stamina to give you what you want."

Dylan took her hand in his and lifted it to his mouth, kissing the top of it. "The only thing I want is your happiness. Merry Christmas, Emma." His lips brushed hers in a brief yet tender kiss. "I'll see you in the morning."

"Merry Christmas, Dylan. Thank you for making tonight special."

Dylan felt like he was walking on air by the time he reached the lobby. After three days of silence, he finally felt hopeful again. His Christmas wish: a lifetime with Emma and her daughter.

Chapter 13

Christmas morning, Emma awoke happier than she had been in years. After watching Dylan with the children last night, she had fallen asleep wondering what it would be like if he were her daughter's father. She had missed Dylan more than she'd been willing to admit, and after spending time with him and his family, she wasn't too eager to go back to the way things were.

She assumed she would hate the silence of the country. She had lived in the city for so long, the twenty-four-hour bustle had become second nature. But the Montana silence had grown on her and she actually found it quite relaxing. It wasn't all tranquility, though. She loved Dylan's brand of loud. Children playing, brothers arguing good-naturedly, a sister-in-law clearly not ready to have a baby. She wanted it all. And she wanted it by Dylan's side.

He still hadn't given Emma an answer to her final proposal. At least she wouldn't accept their last conversation about it as a final answer. That would determine her next course of action.

Or, would it?

She didn't need Dylan's answer to decide if she wanted to make a new life in Montana. It didn't matter either way. Dylan was here. Granted, he could always sell the ranch and move to Wyoming. He had mentioned it once. So what? She could go with him. The spark was still there between them. She had felt the passion last night without the physical touch or the words. Although, she certainly wouldn't thumb her nose at those.

Her parents would probably die of humiliation and her friends would probably try to have her committed, because moving to Montana was insane.

Absolutely…the best idea she'd had in a long time.

Emma's phone dinged. She checked her messages only to find one from Luke. He was heading over to see Billy Johnson's family this morning and said he would take the gifts she'd bought. She originally wanted to bring them there herself then she decided it was best if they were anonymous, the same with the donation her company gave them. Charlie hadn't seen it that way, but he reluctantly agreed. She hadn't spoken to the office since Friday, after agreeing to reconvene on Tuesday morning. She already dreaded it. One more reason to move to Montana.

She had hoped to hear from Dylan since he had mentioned having a surprise for her. She couldn't wait to see what it was. Although, she didn't have anything for him and certainly didn't expect a gift.

Someone began knocking jingle bells against her

door. She flew to it, well, as fast as a woman with twenty-five extra pounds and swollen feet could, and threw the door open.

"Luke, it's only you." She stepped aside so he could enter the room.

"Merry Christmas to you, too."

"I'm sorry, Merry Christmas." She gave him a hug. "I didn't mean to be rude. When you knocked that way I just assumed you were Dylan."

"I haven't seen him yet this morning. Did you get my message? I'm ready to take those packages over to the Johnsons."

"They're right here." Emma waved her arm at the wall. She had originally bought a few things for the children then decided his wife deserved gifts, too.

Luke removed his hat and placed it over his heart. "My word, are these all for the Johnson family?"

Emma hoped she didn't offend anyone with the number of gifts. Due to her predicament, they were the only ones she'd purchased this year. "Yes, they are."

"And you're sure you don't want them to know they came from you."

"Considering the role I played in all of this, I think it's best." Emma enjoyed playing secret Santa and made a vow to adopt a family every year from now on.

"You have a big heart. Thank you." Luke set his hat back atop his head and looked around. "This might take a few trips."

"I can help you bring some of them down."

"You will do no such thing." Luke ushered her toward the door. "Leave me your room key, and I will bring these downstairs while you grab some breakfast before the French toast is all gone."

"Sounds like a plan. The key is on the dresser. I'll see you a little later."

"Oh, and, Emma, you might want to bring your coat and gloves. It's a bit chilly down there this morning. Something's wrong with the heat."

"Okay, thanks. That's kind of rough on Christmas day. The rest of the lodge will stay warm, won't it?"

"Sure. The dining and great room are on a separate system."

Emma slipped on her coat and jammed her gloves in the pockets. If it was too cold, she'd bring her breakfast back to the room. No sense in freezing when she didn't need to.

"Merry Christmas," one of the guests said as they passed her in the hallway.

That was odd. They weren't wearing their coats. As she descended the stairs overlooking the great room, she noticed nobody had a coat on. "What was Luke talking about?"

And then she saw him. Dylan walked through the glass doors and met her at the foot of the stairs. "Good morning, beautiful." He kissed the back of her hand. "And Merry Christmas. Your chariot awaits." He swept his arm to the side, revealing a double-row red sleigh with a team of two Belgian draft horses parked in front of the lodge.

"Merry Christmas." She bounced up and down. "What have you done?"

He held the door open for her. "You're about to find out."

Emma attempted to peek into the second row of the sleigh, but Dylan caught her mid-act. "Everything is covered up back there so you're wasting your time."

She settled beneath the sleigh's blankets, eager to see what he had planned next. Maybe it was the slight drop in the overnight temperature or the magic of Christmas, but Emma swore everything twinkled, from the trees to the ground itself as the sleigh glided across the snow. They stopped at their special place overlooking Saddle Ridge. Even the town sparkled in the morning light.

Dylan reached behind them and lifted a large insulated picnic basket. "This morning we dine alfresco." He sat the basket on the floor. "I will have you know, I had to look up that word just for this occasion."

He withdrew two insulated mugs and handed one to her before setting his on the floor. "Homemade hot chocolate, made by yours truly." And then he handed her a large covered insulated plate. He removed the cover revealing a piping hot stack of French toast with a side of maple syrup. "Also made by yours truly."

"I can't believe you did all of this. Not even in my wildest dreams could I have envisioned breakfast on a horse-drawn sleigh. You truly are a man of many talents."

Dylan smiled at her. "Oh, you have no idea."

After they ate, Emma enjoyed snuggling with Dylan beneath the layers of blankets as the sun warmed their faces. His strong arms enveloped her, making her feel safe and secure against the uncertainty of tomorrow. This was what she wanted. She knew every day wouldn't be French toast and sleigh rides. And that was okay. It was the company of the man beside her that made it special.

She rested her head against his shoulders and sighed at the serenity that had become her new norm. "I never want to leave this place."

Dylan nuzzled his face against her hair. "Neither do I, but I have another surprise for you."

Every inch of her body tingled in anticipation. "You've already done so much. What more could you possibly have planned?"

"Do you want to find out?"

Emma twisted to look in the seat behind them. "Yes, yes I do." Emma thought her face would crack from smiling so big.

"It's not back there. It's waiting for you someplace else." Dylan took hold of the reins and clucked the horses forward.

The majestic beauty of the wide-open spaces nestled between the Swan Range and Mission Mountains was enough to bring tears to her eyes. How could she have ever wanted to take this away from Dylan? Her heart ached knowing she had hurt the man she loved. And yes, she loved Dylan Slade. She felt it all the way down to the tips of her toes.

Up ahead in the distance, Emma saw a large golden package shimmering against the pure white snowy backdrop. As they drew closer, the package appeared even larger. Dylan steered the sleigh alongside it and Emma couldn't believe her eyes. It had to be at least a four-foot square box with a gigantic white bow on top.

"How in the world did you get this out here?" Emma ran her hands across the gold foil paper, testing its rigidity.

"I had a little help from Wes. I wanted to do something special and completely unexpected. I'm pretty sure this will be another *first* you can add to your list." He slid out from under the blankets and walked around to her side of the sleigh. He offered her his hand as she stepped onto the snow. "I will need to help you with this."

Emma rested her hand on top of the package. "But I didn't get you anything."

Dylan laughed at her distress. "Honey, I have what I want for Christmas. You. That's enough for me. Now come on, let's open your present."

He lifted the box, revealing the most adorable rocking horse and cradle. Emma covered her mouth. She had never seen anything more beautiful. She ran her hands over the smooth wood, admiring the craftsmanship.

"I've never seen anything like these. They're absolutely beautiful." Emma wiped her eyes, unable to control her tears. "Where on earth—?"

"I made them."

"You what?"

"I made them for you and the butter bean. I would have liked to have given both of them more detail, but I only had a few days. They're made from solid mahogany so they'll last a lifetime and then some."

"But how?" Emma placed her hands on the seat of the horse, testing the perfectly arched rockers beneath it.

"I have a woodshop behind what's actually my house."

"They are impeccable." Emma patted her chest. "I am touched and honored that you took the time and effort to make something like this for me and my daughter. It's beyond generous."

Dylan closed the distance between them. "I wanted to give you both a part of me. I wanted you to know how special you both are. Every time you use the cradle, know that my hands once lay where your daughter's head rests. When she rocks and laughs on the horse, know I was smiling when I made it. This is my gift to you, to your child, because you both have come to mean so much to me in a short amount of time. Even if we never have tomorrow, know how truly blessed I feel to have had you in my life."

Emma didn't think it was possible to define true love, but Dylan had proved her wrong once again. His gift epitomized it. His words captured the very essence of the emotion. And Emma wanted nothing more than to share her child with somebody who truly loved her daughter as much as she did.

After a perfect Christmas day, Emma agreed to be Dylan's date for Luke and Sandy's evening wedding ceremony. The soft touch of Emma's hand in his as his friends recited their vows caused him to yearn for the same permanence. His next marriage would be forever. His next marriage would be to Emma if he had anything to say about it.

Each time his plane had glided over the mahogany when he was creating the cradle, his love for Emma and her daughter had grown. He knew then, his life wouldn't be complete without them. He wanted them to live with him in Jax's house on the ranch. She had admittedly grown to love Saddle Ridge and he hoped it wouldn't take too much more coaxing to convince her to run the ranch by his side. That is if his idea went according to plan. It was a big if, but after hearing his brother Garrett last night once again talk about wanting to move, he may have found the solution he'd been searching for.

Emma joined him on the makeshift dance floor in the center of the lodge's great room. He sincerely hoped it wasn't the last wedding he'd witness on the ranch.

He loved Emma's idea of an open-air wedding chapel overlooking Saddle Ridge. He'd already begun sketching it in his mind and wanted to build it with his own two hands, so when he said, "I do" to Emma someday down the road, it would be even more special.

"Penny for your thoughts." Emma gazed up at him as they swayed to the music.

"I was thinking about your chapel idea."

"Imagine that. We can actually agree on something."

"I think we have managed to find common ground on quite a few things once we talked them out and understood where the other was coming from. You were right about my stubbornness. I didn't want to hear what you had to say."

"You don't have to say that. I'm ashamed to admit how many times I disregarded your feelings about the ranch. I realize now it's about much more than money. In my line of work, they teach us not to allow our emotions to interfere with the overall vision of a project. After six years of that, my humanity had all but disappeared. You helped me find it again."

Dylan felt a jolt against his lower abdomen. "What was that?" He froze, afraid to move.

"That was the butter bean." Emma smiled up at him.

"You're not going to tell me I bring out the contractions in you again, are you?"

Emma shook her head and laughed. "No, I'm not. This is normal baby behavior."

"It was strong. If that's what it felt like to me, I can only imagine what it does to your insides." Dylan led her off the dance floor and to the couch.

"Believe me when I tell you, the entire center of my

body aches on a constant basis. I will be very happy when the next seven weeks are up."

He sat down beside her. "Would you mind?" He asked, pointing to her belly.

"Go right ahead."

Emma closed her eyes as his hands cupped the curve of her abdomen. He felt the ever slight motion of her daughter moving beneath his palms. It truly was a miracle. A tiny human was living and growing under his hands. The baby shifted again, causing Emma to wince slightly. A more pronounced protrusion poked against him. He imagined it was the butter beans hand reaching out for his. *Soon, little one.* Regardless of where Emma had the baby, he'd find his way there.

"Still no name?"

"No. I read online that many mothers struggle finding the perfect name only to have it come to them the moment they see their child. I have resolved to wait at this point. If something comes to me before then, great. If not, I'm not going to stress over it."

"You've changed a lot over the past week."

"Has it only been a week? I feel like I've been here for an eternity. I don't mean that in a negative way." Emma rested her hand against his chest. "Between the year-long research and time I put into this ranch, I feel much more connected to it now than I had when I barged in here last week."

"I wouldn't exactly say you barged in."

"You're being too kind." She yawned. "I hate to be a party pooper, but I think I've reached my limit tonight."

Dylan rose and helped her to her feet. "I'll walk you to your room." He entwined his fingers with hers as they wished the bride and groom well. Dylan unlocked her door, wanting desperately to follow her inside and hold her in his arms until the sun came up tomorrow morning. But he couldn't. He had a week to save the ranch, and tonight he needed to talk to his brother before he left to go home to Wyoming tomorrow.

"Thank you for making this the most magical Christmas ever."

"I have enjoyed every moment I spent with you today. A week ago, I never thought I'd say that. You are a true joy and inspiration in my life and I look forward to tomorrow. I look forward to every day I'm with you. Merry Christmas, Emma."

"Merry Christmas, Dylan."

He kissed her goodbye before tearing himself away from her door. He had seen Garrett hovering near the buffet line and wanted to catch him before he took the kids back to the house and put them to bed.

Bryce and Kasey were dancing with Ivy and a few other ranch children in the center of the great room while his three brothers stood shoulder to shoulder watching them. Amazingly enough, Wes hadn't absconded with a bridesmaid.

"Got a minute for me to run something by you?" Dylan asked Garrett.

"Sure. What's on your mind?"

"I have a proposition for you," Dylan said.

"Uh-oh, don't do it, man. It's a sinking ship," Wes unnecessarily added.

"Let's talk in Jax's office where we won't be interrupted." Dylan led Garrett down the hallway.

"I have a feeling I know where this is going," Garrett said from behind.

"Before you form any opinions, hear me out. I have a few ideas you might really like, starting with a wedding chapel."

* * *

The laughter and celebrating downstairs kept Emma awake. After an hour, she gave up. She had always hated going home too soon for fear she'd miss out on something good happening at a party. She slipped into her leggings and an oversized sweater. She was sure nobody would mind her rejoining them wearing more comfortable attire. Maybe Dylan would still be there. And maybe there would still be cake. Because she always had room for cake. And maybe they still had one or two of those cheesy puffed pastries. She had room for those, too.

She wandered back toward the party and straight for the buffet. Jackpot. Cake and pastry. She fixed herself a plate and ate as she mingled, keeping an eye out for Dylan. When she spotted Harlan and Belle near the dance floor, she toe-tapped her way across the room. She felt a second wind coming on. Sometimes this happened at three o'clock in the morning. Tonight, it was a little earlier. She could handle earlier. It didn't disrupt her sleep.

"You didn't happen to see if there was any fruit salad left, did you?" Belle asked when she saw her plate.

Emma nodded as she took another mouthful and motioned to the buffet table with her fork.

"Harlan, would you be a dear and—"

"Big or little?"

"Big or little what?" Belle looked up at him.

"Do you want a big or a little bowl?"

Belle tilted her head and stared at him incredulously. "Do you even have to ask?"

"No, I sure didn't. I'll be right back."

"I thought you went to bed?" Belle said as Emma sat beside her on the couch.

"I attempted to. I figured if Dylan was still here, we could hang out for a bit and maybe even watch a movie in my room."

"He's still here. He's with Garrett in Jax's office. They've been in there ever since you left. Poke your head in and see how much longer they are going to be. Harlan and I want to get Ivy home and Garrett's two are getting sleepy."

"Okay, I'll nudge them along for you." Emma and her cake leisurely strolled down the hallway toward Jax's office. She had passed the black-and-white photos on the walls numerous times but had never taken a moment to look at them. The first few were from the early 1900s when they were building the lodge. Log structures had always fascinated her the way they notched and stacked each timber into position. By the time she reached the last photo, she had finished her cake.

"So what do you think?" She heard Dylan say. "Would you consider becoming my partner on the ranch and seeing if we can make a go of it? You keep telling me how much you want to get out of Wyoming. And you know everybody here."

Emma saw Garrett's reflection in the framed photo that hung on the wall opposite the office. "I think your ideas have some strong possibilities. The couples-only packages are a nice touch and I really like the chapel. Offering destination weddings would push Silver Bells into an entirely different category. We can keep it rugged and Western, but still offer some elegance."

Emma couldn't believe it. Those were her ideas, some of which came from her buyout proposal. It shouldn't surprise her, though. He had come right out and told her he wanted to steal her ideas and use them to his advantage. She just didn't think he would, at least not without her.

"I wanted to run it past you before I asked Harlan and Wes if they wanted to buy in. Which I doubt they will, but I have to at least offer. I had also considered offering some of the employees a chance to own a part of the ranch. I think if we band together, we'd have a strong chance of competing with our neighboring guest ranches without becoming an over-the-top exclusive resort."

"I agree. Let's keep Silver Bells in the family."

"Congratulations. You found your solution. I'm glad you both liked my ideas." Emma stood in the open doorway of the office.

Garrett looked from Emma to Dylan. "These were your ideas?"

Emma bobbed her head. "Most of them, some of which I worked a year on developing. Dylan can tell you all about it. I wish you guys luck on your venture."

Emma stormed down the hallway as fast as her pregnant waddle would allow. She had made a mistake. A huge mistake and she couldn't get back home to Chicago quick enough.

"Emma, wait," Dylan called after her.

"Wait for what?" She spun on him. "Wait for you to steal more of my ideas?"

"You're right, they were your ideas. While my original intentions were to steal them, I gave your proposal serious thought. But in the end, it didn't make me want to sell. It made me want to hold on to the ranch even more."

"So you just decided to steal them?"

"I didn't realize they were copyrighted," Dylan retorted. "What's wrong with me implementing some of those ideas? They were good. You should feel flattered."

"Oh, sure. I feel really flattered. I'm the idiot who thought maybe, just maybe, I could run this ranch with you. I even—" Emma stomped down the hallway and back. "I even entertained the idea of becoming your partner. Because I believed in you. I saw how much this meant to you." She twisted her hair off her neck and held it up, suddenly very hot. "What was all this talk about wanting to have me by your side."

"I do want you by my side. I want you to stay here, with me. I thought I made that clear today."

"As what?" Emma sighed when he didn't answer. "I thought you wanted me as a partner."

"I did."

"Did?"

"A few days ago I had planned to ask you to stay and be the new lodge manager."

That wasn't quite the partner she had meant, but that had been part of it. "So why didn't you?"

"Because Barnaby presented me with his proposal a few hours later and I couldn't offer you something not knowing what I was going to do. So, I decided to wait until I had made up my mind."

"Until you made up your mind about the ranch or me?" Emma gave him one more opportunity to tell her how he felt about her.

"The ranch."

Emma waited for him to tell her he had already made up his mind about her, but he didn't. "Then where do I fit into all of this?"

"Honestly…" Dylan shrugged. "I don't know, anymore. I owe it to my brothers to ask them if they want to join in the venture. Until I have their answers, I have nothing to offer you. I had no idea you wanted to be this deeply involved in the ranch. You had already told me your daughter would be born in Chicago regardless of what happened between us. Why would I assume otherwise?"

Emma shook her head. "Because you asked me to stay this morning and I thought that meant something." Like maybe he loved her. "Well, you don't have to worry about it anymore. I will be out of your life soon enough."

"I don't understand why you're so upset."

"Because you left me with nothing. No promotion in Chicago and no job here in Montana. Yet, you and your brothers reap the benefits of my hard work. You cut me out of everything. And I'm still waiting for you to tell me you love me."

When Dylan didn't respond, Emma stormed back to her room. She was a fool for ever believing they could have a perfect little Montana family.

It was over.

They were over.

Chapter 14

Emma had a rough night. After hot sweats, minor contractions and a whole lot of pressure in new places, she phoned the doctor first thing in the morning. They told her to come in right away. Not wanting to bother anyone else on the ranch, she called for car service. On her way out the door, she saw Dylan and Garrett announce the ranch's new plans to the Silver Bells employees. She walked into the cold mountain air as they applauded and celebrated the news. In the end, Dylan had made the right decision and she was happy for the jobs he had saved.

Her exam left her craving the comforts of home. Chicago almost felt foreign to her and the lodge was nothing more than a room. When she said the actual word *home* aloud, Jax's house had immediately come to mind. It would take a long time for her to shake Dylan from her system.

"Emma?" Belle said from a chair in the waiting room. "Is everything all right?"

"How did you know I was here?" Emma asked.

"I didn't. This is my doctor. She doesn't have an office any place else. Just here."

"Oh." Emma sat down beside her. "Where's Harlan?"

"At work." Belle took her hand and gave it a squeeze. "What happened?"

"My blood pressure is back up and I'm almost two centimeters dilated. The baby has already dropped. Here, I thought I'd been experiencing another round of Braxton-Hicks when I noticed I wasn't carrying as high as I had been hours earlier. She gave me a round of steroid shots in preparation for an early delivery. Further travel is out, and I have been ordered to take it easy. Limited exercise, very short walks and no sex."

"You must be terrified."

"I am." Emma fought back the tears that threatened to break free. "The doctor estimates her at almost five pounds, so that's good. But her lungs haven't fully developed yet. Hence the steroids. My baby's not even born and she's receiving medical treatment."

"Mrs. Slade, we're ready for you," a nurse in pink scrubs said to Belle.

"I'm just having a routine checkup. I shouldn't be long. Do you want to wait and we can talk?"

Emma nodded. "Yes, thank you."

She sat back in the chair, attempting to remain calm and think logically. How did millions of women give birth every year, just as they had done for thousands of years, without complications? She thought she had done something wrong but the doctor had assured her that snowshoeing and sex weren't to blame. Neither was her stress. It contributed to her high blood pressure but not the other preterm delivery factors.

As much as Emma wanted to see her little girl, neither one of them was ready. She hated going through this alone. She wanted to call her mom but she couldn't stomach one of her *what's going to be is going to be* speeches. She knew if she called Jennie, her friend would be on the first flight to Montana and insist on staying with her for the next seven weeks. She was that generous of a friend, and Emma wouldn't allow her to jeopardize her job because she was scared.

Belle's exam had taken less time than Emma had anticipated. Harlan was at work and Ivy was visiting her biological mother for the day, allowing Emma and Belle to have the house to themselves.

"How about we make a girl's day out of this?" Belle handed Emma a cup of herbal tea. "We can kick back and watch romantic comedies for the rest of the day."

"I don't think romance is the best thing for me to watch after what happened last night."

"Oh, that." Belle's eyes widened. "Garrett had mentioned that you and Dylan had an argument over the ranch."

"I don't know who I'm madder at. Dylan or myself."

"I don't really understand what happened. Garrett said Dylan had asked him to become his partner on the ranch and you got upset. Full disclosure, he also asked Harlan and Wes to go in with him. Wes said no, but Harlan hasn't made up his mind yet. I think it would be a good idea, but maybe there's something I'm not seeing. Is this about your company not getting the ranch?"

"Yes and no. While I was trying to convince Dylan to sell to me, I decided I wanted to buy into the ranch.

Before I had a chance to tell Dylan, he made the offer to his brothers, which I totally understand. While I can't help but be annoyed that he won Garrett over with my ideas, I'm crushed that I gave him three chances to tell me he loved me and he didn't. I told him I thought he would have said the words, and he just stared at me. So, who's the fool? Me? I feel used. He has everything he wants while I get to go home to a demoted position because once this baby is born, I can no longer afford to travel all over the world. That had been my biggest job requirement. So I'm stuck with a paper-pushing job I hate, at least until I find something else. In the meantime, I'm having my baby in Montana and then I have to move into a smaller apartment when I get back to Chicago. This is not the start to my daughter's life that I had expected."

"So he didn't say the words?" Belle asked.

Emma sipped her tea. "The bottom line is, Dylan and I don't trust each other. That came to a head the night Harlan thought I was going behind Dylan's back when I was just doing what my boss had instructed me to do."

"I was furious with him for getting in the middle of that. I am so sorry for the undue stress that put you through."

"I appreciate it, but I understood where Harlan was coming from, too. Dylan had brought me to a particular place on the ranch a few times. A spot Jax had also shown me. The more time I spent there, the more I had envisioned a beautiful open-air wedding chapel where the ranch could provide destination wedding packages."

"Dylan was telling us about them last night. They sound wonderful. I would've loved something like that.

Both of my weddings were completely unconventional, and I wouldn't mind a third."

Emma set her teacup on the end table. "Okay, so all those ideas Dylan told you about last night, they were mine. Some had been a part of my original proposal package and the rest, like the chapel, were all ideas I wanted to actively be a part of. The more I thought about them and talked about them, I saw myself helping Dylan see them come to fruition. Not sit on the sidelines and watch him do it with somebody else. Dylan kept asking me to stay in Montana so I naïvely thought he wanted me to be his partner in every way. When I heard him ask Garrett to be his partner instead and then mentioned Harlan and Wes, I was crushed."

Belle patted Emma's thigh. "You got your feelings hurt."

"I sure did. Now that I've had a chance to think about it, maybe I overreacted. In the same respect, I don't know what Dylan expected me to do for work if I said yes and moved to Montana. I'm not the type who would be happy answering phones. Not that there's anything wrong with that, it's just not what I want. I want to be a part of the bigger picture. That has been my job for the last six years. I am a commercial real estate analyst. I make a living looking at the bigger picture. After listening to Dylan, it was obvious he didn't see me the same way. He said he had at one point, but once he took on partners, things were different."

"You wanted to be included." Elvis jumped on the couch between them, spun around a few times and laid down. "The dog gets it. He wants to be included, too."

They both laughed, breaking the tension. Emma scratched the dog behind the ears, only to have him roll over on his back for belly rubs. "I think Dylan believes this is about him not selling the ranch, but it's not. I knew he was going to be a tough sell going in. He has every right to explore his options and ask his family to join him. Although, he already told me Garrett had turned him down once before. If he had said, 'I love you,' I could have overlooked it all. I can't move sixteen hundred miles away from my life for a man who doesn't even know if he loves me."

"I would probably have felt the same way."

Talking to Belle made her feel better. It helped justify her feelings and allowed her to see where she may have been a little too harsh with Dylan. In all actuality, he hadn't really done anything wrong. He was looking out for his best interests. Their relationship had been far too new for either one of them to consider her involvement in the ranch. If anyone had the clearer head, it had probably been Dylan for realizing that fact. That didn't make it any easier to accept.

Belle was the last person Dylan expected to receive a phone call from that evening. After she had filled him in on Emma's doctor visit, she clarified why Emma was so furious with him. Belle admitted to violating the girl code by telling him all of it, but she felt they both needed to give the other a second chance before giving up completely. Dylan didn't understand how he could have been so blind.

He checked his watch. It wasn't too late to stop by her room. That's if she would open the door for him. He didn't think any amount of singing in the hallway would change her mind this time after the way he had completely disregarded her feelings.

Surprisingly, she answered after the first knock. "Let me guess… Belle."

"She felt horrible for breaking your confidence, but she's worried about you, and so am I. I owe you a huge apology."

"Dylan, it seems like that's all you've done since I've arrived. No more apologies. We have both made mistakes. I invested too much of my heart into this place and I wasn't even aware I was doing it. I don't know if it was you, Jax, Montana or maybe a combination of all of it, but Silver Bells really grabbed ahold of me."

"It tends to have that effect on people."

"I just wish I had seen it before this visit. Maybe I could have prepared myself better."

"The heart wants what the heart wants," Dylan said. "That's the lesson I've learned since you arrived. I thought I had built up enough resistance to protect myself from ever falling in love again. You can't protect yourself from that."

Dylan noticed her suitcases now sat where the Christmas presents had. He scanned the bed and the dresser. There were no blue and pink bags, no baby clothes lying around, no signs of Emma.

"Are you leaving?" Belle had told him Emma was prohibited from traveling.

"I made open-ended reservations in Kalispell. I think it's best if I put some distance between…us."

"I don't want you to go. And I don't think you want to, either."

"Our relationship happened way too fast. Maybe if time had been on our side and we had met under different circumstances, we may have had a chance. I cannot focus on that or worry about it, anymore. My baby may arrive sooner than later. I need to prepare for the fact I'm having my child in Montana. I don't have any of the comforts of home and before you offer, no. I can handle this on my own."

"What about your job?"

"I have made peace with the lesser position. It's relatively stress-free and will allow me to spend more time with my daughter. I have some money to fall back on so we won't have to move right away, but I will have to move soon. It will all work out in the end. I have a job and a roof over my head, I just need to give birth to a healthy baby."

"Emma." Dylan lifted her hands and held them against his chest. "I understand you not wanting to be with me anymore. But I do love you and I still want to be with you."

"Please don't." Emma looked up at him. The life and fire he had once seen in her eyes was gone. "You're only saying that because Belle told you that's what I wanted to hear."

"That's not true. I mean every word. I don't want you to give up on us, but I understand. I wish you would at least stay here, where you don't have to worry about money. It will be one less financial burden. I don't want you to think of it as a gift, I—"

Dylan noticed the cradle and rocking horse on the opposite side of the room away from her luggage. "You are taking those with you, right?"

"Under the circumstances, I don't think I should. They're beautiful and I think you should give them to somebody you plan on spending the rest of your life with. You worked hard on them."

"I built them for your baby. It doesn't matter what

appens between us now, tomorrow or ten years from ow, these are for your daughter. I want her to have em. You don't have to tell her about me, just…please."

Dylan choked back a tear, an emotion he didn't know e was capable of. He released her hands and stepped way from her. "I will leave you alone now. Just, please, ke the cradle and the rocking horse."

Dylan couldn't escape her room fast enough. He ran own the lodge's stairs and into the cold. He couldn't ear the thought of Emma leaving or never seeing her hild.

How could he have made so many mistakes?

Chapter 15

Emma hadn't expected saying goodbye would be s[o] difficult the following morning at breakfast. She hate[d] leaving all the wonderful people she'd met and woul[d] genuinely miss them. They exchanged numbers an[d] promised to stay in touch. Kalispell wasn't far, so the[y] could still meet on weekends, providing the butter bea[ns] cooperated.

Emma wondered if she would see Dylan before sh[e] left. It would probably be easier on the two of them [if] they didn't. She had three and a half hours before he[r] car service arrived. The rental company had alread[y] come and picked up her car. In hindsight, she should'v[e] done that a week ago.

After breakfast, she headed back to her room. Sh[e] wished she could have checked into the hotel in Ka[-] lispell sooner, but she had to wait until noon.

"Emma." One of the older women who had teased her about Dylan only a few days prior stopped her on the staircase. "Why don't you join us for one last sleigh ride around the ranch before you go? It's just going to be us girls. We've already booked it, and you can be our guest."

"Oh I don't think—"

"Nonsense." The woman hooked her arm in Emma's and steered her back down the stairs. "We have that cowboy hottie, Wes, ready and waiting."

"Oh, okay." Emma allowed the woman to lead her through the lobby. She guessed there wouldn't be any harm since it wasn't Dylan. And how bad could a sleigh ride be with a couple of cowboy-crazy rowdy women? It actually sounded like fun.

The sleigh ride was anything but tame, and Wes egged them on. She had officially heard every dirty joke known to man. Not from Wes. From the women. They even sang dirty songs instead of Christmas carols after stating Christmas was over with and it was time to celebrate being women. Emma began to wonder just how much celebrating they had done before embarking on their little adventure.

Even though her group of rebels was far from romantic, Emma couldn't help but think about the many sleigh rides she had taken with Dylan. She missed him already and she hadn't even stepped foot off the ranch. When Wes reined the sleigh to a stop at the location she and Dylan had made love, Emma thought her heart would shatter into a million pieces.

In the distance, a single draft horse and sleigh approached. To her surprise, it was Dylan. He stepped out of the sleigh and walked toward her, carrying a bouquet of long-stemmed red roses. Wordlessly, he took her gloved hand, helped her out of the sleigh and led her to the future chapel site. The sound of sleigh bells jingled behind them, as Wes and company drove away.

"You all had this planned, didn't you?" Emma asked.

"Yes, ma'am." Dylan tipped his hat. "I couldn't let you leave without showing you how much you and your baby mean to me. I've spent most of my thirty-five years alone. Even though I wanted a family to call my own, I never saw it in my future. And I know your little butter bean isn't mine biologically, but I have this unexplainable attachment to her mother and that automatically led me to fall in love with her, too."

"Dylan, what are you saying?" Emma clutched the roses to her chest.

"I'm saying I love you, Emma Sheridan. I don't want to spend another day without you by my side. I have been so stubborn and pigheaded that I haven't truly seen what is right in front of me. I don't want you to go to Kalispell today. I don't want you to go back to Chicago once your daughter is born. I want you to stay. Here. In Montana with me." Dylan reached into his pocket and knelt in the snow on one knee. "As my wife." He held a diamond ring in front of him. "Will you marry me?"

"Dylan, I'm having a baby," Emma said as tears stung her cheeks.

"And I want to be a part of her life. I want to raise her as my own."

"No." Emma gripped his shoulder. "I'm having a baby. Now!"

"Holy crap!" Dylan pocketed the ring and sprang to his feet. He swept her into his arms and carried her to the sleigh, bundling her in blankets before taking the ins. "It's going to be all right. I'll take care of you. I romise nothing will happen to you or the butter bean."

By the time they reached the hospital, Dylan thought e would have a heart attack.

"I should have taken Lamaze classes." Emma said as ey wheeled her down the hallway. "I should've learned ow to breathe properly." Dylan ran beside her as she queezed the life out of his hand. "I'm sorry I ruined our proposal."

"Don't worry about that. There can always be another proposal. There's only one butter bean."

"Oh, God!" She screamed as she doubled over in ain. "My baby is coming and I still don't have a name." hey reached the delivery room and two women in pink crubs helped her out of the wheelchair and into a gown.

"Is the father staying for the delivery?" one of the omen asked Emma.

"Oh, I'm not the father." As much as he would love ɔ be in the room for the delivery, he didn't want Emma ɔ feel uncomfortable.

"Yes, he is." Emma winced as they eased her onto he bed. "You are her father. I accept your proposal."

"You do?" Dylan ran to her side, unfamiliar tears vetting his cheeks. "You just made me the happiest nan alive."

"Okay, Mr. Happy. We need to get you in a gown, ooties and a cap." Dylan felt himself being spun in nultiple directions. He'd never been in a delivery room efore, let alone a delivery room where he was about ɔ become a father.

"Oh, my God, I'm going to be a dad."

Emma smiled weakly at him from across the room.

"Would you please finish getting dressed and get back over here." It was more of a demand than a question. And he was more than willing to oblige. Dylan bent down and kissed Emma softly on the forehead. "You're doing good, honey. You're about to be a mom."

"Are you sure you want this? Are you sure you want this responsibility for the next eighteen years?"

The idea alone should have terrified him, but he welcomed it. He wanted a family with Emma more than anything else in this world. "There's no one else I would rather spend my life with."

"Okay, Emma," the doctor said. "This baby is coming quickly. I'm going to need you to give me a couple of good pushes when I say so. Are you ready?"

"No." Emma shook her head. "I don't even have a name for her."

The doctor laughed. "You're not the first person that's happened to. You'll figure it out. Now I need you to give me a push on the count of three. One. Two. Push."

Emma squeezed Dylan's hand even tighter as she tried to sit up and push at the same time.

"Keep an eye on her blood pressure," the doctor said to one of the nurses. "Emma, I'm going to need you to push again. She's almost here. On the count of three. One. Two. Push."

Emma pushed again, her breaths more ragged as one of the machines began beeping wildly. Dylan read the concern in the doctor's eyes.

"You can do this, baby, you can do this, baby," he reassured.

"I'm so tired." Emma looked up at him. "I don't think I can." Fear was etched across her delicate features.

"You *can* do this. I have faith in you. I'm right here by your side. You look at me. You look into my eyes and you don't stop looking into my eyes until that baby is born."

"Okay, Emma, this is the last one. I need you to push or we're going to have to deliver this baby by cesarean. On the count of three. One. Two."

"Push," Dylan said in unison with the doctor. "Push, Emma. Push."

"There we go," the doctor said. The sound of a baby's cry reverberated throughout the room as the doctor held her up for Emma to see. "Dad, would you like to cut the cord?"

Dylan nodded, unable to speak. A nurse handed him the scissors, instructing him to cut between the clamps. She was so tiny, but not as tiny as he had feared. And she had a mop of brown hair, just like her mom's.

"She's beautiful, Emma."

"I want to hold her." She reached out her arms.

The doctor carried the infant to a small, padded table and laid her under a heat lamp as a nurse began rubbing her vigorously with a towel. "We're going to clean and examine your daughter. We need to make sure she's healthy since she's six-and-a-half weeks premature."

"Is she okay?" Emma struggled to sit up. "Tell me! Is my baby okay?" Panic crept into her voice.

"Shh, sweetheart. They're taking good care of her." The wait seemed endless as a small team gathered around the table. Dylan had never known fear until this moment. And he hadn't known he was capable of a love so deep.

The doctor returned, carrying a pink swaddled bundle. "Mama, meet your daughter." She placed her in

Emma's arms. "We'll need to run more tests in a few minutes, but she's doing great."

Tears spilled down Emma's cheeks as she held her baby. "Hello, Holly. I'm your mommy."

"I can't believe you're actually here." Emma cradled her daughter. "My beautiful girl." After numerous tests, they had assured her Holly was healthy. Emma couldn't believe how blessed she was.

"She's beautiful, just like you." Dylan brushed Emma's hair away from her face. "And I love her name."

"Holly Jax Slade. I don't remember ever seeing Holly in a baby book, so I'm not sure where I got the idea for the name but somehow it fits. I think it was all that Christmas spirit you showed me. And Jax," she sighed. "He had to be a part of this somehow. I swear he was watching over her today."

"I still can't believe she has my last name." Dylan beamed proudly beside them.

"And I can't believe I'm going to be your wife. Speaking of which, whatever happened to that ring you were going to slide on my finger?"

Dylan reached into his pocket and pulled it out. "It's right here, future Mrs. Slade." Dylan held her hand in his. "Now are you sure about this?"

"Oh, I'm definitely sure I want to be your wife and raise our daughter together," Emma said as he slid the ring on her finger.

* * * * *